The Dark Vineyard

ALSO BY MARTIN WALKER
FROM CLIPPER LARGE PRINT

Bruno, Chief of Police

The Dark Vineyard

Martin Walker

W F HOWES LTD

This large print edition published in 2009 by
W F Howes Ltd
Unit 4, Rearsby Business Park, Gaddesby Lane,
Rearsby, Leicester LE7 4YH

1 3 5 7 9 10 8 6 4 2

First published in the United Kingdom in 2009
by Quercus

A CIP catalogue record for this book is available
from the British Library

ISBN 978 1 40744 819 0

Typeset by Palimpsest Book Production Limited,
Grangemouth, Stirlingshire
Printed and bound in Great Britain
by MPG Books Ltd, Bodmin, Cornwall

FSC
Mixed Sources
Product group from well-managed
forests, controlled sources and
recycled wood or fiber
SA-COC-1565
www.fsc.org
© 1996 Forest Stewardship Council

For the Baron

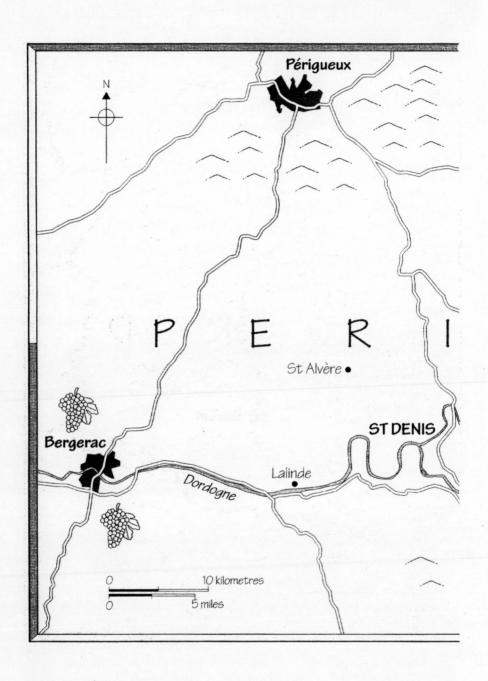

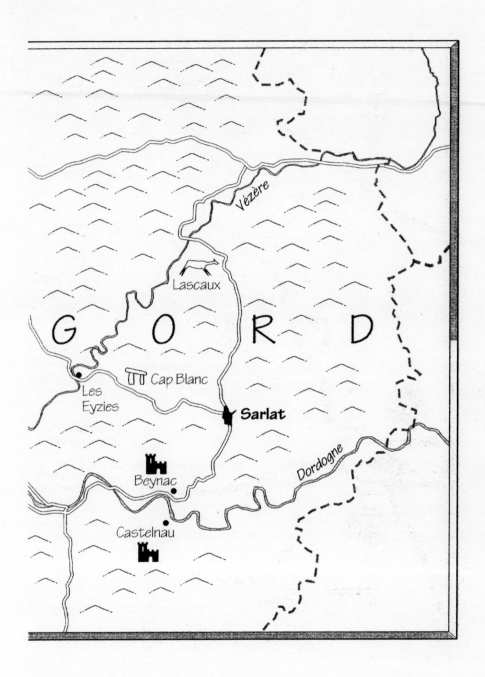

CHAPTER 1

The distant howl of the siren atop the *Mairie* broke the stillness of the French summer night. It was an hour before dawn but Bruno Courrèges was already awake, his thoughts churning with might-have-beens about the woman who had until recently shared his bed. For a moment he froze, stilled by the eerie sound that carried such a weight of history and alarm. This same siren had summoned his neighbours in the small town of St Denis to war and invasion, to liberation and peace, and marked the hour of noon each day. But its swooping whine also served to call the town's volunteer firemen to their duty. Such an emergency invariably required his presence as the sole municipal policeman of St Denis. So, almost relieved at the brusque summons from his gloomy thoughts, Bruno thrust aside the tangled sheets.

As he dressed and swigged from a carton of milk by way of breakfast, Bruno's mobile rang. It was Albert, one of the two professionals who led the town's team of *pompiers*, and he and his truck and his night patrol were already on the road.

1

'There's a big fire up on the old road to St Chamassy,' the urgent voice began. 'It's at the top of the hill, just before the turn to St Cyprien. A barn and a big field. This time of year it could spread for miles if the wind gets up.'

'On my way.' Bruno squeezed his eyes shut to draw on the map of the sprawling commune of St Denis that he kept in his head. It was composed of the roads he patrolled, the isolated homes and hamlets he visited, the farms he knew with their flocks of geese and ducks and pigs and goats that made this into the gastronomic heartland of France. His familiarity with the ground over which he hunted, and searched for mushrooms after the rains, meant that he knew his district as a woman knows her face.

The shout down the phone, tucked between his shoulder and his ear as he tried to fasten his shirt buttons, brought him back to the emergency.

'There's no report of any casualties,' said Albert. 'But you'd better alert the medical centre as soon as you've told the Mayor. I'm calling Les Eyzies and St Cyprien for support. But can you stop at the station and make sure they send up the spare water tankers? Drive one yourself if you have to. We'll need all the water we can find. Now get moving. I'll see you up there.'

'What about evacuation? There are four or five farms around there.'

'I don't know yet, but get the Mayor on to it. He'd better start phoning people to put them on alert. Get a warning out on Radio Périgord.'

Bruno prayed that his elderly van would start first time. He quickly fed his dog, left his chickens to fend for themselves and ran to the vehicle. As if aware of the emergency, it started at once and he drove one-handed down the lane from his cottage towards town, thumbing the autodial to alert first the Mayor and then the doctor, each of them already awoken by the siren. Lights were on and the town was stirring as he drove at speed to the Gendarmerie to tell old Jules on the night desk to call the radio station in Périgueux and to dispatch men up to the fire to seal off the road. As Bruno hurried back out to his van, Capitaine Duroc rushed in from the small barracks, still pulling on his uniform jacket, and Bruno left Jules to explain. At the fire station, Ahmed and Fabien were struggling with the towing rig for the tankers as the other volunteers arrived, enough to man the trucks and tenders. Bruno drove on at the best speed his van could manage, his blue light flashing and the town siren still howling into the night behind him.

By the time he reached the open road by the railway line to Sarlat, he could see the broad glow in the hills above. Bruno shivered with apprehension. Fire frightened him. He had always treated it with a wary respect that had become something close to fear since he'd hauled some wounded French soldiers from a burning armoured car during the Balkan wars. His left arm still carried the scars. Back in his bedside drawer was

3

the Croix de Guerre the government had awarded him, after a lengthy bureaucratic objection that the Bosnian peace-keeping mission hardly qualified as a war.

Bruno wondered if there was anything amongst the jumble in the back of his van that might serve as protective gear. There were gloves and a cap in his hunting jacket, his hunting boots, and some swimming goggles and a bottle of water in his sports bag. He'd probably find an old tennis shirt he could soak and use as a facemask. He tried to push the accelerator harder as the van laboured up the hill. He knew this area well but tried in vain to remember where there might be a barn this high up on the plateau where the land was too poor for farming. It was mainly woods and thin pasture, some tumbledown shepherds' *bories* of old stone, plus the tall microwave tower.

As Bruno rounded the last bend before the plateau, the whole night sky ahead seemed to pulse with red above the trees. He shivered as he remembered the dry summer, the river so low that the tourist canoes had to search out the deeper channels. Automatically he slowed as for the first time he could smell the burning, and then he saw that at least some of the pulsing glow came from the flashing light of Albert's fire truck. Bruno parked off the road. He put on his boots, gloves and hunting cap, looked at his swimming goggles and stuffed them into a pocket, poured water on his tennis shirt and ran up the road to the truck where

4

two *pompiers* stood bracing the spouting hose, silhouetted against the flames.

'Not a barn, just a big wooden shed. We couldn't save it,' shouted Albert against the crackle of the flames and the roar of the truck. He reached into the back of the vehicle and pulled out a heavy yellow fireman's jacket and handed it to Bruno. He looked down at the stout boots on Bruno's feet and nodded approval.

'It could have been a lot worse. We were here in time to stop it spreading to the woods. But the shed's gone, and whatever this crop was.'

More pulsing lights began to grow back up the road as Ahmed came with the second fire truck and the big water tanker, followed by flashes of blue as the Gendarmes arrived. Albert was calling the neighbouring fire chiefs to say their help would not be needed.

'No sign of any people?' Bruno asked when he rang off. Albert shook his head and stomped off to direct the second truck. 'How did you hear about the fire?' Bruno called after him.

'Anonymous call from the phone box in Coux,' Albert shouted back.

Bruno made a mental note of that as he tried to get his bearings. He remembered this road being thickly wooded on both sides, but where he stood was a break in the trees and a dirt track that looked new and which curved into the wide stretch of field and pasture that was burning low but steadily. What little breeze he felt on his cheeks was coming towards him and towards the woods, where the *pompiers* were soaking the brush to deny the flames any fresh fuel. The biggest fire was the ruin of what had been the shed, standing amid the charred crop.

Bruno's foot caught on something. He looked down, and saw a small metal flag, like the one farmers used to identify which seeds they had sown in which rows. He plucked it from the ground and, in the light from the truck headlamps, read the words 'Agricolae Sech G71'. That meant nothing to him, but he stuffed it into his pocket. Shouts came from behind and he turned to see more yellow-clad *pompiers* struggling up with a second hose which bucked in their hands as it filled and a much more powerful jet of water lanced on to the edge of the woods.

'Smell anything funny?' Albert asked, suddenly looming beside him. 'Come on, this way.'

He led the way across the still-smouldering ground and around the side of the shed until they were upwind where it was quieter. Inside the shed were indistinct remains. A metal table, still hot enough to spit as water dripped from what was left of the roof beams, supported some charred machinery. Two smoking roof timbers thrust into the sky, perched on top of what looked like an old filing cabinet. Bruno caught a stink of burned plastic and rubber, and something else.

'Petrol?' he asked.

'That's what I think. We'll send some remains

off to the lab in Bordeaux, but I'll bet this was deliberate. If you go over to the far side of the field, you'll smell it again. Somebody did a proper job, the crops, the shed, the lot. This is going to be a job for you a lot more than for me.'

'If it's arson, it's the *Police Nationale*,' said Bruno. That would mean sealing off the phone box in Coux to check fingerprints.

'If it's arson against crops, it's local. Some farmers' feud, or somebody's been playing games with somebody's wife. And that means the *Police Nationale* won't have the first idea where to start.'

Bruno nodded, peering at the remains inside the hut. 'Albert, that's odd. Have you ever seen a filing cabinet and office stuff like that in a farmer's shed in the middle of a field?'

'No. Could be a computer, but there's no electricity up here. Maybe an old typewriter.'

Bruno turned away and was walking across to the point where the charred crops stopped when the explosion came with a flat crump. Light flared and a rush of heat stunned him as he turned and saw Albert topple to his knees amid the debris of the hut that was bright with new flames.

Bruno ran across, his forearm up to protect his eyes against the searing heat, and grabbed Albert by the collar. Fighting down the internal scream of horror as he plunged into the leaps of flame that seemed hungry to engulf him, Bruno hauled Albert back. The fire chief's legs dragged limply through the flaring wood of the hut and his trousers were on fire. Once they were clear, Bruno speadeagled himself over Albert's legs to douse the flames with the fireproof material of his jacket. And then the other firemen were there, spraying them both with foam from hand-held extinguishers.

Ahmed hauled Bruno off and shone a torch into his face, shouting 'You OK?' while others tended to Albert. Bruno nodded, shook himself and rose a little jerkily to his feet, brushing away the thick foam that covered him.

'A bit scorched, but nothing serious thanks to that jacket Albert gave me,' he said. 'What the hell was that explosion?'

'An aerosol, maybe a can of paint or kerosene. Bastards leave the empty petrol can at the scene and close the cap. It can go off like a bomb once it's hot enough,' Ahmed shrugged. 'Albert should never have got that close. We'd have carried on hosing it but we had to put water on the edge of the fire, stop it reaching the woods.'

'My fault,' said Bruno. 'I was asking him about the equipment inside the hut. How is he?'

Albert had been hauled to his feet and was shaking his head to clear it, flecks of the foam flying off from his helmet and jacket.

'I'll live to make a fool of myself another day. Some damn thing hit me on the ear,' said Albert. He put his hand up to the side of his head and it came away bright with blood. One of the firemen gave him a bottle of water and he drank deeply, spat, and looked across at Bruno and nodded once. 'Thanks,' he said quietly, and handed him the water. Albert's hand was trembling. So, Bruno noticed, was his own.

'How are the legs?' Bruno asked. His voice was hoarse and his throat hurt. The thought of the petrol and of the fire being set deliberately brought a surge of anger. He took a deep breath to control himself.

'Not bad. Flameproof undertrousers, just like the racing drivers,' Albert said, his voice high. He spoke quickly, almost gabbling as the adrenalin rushed through his system. 'I'm OK, just a bit dizzy from whatever hit me. I'll stop by the clinic later. Get checked out. You'd better do the same.'

'Regulations,' said Ahmed. 'You know the rules. You both have to get checked out if we had to foam you.'

More shouting erupted from behind them and another fireman came running up.

'Hey chief, there's a water main. The Gendarmes just ran into a standpipe.'

Albert looked at Bruno and rolled his eyes. 'Probably the first time our Capitaine Duroc ever found anything, and even then he had to run into it.'

They headed back to the road where a jet of water was fountaining high from a broken stand-pipe, and Fabien was doing something violent with a heavy wrench in the light of the Gendarmes' single remaining headlamp. Behind it, Capitaine Duroc could be heard shouting angrily at his men.

Fabien gave a final heave on his wrench and the water stopped.

'We can use this now,' he said. 'There's not much pressure but enough to damp down the embers.'

'Where's that pipe going? Why isn't it on my maps?' Albert demanded crossly, mopping at his bloodied ear with a handkerchief.

'Looks like it goes from the water tower to the microwave station. That's Ministry of Defence so they have a guard post,' said Fabien. 'And this standpipe is here because they have another pipe going off to that shed and the field. Looks to me like there's some fancy irrigation system installed.'

'Irrigation? Up here?' said Albert. 'Somebody's got more money than sense.'

'Funny that the one field that has its own piped water supply is the one that gets torched,' said Bruno. 'You ever heard of this Agricolae?' He reached into his pocket and pulled out the small metal flag he had plucked from the ground.

'Never heard of it. Could be some experimental seed thing, I suppose, but I never heard of anything like that up here.'

They went back to the truck, where the elderly figure of Mayor Gérard Mangin stood patiently by the roadside. Behind him was a row of parked cars belonging to locals come to watch the excitement. The Mayor stepped forward, smiled a greeting and shook hands with Albert and Bruno. A camera flashed. Philippe Delaron must be recording the scene for the local paper.

'Not much to report,' said Albert. 'The danger's over and there's no sign of anyone hurt. Not even me, thanks to Bruno. There's a burned-out shed, a field of crops destroyed and one broken standpipe. I have my suspicions about what started this but we'll have to wait for the lab report.'

'You mean the fire was set deliberately?'

'It looks that way, *Monsieur le Maire*. And I think that explosion you all saw was a petrol can going up. But we'll have to wait and see. Whatever it was, it could have killed somebody. Could have killed me, if Bruno hadn't pulled me out.'

'I hadn't realised this was so serious,' the Mayor said.

'Now I'd better go and see about getting my lads back to the station. Then Bruno and I have to see the medics. But first I'll have that firecoat back, if you please, Bruno. Those things cost a small fortune.'

'Whatever they cost, they're worth every centime,' said Bruno, shedding the coat and brushing away the foam. He turned back to the Mayor. 'There's more to this than meets the eye, Sir. That field had its own water supply and the shed contained what looked like office equipment. Not what you expect to find in a bare upland field in the middle of nowhere. I'll have to inform the landowner, probably have to make a report for the insurance and so on.'

'Have you told the Gendarmes about this?'

11

'Not yet. Capitaine Duroc seems a bit pre-occupied with the damage to his van. It seems they ran into a standpipe.'

'Yes, I saw that.' In the strengthening light of dawn, Bruno watched a smile twitch at the Mayor's lips. 'Well, it seems clear there's been a crime here.'

'Right, and that means the *Police Nationale*, not the Gendarmes. They might even want to send a forensics team.'

Bruno walked on to the row of parked cars and the small knot of local people to tell them there was no danger, the show was over, and please move the cars so the fire trucks could reverse and leave. Big Stéphane the dairy farmer, a friend from the hunting club, was there with his pretty young daughter Dominique. Their farm was just down the hill, probably one of the first to be hit if the fire had spread, and this was normally the hour when they would start the milking. Bruno shrugged off their questions and persuaded most of the onlookers back into their cars. Then he walked over to Capitaine Duroc to arrange for a Gendarme to seal off the phone booth in Coux. It was just gone six a.m. Fauquet's café would be open, and Bruno needed his breakfast.

Bruno walked across to the two familiar cars, an elderly Citroën DS and an even older Citroën *deux-chevaux*, a design that traced back to the 1930s. His friend the Baron, a retired industrialist whose trim figure belied his age, leaned against his car. Beside him stood the owner of a local

12

guesthouse who was known to most of St Denis as the Mad Englishwoman. Bruno had introduced them over a game of tennis, and Pamela and a visiting friend had thoroughly trounced them.

'The Baron woke me with a phone call. I hadn't heard the siren,' Pamela said. A handsome woman whose features were too strong to be described simply as pretty, she was wearing an Hermès headscarf and a battered version of the English waxed jacket that had become highly fashionable in France. Whether she was standing, walking or on horseback, Bruno thought he could recognise her at a distance from her posture alone, the straight back and the proud neck, the bold stride of a woman wholly at ease with herself.

'Where's your horse?' Bruno said, leaning forward to kiss her on both cheeks. She shrank back, laughing.

'Sorry, Bruno. Normally I love this French obsession with kissing, but you smell terrible and look worse. Burned wool and I suppose it's that awful foam all over your trousers. And I think you've lost your eyebrows. It's hard to see under all the black smears over your face.'

'I'm fine,' he said, putting his fingers up to check his eyebrows. They felt like the bristles on his chin.

'I didn't bring the horse,' she said. 'I thought the fire might frighten her. I only came up to see if we'd have to evacuate.'

'What's that building that was on fire?' asked

13

the Baron. 'I thought I knew every inch of these hills but I never knew it was there.'

'Nor me,' said Bruno. 'There's a break in the trees and then a lane that curves away towards the field so you can't see it directly. I want some breakfast. See you back at Fauquet's?'

'Good idea,' said the Baron. 'It's far too late to go back to sleep. Pamela, please be our guest, so long as you promise to prefer our company to your English crossword.'

'But of course, my dear Baron. You're more entertaining than any crossword puzzle. But I think Bruno needs to wash and change first.' She studied him. 'You'd better throw those trousers away. I hope the town pays for a new uniform.'

They turned as two toots sounded from the fire engine. Ahmed was waving to catch Bruno's attention. 'Come on, Bruno, you and Albert are off to the hospital right now. It's the rules.'

14

CHAPTER 2

Even in the age of computers, it was not an easy task to find out who owned the charred field and burned-out shed. Claire, the Mayor's secretary, pored over the *cadastre*, the giant map that listed every building in the far-flung commune of St Denis. It also showed the boundaries of every plot of land, each identified by its own lot number. Until they found this, they could not cross-check the tax list that would show each registered owner.

'There's no building marked on the map anywhere up here,' Claire complained. 'Are you sure you've got the right road, Bruno?'

'Yes, I'm sure.' Showered, shaved and dressed in a spare uniform, and with a clean bill of health from the doctors, Bruno was feeling himself again, except for the eyebrows. He came over to join her at the giant map, careful to keep some space between himself and Claire's ample form. Even though irritated, she couldn't resist flirting with him and batted her eyelashes from sheer habit. The only single man at the *Mairie*, Bruno was used to Claire's ways.

He traced the road he had taken that morning. The microwave tower was there and the water tower over there, so the water line must have run along the road. To that point, he muttered to himself, placing his finger firmly on the spot. He was sure he had the correct lot, but Claire was right. There was no building marked on the map. That was not just very odd, it was also a criminal offence, since it meant the commune had granted no construction permit. And since the land was also served by a water line and a standpipe, the commune was being cheated out of its annual water fee. Still, he had the lot number. He left Claire to roll up the map, and went into the cramped room that was called the registry to check the name of the owner in the tax files.

The owner was a *société anonyme*, a company called Agricolae with a registered office in Paris, and the lot had been purchased from the Ministry of Defence three years earlier. Agricolae – that was the name on the metal flag Bruno had plucked from the ground and put into the pocket of Albert's *pompier* jacket. He'd have to get that back. The file showed that no water fee had been paid, no building tax either, and there was no building permit. That meant the company called Agricolae was in trouble. He was just reaching for the phone to call Albert when Claire peeked around the door to tell him he had a visitor.

'The most important man in St Denis after the Mayor and they still keep you in this miserable

16

hole that they dare to call an office,' declared Commissaire Jean-Jacques Jalipeau, the chief detective of the *Police Nationale* for the *Département*. He took a half-step into the room and at once seemed to fill it.

'Christ, you look terrible, face all red and your eyebrows burned off,' J-J went on. 'Sure it wasn't you started that fire? You certainly got close enough.'

'Far too close,' Bruno replied, smiling at his colleague. 'Heaven help whoever started that damn fire if I get to them first.'

Bruno liked J-J, despite his friend's regular and justified accusation that Bruno's concept of justice owed more to the interests of St Denis than to the *Code Criminel*. They had worked on a couple of successful cases and enjoyed some fine meals together. Bruno led J-J down the ancient stone stairs of the *Mairie*, through the arches into Fauquet's café, where J-J ordered two Ricards.

'How's Isabelle?' J-J began. 'She must be heading up to that new job in Paris any time now.' Isabelle had worked for him as a detective in the regional headquarters in Périgueux before her karate skills and her looks had caught the attention of the Minister of the Interior and secured a flattering photo in *ParisMatch*. J-J had taken a benign interest in the affair that had blossomed throughout the summer, flattering himself that he had played a role as matchmaker.

'She's already left,' Bruno said, trying to keep

17

his voice neutral. 'They said the Minister had some foreign trip coming up and he wanted her on the delegation.'

'Well, you always knew she'd be leaving,' J-J said. 'And you had three happy months.'

Bruno nodded. With the knowledge hanging over them that Isabelle would be leaving, putting her career in Paris ahead of whatever she and Bruno had between them, a constraint had begun to emerge. The walls he had so long kept around his heart, defences that Isabelle had started to dismantle, began to rebuild themselves in a way that he could almost feel. In their last week together, he had lain awake at night, knowing from her breathing that she was also pretending to be asleep, and could almost feel stone piling upon stone within him. Strangely, it had made their love-making even more intense, but the final parting at St Denis's train station had been dry-eyed.

'I miss her,' J-J went on breezily. 'My new inspector isn't much of a replacement. Another woman, but not half so easy on the eye.'

'You're not bringing her in on this case?'

'Not yet. We haven't even got a formal notice of arson from the *pompiers*. But I had one of those discreet calls from Paris just after lunch saying they wanted this sorted out fast. It's not just their usual worry about eco-saboteurs, there's some high-level interest pushing this. What can you tell me?'

Bruno related the events of the night, the unusual nature of the water supply, the former ownership by the Ministry of Defence, and finished with a description of the tax and building permit delinquency of the Agricolae company.

'I'm not sure about the eco-saboteurs, though,' he added. 'Don't they usually want publicity and bring along their journalists and cameras?'

J-J shrugged and swirled the ice cube in his glass, added water and watched his Ricard turn a milky colour. He took a healthy sip. 'I've got a formal letter of request to your Mayor from the Prefect, asking you to be assigned to the case to lend us poor city *flics* your local knowledge. So consider yourself conscripted. I've got a team up in Périgueux, collating all the names of militant *écolos*, and the forensic team from Bergerac will be up at the field by now. What can you tell me about the local *écolos*?'

'Nothing special. We've got one elected to the Council, an elderly hippy who runs a commune in the hills. A sweet man, heart of gold, takes in waifs and strays. Then there's a group that holds protest rallies demanding we close down the local sawmill because of pollution from the chimney. But no real militants. The Greens don't even get ten per cent of the vote. And now let's call at the fire station and see Albert. He won't have the lab reports yet but he should be able to give us some idea of whether this really was deliberate or not.'

'Deliberate?' said Fauquet the café-owner, who

19

was proud of his reputation for being first to hear all the gossip. He leaned over the counter, and slid two coffees towards them. 'On the house, this. Did you say that fire might have been deliberate?'

'No, I didn't say that,' snapped J-J, pushing his coffee back so forcefully that some splashed onto Fauquet's white shirt. A big and burly man, whose rumpled appearance concealed his keen brain, J-J could be very intimidating indeed. 'And if I hear that you did, I'll be back here with an army of suspicious health inspectors and a warrant for your arrest. This is serious police business. Do you understand me, Monsieur?'

CHAPTER 3

Bruno thought that Agricultural Research
Station was a grand name for the modest
single-storey building that had been erected
alongside an old farmhouse on the road to Les
Eyzies. Securing it for St Denis had been one of
the Mayor's prouder achievements. It housed only
four scientists and four technicians and employed
half a dozen locals to run the farm and greenhouses. The Director and chief scientist, Gustave
Petitbon, kept his office in what had been the best
room of the old farmhouse. A tall and very thin
man with a pronounced stoop, he sat perched on
the front of his desk and looked defiantly at the
two policemen.

'I can't tell you what the crop was, not without
authorisation. It's a commercial secret,' he said.
Bruno knew Petitbon slightly from the occasional
attendance at town rugby games and a couple of
mayoral receptions, where Petitbon usually stood
aloof in a corner with a single glass of wine. He
lived quietly in town with his wife and they had
no children to attend Bruno's rugby and tennis
lessons.

'Monsieur Petitbon, I'm ordered by the Minister of the Interior in Paris to conduct this inquiry,' said J-J firmly, his voice starting to rise in volume as he went on. 'I don't think that would have happened unless somebody pretty senior in the Ministry of Agriculture, who are your employers, asked them to get the chief detective of this *Département* to take personal charge of the inquiry. I've put off one murder, two rapes and a bank robbery to come down here. So rather than waste my time, I suggest you call your Ministry in Paris and get whatever authorisation you need before I call my Ministry and tell them I'm going to arrest you for obstructing my inquiries.'

Petitbon looked startled by the sheer volume that J-J's big frame could generate and went behind his desk to telephone. Then he ostentatiously turned his swivel chair so his back was towards them and mumbled into the phone. He listened attentively as the voice on the other end of the line barked what sounded like orders. The phone was slammed down before Petitbon could finish his last deferential '*Oui, Monsieur le Directeur.*' Petitbon jumped slightly, turned and put the phone down.

'What I am about to tell you must go no further than this room,' he began self-importantly, sitting up very straight. 'The crop that was burned was a project of national importance, backed by the Ministry of Agriculture but initiated by the Ministry of Defence. Concern about the implications of climate change led the Defence Ministry to

22

recommend a special project on drought-resistant crops that might flourish on marginal soil. The project included one pharmaceutical and one agro-chemical corporation, and a new private company was formed, Agricolae SA, to organise and fund the research. We have been working with a number of crop varieties – soya and other beans, maize and potatoes, some vines. Those were the crops that were destroyed. It is a matter of urgent importance to establish who was responsible, and indeed, who might have known of the project. It was highly confidential.'

Bruno remembered the little flag that he had recovered from the fire station. 'So a small metal marker that said Agricolae Sech would be yours? I found it at the site.'

'Agricolae Sech – short for *Sécheresse* – that's the drought-resistant strain we are trying to develop. We have some of the crops on the farm here, but we also wanted to do some tests on marginal soil. That's why we planted up there on the plateau. And it looks like it's all gone, along with a lot of files and research notes. Three years' work.'

'Do you have any particular reason to think it might have been deliberate?' Bruno asked, keeping his tone light. 'Any enemies, aggrieved ex-employees, jealous husbands?'

Petitbon smiled, and his thin, almost severe face became quite pleasant. 'I'd prefer the latter. But no, no enemies I can think of, except maybe those crazy eco-saboteur types. Was it arson?'

23

'We're waiting for the lab tests.'

'Well, I may be able to tell you. We had a webcam set up in the shed, playing back to a computer here at the research station so we can go back and check rates of growth, colour, ripeness and so on. It should also have a record of anybody behaving suspiciously in the field or around the shed. Even in low light or night-time, we can probably enhance the image a bit.'

'Wouldn't it have burned? And how did you power it?'

'We had a solar panel up there and that was more than enough. The camera is probably destroyed, but the image will be stored on the computer. I was going to take a look when you arrived.'

'I'm sorry about your three years' work, Monsieur.'

'Thank you. We'd better go over to the lab. That's where the equipment is.'

'Just one thing,' Bruno added. 'These crop varieties you were working on, were they genetically modified, the controversial stuff that people protest against?'

'Of course. That's why it was all kept confidential. And we've made real progress with some of the soybean strains up there.'

'How many people here at the station knew of this project?' J-J asked.

'Just about everybody, I imagine. All the scientists and technicians, and the men who did the actual farming. They're all aware that this is confidential. We were told not even to discuss it with our wives.'

'So altogether, ten or fifteen people,' J-J said.

'Fourteen. And I have no reason to question the loyalty of any one of them.'

'I'll need their personnel files and a room at my disposal here for my team. It will be more discreet here than back in town.'

'Very well,' said Petitbon. 'I suppose you'd better have this room. I can always make do over in the lab. And now let's see what the webcam can tell us.'

But the webcam had little to reveal. Fixed under the eaves of the shed, it showed nothing until the digital timer displayed 03.02 when the first sign of distant movement began on the western edge of the field. At 03.06 there was more movement on the northern edge and then the camera seemed to shudder.

'That could be the intruder trying the door,' said Petitbon. 'It was locked, but from the way that the shaking goes on and gets violent, I suspect the door was forced.'

At 03.09 came the first faint glow of light, very close, and a sudden flare of flame. The webcam stopped transmitting at 03.18.

'Well, at least we have the time,' said J-J. 'Can you make a copy of that for my forensic boys? They may be able to enhance it, get something from that bit of movement. But if you ask me, whoever was spreading that petrol knew exactly where your webcam was and what it did, so the first line of inquiry will have to be whether this was an inside job.'

'Just one thing,' added Bruno. 'Do you have any more of these web cameras?'

Petitbon nodded. 'Yes, we monitor some other crops.'

'Well, I think you'd better put them up around here, around the offices and the greenhouses. Whoever burned your crops may want to come back and finish the job here at the research station.'

CHAPTER 4

After three fruitless days of interviewing the staff of the research station, Bruno had finally been able to relax in the barber's chair for his monthly haircut when the call came from Nathalie, the cashier at the wine shop of Hubert de Montignac. Listed in the *Guide Hachette des Vins* as one of the finest such *caves* in France, it was one of only three places outside the vineyard to boast an unbroken run of Château Pétrus from 1944 to the present. For Bruno, who understood that a great part of the law's duty was to uphold the grand traditions of France and of St Denis, it was close to being a shrine. He leapt from the barber's chair, careless of Baptiste's flashing scissors, tossed aside the sheet that covered him and thrust his official hat upon his half-shorn locks. Pausing only to put the magnetic blue light on the roof, he roared off in his van.

Nathalie had not been very precise about the nature of the emergency, only that it was trouble and he'd better come quick. It took Bruno less than three minutes to force his way through the usual traffic jam at the small roundabout by

27

the bridge and into the courtyard of Hubert's sprawling single-storey barn. Despite the ivy and flowers that tumbled from various old wine barrels it was not, Hubert admitted, the most impressive of entrances to an establishment so renowned. But then, Hubert liked to explain, he spent his money on the contents rather than the showcase. He also spent his money on his appearance, cultivating a countrified English look with tweed sports jackets and Viyella shirts, knitted ties and hand-made brogues that he bought in London on his sales trips.

Bruno saw the usual mix of cars in the court-yard, Mercedes and BMWs, Citroëns and Renaults and Peugeots from all across France. His eye lingered on a green Range Rover with British plates. As a devoted hunter who too often found himself hauling the carcass of a deer through long stretches of rough country, it was the only vehicle that sparked a touch of envy. But he knew he'd be more comfortable with the army-surplus Citroën jeep that he was saving for.

Bruno quickly took in the scene. Nearest the entrance, with one door open and a shouting match under way all around it, was a white Porsche convertible with an extremely pretty young woman sitting in the passenger seat. Hubert himself was standing in front of the driver's door, gripping the steering wheel to prevent a very angry man in bright yellow trousers and a pink polo shirt from climbing in and driving away. Nathalie sat grimly on the Porsche's bonnet, while a younger woman whom Bruno did not know perched beside her, presumably some new employee. With the sun gleaming off the thick ringlets of her blond hair and large dark eyes the new girl was attractive enough for Bruno's glance to linger. She stared back boldly, the kind of frank appraisal he might expect from an older and more experienced woman.

Standing beside the new girl was Max, a handsome youth with blond streaks in his hair whose skin glowed with good health. He grinned at the sight of Bruno, who had taught the boy to play rugby. Now at the university in Bordeaux, Max had a summer job working for Hubert. As backdrop to the scene around the Porsche, a small audience of enthralled customers was gathered in the door of the *cave*.

His blue light still flashing, Bruno had stopped with the front of his van almost touching the Porsche, blocking its getaway. He took out his notebook and made a note of the licence plate. It ended in 75, which meant Paris. He strode up to the group, which now fell silent. This was no time for the habitual round of kissing and hand-shaking. It was an occasion for the anonymous majesty of the law.

'*Messieurs-Dames*,' he began, touching his peaked cap in salute and taking in the scene. 'Chief of Police Courrèges at your service.'

Bruno took a good look at the strangers and

their expensive car. The man in pink and yellow must have been in his late fifties. He had a magnificent head of long, curling white hair, a small paunch, and he wore a gold wedding ring. The woman in his Porsche looked in her twenties. She was wearing big sunglasses and shoes that had cost – Bruno guessed – at least two weeks of his pay. He noted that she wore an impressive collection of diamonds on her fingers but no wedding ring. An exquisitely groomed small white poodle with a diamante collar sat at her feet.

'He dropped the Château Pétrus Eighty-two and is refusing to pay for it,' declared Hubert, in tones suitable for the announcement of a death in the family.

'You mean, he broke it?' Bruno was awed. 'A bottle of the Eighty-two?' This was indeed a death in the family.

'Two thousand two hundred euros worth of wine, smashed on the floor,' chimed in Nathalie.

'It was an accident,' said the man in pink. 'The bottle was slippery, greasy. It wasn't my fault.'

'And you are, Monsieur?' inquired Bruno.

'Just a tourist, a short vacation.'

'Your papers, please.'

'Look, I'm just passing through. I'll be on my way once these people stop blocking my car . . .'

'Your papers, Monsieur. And yours, please, Madame.'

'Mademoiselle,' the well-groomed young woman corrected him, fishing in her purse for her identity card. Bruno recognised the distinctive Chanel logo.

'Apologies, Mademoiselle – ah – d'Alambert. This is still your address, Boulevard Maurice Barrès in Paris?'

She nodded. Bruno copied it all down in his notebook. She was twenty-four and had been born in Lille. It was quite a jump from that industrial city in northern France to Boulevard Barrès, overlooking the Bois de Boulogne, a celebrated street in the richest part of Paris. Her profession was listed as model.

'Monsieur,' he repeated. 'Your papers.'

The man pursed his lips as if to object, shrugged and reached for his wallet, an expensive slim model of crocodile skin, and handed across his identity card and his driving licence.

'Monsieur Hector d'Aubergny Dupuy, of Avenue Foch, Paris, Sixteenth *arrondissement*. Is that right?' the man nodded. Avenue Foch was a grand address, and but a pleasant stroll from the Bois de Boulogne and Boulevard Barrès.

'And if I am to telephone to your home, Monsieur, would someone be present who could confirm your identity?' Bruno paused, and glanced at the girl in the Porsche. 'Perhaps a Madame Dupuy?'

Dupuy coloured, his face starting to match the pink of his polo shirt. 'I doubt it, not at this time.'

'And your business address, if you please.'

He opened the wallet again and fished out a

31

card that identified him as *chef d'entreprise*, the boss of a business consultancy named after himself, with an office on the Avenue Monceau. Bruno pulled out his mobile phone. 'And there would be somebody at this number in Paris, Monsieur, to vouch for you and certify that the car is yours?'

'Yes, my secretary. But I have the car's registration papers and insurance and . . .'

Bruno held up a hand, turned away and dialled the number of Philippe Delaron, who took photos of weddings and wrote up the local sports results for the *Sud-Ouest* newspaper, to suggest that the part-time reporter come with his camera. Bruno turned back to the now silent group.

'I'm not sure that any crime has been committed, but there's clearly the prospect of a civil lawsuit to which I would most certainly be called as a witness. So I must ask your patience while I satisfy myself that I understand what has taken place,' he said with a deliberately ponderous delivery. 'And because of that, I have asked a local photographer who sometimes helps the police with recording scenes of dispute to join us.'

'You mean Philippe, who takes pictures for the newspaper?' inquired Nathalie. This time, Bruno noticed with satisfaction, Dupuy's pink face was turning white again. Bruno looked at the employees of the wine shop clustered around the bonnet of the Porsche.

'Perhaps, Madame, you might descend from the

front of the car now that everything is calm and under control and attend to your customers inside the shop.' Nathalie flounced off, and the pretty young stranger beside her slid off rather less gracefully. Bruno noted that Hubert reached quickly forward to help her, only to be beaten to the task by Max. Nathalie, Hubert's long-time mistress, had also noticed Hubert's protective move and her jaw tightened.

'I don't believe you have met our new *stagiaire*, Mademoiselle Jacqueline Duplessis from Québec. She's a quick thinker – the first one out to sit on the car after the bottle broke and the customer tried to leave,' Hubert said. 'She's been studying wine in California and she'll be working with us for this year, learning our ways. Her family in Canada make a very interesting dessert wine.'

Bruno shook hands with the young woman, who held his hand a moment too long, greeted him in the curious accent of French Canada and almost stroked his palm as she released it. Bruno clasped his hands firmly behind his back and murmured a pleasantry before turning back to the entrance, weighing how best to proceed. The first thing would be keep this as private as possible.

'There's no more to see, *Messieurs-Dames*,' Bruno called to the little audience in the doorway. 'Please return inside and continue your shopping.' He moved forward, arms outstretched but with a smile on his face, steering them inside. Then he resumed his official expression and faced the white-haired gallant from Paris.

'Monsieur Dupuy, you agree that you handled the bottle of Château Pétrus and that it fell from your hands?'

'Well, it slid. It was greasy.'

'Then let's go inside and examine the remains of the bottle. With your permission, Monsieur de Montignac?'

The *cave* was one of Bruno's favourite places. Directly ahead lay Hubert de Montignac's own wines, which were the source of his success. He had started by blending the wines of various local growers into his own brand of Bergerac whites, reds and rosés. Then he'd bought a small vineyard near the castle of Monbazillac to produce his version of the sweet and golden dessert wine. Later came the partnership with an English businessman who had bought a run-down château and vineyard outside Bergerac and produced a wine that won prizes at the great fairs in Dijon and Paris. To the right lay the seat of the *cave*'s reputation, row upon row of the finest wines of Bordeaux, year after year after year of Latours and Lafites. Cheval Blanc and Angélus, and the famous unbroken run of Château Pétrus. To the left was what was said to be one of the finest selections of malt whiskies outside Scotland and one of the best collections of vintage Armagnacs in France.

Between these two wings was the heart of the

place, six tall plastic cylinders. These gigantic vats, with their petrol pumps attached, sold wine in bulk. All comers were invited to buy their Bergerac white and red and rosé, their *vin de table* and their sweet white wines for one euro a litre or less, so long as they brought their own plastic containers and did their own filling. This was where Bruno bought his everyday wine. The air smelled of wine, old wine and new, fresh spilled and freshly opened, and at least some of it breathtakingly costly. Knowing the way to the shelf of Pétrus, Bruno led his small entourage to the altar of this temple to wine, and stopped, looking down mournfully at the smashed bottle on the tiled floor. Château Pétrus '82. In respect, he removed his hat, and knelt to see it more closely. The price, carefully written in delicate thin strokes of white paint, was 2200 euros.

He peered closely at the largest shard of glass. There was indeed a grease mark, more of a long smeared thumbprint. He turned and looked at Dupuy's glistening face.

'Monsieur, I noticed in the pouch by the driver's seat of your car a tube of sunscreen, a very sensible precaution when driving a convertible, although it can be somewhat greasy. How recently did you apply it to your face?'

Dupuy shrugged, and the door opened and Delaron walked in, his camera around his neck.

'Monsieur Delaron, perhaps you would begin with a photo of the Porsche outside, and be sure to get the number plate, and of course the passenger,' Bruno began. 'It may make a story for your paper, the sad death of a bottle of Pétrus Eighty-two . . .'

'I'll pay for the bottle. It may have been my fault,' interrupted Dupuy, and handed a black credit card to Nathalie. 'Then let's forget about the whole thing.'

'You're lucky it wasn't the Sixty-one,' said Nathalie. 'That's four thousand one hundred euros. By the way, Bruno, what's wrong with your hair?'

'This is a most handsome gesture, Monsieur, just what we might expect from a gentleman,' said Bruno, ignoring Nathalie but hurriedly replacing his hat on his half-cut hair. 'It's a pity there aren't more like you. And I'm sure that, in a spirit of reconciliation, Monsieur de Montignac would like to offer you a small glass . . .'

Hubert was already behind the counter pulling a bottle from the cooler. 'I was planning on tasting a new shipment of the Krug Ninety-five, if Monsieur Dupuy would care to join me, and Mademoiselle, of course.' He tapped the bottom of the bottle to prevent it from bubbling over, and removed the cork with a restrained but festive pop. Jacqueline scurried forward with glasses and Nathalie stood sternly by the door with the credit-card bill for Dupuy to sign. Max emerged from the vast warehouse at the rear with a mop and dustpan and began cleaning up. Bruno went outside and invited the bored-looking

Mademoiselle d'Alambert to join them for a glass of champagne. She left the car with impressive speed and a flash of thigh, leaving the poodle behind.

CHAPTER 5

His interrupted haircut completed, Bruno took the ancient stairs of the *Mairie* up to his office, wondering as he often did just how many feet it had required over the centuries to wear away the stone steps into such deep curves. The usual mail and paperwork awaited him, along with the endless to-do list that had piled up while he had been working at the Research Station with J-J. It ranged from certificates of good conduct for people applying for jobs and university places to contracts for the musicians who would play at the civic ball on the night of the fair of St Louis. As secretary of the Council's sports committee, he had to sign the cheque for the first stage of the re-painting of the rugby stadium in time for the new season. There was a faxed notification of death from the *Préfecture de Police* in Paris, advising him that a resident of St Denis had died in the jurisdiction of Paris, and would he please inform the family. The name of the deceased was unfamiliar, but the address was that of the hippy commune that had survived in the hills since the 1960s, probably because they

38

produced the best goat cheese in the market. He would have to find time for that call before the end of the day, but he would use the occasion to put some questions about GMOs and militant *écolos*.

His hat went on top of the bookcase, beside the FBI baseball cap that a friend had brought him after a holiday in New York. Bruno squeezed between the filing cabinets and the wall to get behind his battered metal desk. He sat, hearing the familiar squeak of the swivel chair, and looked down through the window at the busy roundabout and the bustle of the main shopping street behind it.

Most of the people he could see were tourists, studying the houses for sale in the estate agents' windows. That was the new St Denis: four bakeries, four women's hairdressers, four estate agencies, three banks, three shops selling *foie gras* and other local delicacies, and only one grocery and one butcher's shop. The fishmonger had long since given way to an insurance agency. The other grocery had been replaced the previous winter by a place that serviced computers and sold cellphones and DSL lines for the internet, and the other butcher had retired in the spring and now rented his premises to an estate agent. It was no longer the St Denis Bruno had first come to, a decade ago, when the small towns of rural France still retained the shops and texture he remembered from his boyhood. Now people shopped at the supermarkets on the outskirts of town, or

39

drove to the complex of shopping malls and hyper-markets outside Périgueux, forty minutes away. He sighed, and turned back to his desk.

He filled out the good conduct forms, signing and stamping each one with his required seal, and completed the musicians' contracts. He completed the paperwork for two death notices to be sent to the Préfecture, and phoned Father Sentout to confirm the church for the funerals, and then something jogged his memory. There had been another batch of the good conduct forms that he had signed earlier in the year. He looked at his file of copies, and there it was: an application for a summer job as a lab assistant at the Agricultural Research Station for Dominique Suchet, Stéphane's daughter. He and J-J had interviewed the permanent staff, checking the backgrounds of the technicians and the farm workers. He hadn't thought about the summer jobs or any of the school-leavers on work experience or internships. *Putain*, that meant more work, but it had to be done.

Bruno paused. Dominique had been at the scene of the fire with her father, natural enough since their farm was just down the hill. Still, it was an inter-esting coincidence. He looked again at Dominique's good conduct form, which contained a recommend-ation from her old headmaster at the town *collège*, the secondary school where the kids went before going on to the *lycée*. He picked up the phone again and called Rollo, the headmaster, still working despite the school holidays.

Rollo told him she was a very promising girl, good at maths and science. She'd done well at the *lycée* and was now studying computer science at Grenoble university. Proud of his pupil as a hard worker and captain of the school swimming team, Rollo went on to recall a mock election. Bruno suddenly began to scribble notes as Rollo described how Dominique and her partner had plastered the school with posters, held meetings about global warming and melting icecaps and defeated the Socialist favourites to pull off a victory for the Greens. The partner, Rollo responded to Bruno's question, had been Max, the lad from Alphonse's hippy commune who was working at Hubert's wine shop.

Bruno put down the phone. The prospect of a militant young Green at the research station, doubtless knowing about the GMO project, with a father whose farm was near the research crops, was by far the best lead in a case that was making no progress. But Stéphane was a friend. He'd have to make some inquiries of his own before talking to J-J, at least to establish whether the girl had a decent alibi for the time of the fire. He rose and was reaching for his cap when Claire put her head around his door to say the Mayor needed to see him.

'I like the new haircut, Bruno,' she added, lingering in the doorway.

'It's the same one I get every month,' he said, grabbing his notebook.

41

'No it's shorter,' she said, edging by the door so that he had to squeeze past. 'It makes you look younger.'

'But I'm even older now than I was when it was cut,' he said, and left her puzzling out his meaning.

His spirits rose as they always did when he entered the Mayor's office. The rich colours of old wood and panelling and faded rugs could hardly have been more different from his own cramped and functional office, nor from the modernised reception area where the public came. The Mayor kept to the old ways, preferring his fountain pen to a computer terminal, and the traditional system of manila files bound with green and red tape over some electronic database.

'*Bonjour*, Bruno. I had a call earlier from the American Embassy in Paris, commercial section, following up on a letter they sent, but somehow Claire seems to have misfiled it. Can we receive some distinguished businessman who wants to discuss a possible investment in our region.'

'What kind of investment?'

'They didn't say. But I'd be glad of anything. We need the jobs. The meeting is here in my office, tomorrow at nine a.m. I'd like you to be there, along with Xavier.' Xavier was the *Maire-adjoint*, one of Bruno's tennis partners, and probably the future Mayor when Gérard Mangin eventually stepped down.

'Did we get a name?' Bruno asked.

'Only if Claire finds that letter.'

'If the meeting is at nine, they'll be staying in a hotel near here. I'll ring around, find out the name and then see what we can dig up.'

'It could be just some big donor to a presidential campaign looking to buy a château. You know these Americans,' grunted the Mayor. Bruno knew him to be a wily old politician who had learned his skills as an aide to Jacques Chirac about the time Bruno had been born. 'Still no progress on the fire?'

'Only that we got the lab report confirming the presence of petrol. It was arson, all right. But we're no nearer knowing who or why. The staff all seem to be in the clear, so J-J is working on possible competitors and I'm supposed to make discreet inquiries among the locals, starting with the *écolos* and then the nearby farmers who might have been worried about contamination of their own crops. But first, I want to find out a bit more about the anonymous phone call that gave the first alert of the fire. It came from the call box at Coux. It's a long shot, but somebody may have seen or heard something.'

CHAPTER 6

Back in his office, Bruno tracked down the American businessman at the Centenaire at Les Eyzies, the grandest hotel in the district with a restaurant that boasted two Michelin rosettes. Thérèse on the reception desk had a daughter in Bruno's tennis class, so he scribbled hasty notes as Thérèse told him everything she knew. A young man named Fernando Bondino had arrived in a big Mercedes and taken the Presidential suite at a cost of nearly a thousand euros a night. He had demanded an internet connection the moment he checked in, eaten the *menu dégustation* with a bottle of Château Pétrus and then the best Armagnac. The booking had been made by the Dupuy management consultancy in Paris, address on the Avenue Monceau. Bruno checked his notebook for the names he had scribbled down at the wine shop. The address and the phone number were the same. A Monsieur Dupuy was booked to join Bondino that night.

Bruno fired up his computer, typed in google.fr and looked up the name Bondino. A flood of page references came up, starting with Bondino

Wines Inc, in English and Spanish. He understood enough to see that they ran vineyards in California, Chile, Australia and South Africa and were clearly a very large and rich company. He turned back to the main Google page and found articles in French from *Figaro, Marianne* and *Les Echos*, the business paper. The *Figaro* piece was an interview, which he printed out, marking the passage in which the head of the company, Francis X. Bondino, was asked if his global wine empire would ever spread to France.

'France and Italy are the homes of great wine, and our ambition will not be complete until we return to the source of our craft in these great countries,' Bondino was quoted as saying. His son Fernando had added: 'And frankly, the wine industry in these countries is suffering from too many small vineyards overproducing too much indifferent wine. They have not yet followed the United States and Australia into a rationalisation of the industry with new techniques and modern marketing. Opportunities for reorganisation are enormous.'

Bruno read on in *Marianne* about a family feud that had split the business a generation earlier, with prolonged lawsuits and much bad blood, and a brother and his wife disinherited. *Les Echos* had a story about the company buying new vineyards in South Africa the previous year that contained some figures that startled him. They had turned down an offer to buy out the company for 600 million euros, and had nearly 3,000 employees worldwide – roughly the population of St Denis – and had made a profit the previous year of thirty-eight million euros. Marvelling at the amount of instant information that the computer brought to his desk, he printed out the story from *Les Echos* and prepared a small dossier of his researches for the Mayor, while wondering what exactly a firm so large might want from his little town. He turned to his telephone and rang St Denis's own expert on the wine trade, Hubert de Montignac.

'Bruno, my dear, I've put aside a fine bottle for you to show my appreciation of your tact and good sense,' Hubert began as soon as he heard Bruno's voice. 'Really, I owe you a big favour.'

'Just doing my duty. Listen, what can you tell me about an American wine corporation called Bondino?'

'Bondino are very big, up there close to Gallo and Mondavi among the American giants. Worldwide operations, Australia and South Africa, and there was a rumour that they're sniffing around one of the big Bordeaux châteaux. They make their money with mass wines they call varietals.'

'What are these varietals?'

'It's just the name of a grape like Chardonnay or Cabernet Sauvignon, with each brand made from a particular grape. It's mass production, exactly the same product year after year, whatever the weather and terrain. But come on, why are you asking about Bondino?'

46

'Just that Bondino is coming in to see the Mayor. That's all we know, so I thought I'd call you. What would they want with us?'

'Could be a number of things. They don't have much of an operation in Europe and it might not be a bad idea to look around here. As you know, we used to be a big wine-growing area, before phylloxera, when we started growing tobacco instead. Now the tobacco trade is dying so land is pretty cheap. There's no *appellation contrôlée* in this valley to drive the price up. Funny you should mention this, because that guy who dropped the bottle, Dupuy, was asking me about wine and land prices around here just after you left. I let him try a glass of that stuff the Domaine produces, a bit overpriced but it's not bad.'

'You mean Domaine de la Vézère? But that's just a house wine that Julien makes for his hotel and restaurant. It's not bad, but it's not exactly a viable operation.'

'You'd be surprised, Bruno. Julien bought some of that neighbouring land across the commune boundary, so you may not have known about it. He must have eight or nine hectares by now, and that's enough to make forty thousand bottles a year when the vines mature. The land is all on a south-facing slope on a chalk hill with good drainage so there's no reason not to grow decent wine. And his hotel and restaurant is a captive market.'

Bruno had never had much to do with business,

but he suddenly got the point. A small grower in a standard part of Bordeaux would be lucky to get even one euro a bottle when he sold to a *négociant*, but at the restaurant Julien could sell every one of his bottles for eight or nine euros.

'When I realised what he was up to, I bought a few hectares just along from the Domaine, reckoning I'd get a good price from Julien the next time he expands,' Hubert went on.

'You mean Philibert's old farm, off the Limeuil road? I thought you bought that as a place to house your staff.'

'Sure, but it was mainly an investment in the land, and I'll be planting my own vines there in November. Don't forget that I have some of the same advantage as Julien at his hotel. I can bottle it as *vin du pays* and sell it in the *cave* for three euros.'

'What about Dupuy? What did he want to know?'

'Well, he calmed down a bit with the champagne, and then I presented his girlfriend with a bottle. Not the Krug, but I thought, hell, he'd paid out a lot of money. He obviously knew a lot about wine and is obviously pretty rich so I thought I might try and turn him into a regular customer. Why do you ask?'

'Dupuy's office in Paris made the hotel reservation for Bondino and Dupuy is booked into his hotel tonight.'

'Don't tell me, the Centenaire. Nothing but the best for Bondino.'

'That's right. But Dupuy got a single room, so where does that leave the girlfriend?'

'He said he had to put the girl on to the Paris train at Périgueux. She didn't have much conversation but she was certainly decorative. It looks like that little romantic interlude is over.'

'And now it's time for business,' said Bruno. 'Let's stay in touch on this, because the Mayor is going to need your knowledge of the wine trade. They probably think we're a bunch of country bumpkins down here, and when it comes to me they're not far wrong.'

'Sure, I'll help however I can. But let's keep me out of it, at least in public. We need to know what they're really up to.'

'Just one more thing. What's the price of land around the Domaine? Land that you might use to grow wine, I mean.'

'Well, you know what I paid for Philibert's place, a hundred and twenty thousand euros, for just over three hectares and the old farmhouse.'

'I know what you paid officially for tax purposes,' Bruno said. 'I don't know what you paid under the table when the *notaire* left the room.'

Hubert chuckled. 'The usual ratio. Only the greedy go for more than a third off the real price.'

'So you paid about a hundred and eighty, and the farmhouse alone is probably worth that. What are we saying, four or five thousand a hectare for the land?'

'Somewhere around there. Maybe five or six,

depending on what the land is used for. Straight farmland, maybe as little as two or three. With zoning permission for building, twenty or more.'

'What would it be worth if it were proper wine land, with the *appellation contrôlée*?'

'It depends. If this were Champagne you're talking about six or seven hundred thousand a hectare. But a vineyard in the Bordeaux with any kind of decent reputation would be fifty thousand a hectare and up. In the Bergerac, maybe ten. I think Julien paid about three thousand a hectare for the extra land he bought.'

'What's his place worth?'

'Taken all together, the château and the winery and the big restaurant, at least three million euros, probably more. It's a good business.'

'Christ, I must be the poorest man in St Denis,' said Bruno.

'Well, after today, you're richer by a lovely '89 Cos d'Estournelle from St Estèphe. That's my way of saying thanks for that business earlier today.'

'You don't have to do that. You more than repaid me with all this information.'

'My dear Bruno, it's in my interest to know what this Bondino wants. As for the wine, let's make a date for me to bring it up one night to your place. You can make me one of your truffle omelettes and we'll enjoy it together. Perhaps we should invite some friends and make an evening of it.'

CHAPTER 7

Coux was a quiet place with a bakery, a *tabac*, a café and a small hotel where Bruno would occasionally join friends for Sunday lunch. It lay outside the commune of St Denis, so he did not know it well. Thinking his jurisdiction was therefore somewhat thin, he left his cap in the van.

The phone box stood in front of the tiny *Mairie*, a scrap of yellow police tape still fluttering from the handle where it had been sealed. Bruno peered in, took a note of the number, and saw that it was one of the modernised ones that took no coins, only phone cards. France Télécom might have a record of the card used, but J-J's forensics team would doubtless have checked that. Off to one side was a bicycle stand and a small parking area, enough for perhaps two cars and a motorbike. Bruno scanned the ground. There was a patch of oil that looked fresh. He took a tissue from the pack in his car and gently pressed a corner into the edge of the stain. The thin paper went translucent, so the oil was recent enough to be interesting. Bruno strolled down to the small hotel to take a coffee with Sylvestre, the owner who was also the chef and bartender. He asked if he'd seen anything on the night of the fire.

'Three in the morning? I'd have been fast asleep,' said Sylvestre, But from the cash desk, where Sylvestre's wife was poring over the books, came a sniff. 'Snoring like an ox, more like,' she said. 'But I heard nothing. You might try the baker. He's usually up about four to start the oven.'

But the baker said he slept deep until the alarm woke him at four. Bruno shrugged, resigning himself to making inquiries up and down the long main street, when the baker jerked his thumb across the road and suggested Bruno try his uncle, a retired postman, who always complained of waking early and seldom getting back to sleep. 'But you'll probably find him in the café,' the baker added, as Bruno turned to go. 'His name's Félix, Félix Jarreau. Buy him a drink and he'll tell you anything he thinks you want to hear.'

Every café in France seemed to have the same group of old cronies playing cards around a small table at the back of the room, their glasses of *petit blanc* beside them and a TV blaring away ignored above their heads. Bruno recognised Félix Jarreau from his postman days, and like most people in the valley Félix knew Bruno by sight. Bruno was introduced and shook hands all round, waited until invited to sit, declined the offer of a drink, and explained his task. The bartender's inevitable curiosity brought him across to their table with a bottle to refill the glasses and then to hover as Félix said he had indeed heard something.

'Just after three-thirty, and I know because I looked at the clock when I woke up, I heard a motorbike coming down the street and then stopping by the *Mairie*. I looked out and there was the bike parked and someone going into the phone box. But he wore a helmet, one of those big ones with a chin piece. He came out and went off down the hill.'

'Did you see his face? Would you know him again?' Bruno asked.

Félix shook his head. 'Not in that helmet.'

'Didn't he take it off to make the call?'

Félix shrugged. 'You can't see that from my window. I didn't look out for long, just went back to the kitchen to make some coffee.'

'What about the bike? Anything about it you remember?'

'It was a modern one, the kind they use for motocross, tiny mudguards, fast-revving engine, noisy. All the youngsters drive them these days.'

'Did you see him drive off?'

'No, didn't hear him either. He could have free-wheeled down the hill.'

The heat finally beginning to fade from the late summer day, Bruno climbed into the furnace of his van. He opened all the windows and pondered the delicate tasks ahead. First he would have to interrogate Stéphane, a close friend, and then he

53

would have to pass on the news of a death to someone at Alphonse's commune. Sighing, he set out, taking the same winding road up the hill that he had taken on the morning of the fire. He turned off over a small bridge by a wayside shrine that commemorated two young Resistance boys, *Fusillés par les allemands*, one of them Stéphane's uncle. This road led past a steep and muddy hollow that seldom saw the sun, which Stéphane rented out to the local motocross club for their trail bikes. Beyond the hollow, with its constant buzzing whine of straining engines, Bruno came to Stéphane's pastures and the old farm, now almost over-whelmed by the new dairy and cowsheds and cheese barn.

He had spent many a happy evening here, enjoyed long Sunday lunches, brought back game from his hunting days with Stéphane, and every February had helped the family kill and clean the annual pig. He had taught Dominique how to rinse out the intestines in the swift brook of running water that led down to the shrine. Stéphane's friendship would be a central part of Bruno's life long after the ministers of the Interior and Agriculture had been voted out of office. He would handle this meeting with great care.

'*Salut*, Bruno,' said the big farmer, greeting him at the entrance to the milking shed, a broom in his hand, while Dominique played a running hose over the floor. She turned it off and clomped across in her big rubber boots to hug him.

54

'We're just finishing,' said Stéphane. 'Care for a little *apéro*? I always reckon I deserve a Ricard after this job.'

'Not this time, thanks. I'm on business, checking into that fire. It looks as though it was started deliberately, so I'm checking with everybody nearby to see if they heard or saw anything at about three that morning.'

'That's a bit early, even for me,' said Stéphane. 'I was up about four-thirty, as usual, and then got the phone call from the *Mairie*. I looked out and saw the glow. I got Dominique up and we left the cows in the barn and took the truck up to the fire. That's where we saw you. I didn't hear anything. What about you, Dominique? You were fast asleep when I woke you.'

She shook her pretty head, her cool grey eyes and clear complexion the very image of youthful innocence. 'I heard nothing, not even the phone.'

'Did you know the place at all, from when you were working at the research station?'

'Sure, I was up there once or twice a week to bring back samples and take up testing equipment. We never left expensive stuff there overnight. And every time I was there, I had to fill in the log, but that must have got burned.'

'So you knew what they were growing up there.'

'You mean those GMO crops? They used to scare me stiff, but not now that I know more about it. The only thing that worries me now is contamination, seeds blowing over into our fields and

55

getting into the crops and maybe into the milk. One of the projects I worked on was seeing whether we could test milk for GMO traces. I remember thinking that could wipe my dad out if customers thought they were getting these Frankenstein foods in his milk and cheese.'

'I suppose it could. Did you tell your dad?'

'We talked about it a lot,' said Stéphane. 'But there's that big bank of trees and the woods between their field and my land, and Dominique said the stuff they were testing was pretty obvious and it's not what the cows tend to eat anyway. She said not to worry.'

'Well, I'm no expert but I can't say I'm feeling very reassured,' said Bruno. 'Still, it seems there wasn't anything secret about what was being grown up there.'

'All of us who worked there knew, naturally,' said Dominique. 'And of course I told Dad, but like I said it wasn't in his interest to spread the word around. And it's not as though there were any farms up there with crops at risk, the land is too poor.'

'So you're less worried about this GMO stuff now, is that right? I remember you used to be a real *écolo* when you were at school, you and Max winning that mock election.'

'I'm still a real *écolo*,' she said, almost snapping. 'And so's Max. It's just that there are bigger things to worry about – global warming, the icecaps, millions of refugees as the sea levels rise. That's when we'll need GMO crops to feed people. Did you know the Rice Research Centre in the Philippines has developed a gene that will let rice plants live for twelve days after being flooded with salt water? That could save millions of lives in Asia.' She turned to her father. 'Remember how I used to be dead set against nuclear power? Well, these days I can't wait for them to build more reactors because it's better than carbon. The Green movement has grown up, Bruno. We had to.'

Bruno had to smile. She looked very fine, young and fiery. 'You sound like you should go into politics. I'd vote for you, Dominique. We need some of that passion around here.'

She grinned at him, suddenly looking even younger. 'You think I'm passionate? You ought to hear Max.'

'You two are still friends, even with you at university in Grenoble and him in Bordeaux?'

'We talk most days – email and instant messaging and VOIP. It's all free, over the internet, and we're in the same chat forums on ecology. He's really into organics, not surprising since he grew up on the commune. His dad Alphonse was the first real Green I ever met.'

'Did you tell Max about the GMO crops?' Bruno asked, keeping his voice light.

'Not exactly,' she said hesitantly, picking her words with care. 'Well, not in so many words. We were having an argument about GMOs and I was saying my views had changed, now that I'd been

57

working with them. And he knew where I was working this summer, so I suppose he could have worked it out.'

'What about his views? Is Max still against GMOs?' His question jolted her, and he could feel Stéphane start to eye him quizzically.

'You'd better ask him, Bruno,' she said. 'This is beginning to sound like you suspect something here. You're not going to start behaving like a cop, are you?'

'Come off it, Dominique,' he said. His affection for her helped damp down the irritation tinged with guilt that came when friendship interfered with police work. He had known this girl since before she wore braces on her teeth. He smiled at her, gaining a little time as he wondered how to make her realise how serious this could be.

'I've been a policeman for as long as you've known me, which is most of your life,' he said. 'But I work for St Denis, not for anybody else, and there are some much tougher policemen down here under pressure to make an arrest. The chief detective of the *Département* for one, and I wouldn't be surprised to see some security people down from Paris. And you'll be right in their sights. You worked at the station, you knew about the GM crops, your dad's farm could be at risk, you're a passionate *écolo*. You're an obvious suspect. And arson means a prison term.'

'Are we going to need a lawyer, Bruno?' asked Stéphane. At least he understood.

'Not yet, but I'll let you know. And in the meantime, if you have any documents or something that shows you're not against GMOs, this would be a good time to get them together.'

'That I can do,' she said thoughtfully, sobered by his speech. 'We had a whole debate about them in our chat group and I wrote a piece about them for *Grenoble Vert*, the Green newsletter at the university. But what about Max? What should I tell him?'

'That's up to you. But he didn't work at the station so there's no reason for him to come under suspicion. But you're in a very different situation. What's the name of that chat group, by the way?'

'*Aquitaine Verte*, the same as the organisation. It just sort of grew out of their website and I've been in it since I was at school. Well, thanks for the warning. But I haven't done anything wrong, so I'll be fine.'

'Let's hope so. Whatever you wrote for that newsletter, email a copy to me, just in case. It might come in useful,' said Bruno, closing his notebook. 'By the way, you might like to know that your boss there thinks very highly of you. Petitbon told me earlier that he'd like to offer you a permanent job once you get your diploma.'

'So he must be sure I had nothing to do with it.'

'Right – you've got a witness for the defence already,' grinned Bruno.

In a slightly easier frame of mind, Bruno went on to his next errand, wondering who the dead woman might be who had given the commune as her address and whether he had known her. He took the back road towards St Denis over the railway crossing, skirted the new cemetery and turned on to the small single-track lane that led out of the town and up the hill to the water tower. Beyond it lay the rolling wooded countryside where the hay was freshly harvested and the golden Limousin cattle grazed contentedly in the early September sun. He drove on up the gentle slope to the high plateau where the land was cheap and the farming difficult. Bleak and windswept in winter, these high lands had a certain austere grandeur now at the tail end of summer, and spectacular views over the river valleys on either side.

Further along the ridge, the ruins of the château de Brillamont stood watch over the confluence of the rivers, the nearest of the chain of medieval fortresses that marked the shifting frontier between the English and the French. The war had lasted over a hundred years, until Jeanne d'Arc restored the French morale and Bernard du Guesclin devised an artillery train that was light enough to be moved and heavy enough to batter the English castles into submission. Despite what he had been told in school of the national heroine, Bruno knew from his army days that it was the gunpowder that had been decisive. It usually was.

CHAPTER 8

Bruno turned off at a half-rotted and unreadable wooden sign that pointed to an unmade track. He heard the blades of grass between the tyre ruts swish against the bottom of his van as he followed the lane through an avenue of trees into a broad and protected hollow. He sounded his horn as he came to a wooden gate across the track, turned off the ignition and walked on alongside a large and well-kept vegetable garden. It led towards the curious assortment of buildings that faced the sun from the northern slope of the hollow. A woman he recognised was weeding, while two of the children from his tennis class were picking tomatoes. Briefly he paused at the sturdy fence of chicken wire that surrounded the plot, greeted them and accepted a gift of two plump and perfect cherry tomatoes.

'*Salut*, Bruno. What brings you up here?' called Céline, a grandmotherly type who had been with the commune from the beginning. 'Have you come to help?'

'Too busy with my own garden these days, Céline. Is Alphonse around?'

'In the cheese barn.'

Bruno nodded and turned away to view the small village that the young revolutionaries of 1968, the *soixante-huitards*, had built in the nearly four decades since their first arrival. Even if he had not known the steady parade of healthy youngsters they had sent through the schools and sports clubs of St Denis and seen Alphonse elected as the first Green member of the town council, he would have been impressed. In pride of place stood a traditional stone farmhouse, with ivy covering most of the side wall. It was topped with the usual red tile roof shaped like a witch's hat, native to this part of the Périgord. Beside it stood a tall and spindly windmill which seemed to provide enough power for the needs of the dozen or so people who usually lived here. Closer to Bruno and the lane stood a large log cabin with a shaded porch, where a middle-aged woman with long straight hair sat cross-legged, her eyes closed and her back straight. The gaps between the logs were stuffed with clay, and the roof composed of two layers of planks separated by thick sheets of polystyrene foam, all covered by solar panels to heat the water.

Then came a wide and deceptively large building that Bruno knew from previous visits to be constructed of home-made bricks of mud and straw, and then covered with earth and dug into the side of the hill so that the doors and windows appeared to peek from the living turf. A goat

62

grazed on the roof and two children were seated on benches in front of the building, where they appeared to be playing chess. To the right was the barn, a simple but sturdy A-frame building made of abandoned planks of wood and some salvaged iron piping, welded into bracing triangles for strength. Bruno's favourite building was the dome, perched on the grass like half of a gigantic multi coloured golf ball, all composed of triangles, some of glass, some of wood painted in various hues, some in plastic and some in shards of mirror.

To one side of this dome was a wooden frame-work over which grape vines had been trained for years to make a shaded terrace. It was floored in stone, and housed a long wooden table with a variety of chairs and benches, and a remarkably wide and ornate hammock that was festooned with sashes and ribbons. More goats lounged around this hammock like courtiers waiting on the empty throne of their monarch. Standing in the doorway of the dome as if awaiting Bruno's arrival was a naked toddler, the little boy's arms resting on the neck of a kid goat about its own size. The kid bleated and the toddler waved. Bruno waved back.

Alphonse emerged from the A-frame barn, wiping his hands on a long apron. His face was looking older these days, but he was still spry with his long grey hair braided into a pigtail. He wore jeans and rubber thong sandals, the top half of a pair of braided pyjamas from India, and topped off this unique confection with a multicoloured silk bandanna that glinted with gold threads.

'Bruno, welcome,' Alphonse said. 'Some tea perhaps? A home-made beer? Or have you come to try the new cheese?'

'Nothing thanks, Alphonse. I'm here on business and I hope it won't be too sad. Do you recall a woman named Mireille Augereau? She claims this as her address.'

'Mireille, yes, she was here about ten years ago for a whole summer, nearly a year, and then moved on. She first came as a student with one of the originals who had become her professor. But I haven't heard from her for years.'

'And Maximilien Augereau? Would that be the Max I know?'

'Sure, that's her son, only he calls himself Vannes after me. I suppose because I brought him up and he never heard much from his mother after she left. Mireille was a pretty thing when she first came here. What's happened?'

'Well, we just got word that she died yesterday in a car crash outside Paris. Her licence and identity card gave this place as her address and listed Max as next of kin. It seems that some money may be involved. She was working in a municipal nursery school, so she had life insurance, and Max was listed as beneficiary.'

'Well, he may not have known much of her but I suppose it's bound to be a blow, losing your mother. I think he got a birthday card once or twice, whenever she sobered up and got off the drugs.'

'She just left the boy here, with you?'

Alphonse nodded. 'She met some guy in the market. It was just after we started selling the cheeses and she was good in the markets. A pretty face always helps and she had a bit of English for the tourists. She said she was going off with him for a weekend at the beach and she never came back. That was it. And Max, well, he was part of the family by then, even if he'd had anywhere else to go.'

'Was there a father? A birth certificate? What's on Max's identity card?'

'I'm listed as the father, since I raised the lad. She never mentioned the father. She was a wild one, Bruno, slept around a lot. She might not have known for sure who the father was.'

'Where's Max now? Still working at Hubert's *cave*?'

'By now he'll be over at old Cresseil's place, helping him with the vineyard. It's what Max most likes to do, along with playing rugby and computer games and chasing girls. He's really interested in wine as a career, so he'll help Cresseil bring in the crop before he goes back to university. He's a fine boy, Bruno.'

Bruno nodded. He liked Max, who kept all his violence to the rugby field and had no enemies. Fast and slippery, and a determined tackler, he played centre for the second team whenever he was home.

'I'd better go over and tell Max the bad news,' Bruno said. 'He may not have known her well, but it's still hard to learn your mother has gone. Unless you'd rather do it?'

'Let me come with you. I have to get something in town anyway. Try a bit of the new cheese while I clean up. You know where it is, and you'll find some bread on the counter.'

Alphonse ducked into the dome and Bruno headed into the dark barn, which smelled of goats and urine and the warm tang of ripening milk. Most of the cheeses were stored in the cooler room at the rear, but here in the workroom Alphonse had left row upon row of fresh *crottins*, the small disc-shaped cheeses that could be sold fresh or in varying states of dryness. On a wooden board stood one of the big round loaves of brown bread that were the commune's speciality. Bruno took his Laguiole knife from his belt, cut himself a slice of bread and half a *crottin* and leaned back against the counter to enjoy it. To one side he noticed a brown cardboard box with a small tap and he turned it to the window. South Africa Pinotage. There was an empty glass beside the box so he poured himself a taste. No nose to speak of but not bad in the mouth. He looked at the price tag. Four euros for five litres. No wonder the French couldn't compete.

'You found the South African wine,' said Alphonse. 'Not bad, is it? Max bought it, like he bought the Australian and the stuff from Chile, trying all

66

the different wines. Research, he called it. But here, try a glass of this.'

'The cheese is really good,' said Bruno, holding out the empty glass to the anonymous bottle of red wine that Alphonse was pouring. He took an appreciative sniff, and a good sip to taste, smacking his lips and then nodding a cautious approval.

'It's our own, and a lot better than the crap we used to make up here, thanks to Max. The techniques aren't much different – it's just better when he does it, like a gift.'

'It's a lot better than your old plonk, and now I can tell you that I only used to drink it to be polite. This is very drinkable.'

'All organic, too. I got him on to that. Now he says it's the future of the wine business, as if it were all his own idea,' Alphonse said fondly. 'If you're finished, let's go and break the bad news.'

Bruno slowed the van and stopped as the road emerged from the trees and reached the top of the ridge. He loved this view above all others, he explained when Alphonse turned to him, raising his eyebrows in a silent question. The familiar view down the valley of the Vézère and the hilltop villages on the far ridge was splendid in its lavish sweep. Immediately below him stood the small château that was the heart of Julien's Domaine de la Vézère. Bruno looked carefully at the rows of new vines that Julien had planted. He brought his eyes back to the Philibert farm that Hubert had bought, and to Cresseil's ramshackle place beside it. It boasted the farmhouse, not much more than a shepherd's cottage, where the old man lived, with two barns, a kitchen garden and perhaps twenty rows of vines. Cresseil had not been mobile enough to farm the place for years, so the rest of the land down the slope to the river was left to grow hay for Cresseil to sell. A dozen of the giant cylinders of compacted hay, wrapped tightly in black plastic, lay in the shorn field where the combine harvester had left them.

He tried to estimate the extent of Cresseil's holding. Long and narrow, it was a bit more than half of the size of the Philibert farm, maybe even two-thirds the extent. Looking back to St Denis a couple of miles up the river, and then down to the river bend where it began the long sweep to join the Dordogne, he could not begin to estimate the full extent of the south-facing slope that Hubert de Montignac had suggested might grow decent wine. There were places where the slope steepened sharply to become the sheer chalk-white and limestone cliffs where people had taken shelter in the Middle Ages, and where prehistoric men probably lived. But the Domaine itself took up no more than a fraction of the length of the gentle hillside, so if Hubert was right to suggest that the Domaine was worth three million euros the overall value could be enormous.

'You don't know your own valley yet?' called

Alphonse from the van window. Bruno turned back.

'How did Max come to know Cresseil?' he asked, leaning against the side of the vehicle while Alphonse rolled himself a cigarette.

'Through the *collège*, that scheme Rollo started of getting each of the older kids to adopt one of the old folks in the retirement home.' Alphonse broke off to lick the paper and light up. 'Max was visiting old Madame Cresseil just before she died, must be three years ago now, and the old chap took a shine to him. He finally got a new audience for his old stories about the war, I suppose. Then Max started helping him out in the garden, doing a few repairs around the house, and Cresseil started teaching him about wine-making. And he let Max have the old motorbike that hadn't run for years. He got it running again, what's more. Max likes the old boy, says it's like having a grandpa.'

So Max had a motorbike, albeit an old one, Bruno thought, not the kind seen by the postman of Coux. Perhaps he also had access to a more modern one. Bruno filed the thought away.

'Old Cresseil didn't have any kids of his own, as far as I know.'

'Just the one who got killed in the air force, some plane crash in Africa, long before your time, Bruno.' Alphonse pinched out the half-finished cigarette between his horny fingers, and put it carefully back into his tobacco pouch. 'Come on, let's go see Max.'

'Alphonse, there's something I have to ask you, officially.' Bruno explained the background to the fire and asked Alphonse, as a committed local Green, whether he knew of any militant *écolos* in the area daft enough to do such a thing.

'You're not joking, are you?' Alphonse said, more resignation than question in his voice. 'I was wondering if it might get around to this. Any real *écolo* might trash a crop if he thought it was some GMO business, but he'd never start a fire. And nasty rumours are going around about that crop. I had some people calling me from Bordeaux, asking whether as a councillor I could check whether a special GMO permit had been issued. So I checked into the law because I'll be bringing this up at the next council meeting.'

'There's no permit, Alphonse. The Mayor and I are as much in the dark as you.'

'Well, there should be a permit from our own council. If that was a GMO crop and our town council knew nothing about it, there's going to be a scandal, I'll promise you that. This is not just me, Bruno, the whole Green Party will kick up a stink, arson or no arson.'

'I can't say I'm a fan of this GMO stuff,' said Bruno. 'But arson is a crime. I'll pursue that, GMO or no GMO. And I'll expect your help, Alphonse. We can be on the same side about that just as I think the whole council and the Mayor will be on your side about GMOs and permits.'

Alphonse gave a cursory nod.

'One more thing. Alphonse, a bit of advice. There are so few leads on this case that the detectives are getting worried. So it won't be your old friend Bruno making inquiries but some serious cops looking for leverage. If they have to pin something else on you to make you cooperate, that's how they work. And an old hippy commune is just asking for a drugs raid, so if there's anything up there that shouldn't be, you'd better get rid of it fast.'

'It's not a hippy commune,' Alphonse protested.

'You know that, and I may know it, but the Gendarmes don't and that Capitaine Duroc is hungry for promotion. Think about it, and now let's go down and find Max.'

CHAPTER 9

Max was a good-looking young man. Bare-chested and tanned, his long fair hair sun-streaked, he was energetically wielding a hoe on the weeds of the kitchen garden when Bruno pulled up in front of the barn. He was not alone. Beside him, in shorts and T-shirt, was the French-Canadian girl Bruno had met at the *cave*. As she stood from the weeding to eye the new arrivals, she was almost as tall as Max. She wore a low-cut T-shirt that revealed the tops of her tanned breasts and her shorts were very short indeed. No wonder Max always seemed to be wherever she was, Bruno thought.

Cresseil was sitting on an elderly wooden chair, resting his chin on his walking stick and watching the youngsters work. A Porcelaine, one of the classic French hunting dogs, lay ancient and asleep at his feet. The old man turned to see them approach, leaned back and nodded and held out a gnarled right hand.

'Alphonse, Bruno . . .' he said. 'Welcome to you both. A little *apéro*? Hey, young Max, time to stop work. Your dad's here.'

'Thanks, I'll take a glass of that wine you made last year,' said Alphonse, before Bruno could say this might not be the best time to sit around drinking, at least not until Max had been told of his mother's fate. 'Give it a try, Bruno,' Alphonse went on. Max put down his hoe and came up, murmuring greetings, kissed Alphonse on both cheeks, and then did the same to Bruno, whom he'd known since boyhood.

'You remember Jacqueline from the *cave*?' Max said as she came forward to shake Bruno's hand and to embrace Alphonse. That was interesting, thought Bruno. The girl knew Max's family already. Again, she held on to Bruno's hand slightly too long and her appraisal of him was slightly too frank, her pose almost brazen in the way she breathed in to push her breasts forward against the cotton of her T-shirt. It's automatic, Bruno realised; she may not even know the kind of signals she's sending.

'Bring our guests some wine, lad,' said Cresseil, and Max slipped his shirt on over his broad shoulders and went into the house, followed by Jacqueline.

'You've got him working hard,' said Bruno.

'It does him good. The devil finds work for idle hands,' the old man replied, pulling an ancient pipe from the pocket of his waistcoat and striking a match. Between puffs, he squinted at Bruno. 'What brings you here? Bad news?'

'Not good,' said Bruno, and the three men

73

waited in silence until Max returned with a small table under one arm and two folding chairs swinging easily from the other. He set them down as the girl came out with a tray, poured the drinks and the two youngsters sat cross-legged beside the old man. The dog stirred, rolled over and put its head on his master's foot.

'Bruno has some bad news,' Alphonse said when they were settled. Bruno took a breath to steady himself. He'd never had to deliver a death notice quite like this, to the abandoned child of a long-gone mother. Nor had he ever before had to confuse the matter with a police inquiry.

'I got word from Paris. I'm afraid your mother Mireille has been killed in a traffic accident. I'm sorry,' Bruno said. He paused a moment and went on. 'There will probably be a bit of paperwork since she had you listed as next of kin, but I can take care of a lot of that for you and help you with the rest.'

Max stared at him blankly, pursed his lips and then looked away across the river. Jacqueline put her hand on his arm but kept silent. 'I hardly knew her, so I can't say I feel very much. I always thought I'd meet her later, as two adults, when we each had our own lives and could talk calmly.'

'We can have her buried up at the commune, if you want,' said Alphonse.

'I never saw the point in burials,' said Max. 'I'm not religious and cremation always made more sense to me.' He turned to Bruno. 'Should I come to your office and sign something?'

'Not yet. We'll have to wait for the paperwork from Paris. You don't have to decide anything now, but if you want we can arrange for the cremation to be done up there.'

The young man nodded, vaguely, then took a long sip at his wine and held up his glass. 'What do you think of it, Bruno? It's last year's, the first wine I helped Cresseil make.'

'I didn't do much,' grunted Cresseil. 'Just sat here and watched while you did all the work.'

Bruno twirled the glass and took a sniff, then a sip. 'It's pretty good, Max. But then the wine you made up at the commune was pretty good as well. Alphonse let me try a glass.'

'This year's will be better. Jacqueline is going to help,' Max said, and rose to his feet in a single, supple movement, bringing the girl upright with him. He looked at Alphonse, making it clear that he wanted to leave.

'Just a minute, Max,' said Bruno, shifting uneasily in his chair. It was terrible timing, but he knew the question about Max's whereabouts on the night of the fire had to be put.

'I'd have been in bed asleep,' Max replied, still standing, still poised to leave. He gave Bruno a nervous smile and then glanced at the girl beside him.

'Up at the commune?' Bruno pressed.

'No, you stayed here that night,' interrupted the old man. Cresseil turned to address Bruno. 'I don't sleep too well these days. Max was here that night because I'd have heard if he left. Half the valley would have heard that old motorbike.'

Bruno looked at the old man. It was an alibi that would be hard to shake, but Bruno felt himself wondering whether he believed it. The interruption had been too quick, Max's response too glib. Bruno was not accustomed to being lied to. J-J had once told him that a policeman had to assume that nobody ever told the real truth, but Bruno wasn't that kind of policeman. He knew almost all the people in St Denis and assumed most of them told him the truth most of the time. If Max was lying, Bruno wasn't sure he could tell, even though he'd spent hours with Max on the rugby pitch and watched him grow. Bruno scratched his head and scrutinised the youngster. Something rang false. It was time to push Max a bit.

'You didn't have to use the bike. You could have walked out quietly, even walked up through the hills to the field. It's not that far,' he said. 'You're fit enough, you could even have run . . .'

'I could, but I didn't,' Max snapped at him, his eyes fiery. Then stopped himself. 'Sorry, Bruno. You don't really suspect me, do you? It's just you being a *flic*.'

'Have you seen my eyebrows, Max?' Bruno said. 'See where they're burned off. And I still cough in the mornings from the fumes I breathed in. I'm taking this fire very personally because it could have killed me. So, yes, I'm being a *flic*.'

'Sorry, Bruno,' Max said, scrutinising Bruno more closely and looking chastened.

'Whoever set that fire left a kind of bomb in there that went off just as the firemen got close. Did you know that?'

'That's not . . .' Max began fiercely but then seemed to catch himself, and Bruno wondered what he'd been about to say. '. . . that's not what was in the newspapers. I hadn't heard anything about a bomb.'

'Set a fire with the petrol, then screw the cap back on the empty can and you have yourself a bomb that goes off quite a bit later, when the fire gets hot enough. Arsonists know that and some of them do it deliberately to hurt firemen. That's why it carries such a long prison term.'

Max froze for a moment, as if the thought of prison had shocked him. Then he braced himself and shook his head firmly. 'I know nothing about it,' he said, and the girl looked at him, rather anxiously, Bruno thought. There was not a smidgen of proof, but Bruno suddenly felt with dismay that he could be looking at the culprit. He pulled out his cellphone, as if checking for a message, but instead hit the speed dial to call his office phone, which would record the rest of this conversation as a message.

'You haven't heard any gossip about it among the *écolos*?' Bruno went on, holding the phone casually in his hand. 'People must be talking about it. What about your old girlfriend, Dominique? You must have talked about it with her.'

77

'Sure we're talking about it, I told you that,' interrupted Alphonse. 'Some of us were getting very suspicious about that place.'

'I was asking Max the question,' Bruno interrupted, his eyes firmly on Max.

'We talk all the time, email and instant messaging, texting. Dominique's always been my best friend, but never my girl-friend. We know each other too well, I suppose, going through school together.' He turned to Jacqueline with an encouraging smile and took her hand. They made a handsome couple. The girl quickly glanced at Bruno before turning her eyes back to Max.

'So what did you and Dominique exchange when you talked about the fire? I'm trying to find out if there are any *écolo* crazies who'd do something like this. It wasn't just me and the *pompiers*. It could have burned down Dominique's family farm.'

'Do you think so?' asked Max, real concern in his voice. 'It was that dangerous?'

'A bit more wind, a bit of delay in the *pompiers* getting there, and we'd have had a real disaster,' said Bruno. 'So, any ideas?'

Max shrugged.

'And why burn down the hut, rather than just the crop?' Bruno pressed.

'How should I know? Maybe whoever started the fire wanted to destroy the files . . .' Max broke off. 'Whatever it was they had in there. It said office equipment in the paper.'

'Did Dominique tell you about the office?' Bruno could hear the harshness in his voice and took a breath to calm himself. *Sud-Ouest* had indeed mentioned a destroyed typewriter, but the paper had reported nothing about files.

'She said she was keeping files up to date when she went up there. She's furious about the fire. Since working at that place, Dominique has started thinking GMOs made sense. That's mainly what we talked about.'

'You agree with her?'

Max shrugged again. 'I don't know. It's technical, very complex. I mean, most of the vines in France are transplants, based on Californian rootstock. And to do that you have to graft your cutting on to the root of another kind of vine. Isn't that genetic modification? In its own way, I mean?'

'So what do you think about the fire?' Bruno wasn't going to let it go.

'It must have been a really foolish, dangerous thing to do. So if I learn anything, I'll let you know,' said Max. He draped his arm around Jacqueline's shoulders and turned to go. 'If that's all, I'll see you at the rugby practice, Bruno.'

Max put his hand on Cresseil's shoulder in farewell and walked off with Jacqueline to the barn, where he pulled out Cresseil's old motorbike. It looked like a World War Two vintage. Alphonse shrugged an apology and followed, preparing to clamber aboard the pillion seat. Bruno decided to turn a blind eye to the absence of helmets. He turned his phone off as he watched Max embrace the girl before she pulled a battered bicycle from the hedge and began pedalling away alone.

CHAPTER 10

'You seem to have grown fond of Max,' Bruno said when the roar of the bike and the clouds of blue smoke had faded up the lane. He was wondering how tough it would be to break the alibi that Cresseil had given him. Without that, Max would be the prime suspect.

'If it weren't for him, they'd have had me in the old folk's home by now.' Cresseil rummaged in his pockets for his matches, and lit his pipe again. 'He helps with my bit of shopping and gardening and he fixed the roof. I couldn't do without him, to be honest. And he won't take anything, no money, nothing. Even that old bike he fixed, he says he's only borrowing it and he'll let me have it back when my leg's better.'

'How's your leg these days?'

'I can get around, just. But I don't think I can take another winter here. They'll get me into that home of theirs yet.'

'It might be for the best.'

'Bugger off, Bruno. I may be old, but I'm not a fool. I'll go into that home when I have no other choice because you know and I know the only

81

way I'll leave that place will be feet first. It's death's ante-room and no mistake. They won't even let me have my dog in there, best hunting dog in the valley. Mind you, he's on his last legs, just like me.'

He reached down with his walking stick and poked the sleeping dog gently in the side. One eye opened, and old man and old dog looked at one another for a long moment, exchanging some deep but unspoken communication. The dog squirmed across the grass to nestle against old Cresseil's legs and then closed his eye again. Bruno smiled to watch them.

'Max seems to have got himself a girlfriend,' Bruno said. 'She's a good-looking one.'

'They work together at Hubert's *cave* and she's studying wine, just like Max. He's daft about her, and I can't say I blame him. He's brought her round here a few times to help with the vines.' His eyes twinkled, and he winked at Bruno. 'Takes years off me, just looking at a woman like that. I don't suppose I'll see many more young beauties. I've got a feeling I haven't much time left.'

'What about this place?' Bruno asked. 'Have you got family to leave it to?'

'There's always family somewhere, cousins or some such, but none that I can say I'm close to, none that I'd want to have the place. I was born in this house, Bruno, and lived here all my life, over eighty years on this bit of farm, and I'm very particular about what I want to happen to it. I've been thinking about it, and I know what I want. I just don't know how to go about it. I was going to ask your advice.'

'Ask away. If I don't have an answer we'll find the Mayor, or I'll find someone who does.'

'Well, I was thinking about Max. Whether I could leave it to him when the time comes.'

Bruno whistled softly. That would be quite an inheritance for a young man. It could also mean a lot of legal complications. It was almost impossible under French law to exclude someone with a right of inheritance by family. It also meant, Bruno thought, that he could neither refute nor rely on the old man's alibi for Max on the night of the fire.

'You know the inheritance laws,' Bruno said. 'Family comes first, however distant.'

'I know, and I thought about that. But what if I were to adopt the boy? He'd be family then, wouldn't he?'

'I suppose he would. I don't even know if you can adopt somebody over the age of eighteen. In any event, he'd have to agree, and he's an independent young lad, ambitious too, going off to university. He might not want to get locked into the land.'

'We've talked about that, not the adoption, but the land. Max likes this terrain, likes the house. He says this whole stretch down to the river can grow good wine. He wants to try planting some new vines, different varieties, when he comes back at Christmas. Just to see how they take in the soil. I haven't had the heart to tell him I don't think I'll be here at Christmas. And when that happens, I'd have to sell the farm to pay my way at the old folk's home. I'd rather the boy had it.'

'Well, keep it to yourself for a bit, until I can find out the law about the adoption and come back to you. And the boy won't want any more shocks for a while. I know he wasn't close to his mother, but it will take some getting used to.'

Cresseil nodded. 'His new girlfriend will help with that. She's a pretty thing, that Jacqueline, but she's got a sharp mind. Wise beyond her years.'

'Maybe a bit too sharp for Max, you mean?' Certainly too sharp for me, Bruno thought to himself. And too flirtatious. 'Do you want a hand up?'

'No, I can totter off on my own. But I'd be glad if you could take the table and chairs back to the porch. And the glasses. You can have that wine, if you like. It's not bad is it?'

'Not bad at all, but it tastes pretty much like your wine always did. Still, it's a damn sight better than some of the stuff they used to give us in the army.'

The old man grinned. 'You ought to hear young Max go on about the way we make the wine around here,' he said. 'He's read all the books and goes on about cold fermentation and stainless steel vats and malo-lactic something-or-other that I never heard of. I tell him that old wooden wine

84

vat was good enough for my father and for his father before that and it's good enough for me.'

'I suppose all this new equipment would cost quite a lot.'

'It's not so much that. I'm not a wine maker, just always made a bit for myself and the family and a bit over for friends. That was how everybody round here did it in the old days, and we all got together and helped each other pick the grapes and we'd all tread them together, all the young people, and then we'd all come together again for the bottling. They were happy times, young Bruno. That's how I got together with my Annette, treading the grapes together. That's why most of the babies used to get born in May, nine months after the vendange. Did you know that?'

Smiling, Bruno shook his head. He hadn't known that, but he could understand how it must have been.

'It was the harvest of the Liberation, September of '44. Most of us lads had been with the Maquis but the Germans had been kicked out and De Gaulle was back in Paris. It was a great time, and a great harvest that year.'

The old man paused, his eyes looking across the valley into a distant past, a smile playing gently among his wrinkles.

'Of course I'd known Annette before as a schoolgirl, she just lived up the valley,' he went on. 'But treading the grapes that September, seeing her fair hair tumbling down around her shoulders and her

85

lovely white legs with the grape juice running down them. I could have licked it all off, I tell you. Ah Bruno, she was a real beauty, so delicate, and you could tell from the way she liked treading the grapes that she was a lively one. And I was young and strong and proud of myself after being in the Resistance, and all the girls looked up to us lads who had fought the Germans. Well, you can imagine. We got married in the November and the baby came along the next May. I was in the army by then, in Germany.'

'So what did it do for the wine, all those bare legs and passion in the vats?'

'I don't know what it did for the wine, but it certainly made me feel a lot better about every glass when I thought about my Annette's legs each time I had a drink. It still does.'

CHAPTER 11

Bruno was looking forward to meeting the business consultant from Paris again. But he kept a straight face as he shook the hands of the American, Bondino, and then watched Dupuy blush as he announced to the room: 'But of course I know Monsieur Dupuy, and his reputation as a connoisseur of fine wines.'

They were gathered in the council chamber, a long glassroofed room that had been built on to the wide balcony of the *Mairie* and which looked down to the old stone bridge and the length of the river's slow bend. Bruno noted that the heir to the Bondino company, Fernando, was about his own height, but sleek and slightly plump with thinning dark hair cut very short. Close to thirty, Bruno estimated, perhaps a little younger. He was dressed in a black linen suit with an open-necked white silk shirt and he wore what looked like a very expensive watch. Bruno had never cared for jewellery on men, and Bondino had a chain bracelet of white gold dangling from his other wrist and a large ring on his right hand. He pulled a slim laptop from his briefcase, turned it on and slowly ran his index finger over a small sensor below the keypad.

He noticed Bruno watching, held up his finger without smiling and said: 'Security.' It must be one of those devices that read fingerprints, locking the computer until it identified the correct digit. He leaned back casually in his chair, letting one leg dangle over the other as if to show off his black moccasins, the leather so thin they could have been slippers. Bruno felt the start of an instinctive dislike for the man.

'Might I begin, gentlemen, by asking your assurance that this meeting is confidential and that nothing that we communicate to you will be said outside this room?' Dupuy began. He wore large, black-rimmed spectacles and a severe blue suit with a bright pink tie. '*Monsieur le Maire?*'

'We're accustomed to commercial discretion, Monsieur,' the Mayor said. 'Perhaps you would ask your colleague with the machinery to be careful with that table. It's said to be nearly seven hundred years old, which may be an exaggeration but it is certainly older than all of us in this room put together.'

Bondino took a glossy magazine from his briefcase and slid it beneath the computer. It was *Marie-Claire Maison*, Bruno noted, a French magazine of décor and design that suggested he might be fluent in the language. Of course, he might just be looking at the photos.

'Bondino Wines was founded in California by the

grandfather of the present Chairman Francis X. Bondino . . .' Dupuy began.

'In 1906,' interrupted the Mayor, addressing the room but turning to look directly at Bondino. 'I should say, *Messieurs*, that Bondino Wines needs no introduction, even here in rural France. We know of your interests in South America and South Africa, of your three thousand employees, so we may be able to dispense with your introduction and come directly to the point.'

Dupuy seemed about to speak again when Bondino held up his hand. Dupuy sat.

'It all comes down to one question.' Bondino spoke heavily accented but serviceable French, and kept his eyes on the Mayor. 'Do you have the political juice to get this valley made into an *appellation contrôlée* region within the next twelve months? Our Embassy is pretty well plugged into Paris and Dupuy makes a living at this stuff and they both tell me that you have the political connections to do it.'

'And if I do?'

'Then I'm prepared to invest an eight-figure sum in your district. That means over ten million US dollars. Correction, I mean over ten million of your euros. That's a lot of jobs and a big new tax base for St Denis.'

'And you would do what with that large sum of money?'

'Buy land, build a state-of-the-art modern winery with a visitor centre, run a hotel, grow vines, make fine wine and export it all over the world.'

'How much land would you need and how much wine would you intend to produce?'

'Our business plan calls for a minimum of a million bottles a year within seven years. That means about two hundred of your hectares.'

'And how many jobs?'

'Full time, probably about fifty when the visitor centre is up and running, plus some seasonal employees.'

Bruno was intrigued by the way Bondino and the Mayor appraised one another. Although each kept his eyes fixed on the other man, there was no staring match, no little play for dominance, just two serious and experienced men coolly taking each other's measure without any apparent emotion. He was suddenly aware that the American had doubtless had dozens of meetings with politicians, and that his Mayor had held just as many meetings with businessmen. Bruno began to temper his dislike with a little respect.

'I see. That's a very ambitious project,' the Mayor said. 'And the entire plan hinges on your ensuring that this valley is designated *appellation contrôlée*?'

'That's right. And I know what that will do to improve land values for a lot of your voters, so I'd like no property taxes for the first seven years.'

'And what else?'

'A lot of help in acquiring the land discreetly.

Once this is known, land prices are going to go through the roof. If that happens, the deal is off.'

'Do you know which land you want?'

'Dupuy, pass the Mayor the aerial photos and the map. Put it up on the screen as well so we can all see it.'

It was, as Bruno and the Mayor expected, the Domaine and all the land along the south-facing slope above the river.

'Just so you know how serious we are, I have an option to buy this hotel and vineyard complex, the Domaine de la Vézère. I'm sure you know the place. I also have an option to buy the canoe landing stage and the campsite and grill bar on the far side of the river. We have also done very discreet but detailed soil and drainage tests on the land. All this was arranged by our good friend Dupuy here, and the diplomats assure us that we would get no objections from the relevant ministries of the government in Paris.'

'When you ask for a tax holiday for the enter-prise, do you mean that we'd lose the taxes the commune currently receives from the Domaine and from the other properties you intend to buy? That would be a big hole in our budget,' said Bruno.

'I understand that, and I know that this whole scheme will only work if we in this room come together in a willing partnership,' said Bondino, with a smile that Bruno did not find convincing. 'So I'm prepared to negotiate on this to minimise any negative impact on your revenues. You help me out on the cash flow and I'll do my best for you.'

'I'm a politician who needs to get re-elected, Monsieur,' said the Mayor, his relaxed posture as he leaned back in his chair belying the firmness in his voice. 'If my opponents could say that I have conspired with an American corporation to buy up land cheaply so that the Americans can benefit from increased land prices, I would lose the next election. And I would deserve to lose it because it would be a scandal. So even if I were prepared to do this, you would not have your partner here in the *Mairie* for very long.'

'I think it's important to bear in mind that Monsieur Bondino is not trying to speculate in land prices but to build a thriving local wine industry,' said Dupuy smoothly. 'Perhaps we can put the matter of land ownership to one side while we explain the other benefits . . .'

Bondino help up his hand. 'What about a lease with an option to buy. Could that work?'

'You could lease the land for a minimum period of say five years, with an option to buy at the end of the lease,' said the Mayor.

'Is that right, Dupuy?' Bondino asked, not bothering to look at the consultant. He was leaning back in his chair, tilted on its two rear legs.

'Yes, Monsieur. The lease contract can also be written to impose a maximum selling price at the end of the lease period. But you could give each landowner share options in your company as a way to ensure they benefit from the growth in value. There are tax advantages in that, for them and for you.'

'How's that sound to you, Mister Mayor?' the young man said, almost insolently. 'Reasonable?'

'I think it has some very interesting possibilities.'

Bondino brought out from his briefcase a document, encased in a plastic sleeve, and slid it across the table to the Mayor.

'Just so you know I'm serious. There's my letter of credit for ten million euros, certified by the Paris branch of Citibank and waiting to be put to work.'

As the Mayor studied the letter of credit, Bondino spoke up again. 'One other thing. This fire that was in the local paper, we don't like the sound of that. We're not going to invest in some area where you've got militant environmentalists trashing the local McDonald's or destroying crops to make some sort of political statement. One reason why we've come to you is because we were told this was a nice, law-abiding place. So we hope to see some arrests pretty soon. We are not going to take any risks with ten million euros. I hope that's clear.'

CHAPTER 12

It was a courteous summons, but Bruno knew it was an order just the same. The presence of the Chief of Police of St Denis was requested at his earliest convenience at the Gendarmerie where a senior officer from the Ministry of the Interior desired to see him. As he crossed the square where the old men played *boules*, Bruno saw a large and official-looking black Renault parked opposite the Gendarmerie, a driver still waiting at the wheel. Inside, he was shown to Capitaine Duroc's austere office with its view over the old cemetery. A middle-aged man in civilian clothes but with a distinctly military bearing occupied Duroc's chair. Bruno was steered to a plain wooden chair before the desk, but remained standing. Duroc perched on a windowsill.

'Brigadier Lannes, may I present the municipal policeman Courrèges,' said Duroc coldly. 'The Brigadier has been sent down from Paris, from the Ministry of the Interior.'

As Bruno saluted, and felt himself being studied by a very penetrating pair of dark eyes, he recalled that J-J had warned him this might happen.

'You're the man with the Croix de Guerre and the local knowledge,' said the Brigadier, standing to shake his hand. 'People have been telling me about you. Well, you'd better tell me where we are. It's been nearly a week since the fire and the head of the local detectives says they've not been getting very far in their inquiries.'

'We don't have many new leads, except that forensics was able to analyse the petrol, the regular Total brand,' said Duroc. 'There was nothing from the fingerprints in that phone box in Coux. The culprit must have been wearing gloves, or used a pencil to press the buttons.'

'It's a phone box that takes cards,' Bruno intervened, thinking he'd keep the postman's evidence to himself for the moment. 'I know that Commissaire Jalipeau from the *Police Nationale* was checking with France Télécom to establish where the card was bought.'

The Brigadier glanced quickly, almost reproachfully, at Duroc, as if this had been left out of his briefing. Then he reached into his briefcase and pulled out a printout from a website and said: 'There's been a development.

'*Aquitaine Verte* is an *écolo* newsletter published in Bordeaux by some militants in the Green Party,' he went on. 'Chief Detective Jalipeau is interviewing them now in Bordeaux, because their new issue which was emailed out to their members last night is almost entirely devoted to your Research Station and the GMO tests. They have a lot of accurate details, and apparently have copies of test results that seem to have been taken from the barn that was burned. They also have a number of quotes from one Alphonse Vannes, a councillor here in St Denis for the Greens. He says that no permit for the crops in question was ever issued by the *Mairie* nor by the *Conseil-Général.*'

'That's true,' said Bruno. 'The Mayor is not happy about it.'

'Well, that's not my concern. I've been brought into this because this was a discreet government-backed research project. It now looks likely to become a national scandal, and all the more embarrassing if we can't find who was responsible for the fire.'

'Excuse me,' said Bruno. 'I just want to be sure I understand. You are a Brigadier of Gendarmes, assigned to help J-J – I mean Commissaire Jalipeau – of the *Police Nationale?*'

'Brigadier of Gendarmes is my rank and I report to the Minister of Defence, but I'm attached to the staff of the *Renseignements Généraux.* I've been given the authority to take over this investigation by the Minister of the Interior. J-J will work under my orders, and I'm sure you two gentlemen will give me your full cooperation.'

'Yes, Sir. Completely,' said Duroc.

'I'll be happy to cooperate all I can, but you understand that I'll have to consult my Mayor. He's my chain of command,' said Bruno formally, not liking this at all. The *Renseignements Généraux* was officially the intelligence arm of the French police, under the Minister of the Interior, with a special mission of counter-terrorism and a sinister reputation.

'J-J told me you'd say that,' said the Brigadier with a grin that surprised Bruno. 'He also said I should call you Bruno and tell you I really need all the help I can get. Why not just tell me whatever you feel you can about possible suspects and why you thought they weren't guilty.'

Bruno considered this. It was a reasonable request, courteously presented, from someone who probably had and could certainly obtain whatever authority he needed. This Brigadier appeared to be a decent fellow or at least making the effort to act like one. Knowing something of brigadiers, and the kind of pressure for a swift result that Paris would bring, Bruno reserved judgement. Protecting his town and his people, as far as he could, was his job.

'There was a possible suspect, Dominique Suchet, a university student who had a summer job at the station and who is very *écolo*. But first she has a strong alibi for the time of the fire from her father. And second, she's actually a supporter of GMO crops and of nuclear power. A very thinking *écolo*, and if that fire had spread, her family farm would have been next to go. So I don't think she's likely. The most promising line of inquiry is through this *Aquitaine Verte* group in

Bordeaux. If they have the documents from the burned-out shed, that's the obvious connection.'

'I'll bet you a beer that they'll tell J-J that the documents arrived anonymously by post,' said the Brigadier. 'Tell me more about this Alphonse Vannes.'

Bruno tried to explain Alphonse's background and the unusual but on the whole successful commune in the hills. But he knew from the start that it was hopeless, with Duroc snorting contemptuously from the window ledge. Even when Bruno suggested they call on the Mayor to confirm that Alphonse was a model citizen, the Brigadier's eyebrows rose in what looked like mockery. 'He's a responsible type so he may be prepared to help us if we treat him right,' Bruno concluded. It sounded lame, even to him.

'You may be right, but we don't have enough time to treat anybody with kid gloves. If he knows anything, I need to know it now,' said the Brigadier. 'How did word get out about the GMO crops?'

'Possibly through Dominique Suchet or one of the other employees at the station,' Bruno said, wondering how he could explain what he knew about his local people to an outsider who simply wanted to make an arrest and move on.

'Dominique told me that she's part of an *écolo* chat group on the internet and she suddenly started arguing in favour of GMOs on the basis of her own experience at the station,' he said. 'It

98

wouldn't be difficult for anyone in that chat group to put two and two together.'

Bruno scratched his head, half-remembering something, and then took out his battered notebook and looked for the notes he had scribbled after seeing Dominique. He looked up. 'This is interesting. She called that chat group *Aquitaine Verte*, so there must be a connection with this newsletter in Bordeaux.' Suddenly he felt more cheerful. It looked as if the focus of the inquiry might be shifting away from St Denis. 'I'd better phone J-J and let him know.'

'That's already taken care of,' said the Brigadier. 'There's a whole floor of an office building in Paris filled with computer experts who have since this morning been trawling through *Aquitaine Verte*'s entire history on the net. Emails, phone numbers, call histories, credit card records and web searches. You have no idea of the resources of the modern state when the decision is made to focus its efforts. We'll have every exchange on that chat site, so if our fire starter learned about the GMOs from your Dominique Suchet's indiscretions, we'll find him.'

'Capitaine Duroc, I'm going to need your office,' the Brigadier went on. 'I also need your men to bring in Alphonse Vannes and Dominique Suchet. I'll start by talking to them.'

'Are they under arrest?'

'No, of course not. Just helping us with our inquiries. But I'll want their computers.'

'And if they don't want to come?'

'You'll have to find a way to persuade them.' He turned to Bruno. 'Most of these old Sixty-eight types usually have some drugs around. That would do nicely as a holding charge. What do you think?'

'Alphonse must have grown out of it by now,' said Bruno. 'And the youngsters up there are too keen on their rugby. A raid might be counter-productive. It might be more useful to keep Alphonse cooperative.'

The Brigadier studied Bruno in silence for a long moment. 'Just so long as you don't forget which side of the law you're on,' he said, and turned to Duroc. 'Take a long hard look at those rugby-playing youngsters. They were probably brought up to be zealous little *écolos*. And when we've done that, we'll go through the rest of St Denis, one by one until we get our result. And make a special note of every France Télécom phone card you find.'

Bruno felt a chill as the Brigadier turned away to pull a toughened laptop from his case, plugged it into the wall socket and settled down before the screen. Duroc and Bruno were dismissed. Duroc went to the front desk to organise a car to fetch Alphonse and Dominique. Bruno walked thoughtfully back towards the *Mairie*, thinking about that room full of computer experts in Paris trawling through emails and tracing phone calls and probably listening in to numbers of interest. By now, that would probably include Dominque's cellphone.

100

His instinct was to give Stéphane a warning call anyway. But any sign that Dominique was prepared, or that she had called in a lawyer, would just deepen the suspicions against her.

CHAPTER 13

Bruno felt miserable as he took the short stroll from the Gendarmerie to the fire station, but felt his spirits restored by the cheery greetings from the throng on the pavement outside the infants' school. As they always did this close to noon, young mothers and their prams and shopping bags massed and gossiped and showed off new babies as they waited for the morning classes to end and their children to pour out from the gates in a happy, shrieking horde. If the birth rate alone was the sign of a town's health, St Denis was in fine shape, Bruno considered, as he tipped his peaked hat to the assembled mothers and stepped into the road to pass them.

Ahmed was in the fire station, as arranged, and the two of them went up to join Albert in his office to try Bruno's experiment. It was Ahmed who had taken the alarm call on the night of the fire, and although the call had not been recorded, Bruno thought it worth taking a chance on Ahmed's hearing and his memory.

'I don't know how much I can help, Bruno,' said Ahmed as they stood by Albert's crowded desk.

'I told you it sounded to me like there was a cloth stuffed over the mouthpiece. The voice was muffled, hard to make out.'

'But you remember what the caller said?'

Albert pushed towards Bruno the note pad on his desk. 'Here's the note Ahmed scribbled down as he took the call. It was just a list of single words – "Fire. Barn. Field. Behind woods. St Cham road. Before St Cyp turn."'

'That's pretty much all he said,' Ahmed confirmed. 'Then when I asked for his name and address he just said the Coux call box and rang off.'

'Well, try and remember the voice and then listen to this,' Bruno said, picking up Albert's old rotary dial phone and calling the message box at his office. 'The quality isn't brilliant and you'll hear me talking a bit but there's another man's voice and I want to know if it sounds like the caller from Coux.'

Ahmed took the phone and listened, closing his eyes in concentration. 'Can you play it again?' he asked when the short conversation at Cresseil's farm was over. 'It's a bit faint.'

Bruno rang off and dialled the message box again. This time Ahmed's eyes were open and his lips moved as if he were reciting the words to himself. Albert sat motionless behind his desk, his eyes fixed on Ahmed, and there was no other noise than the tinny crackles of sound that leaked from the phone at Ahmed's ear. Bruno realised he was holding his breath in response to the tension that was building in the room.

'One more time,' Ahmed said, handing the phone back to Bruno. 'There's something familiar about the voice. Maybe it's just someone I've met once or twice. But try again.'

'As often as you like.' Bruno dialled again.

'You think it's him, don't you?' said Albert. 'You think it was the caller who set the fire.'

'Maybe,' said Bruno, handing Ahmed the phone for the third time.

Again, the voices leaked from the phone into the silence and tension of the room. From outside the window came the voices of the children liberated from school, followed by the opening howl of the noon siren.

'I can't swear to it,' said Ahmed. 'But I think it's him. It's the way he says the word 'fire'. But when he says he knows you and he'll see you at rugby, maybe I heard the voice there at the rugby club. He's one of us, isn't he, from St Denis?'

'Don't worry, Ahmed. I won't try to get you to testify in court about this,' said Bruno. 'I'm just trying to narrow things down a bit.'

'Maybe this will persuade the Mayor to let us have a new phone system in the next budget,' said Albert. 'One that records calls automatically.'

'Not until I get my new van,' said Bruno.

As he climbed the familiar steps of the *Mairie*, Bruno had the uncomfortable feeling that he was losing his grip on the affairs of his town. It wasn't just the arrival of the Brigadier but also the coming of Bondino and the scale of the change the venture would bring to St Denis. But his immediate problem was the Brigadier. It felt like a personal humiliation, knowing that Dominique and Alphonse, people under his care who had given him their friendship, were now to be hauled in for a less-than-gentle grilling by the big guns from Paris. And his own hardening suspicions against Max made the fate of the other two seem all the more unfair.

Bruno paused at the top of the stairs, knowing it could get a lot worse. This wouldn't stop with Alphonse and Dominique. It probably wouldn't even stop with Max, when the Brigadier got round to him as he surely would. Once the Paris politicians got worried, the people of St Denis became just so many pawns. His anger brought back the old bitterness that he'd hoped to leave behind when he left the army. It was all part of the same rotten system. The people of St Denis were going to be treated just as he and his fellow soldiers had been used and abandoned when they were sent into Bosnia as barely armed peacekeepers where there was no peace to be kept, no orders to fight, no honour in the duty. Only humiliation, and mortar rounds, and the sniper who put a bullet into Bruno's hip.

He stayed there at the top of the stairs, staring at the old stone wall. The door to the offices of the *Mairie* and to his duty remained closed. The only way to protect St Denis now was to solve the case quickly, and to do it himself. He knew that Max was his obvious suspect. That meant breaking Cresseil's alibi, forcing or tricking a confession or setting a trap for Max. Bruno let out a deep breath. He didn't like it but he now knew the course he'd have to take. He pushed through the heavy door into the offices, barely nodded to Claire's cheery greeting from the reception desk, knocked on the Mayor's half-open door and put his head around to ask about working with the Brigadier.

'Better cooperate,' the Mayor said. 'I already approved your assignment to work with J-J and it's the same case. And after that final remark by Bondino about getting the fire cleared up, the sooner we do so the better. I'm glad you came by because I wanted to ask about this adoption request. I don't want to stand in Cresseil's way, but this may be a problem. Cresseil's land is part of the slope Bondino wants us to help him buy. Perhaps you could have a quiet word, just explore what Cresseil plans to do. From the look of him, we'll have him in the retirement home before the year is out. And maybe you could talk to Bondino's people about some promise of a job or a scholarship or something for young Max. If he wants to go into the wine business, it could be a good opening for him.'

Heading back to his office, Bruno pondered the Mayor's ploy and its subtle hints of carrot and stick.

The prospect of a Bondino scholarship for Max could be an attractive idea, unless he was arrested, but it also carried the implicit threat of the Mayor blocking the adoption request. Clearly the Mayor had decided to go ahead with the Bondino project. And if it worked, it could secure the economic future of St Denis for generations. So why did he feel so wary of the plan? Was it just his suspicion of change or his affection for St Denis as it was? Or rather, as the place used to be, he corrected himself as he fired up his computer. There at the top of his list was a message from Isabelle in Paris: 'Coming to Périgord. Are you free this weekend?'

Bruno sat back, surprised and taken aback by the sudden rush of emotion that flooded him. I'm a grown man, he told himself, not some teenage innocent in the grip of his first affair. I'll be forty on my next birthday and we had a very grown-up and responsible conversation about how Isabelle's career ambitions and my love of this place could never blend happily. And now she comes to visit and my heart beats faster. There's a surge of excitement in my veins and I want to stand up and cheer.

He read the email again, analysing the eight short words for some deeper meaning. There was not the slightest hint of affection, even less of passion, only the raw data. She was coming and wanted to see him. For a whole weekend? Perhaps. Should he reply in similar neutral terms, or add something personal? And did he really want to repeat the cycle of joy and disappointment that he had known with Isabelle already? His fingers rested lightly on the keyboard. He would have to send some kind of reply. How best to phrase it? He closed his eyes in thought and then quickly opened them, tapped out 'Wonderful news. For you, of course I'm free' and hit the button marked Send.

CHAPTER 14

When Bruno arrived at Cresseil's cottage, the first thing he saw was a familiar white Porsche. Dupuy and Bondino were standing on the porch facing the seated Cresseil and Max, standing protectively at his side, his hand reassuring on the old man's shoulder. Cresseil's venerable dog was growling and trying to stand, its hackles raised but its rear legs crumpling at his master's feet. All their faces had turned to watch Bruno's arrival. He had interrupted a far from amiable scene. Leaving his hat in the van to appear less official, he walked in silence up to the porch, ignoring Dupuy and Bondino, shook hands with the old man and Max and then knelt to let the dog sniff his knees and his hands before it consented to be stroked by an old friend. Only then did he look up at Dupuy and Bondino to offer a curt greeting.

'These men were just leaving,' said Max angrily. Cresseil looked very tired, but nodded firmly.

'Well, Monsieur, I trust that you will consider our proposal,' said Dupuy. 'Perhaps I might call again when you've had time to consider . . .'

'No considering needed,' said Cresseil. 'The answer is no today and it will be no tomorrow. You won't be welcome if you try to come again.'

Bondino made to speak, but Dupuy put a quick hand on his arm and steered the young man back towards their car.

'You,' said Bondino, addressing Bruno. 'You talk to them. Make them understand. Tell them how this is.'

Bruno, wishing that he had worn his hat, stood and faced them impassively. When Max started forward to say something, Bruno put a restraining hand on his arm. The lad was trembling with emotion. As the two men approached the Porsche, Bondino pushed Dupuy away from the driver's door and climbed in to take the wheel. Looking back at Bruno, Dupuy shrugged, and walked round to the passenger door of his own car, whose engine Bondino was already revving aggressively. Dupuy had barely taken his seat and had not even closed his door before Bondino took off, sending gravel spurting as the wheels tried to grip, the expensive car lurching and bouncing up the rough lane.

'What is this shit?' said Max angrily, speaking directly into Bruno's face. 'They said the Mayor is with them and they want our land. And why do they expect you to talk sense into us?'

'Maybe I'd better sit down,' said Bruno mildly. 'Is there another chair? Then you can tell me what's going on.'

110

'They said they were going to buy us out. Not asking. Telling,' said Max.

'Max, a chair for our friend,' said Cresseil, leaning back and reaching for his pipe. 'And I'd like a glass of something. You too, Bruno?'

Max breathed heavily, but went inside and came out with a chair which he scraped noisily on the stone of the terrace before going back to fetch two glasses of wine.

'The boy's right,' said Cresseil, puffing. 'They also said that there was no point in my arguing because the Mayor would make sure I sold the place, that it was all arranged. Is that right?'

'No,' said Bruno. 'You know the law. This is your property and you can do with it what you will. What did these two guys tell you?'

'They made an offer, not to buy the place, but to buy an option,' Max said. 'The young one showed a fat wad of notes, said it was ten thousand, just for an option to buy at the end of the year for the market price. We said no, and then they got nasty and said we'd find we had no choice, that the Mayor would take care of it.'

Bruno cocked an eye at Cresseil. The old man nodded confirmation, than looked at the youth he wanted to adopt. 'They only got nasty after you laughed at them. That never helps, Max. Always leave a man his dignity.' He turned to Bruno. 'So why don't you tell us what's going on here?'

Bruno explained, only to be interrupted by

111

Max's scornful demand to know where the fifty jobs were supposed to come from.

'And they'd want control over the grapes, the plantings, the wine-making and selling, the lot,' said Max. 'Why do they want to come here? What's in it for them?'

'Water,' said Bruno, who had learned a lot from his surfing of the *écolo* websites. 'I read about it in Hulot's newsletter, you know Nicolas Hulot, the ecology guy on TV. He had a long piece on world water shortages. That's what this is all about.'

'What do you mean, water shortages?' asked Cresseil, pulling some reading glasses from his waistcoat pocket to scrutinise Bruno.

'Bruno's right. We have water, but everywhere else it's getting short,' chimed in Max excitedly. 'The Australian wine crop has halved because of their drought. A big group like Bondino must be thinking about climate change. South Africans are getting worried about water and the Chilean glaciers are shrinking fast. California has its own water problems, and I read about drought in Spain last year. But we've got decent rains, and the river. That must be it.'

'Well, it would explain why they're interested,' said Bruno. 'But that still leaves the question whether we all want to go in with Bondino. They've got the money to pay top price, if you want to sell.'

'It's my own wine I want to make here, organic

wine, quality wine. Not the mass-market stuff they'll produce.'

'This will take some thinking about,' said Cresseil, putting his spectacles away. 'The boy and I will talk about this.'

'One thing you might also want to think about,' Bruno said, leaning back in his chair and preparing to lay out the bait of the little trap he had prepared. 'Max, if you really want a career in wine, you could do worse than start off with Bondino, get them to train you, send you off to their operations in California and Australia.'

Max was silent, but his eyes never left Bruno's face. This was what Bruno was counting on. He'd seen Max playing rugby dozens of times, observed how the young man applied his intelligence to the game, thinking even in the heat and flurries of the match. Bruno was sure that Max would be thinking now, turning over the options in his head.

'Think of Jacqueline,' Bruno went on. 'She's studied wine all over the world. You'd certainly have the leverage to make Bondino back you. When you really know the trade, that's the time to come back and make your own wine, as organic as you like. A couple more years at the university, get your diploma, and then you'd be pretty useful to the Bondino group. Think about it.'

'That Jacqueline! It's all he thinks about,' chuckled Cresseil. He turned to Bruno and winked. 'The lad thinks he's in love. Can't say I blame him.'

'The problem is, it might not go like that,' Bruno went on, closing the trap. 'I was surprised to see Bondino here because the last I heard, he was threatening to pull out. It's the fire that worries him. He told the Mayor straight, any more trouble with militants and the deal's off. He'll go somewhere else with his ten million and some other bright young students will get to make their start in the wine business. You might even find Jacqueline signing up with Bondino.'

Max looked thoughtful, but Bruno wasn't done yet.

'Just one more thing, Max.' He pulled a small tape recorder from his pocket and turned it to record. 'Just read those words aloud into the recorder, if you would.'

He handed over the paper on which he'd copied down the notes that Ahmed had taken on the night of the fire. 'And then you too, Cresseil. We're getting every man in St Denis and environs to do this, just to see if we can identify the caller.'

Max had gone white as he read the paper, but in a halting voice he read out the short list of words, and then Cresseil followed suit.

'There's no point in this,' Cresseil protested when he'd finished. 'I told you Max was here with me and you know how bad my legs are. I couldn't get anywhere near Coux.'

'Who said anything about Coux?' Bruno inquired mildly, turning off the recorder.

CHAPTER 15

The *plat du jour* at Ivan's was kidneys in red wine with *petits pois*, which Bruno felt was a small compensation for Ahmed's refusal to confirm that Max's voice on the new recording had been that of the anonymous caller. Bruno was just wiping the last of the sauce with a slice of bread and was about to finish off the small carafe of Bergerac red with his friend the Baron when his phone rang. It was Dominique, sounding excited.

'Bruno, I've just had a text message from *Aquitaine Verte*, the kind they send out to all their members. They've organised a demo at the Agricultural Station here this afternoon at five. They've arranged a couple of buses from central Bordeaux, leaving at two thirty, and two others from from Périgueux and Sarlat.'

That would be well over a hundred people, Bruno calculated, plus whoever used their own transport, plus however many came from St Denis. It could be a couple of hundred, and the Research Station was right on the road with nowhere for buses to park or people to gather. They'd be blocking the main road to Les Eyzies just as the rush hour was starting, which was probably the disruption they wanted.

'Thanks, Dominique. Can you alert Petitbon at the Research Station? He needs to know about this, and tell him I'll be along shortly. And by the way, will you be there? It could be useful if we have to calm things down.'

Dominique agreed, and Bruno closed his phone and opened it again. He shrugged an apology to the Baron, waved away Ivan bringing the cheese course and called the Mayor and explained the situation. The Baron called the cheese course back and helped himself to a double portion, winking at Bruno as he did so. Bruno focused on his call. Could the Mayor call the Prefect and ask for some extra Gendarmes to be on duty? And perhaps also call Alphonse to see if he knew about it.

'Any suggestions, Bruno?' the Mayor asked.

'Just one you might want to think about. People at a demo want some kind of result. We could give them one, if you were to announce that you were bringing charges over the nonpayment of taxes. You needn't specify whether you're targeting the Research Station or the company that owns the land. But it would make the demonstrators think they'd achieved something, and it would get Alphonse on our side. I think he might be the key to this.'

'I like it. I'll get the paperwork moving and see you at the Research Station a bit before five.'

116

Next Bruno called the Gendarmerie, where Jules reported the welcome news that Capitaine Duroc had the day off and had gone to the cinema in Sarlat. That made things much easier. Bruno explained the situation to Jules, and asked for a patrol on the main road from Périgueux and Bordeaux to check all coaches and order any likely ones to park in the square by the Gendarmerie. That would ease the traffic problem. The remaining Gendarmes should gather at the Research Station. As he rang off, his phone trilled again. It was the Brigadier.

'Something's up,' he began.

'You mean the demo at the Research Station?' Bruno asked.

'How did you know about that? My computer guys just picked it up from their website.'

'Dominique Suchet, one of your suspects. She rang to warn me. As I told you, she's a responsible young woman.'

'How do you want to handle it?'

'The Mayor's asking the Prefect for more Gendarmes. And we'll handle it softly. People have a right to demonstrate peacefully.'

'You'd better hope it turns out to be peaceful, but I doubt it. From the cellphone traffic, some of the militants who trashed the McDonald's are going to be turning up. Leave them to me. That's an order. One more thing, we traced the phone card. It was one of a batch of five-euro cards sold in the *tabac* here in St Denis and hasn't been used

117

for any other calls so far.' He rang off, leaving Bruno staring worriedly at his phone.

'Sounds like trouble. Anything I can do?' asked the Baron, relishing his cheese course. Bruno found a steaming coffee before him and he sipped it gratefully. 'Maybe call some of the lads in from the rugby club. Get them chanting "Save Our Research Station". Just in case there's any trouble from these outsiders.'

Bruno eyed his friend thoughtfully. 'As I said, people have a right to demonstrate peacefully, particularly in their own town. And you're the big shareholder in that building yard. Maybe some of your heavy trucks could cruise up and down slowly past the Research Station, make sure the demonstrators stay off the road.'

The Baron winked at him again.

Bruno watched as the demonstrators straggled in on foot after the long walk from the square where their coaches had been parked. He was not altogether confident, but he was calm. His objectives were clear. He had rallied his forces and organised a reserve. He had prepared the ground, made his dispositions and he had a plan. All the tactical requirements the army had taught him had been fulfilled.

He stood before the closed iron gates of the Research Station, five Gendarmes alongside him and the Mayor at his elbow. Another dozen Gendarmes from Périgueux were inside the gates with Petitbon and some of his employees, and four more were directing traffic. Across the road, the Baron and a small knot of rugby players were grinning and waving some hastily inked placards that said 'Save Our Research Station' and 'Hands Off Science'. Heavy trucks loaded with sand and building supplies ground slowly by, forcing the marching demonstrators into a single file along the grass verge. Bruno looked down. The bullhorn stood ready behind the folding steps he had placed before the gates, and the Mayor had a file of papers under his arm. The forces of order of St Denis were as prepared as he could make them.

'You knew we were coming,' said Alphonse as he approached at the head of the marchers, Céline at his side. He carried a baton on his shoulder with a placard that read '*ARRETEZ-OMG*'. There was resignation and perhaps a touch of relief rather than accusation in his voice.

'You're a town councillor. You don't want trouble here any more than I do,' said Bruno. 'Let's keep this calm and dignified. The Mayor thought you might like to say a few words, tell your demonstrators why they're here. And then the Mayor has something to say.'

Alphonse went back to confer with two of the older men who led the group of marchers. Well-groomed and wearing town shoes, they did not look to Bruno like troublemakers. He eyed the rest of the demonstrators, noting that Max and Jacqueline were among them, Max waving cheerfully at his

119

rugby friends across the road. There was no sign yet of Dominique. Bruno counted maybe a hundred and fifty, at least a third of them women and perhaps twenty kids he knew from the St Denis *collège* and all the local Greens. The only ones that worried him were shouldering their way from the long straggle of marchers to the front, all young and carrying placards, some of them wearing heavy boots and hooded sweatshirts and carrying suspiciously heavy bags over their shoulders. Bruno turned to Jules, the senior Gendarme present, and quietly pointed them out. Jules nodded, and passed the word to his men.

Bruno strolled over to where Alphonse was talking urgently to the two men. One of the young toughs with a heavy bag joined them. Bruno casually turned so his arm jostled the bag. It seemed to squash on contact like liquid rather than anything solid. At least it wasn't bricks.

'Ready, Councillor?' he asked Alphonse, who nodded, handed his placard to one of the two men and began to turn towards the gates.

'Perhaps you'll introduce me to your friends. I presume they're from *Aquitaine Verte*,' Bruno said pleasantly.

'Well, perhaps . . .' Alphonse began.

Bruno was already shaking the hand of the first man and introducing himself as the municipal policeman, welcoming them to St Denis and wishing them a pleasant and peaceful stay. They mumbled polite replies and Bruno made a mental note of their names. One, he learned, was an elected member of the *Conseil Régional*, the other a parliamentary candidate. The young tough backed hastily away into the crowd. Alphonse began squeezing his way through to the gates and Bruno walked slowly across the road to the lads from the rugby team.

'Any trouble, grab those lads in the hoods and keep them out of action, peacefully as you can,' he told the Baron quietly, and strolled back to stand beside the small stepladder where Alphonse and the Mayor had their backs to the crowd, talking with animation. Bruno didn't bother with the bullhorn, ascended the steps and began in the parade-ground voice he had learned on the barrack square.

'Welcome to St Denis, where we take very seriously the right of every citizen to demonstrate peacefully on matters of public concern. I repeat, peacefully. We're proud of our scientists and technicians at our research station whose work we believe will help feed a hungry world and keep our home of the Périgord as the agricultural heartland of France. Our respected town councillor, Alphonse Vannes of the Green party, who is known to most of you, will now say a few words on the issue that brings you here. He will be followed by our Mayor, who has some news of great interest.'

Bruno stepped down, gave Alphonse the bullhorn, and helped him up the steps. At the back of the crowd he saw Dominique on a bicycle overtake one of the slowly grinding trucks. She turned

121

off to leave her bike with the rugby boys, most of whom had been at school with her.

Alphonse began. He was not a born speaker, and had trouble with the bullhorn, which squeaked and burped whenever he became animated. This was not often. Bruno had ensured that Alphonse would be the main speaker, knowing that he wouldn't be an incendiary one. Alphonse began citing some vague statistics about the dangers of genetically modified crops and the charm of organic foods and what little energy had been in the demonstration began to leak away. Sensing this, he changed his tune, and began condemning the Research Station for illegal plantings and operating without a permit. This had little effect, but it seemed to stir up some of the militants, who began chanting '*Arrêtez OMG*.' Feeling drowned out, Alphonse joined in the chanting and the crowd began to join in, the young toughs turning to the crowd and waving their arms to get everyone chanting and a rhythm going.

Bruno tugged at Alphonse's sleeve. 'Calm them down,' he urged. Alphonse nodded and stopped chanting, but a momentum had built among the crowd and they were moving forward, their faces red and voices climbing in pitch. Bruno tugged at Alphonse once more and he began to speak again, but somehow the bullhorn had been turned off and he was drowned out. Bruno kept his eyes on the young men in hoods who were now out of the front line and pushing others forward. He clambered up the steps alongside Alphonse and waved across their heads to the Baron, and the rugby team began to move in.

From the middle of the crowd something black was hurled into the air and then another. Bruno whirled to see. It seemed to have a tail and be heading off to one side, way over the heads of the Gendarmes and towards the long row of greenhouses that flanked the Research Station. Were they trying to break the glass? He pulled Alphonse down the steps, grabbed the bull-horn, turned it on and shouted for calm. Three, four, five more projectiles were in the air when the first one landed with a great splash of red paint across the glass panes. Another bag seemed to open in mid-air, scattering splashes of paint over the Gendarmes and the research staff inside the gates.

Bruno noted the location of the paint-throwers – that was what they'd been carrying in those shoulder bags – and handed the bullhorn to the Mayor. He turned to Jules and the Gendarmes, shouting 'Get them,' and pushed his way through the crowd. The one he had jostled was drawing his arm back for another throw. Bruno grabbed the arm and pulled him backwards so that he fell, the paint bag splashing over the marchers behind him. Bruno grabbed the shoulder bag, pulled out a bag of paint and upended its contents over the face of the sprawled youth. He turned and threw a second bag at another of the young paint-throwers, half of it catching a Gendarme who was trying to collar the man.

123

Jules had one hooded youth in a bear hug and another was ducking away from two more Gendarmes. The rugby lads had moved in to grab some of the others. Red paint was splashing everywhere. The chanting had stopped and most of the marchers were scuttling away from the mess of paint. One young tough ran at Bruno, his placard held out ahead of him like a lance and Bruno stepped quickly to one side, tugged at the baton so that the youth lurched forward, and pushed him sprawling to the ground.

Suddenly it seemed to be over. The Mayor was standing on the steps, speaking calmly into the bullhorn about his lawsuit and waving the legal papers he had brought. Nobody was listening so he began asking the crowd to disperse. Max, his arm protectively around Jacqueline, was escorting her back towards town. Dominique was helping a middle-aged man who was holding his head and sitting on the ground. All of the paint-throwers were pinioned either by a Gendarme or a rugby player.

Bruno turned, almost losing his footing on the lake of fresh paint that seemed to cover the ground, and camera flashes went off. Of course the marchers would have tipped off the media. Bruno began steering the captives and their escorts through the gates where the remaining Gendarmes could hand-cuff them.

The braying siren of a klaxon sounded and with a squeal of brakes a large dark blue bus with darkened glass windows rocked to a halt on the road. The door opened and standing by the driver Bruno saw the Brigadier, clutching a handrail to keep his balance. Two by two, the squadron of thirty black-clad figures jumped out and drew up in a disciplined line. They wore helmets and leg-guards and carried shields and clubs. The *Compagnies Républicaines de Sécurité* were France's feared riot police, tough and trained and ruthless.

The crowd began walking and then running back towards town and their parked coaches. Abandoned bags of paint bombs lay leaking on the road behind them. The two well-groomed politicians, their hair and clothing splashed with red paint, stood staring at the motionless ranks of riot police and at the Brigadier, who now descended the steps from the coach and eyed the scene, nodding affably at Bruno.

'You seem to have handled this without our re-inforcements, but I thought it best to be on hand if needed,' he said, eyeing the lake of red paint. 'Let's hope nobody tries to claim that the riot police left a sea of blood on the road.'

'We had the Research Station security cameras running the whole time. They'd look silly if they tried.'

The Brigadier nodded. 'I'll take over the arrests. How many have you got? It looks like eight or nine. Criminal damage and making an affray, it should be good for three years each. And I get to interrogate them all, search their homes and confiscate their cellphones and computers. Lots of address lists. Many thanks, Bruno, for a gratifying haul. All this, and your little town stays remarkably calm, considering.'

'I hope you note that your suspects Alphonse and Dominique were not part of this.'

The Brigadier raised his eyebrows and turned to wave the riot police into the Research Station compound. They trotted dutifully forward to take custody. The Brigadier turned back to Bruno. 'And now perhaps you'll introduce me to your Mayor.'

CHAPTER 16

Bruno had a special attachment to the knowledge that while almost any French village can boast a weekly market, the proud and venerable town of St Denis had two. But he was usually too busy to enjoy the justly famous market of the royal charter, which had been held every Tuesday since 1347. He preferred what St Denis called the new market, held on Saturdays since the relatively recent date of 1807 when one of Emperor Napoleon's new Prefects had a bright idea. He was running out of money to complete the new stone bridge, and his wife's cousin was running out of customers for the output of his new textile mill. So the prospect of a second market, which would double the income from tolls on the new bridge and provide twice as many buyers for the woollen cloth, made eminent commercial sense. That was the theory. In practice, the Saturday market had never lived up to his hopes, failing to attract as many stalls and merchants as expected.

The Saturday market did survive, however, not as a great business success but as an agreeable and useful addition to the amenities of St Denis. Bruno admired the stubborn patience of the citizens in keeping it going. While the grand Tuesday market could attract over a hundred stalls and stretch from the main square in front of the *Mairie* all along the Rue de Paris to the parade ground in front of the Gendarmerie, the Saturday market was a more intimate affair. Bruno seldom saw more than a dozen stalls, all manned by locals, and they never overlapped the small square that was on other days the parking lot for the Mayor and his staff. In winter, the entire Saturday market could be accommodated under the arches of the *Mairie*, benefiting from the warmth of the brazier that Bruno lit, his own small effort to ensure the tradition did not die out. On this quiet September morning when the tourists had mostly gone the market still spilled over into the parking lot.

For Bruno, it was a gathering of friends. Stéphane was there with his milk and cheeses and yoghurts, with young Dominique to help out at the stall, alongside Raoul the wine merchant and Yves with his fruit and vegetables. The fishmonger and *charcutier* were squabbling over which of them got the prime location at the corner of the bridge. Old Marie with her ducks and eggs and *magrets* was in her usual place under the arches and close to the café, the dubiously legal fat goose livers tucked discreetly out of sight in a cool box. Fat Jeanne, her leather cash bag dangling from her shoulder, passed through the stalls exchanging kisses and gossip as she took the modest fees the town charged the merchants.

The air was fresh and the sun warm but not oppressive. Fauquet had not bothered to open the sun umbrellas over his outdoor tables, where people were lingering over their croissants and newspapers. Light glinted on the ripples where the river shallows danced over the pebbles on the near shore. Far downstream, a group of pony-trekkers waited patiently as their steeds drank their fill while a flotilla of ducks paddled by. The golden stone of the old bridge and the local buildings glowed warmly in the mid-morning light. The clock on the *Mairie* pointed to ten a.m. and the bells of the church in the Rue de Paris began to strike.

Bruno, still feeling a glow of satisfaction from the way his town had emerged unscathed from the demonstration, surveyed the familiar scene from the steps of the *Mairie*. He enjoyed the familiar rhythms of the town that had become his home, where he knew all the stallholders, most of their customers and some of their secrets. How much of this would survive the changes that the Bondino enterprise would bring? There would be more jobs and money and probably more American tourists and a handsome stall in pride of place selling Bondino wines. All that would be good. But Raoul's modest little wine stall, selling his choices of the local Bergerac wines, would face stiff competition. That was not much of a price to pay. So why did he have so many doubts about this project? Why did it feel like an oversized and alien intrusion that would change St Denis's way of life?

With a small start, he noticed that one of the shoppers pausing at the stalls was Bondino. Bruno wondered if he had seen the previous day's *Sud-Ouest*, with its front-page report headlined 'Riot in St Denis' and a photo of the riot police pushing men in handcuffs into the coach. Bondino was wearing jeans and a polo shirt, with a camera around his neck, looking like just another tourist rather than the sleek global businessman Bruno had disliked on sight. He was buying honey and beeswax candles from Margot, the housekeeper at the home for retired priests in St Belvédère, who was almost as old as her charges. Then he stopped to purchase some of the small *crottins* of goat cheese from Alphonse, walked quickly by the man selling mussels and oysters from the bay, and came up to Bruno.

'*Bonjour*, Monsieur,' he said, putting out his hand to shake. Bruno returned his greeting. 'I like this market,' the American went on. He smiled an apology. 'I speak French not too well, I regret. St Denis has much charm.' He gestured with a look of puzzlement at the stall behind Bruno. 'What is it?' he asked.

Now that Pierrot had his driving licence back, he was in the market once more with his ancient Citroën bus whose side folded down to display some of the oddest merchandise in France – widows' weeds, felt slippers, long black skirts and shawls, and the gaudy wrap-around aprons that farmers' wives used to wear. In tiny cubbyholes beneath came the useful items that could be found nowhere else: typewriter ribbons and crochet hooks, little gas mantles for paraffin lamps, knitting needles and smooth wooden domes used to darn socks.

'The farmers and their wives find Pierrot very useful,' Bruno explained. Bondino smiled and moved on to buy some late strawberries, with a last look at Pierrot's display of hand-operated mixers and tin openers and the blowpipes the farmers used to shoot medicine pills deep into the throats of their live-stock. Pierrot hardly bothered to attend his wares, spending his time in the café or helping Raoul's customers taste his wines, which was why he had lost his driving licence six months ago.

As Bruno headed for Fauquet's café, Jacqueline appeared around one of the stalls. She stopped, smiled and held out her hand. He tipped his finger to the brim of his cap and then shook her hand.

'Not shopping yet?' He gestured at her empty bag. She shook her head.

'Meeting someone for coffee,' she said, appraising him. 'You were brilliant at the demo, taking charge like that.'

'Max seemed to get you away without any trouble,' he said.

She shrugged. 'Not my kind of scene, but Max

gets so passionate about this GMO stuff. How about you? On duty again?'

He nodded. In fact he was about to take a coffee and then go to his office to see if Isabelle had sent another email. This was the weekend she was supposed to come down but there had been no more word from her. His cellphone number had not changed. She knew how to reach him. But he wanted to check the emails, just in case.

'I'll be heading off to a friend's vendange soon,' Bruno told her. 'It's probably too early, but he picks his grapes at the same time every year and feeds us all a grand lunch of cassoulet.'

'Does he take volunteers?' She spoke in correct and fluent French but with an unmistakable Québec accent that still carried memories of the eighteenth-century Bretons and Gascons who had planted the *fleur-de-lys* in the new world. 'I'd love to take part in a French wine harvest. It would be a first for me.'

She was better like this, Bruno thought. For the first time since he'd met her she seemed genuine, with all the eagerness of youth. It made her easier to like. He smiled at her. 'I'm sure there's always room for one more. Come and have a coffee so I can explain what you're letting yourself in for. Have you picked grapes before?'

'Often, back in the States. And in Australia, where I studied wine-making.' She was wearing jeans tucked into long boots, and carrying what looked like an army-surplus shoulder bag.

'OK, Jacqueline. I could come back and pick you up here in the café at about eleven, but you might wish to change first into working clothes. Or I could entrust you to my Communist friend Montsouris here, a fierce revolutionary who wishes Stalin were still alive. But he'll probably be heading for Joe's before me, and I'm sure he'd be delighted to escort you.'

Fauquet's was already filled with the usual market crowd taking coffee before going back to man the stalls. Fauquet himself, brisk and dapper in his white chef's blouse and little white cap, came from behind the zinc counter to shake Bruno's hand and inform him that the latest batch of croissants was still piping-hot from the oven.

'Not today, *mon vieux*. Just a quick coffee. I'll need to keep room for Joe's feast.' Bruno passed along the counter shaking hands with the usual crowd, introducing Jacqueline as the new *stagiaire* from Hubert's wine shop. The men greeted her with ponderous gallantry, bowing over her hand as they shook it. Pierrot instantly ordered a *petit blanc* for the new arrival and Pascal offered her a *café crème*. Fauquet swept off his chef's hat and Montsouris used a paper napkin to wipe the seat of a bar stool for the young woman to perch on amid the circling admirers.

Laughing, she took her place on the stool and chatted agreeably, but Bruno could not help but notice that her eyes kept glancing out of the window. Following her gaze he saw Max appear at Alphonse's

133

stall. Jacqueline began to step off her stool as if to leave. Then Bruno saw Dominique walking across from her father's stall to embrace Max and steer him off behind one of the columns that supported the *Mairie* for what looked like a private and urgent conversation. Probably talking about the fire, thought Bruno, or perhaps the demo, wishing he could overhear them. Jacqueline had sat down again. A lovers' tiff seemed to be brewing. Bruno watched the assured way that Jacqueline drew the men at the bar back into her orbit.

'I gather this is the day Joe picks his grapes and makes his cassoulet,' she said.

'The day we pick his grapes, you mean,' rumbled old Pierrot. 'Joe's a clever old sod, getting everybody else to pick his grapes when he just stays at home and cooks.'

'You can't complain, Pierrot,' grinned Fauquet, with a wink at Jacqueline. 'At least you drink Joe's wine, which is more than most of us can say.'

'Be fair,' said Bruno. 'We all use Joe's wine for the *vin de noix*, and for the *eau de vie*. Where would we be without him?'

Bruno was accustomed to the chorus of amiable jeers that met his defence of Joe, his predecessor in the post of police chief of St Denis. His vineyard, tucked between the town's rugby field and its tennis club, was small and poorly drained. But it was the first piece of land that Joe had ever owned, and Bruno had to admit that his wine was no worse than the *pinard* he had been given to drink as a young recruit in the French army, the litre of rough red wine a day that had sustained the *tricolore* throughout the ups and downs of French history.

'Don't be naïve, Bruno,' said Montsouris, the Communist member of the town council, a big and burly railwayman. 'Joe's just hanging on to that plot of land to force the rugby club to pay more to get the second pitch. He knows he can get a higher price so long as he claims it's a vineyard, whatever crap he makes.'

'And here's another North American who's visiting our town, Monsieur Bondino,' Bruno said, as the American walked into the bar, loaded down with shopping bags. He stopped in his tracks when he saw Jacqueline. She gave Bondino a cool appraising look and then her face broke into a broad smile, almost as if she recognised him. They shook hands and exchanged bursts of American-English too fast for Bruno's limited command of the language, though he heard the words 'wine' and 'Bondino', so she evidently knew the family name and business.

From the doorway, Bruno smiled his farewells, a smile that became all the broader as he saw Montsouris's wife heading with her usual determined stride through the market towards the café where her husband was paying court to Jacqueline. Madame Montsouris, far more rigid in her Communist ideology than her husband, held equally strict views on marital fidelity. Thank God he was still single, Bruno told himself, and assumed that he, rather than poor Montsouris, would be responsible for taking Jacqueline to the little vineyard beyond the rugby field. Bachelor or not, he could not help smiling at himself as he ran up the stairs to check his email and for the third time ensured that his phone was on and its battery full. But there was still no message from Isabelle.

CHAPTER 17

Joe was not particular about the grapes that went into the ancient wooden vat for the pressing. So as well as the bunches from the forty rows of vines in his own vineyard, he welcomed grapes from the shady terraces and hedges of his neighbours. To Joe, grapes were grapes. Nor was he averse to the occasional handful of blackcurrants.

'Mainly Cabernet Sauvignon, a couple of rows of Merlot which is about what I'd expect around here, along with the odd foot of Cabernet Franc,' said Jacqueline, casting what was evidently an expert eye over Joe's pride and joy, where men and women of all ages and several children were dragging blue plastic boxes between the rows of vines and yelling greetings at Bruno as they carried the full boxes to the trailer behind Joe's old tractor.

Bondino, who'd been sitting over a coffee with Jacqueline when Bruno returned to Fauquet's to collect her and had asked to come along, stared bemusedly at the scene. 'It's like history, like the nineteenth century,' he said. 'No machines.' He bent to look at some of Joe's undistinguished bunches of grapes and shook his head.

'Don't let Bruno get you into his cellar, Mademoiselle,' called out Jeanne from across a dozen rows of vines after Bruno had shouted out a brief introduction of Jacqueline and Bondino as new volunteers.

'There's a couple of feet of Mourvèdre and Cinsaut and even a Petit Verdot, but it's really too soon to pick that,' Jacqueline went on. 'And Lord bless my soul but I think that's a Carignan, although I've never actually seen one before. Where on earth did Joe get this job lot of vines? This isn't a vineyard, it's a vine museum.'

She had changed into sneakers and a baggy cotton sweater that was emblazoned with the letters UCD and her abundant hair was swept back into a loose bun. The tight jeans she had worn in the café had been replaced with some loose cargo pants that seemed to have pockets everywhere. From one she took some very fine latex gloves and from another a pair of curiously curved scissors that were evidently designed to cut the bunches of grapes. Bruno was always content to observe a real expert, any expert in anything, so he listened carefully.

'The soil is terrible for wine,' she went on. 'No drainage, a lot of clay, not enough pebbles, too much water too close to the surface and the soil nutrients are probably too good for vines. Weeds everywhere and I'm not sure that our owner has ever heard of pruning. The foliage is far too thick for the sun to get to the grapes.'

She delivered a burst of English to Bondino, too fast for Bruno to follow, but since she was pointing at the various vines, it seemed to be a translation of what she had told Bruno. Bondino nodded appreciatively.

'You can tell all those different varieties of grape by sight?' Bruno asked.

'Well, I cheated on the Carignan. Back in the hotel I checked up my reference books on the kinds of grapes that are grown in south-west France. But I can tell most of the varieties. I grew up on vineyards and then did four years at U of C Davis.'

'U of C?' Bruno asked.

'University of California, and Davis is the campus that specialises in wine. Then I took a year at Adelaide, the best place to study wine in the southern hemisphere. My family takes wine very seriously and if you want to make it in the family business, you have to know your stuff. By the way, Bruno, I wanted to ask you, since you evidently know everything that happens in St Denis. I really don't want to stay at the hotel too long. If you hear of any rooms to let or a small, cheap apartment, could you let me know? Anything that's not a hotel would do fine, as long as it's not too far from town. That nice man at the bicycle shop let me have a cheap old bike so I can travel a bit.'

Her voice trailed off as she looked over his shoulder. Turning, Bruno saw Max and Alphonse arrive, cheerfully greeting the other grape pickers. Max began heading toward them, waving at Jacqueline, but she turned her back and bent to the next row of vines with Bondino.

Bruno went off to collect a blue plastic basket for each of them and a pair of Joe's rusty old wine scissors for himself and Bondino. As he approached the truck, Max brushed past him, barely grasping his hand with a quick '*Bonjour*'. Bruno assumed he was still nervous at being under suspicion until Max moved on quickly to Jacqueline, only to be taken aback by her frosty response.

Has there really been a row, Bruno wondered, or is she just playing off one man against the other? Max was looking hesitant, furious and baffled, all at the same time. He had a lot to learn about women. But then so did he, Bruno reflected ruefully as he caught himself checking his phone yet again and wondering if Isabelle was ever going to call. And how would he respond if she did appear? Could he possibly assume that all would be as it was, that they would fall into bed and make passionate love? More likely he'd be tongue-tied and nervous, but trying to conceal it with some light bravado. And what of Isabelle? Would she too be uncertain at meeting again, a little reserved, suggesting that she was not prepared to jump into bed at the sight of him?

Time would tell. She had made the approach, coming down again to St Denis, to Bruno's turf. But it was her meeting, her choice about the way it would develop. So he'd take his cue from her, and try to fathom if he could find the real Isabelle again behind whatever mask she'd be wearing for the delicate moments of reunion. Snipping away at Joe's grapes, Bruno wondered whether it was the policeman in him that made him so interested in how other people presented themselves to others. In his experience, and indeed in his own case, what the public saw might have been very different to the real person, but it was full of useful clues about the way the person would truly like to be. Bruno would love to be as calm and self-confident as he had taught himself to seem, and to be even a fraction as wise and as patient as he sought to appear.

The reality, Bruno knew, was that he tended to be lazy and self-indulgent and required the imposition of a clear routine and self-discipline to function even tolerably well. He assumed that it was much the same with others, and that one's own faults loomed far larger than they usually appeared to the outside world. The superficially poised and self-assured Jacqueline was probably far less sure of herself than she appeared as she played off her two admirers against one another. Bruno watched as she chatted happily to Bondino in English, and gave curt replies in French to the crestfallen Max.

Jacqueline lifted some vine leaves and peered

through at Bruno. 'Does your friend ever trim these vines? I can't imagine what kind of wine he produces.'

'It is an acquired taste,' Bruno said. 'But I doubt that you'll acquire it. I never have.'

'Nor me,' said Max, working alongside Bondino at the next row of vines. 'It's probably the worst wine I've ever tasted.' He looked sourly at Bondino. 'Except for some of that mass-produced *merde* from the new world, sugary grape juice with added alcohol.'

Aha, thought Bruno. The young bulls are starting to face off.

'So why do you do this? He pays you?' asked Bondino. Bruno wasn't sure whether he was ignoring Max or simply didn't understand.

'Not in money, but in food and good fellowship,' Bruno replied. 'Joe has been a good friend to me and he helped me in this job. He did it for years before I came to St Denis. All the people here are his friends and family, and they come every year for the vendange.'

'But why bother when he takes no care of his vines and the wine is no good? I don't get it,' asked Jacqueline.

'You missed that bunch,' Bruno said. 'And that one back there.'

'No, I didn't,' she said primly. 'I left them on purpose. Some of them were already rotten.'

'So cut those off the bunch and put the good ones in the plastic bin with the rest. Joe is not particular.'

She flounced her head, ignoring him. Bruno went back and cut the bunches she had left. Only a few of the grapes had burst and some were shrivelled. Bruno shrugged, cut off the worst and tossed the bunch into the bin.

'If we were in California, I'd fire you,' she said when he returned, her voice rising in tone at the end of the phrase, as if it were a question. She did this a lot, Bruno noted.

'If we were in California she'd probably shoot you,' grinned Max.

'If we were in California I would not be working in a vine-yard,' Bruno said. 'Unless a friend asked me to help. And then for cutting the grapes I would follow his rules, or hers. Here, I follow Joe's rules. So should you.'

CHAPTER 18

Still conscious of Joe's cassoulet lying comfortably behind his belt, Bruno waited in front of the *Mairie*. With a wedding scheduled at three p.m., the Mayor had agreed to fit in the formal *attestation* of adoption at 2.45 as a favour to a fellow member of the town council. Never having bothered to register Max's status, beyond agreeing to be listed as next-of-kin on the boy's identity card and his university application, Alphonse had been enthusiastic for Cresseil's plan the moment he heard it.

'Can you think of a better way to keep the lad here in the neighbourhood than by giving him some land of his own?' he'd asked Bruno. 'I'd always thought that once he had his university diploma, he'd be off, Paris or California or somewhere like so many of the kids.'

The guests for the wedding were already gathering in the car park beside the *Mairie* when Alphonse's car pulled up. For once, this was not a marriage that Bruno needed to attend. Two of the temporary workers from the Royal hotel had decided to marry after a passionate and hard-working

144

summer, and one of them had been kept on as the barman. Bruno shook hands with some members of the wedding party he knew, and then stopped as he recognised Pamela in a wide straw hat with a red satin scarf tied around the brim.

'You look magnificent as always, almost regal,' he said, kissing her on each cheek. 'But then you English have a special affinity for royalty.'

'My dear Bruno, you have evidently lunched extremely well,' she replied in her excellent French. 'I presume you were at Joe's *vendange*?'

'And like all the men of the village, heartbroken not to see you there.'

'That's the wine speaking, Bruno, and I know it. Young Marie stayed with me overnight before going off tonight to her husband's bed.'

'Marie the bride? I didn't know she was a friend of yours.'

'She helped out a bit in the summer on my hectic changeover days, so I've known about this romance from the beginning. And that meant I had to help dress the bride so I sent Joe my apologies.'

'Well, you'll have to attend the wedding party so you'll miss the pressing of the grapes this evening. Now I must go. Business at the *Mairie*. Oh, and there's something I need to ask you. There's a Canadian girl working at Hubert's *cave* and she's looking for a place to rent. I thought one of your *gîtes* might be free. Let me know, or call her at the *cave*, her name's Jacqueline. Sorry,

I have to dash but see you soon.' He turned to run up the ancient stairs and arrived at the council chamber just as Cresseil was limping slowly from the elevator. The Mayor, wearing his *tricolore* sash and his *Légion d'Honneur* button in his lapel, came forward to greet them.

'We need another witness, Bruno,' the Mayor began. 'Alphonse won't do. He's listed as a next of kin.'

'Does it have to be a French citizen?'

'No, anyone with an address in the *Département* will serve.'

Bruno nodded, went back down the stairs to find Pamela and hastily explained why her presence was needed as he took her by the hand to steer her upstairs. His request seemed to fluster her but she quickly recovered her poise and politely shook hands with the group. Alphonse and Max she knew from the market, but not Cresseil.

'François Pontillon Cresseil,' the Mayor began once they were all gathered in his office. 'Do you formally adopt this young man present, Maximilien Alphonse Vannes, as your son and inheritor, assuming your name and taking upon yourself all paternal responsibilities under the *Code Civil* of the Republic?'

'I do, freely and willingly, as a citizen of the Republic,' said the old man. Bruno noticed the pride in Cresseil's eyes as he watched Max make the ritual replies, and pondered again his suspicions about the fire. Max had shown no sign of hatred for the

146

genetic crops at the demo, had simply been there taking care of Jacqueline. Perhaps Bruno's suspicions were misplaced, and his trap was just a waste of time. Worse still, he was right, and this touching scene was just the prelude to Max's arrest and Cresseil's heartbreak.

'Then please come forward and sign in turn, and then Bruno and you Madame in the space below for the witnesses.'

Alphonse brought out a small camera and began to take snaps of the singing, and the Mayor brought out a bottle of his own *vin de noix* and began filling the small glasses that stood waiting on a tray.

'We still have some moments to toast the new family before the ceremony of marriage,' the Mayor said. 'In the name of the Commune of St Denis and of the Republic let me be the first to welcome this new family. The adoption will not, of course, be wholly legal until it is ratified and registered by the court in Sarlat, a formality that should be completed in the course of this week.'

Max kissed the old man on both cheeks, and then embraced Alphonse, Bruno and Pamela, who congratulated everyone and allowed old Cresseil to hold her hand as she declared it was quite the most charming adoption she had ever attended.

'I might as well stay up here since I think I hear the sound of the wedding guests on the stairs,' Pamela said. 'But Max, I shall be most disappointed if this means you stop selling the best goat cheese in the market. I'm sure some of my guests come and stay only for your cheeses.'

'I hope soon to be selling your guests wine as well, Madame,' Max said. 'I've an idea that might interest you and other businesses in the area. With my computer I can print special labels for your guest house, your own private *cuvée*, and I can offer you a very good price for the new vintage of Domaine Cresseil, a completely bio-organic wine.'

'Sounds interesting. I'll come round for a tasting. And now forgive me, I have a wedding to attend. And Bruno, tell the girl to call me. I'm sure we can work something out.'

They shuffled out, squeezing past the guests in the hall, Max explaining his plans for the vineyard. Bruno felt a tug on his arm. The Mayor hauled him back into his office and closed the door.

'Is the boy serious about making Cresseil's land into a vineyard, into a business?'

'It looks that way, but he's heading off to university. I don't see how he can until he finishes his studies.'

'I'm tempted to hold off sending those adoption papers to the court at Sarlat for the moment,' the Mayor said. 'I'm not going to let the fancies of an old man and a youngster who thinks he's a *vigneron* block the best chance this commune has of fifty good new jobs.'

'I'm not sure that's a good idea,' Bruno said carefully. 'Cresseil is one of us and so's Max. Our obligation is to them, not to Bondino, and his investment isn't even certain yet. Keep in mind that by the end of this week, Alphonse could be asking in Council where his court papers are, and if it turns out we sat on them, it won't look good. It will certainly make it harder to get Max and Cresseil to see things our way about selling the land to Bondino.'

The Mayor squeezed his lips together and looked cross. Then he took a deep breath. '*Putain.* You're right. But so am I, and you know it. *Tiens*, I must get to this wedding ceremony. I won't bury the papers. I'll just delay them a bit, buy some time for you to sound them out. It's natural enough, squeezing in an adoption at the last minute before a wedding ceremony. No wonder the papers got mislaid for a day or two. If we can't get those land sales guaranteed, this whole project collapses, and then the council will be really upset.'

'But the council don't know about this yet,' Bruno objected.

'Bondino knows how the game is played. The best pressure he can apply is to get the rumour going that I'm blocking an opportunity that's going to raise land values for a lot of people. That's what I'd do in his place, and he's shrewd enough to know that. We don't have much time. Let's meet tomorrow, with Xavier, and talk all this through.'

Sick at heart at this first real breach with the Mayor who had been his patron for a decade, Bruno walked heavily down the stairs and into the sudden sunlight. But his heart leapt and his mood changed in an instant when he saw, leaning against the door of his official van, a familiar slim figure, watching the door of the *Mairie* for his appearance and brandishing a shopping bag.

'Steak, salad, cheese and a bottle of St Emilion,' said Isabelle as he stretched out his arms to approach her. 'Just like the first time. And I also have a bone for Gigi.'

And then she was in his arms, fitting easily all the length of him as she always had, tall enough to put her cheek against his and to whisper in his ear: 'I've missed you more than I thought possible.'

All his gloom had gone and all his worry about how they would meet and what they would say and how reserved she might be and he felt that they had all the time in the world.

'Tell me,' he said, kissing her. 'Have you ever trodden grapes?'

'No,' she said, leaning back to examine him, and tracing his lips with a gentle finger. 'But if I'm going to tread anything, I want to practise on you first. It's been too long, Bruno. Let's see how fast this old van of yours can get us back to your place.'

CHAPTER 19

The party was still under way when Bruno and Isabelle arrived much later that same afternoon. Their hair was still damp from the shower, their desires for one another slaked but hardly sated. The accordions of Joe's favourite 1930s *bal musette* music were blaring from the speakers and a throng of bare-legged people was gathered around the outbuildings at the bottom of the yard. Around them scampered the chickens from Joe's hencoop, pecking at the floor between the feet of the revellers and fluttering fussily out of the path of the humans with whom they had always shared the courtyard.

Montsouris the Communist sat with young Karim and his wife Rashida from the roadside café at the entrance to St Denis, tickling their new baby under the chin. In swimming trunks and T-shirt, and with a big smile on his face as he played with Karim's new son, he could not have looked less like the fiery trade union militant Montsouris liked to play at the council table. Stéphane from the market, his vast thighs like tree trunks, had one arm fondly around his wife and his other hand

151

gripped a large tumbler of wine. Brosseil the town notary was locked in conversation with Gérard, owner of the local campgrounds, his white and spindly legs looking as if it were their first time in the open air this year. Rollo, headmaster of the local *collège*, was pouring out more wine.

A cheer went up as Bruno and Isabelle joined them, hand in hand, a languid almost dreamy look on their faces that signalled the way they had spent the afternoon and raised fondly knowing smiles from his friends. Bruno bent down to take off his boots and socks and trousers and took his place in line at the tap to sluice off his legs. Like most of the men coming for this annual ceremony of treading Joe's grapes, he wore swimming trunks beneath his trousers, and with his T-shirt he was dressed as if for a game of tennis. But the familiar sight of his bare legs sent the women into bursts of bawdy laughter.

'Ooh, there's a hairy one,' hooted Monique, who worked at the town swimming pool and spent her life with half-naked men, and she pirouetted before a bunch of giggling friends, her skirts tucked into her pants to reveal her tanned and brawny legs.

'That's why he's Bruno, Bruno the hairy bear,' called out Montsouris's wife, arm in arm with Josette from the flower shop. 'You just control yourself in there. If you've got any energy left, that is.'

Isabelle, slipping off her shoes and sliding her

152

jeans down her shapely legs to reveal the sleek swimsuit she had donned in Bruno's bedroom, was laughing openly as she joined Bruno at the hosepipe. 'These women are terrific,' she said, putting her arm on his shoulder and turning to watch them.

There was something about these events that turned the usually staid and capable women of St Denis into so many jolly wenches, hooting with derision at the knock-knees of each other's husbands, making saucy jokes at the young men and flouncing their skirts over their bare thighs as they paraded up and down, singing along to Joe's old songs after their turn in the vat. It was the kind of evening that made Bruno aware that he was a bachelor, for the husbands seemed entirely pleased with the liveliness and raucous sisterhood of their wives, as if the woman they knew in private was treating herself to a rare public appearance. The single men by contrast seemed startled, even a little shy at seeing the worthy women they knew from the shops and markets and weddings and funerals acting so out of character.

Bruno, who had learned in almost ten years as the town's policeman that very little was really out of character for anyone, relished this event each year. If the men of St Denis could let their hair down at the rugby club and the hunting dinners, their womenfolk deserved a similar licence. Bruno smiled to himself, remembering old Cresseil's remark about the number of children born nine months after the vendange. Probably the reason why the married men were all grinning at their wives' performance was that they took the bawdy mood home with them. He exchanged glances with Isabelle, twining his fingers into hers. 'We won't stay long,' he murmured.

'Come on out of that vat, Jacquot,' Josette shouted to her husband through the doorway. 'I don't want you tiring yourself out in there. I want you on form later.' The women around her collapsed into happy hysterics. Scenes like this had gone on in these parts for centuries, thought Bruno happily, suffering a number of slaps on his rump as he squeezed through them to take his place in the vat after Jacquot.

The scent was heady, fresh human sweat with the intense sweetness of the grape juice, blended by the large electric fan that Joe had whirring at the edge of the vat. There was a sound of youthful laughter from the vat and Joe, dressed in shorts and a singlet, played the hose over Bruno's and Isabelle's legs as they waited.

Gingerly, because the top step was slippery, Bruno eased himself into the giant vat, nodding at Joe's pretty great-niece Bernadine as she made way for Isabelle and noticing without the slightest surprise that Bondino had managed to join Jacqueline. The girl seemed delighted in his company, her arm and his intertwined as they braced on the wooden rim and their legs trod rhythmically in the purple foam. They were talking

154

fast in English, but he noticed that Bondino's eyes were riveted on Jacqueline's face. Max's girl seemed to have made a new conquest and he might have cause to regret having to attend the celebration of his adoption up at the commune.

Beneath Bruno's trailing fingers, the purple froth still felt greasy rather than clear, the old telltale of the *vignerons* to know when the pressing was done. He felt around with a foot, looking for a whole bunch for the tactile pleasure of treading on it and feeling it burst through his toes before starting the steady tramping motion that was the approved style. Once the novelty wore off, it reminded him of marching in the army.

Bruno had done this for years and knew the ritual, and Isabelle quickly followed his lead, holding the rim with one hand as they faced one another and moved back and forth in unison, then turned to stand sideways with both hands on the rim. He beamed at her, admiring her readiness to try anything. Isabelle grinned back at him, and then looked down to see the grape juice splashing her tanned thighs.

'They'll never believe this in Paris,' she murmured, and leaned forward to kiss him. 'I think you set this up for my return, back to the real France. Back to my very real Bruno.'

Bruno laughed aloud at the incongruity of it, exchanging kisses and the sweet words of lovers as they tramped up and down like a pair of old soldiers amid the rich and heady scent of the

155

grapes. Somewhere in the back of his mind he knew that this wondrous moment would not last, that she would go back to Paris and he would stay. But it didn't matter. She was here and her eyes were huge as they drank him in and her hand came up to touch his face, careless of the other couple.

'You done up there?' called Joe from the bottom of the steps. 'You taught them what to do, Bruno?'

Next it should have been time to change partners, for Isabelle and Bondino to move together, but the young couple seemed fixed to their respective spots.

'Time to move out, Bondino,' Bruno said, giving him a friendly push towards the ladder. 'Let someone else have a go. You've been in here too long.'

Bruno felt the spume as Joe clambered into his vat. The consistency had changed, the slipperiness had gone and it was thickening. There was no sense of anything but liquid underfoot. Joe held on to the rim with both hands, probing with a foot, and he nodded.

'That'll do. Out you get, Bruno, and you too, Canada. We'll leave her overnight, see how the cap is in the morning.'

'That's it?' asked Jacqueline, following Isabelle down the steps to where Bondino waited for her. She flashed the American a quick smile. 'You don't run off the first pressing, you just leave it all in together overnight?'

'Always have and I'm not changing my style now,' said Joe. 'Can you take care of the hose, rinse us off as we come down the steps, and pass us one of those towels?'

'Of course.'

'Do you feel a little light-headed?' Joe asked when they were all down and rinsed off. 'That's the carbon dioxide coming out as the fermentation starts. That's why I have the fan going.'

'Do you add any yeast?' Jacqueline asked.

'There's enough yeast spores in the walls of this barn to ferment half of the wine in the Bordeaux. So we just leave the yeast to Mother Nature, as our ancestors have for hundreds of years. Come on, I want you to try last year's wine, get a sense of just what you've been helping to make. Just bring us a couple of those glasses from the table there.'

He pulled a bottle with no label from a horizontal rack, and opened it with an elderly corkscrew with a handle of olive wood. He splashed some of the wine into a glass for each of them and raised his glass.

'To the new vintage,' he declaimed, and then emptied his glass in a single gulp, like a Russian downing vodka.

Jacqueline was staring at the sludgy liquid in her glass. Gingerly, she put her nose close and gave a very small sniff. Her eyes widened. She took a sip, swirling it around her mouth and then spitting it out as if she were at a wine tasting. Then noticing

Joe's horrified glance, she took a discreet sip, rolled it around her mouth and swallowed. Bondino was staring at his own glass in disbelief and Isabelle discreetly placed hers back on top of a barrel.

'So what do you think of my wine, Mademoiselle Canada?' Joe asked.

'Very authentic. Very true to its terroir, and to its maker, Sir.'

'You're very kind. Unlike your friend Bruno here, you are clearly a connoisseur who knows what she's drinking. I'll save you some bottles.'

Bruno tried to restrain his chuckle. Joe was no fool, and knew what kind of rough old wine he turned out, but he'd be amused to see if he could tease a polite young woman into praising his *pinard*, and talking herself into having to drink more of it.

'Oh, but I couldn't possibly. I've heard how much everyone in town depends on your wine for the *vin de noix*, and I'd hate to rob them of your speciality.' The girl had passed that one with flying colours.

'Let's get back to the party,' said Bruno. 'It's time for the dancing.'

'Not too long,' said Isabelle, fastening the belt of her jeans.

CHAPTER 20

Bruno awoke slowly, only just aware of Isabelle's arm across his chest and his deep sense of contentment at the ease of their reunion and the teasingly delayed pleasures of the night. He turned his head to study her. She was deeply asleep, her lips slightly parted, the calmness of her face all the more striking after the passion of the night. How long would she stay this time? It was a question they had carefully avoided the previous day and one with no real answer.

She wanted him to change his job, change his life and join her in Paris. But the life of a big-city policeman held no attraction for Bruno. In his heart, he wanted to wake up with Isabelle for all the mornings that stretched ahead. In his mind, he suspected the decision had already been made when she transferred from the *Police Nationale* in nearby Périgueux to the high-powered job on the Minister's staff. So was that what lay ahead of them? Snatched weekends interrupting their separate lives, into which other lovers would doubtless come and go? That was not a future that appealed to him, not when compared with that vague assumption that always lay at the back of his mind that some day there would be a wife in this cottage he had built, and children that he could teach to hunt and play tennis and watch them grow and explore his woods in this placid heartland of France. And he could never see Isabelle in that misty mental image.

Bruno sighed gently. What would be, would be. He lay back with his hands clasped behind his neck and let his thoughts wander. No matter how long Isabelle stayed, eventually she would head back to Paris or dart away to some new mission. But it was clear from his meeting with the Brigadier that catching the arsonist was only part of a wider agenda that included gathering intelligence on all the militant *écolos* and protecting whatever interests were involved in the Agricolae operation. That wasn't Bruno's job. And he didn't much like the kind of France the Brigadier represented, which meant that Bruno and Isabelle had different objectives.

His thoughts drifted to Max. His feeling that Max was in some way involved in the fire had grown. The fact that Max had not joined in with the paint-throwing militants at the demonstration meant nothing. Max was a loner. He even played rugby that way. Max would never join a group. He'd do things his way, acting alone, and he'd see them through, which was why Bruno had a hunch that the cameras at the research station could yet be useful.

Damn it, the real problem was that he liked Max and didn't want to see a promising young life wrecked by a prison term for a crime that was also a foolish act of political idealism. And how would Max react to losing Jacqueline, or having a rival for her, Bruno wondered, remembering the way Jacqueline and Bondino had left Joe's party together at about the same time as he left with Isabelle.

That thought took him to his deeper worry, the Bondino proposal. He did not trust the sleek Dupuy, and he didn't much like Bondino. And something in Bruno rebelled against the idea of St Denis doing any deals behind the backs of its own people. Even if some fancy lease arangement could guarantee a future share in theoretical profits, it was not right to press the locals to sell their land for less than it might be worth. It simply felt wrong, and the Mayor had to be made to see that. And now, said Bruno to himself, comes the real question: what if he failed, and the Mayor insisted on proceeding with the scheme? That was the issue that kept him from kissing Isabelle awake and into renewed embraces, kept him fretting in bed on this fine September morning.

Bruno firmly believed that life always looked a little better after a shower, a shave and a shampoo. It was a hangover from his army days. So he slipped gently from his bed, his eyes lingering a little on Isabelle's sleeping form, and went to the porch to greet his dog. Together they made the usual rounds of his vegetable garden and his hen-coop to feed the ducks and chickens before Bruno performed his familiar military exercises, turned on his kettle and headed for the bathroom. Cleansed and refreshed, and dressed in shorts and T-shirt, he looked in at the bedroom where Isabelle still slept. He went back into the kitchen and sliced the previous day's baguette in half and put the slices in the toaster while he prepared his coffee and ate the apple he had just plucked from the tree. Then he spread some of his own raspberry jam on one half of the bread and shared the other with Gigi.

The basset hound's official name was Gitan, or gypsy. But having awoken hungover to find this adoring puppy in his bed on the morning after his house-warming party, Bruno had immediately shortened the name to Gigi, much to the surprise of the Mayor, whose gift it had been from the litter of his own renowned hunting dog. On the hour, Bruno checked the news on Radio Périgord and heard nothing that mattered or needed his attention.

He made a fresh pot of coffee and put the slice of toast and jam on to a tray. He went to the garden for another fresh apple, picked a late white rose from the bush by the door and returned with Gigi to the bedroom. Whether it was the smell of coffee or the heavy breathing of Gigi, his front paws perched on the side of the bed, Isabelle awoke and turned to look at him.

'Hello again,' she said, smiling, and then disappeared under Gigi's happy welcome as the basset hound clambered on to the bed and nuzzled her ear.

'How is a woman meant to look languorous and romantic with a dog like this in her bed?' she protested, laughing and stroking Gigi's long ears. She sat up, her lovely delicate breasts appearing above the sheets, ran her fingers through her hair and grinned broadly.

'Breakfast in bed. Bruno and dog. Fresh coffee. A rose. *Mon Dieu*, Paris is never like this.' She settled the tray across her lap, put the rose behind her ear and patted the bed beside her. 'Come and join me. We have the whole day together.'

'You forget the duties of a country policeman,' he said, and leaned down to kiss her. Gigi wriggled aside to make room for him and Bruno lay down on his side, enjoying the sight of Isabelle sipping her coffee. She broke the grilled baguette into portions, one for her, one for Gigi and another for Bruno.

'I have a rugby class for the *minimes* and then a quick meeting at the *Mairie* before I'm free. I thought you might like a walk in the woods before I go to the rugby club. Then we could go out to lunch and have the day to ourselves.' He kissed her again, and then put the question that had been on his mind since her first email. 'How long can you stay?'

'Until you find the arsonist,' she said. 'I'm

attached to the Brigadier's team. The Minister wants one of his own staff on this inquiry.'

'So you're here on business?'

'Yes, but I was planning on coming down anyway, since the only time I'm ever likely to see you in Paris is when you come up for a rugby international.' She leaned forward to kiss him, the tray wobbling, to take any sting from the remark. 'How long do we have before your rugby lesson?'

'Long enough,' he said, and moved the tray from her lap to the floor and shooed a reluctant Gigi from the room.

'Oh good,' she said, and lifted the sheet to invite him in.

Bruno understood his dog well enough to have accepted that a human never walks a basset hound. The dog and the human go for separate strolls, which always coincide at the beginning, sometimes at the end, and rarely in the middle, unless Bruno gave the special hunter's whistle. Gigi knew every inch of the woods that backed on to Bruno's cottage, and was on nodding terms with every tree, to most of which he gave a token watering as he followed the various beguiling scents that arose to his nostrils, stirred up by his long trailing ears. Bruno, happy to be showing Isabelle his land again, took her hand as they followed Gigi through the well-spaced assortment of beech and chestnut.

'There's something on your mind,' she said,

squeezing his hand. 'Not just me and not just about us. And I don't think it's about the fire. You want to talk about it?'

Skirting the thick entanglements of brambles, he explained his doubts about the Bondino project and the prospect of a row, even a breach, with his Mayor.

'What nags me most of all,' he said, as he led the way through the thin brush and on to the ridge that let them look down the valley to the town, 'is the thought that Bondino could change St Denis beyond recognition. It's like being in bed with an elephant, an international firm worth tens of millions, dominating our life. But as the Mayor says, if we don't get jobs then St Denis could be finished anyway.'

'So what's the worst that can happen?' she asked, looking down at the view. 'You have a fight with the Mayor, resign or get the sack and this wine project goes ahead anyway. You'll walk into a police job in Paris, J-J and I will see to that, and then you move in with me. We come back here every holiday to your cottage. Does that sound so bad?'

She turned to face him, still holding his hand. 'You can say I'm being stubborn for not giving up my career in Paris. And I can say you're being stubborn because you won't give up your country life in St Denis. And so two people who make each other happy are going their separate ways. But what if St Denis gives you up, Bruno? What then?'

Her eyes searched his face but he had no answer. The thought of it was tantalising, a new life in Paris with Isabelle. Marriage and perhaps children. It sounded beguiling but somehow he couldn't bring himself to believe in it. Bruno knew himself well enough to understand that much of his need for St Denis was that it had become the family his orphaned childhood had never provided and with the Mayor as father figure. Here was the prospect of a family of his own and it frightened him. Yet there had never been a woman with whom he could talk like this, a woman whose judgement he trusted, a friend as well as a lover.

He drew her to him and hugged her close. 'Let's see how things go these next few days,' he said. 'Will you be staying here at the cottage?'

'I can't, damn it,' she said huskily, speaking into his shoulder. 'They've based me in Bordeaux. I have to get back for a nine a.m. meeting tomorrow. *Merde*, Bruno, I never cry,' she said, turning away and putting a hand to her eyes.

Gigi came running to snuffle at their feet and gaze up inquiringly as Bruno embraced her and stroked her hair. He was going to be late for his rugby lesson for the *minimes*, and he felt his face relaxing into a smile as he recalled how much he enjoyed teaching them and watching them learn and grow. That was one of the satisfactions of being here, in this position that was far more than a job to him. Was it a position that he was prepared to put at risk? He honestly did not know.

CHAPTER 21

Bruno had a theory that a country displayed its deepest national character in the way it played rugby. The English relished wars of attrition in the mud, grim battles for inches between bloodied forwards under grey skies. The Welsh played like quicksilver, the dashing break through the line by a nimble fly-half dancing his way through the defence. The Scots loved the heroic charge, even when it looked most hopeless, the brave sprint down the wing with the full-back and every man hurling himself into the line. The Irish loved cunning and played with creative trickery, suddenly switching their line of attack or kicking ahead to frustrate the stolid English forwards.

But the French played with unique flair, ready to use their running backs like forwards to power through on the wing. Even better, they loved to play their forwards as if they were wingers, constantly passing the ball to each other and over-whelming the defenders as they sidestepped and broke tackles and moved and thought too fast for the other side to react. And that was how Bruno taught his ten-year-olds, drilling them constantly into the habit of always being just three paces behind the boy with the ball, ready to take the pass.

'Now turn and pass, turn and pass. Make each pass clean,' he panted as they ran the length of the field and back again. 'Tackle low, you defenders. Get his ankles and he'll come down. That's how you stop 'em. Don't grab his arms. Go low. The lower the better.'

By now the older juniors and the reserve teams were drifting through the entrance gates and past the stadium heading for the changing rooms for their training sessions. A small knot of girlfriends took their seats in the stadium to watch and he saw Jacqueline arrive with Max. A busy girl, he thought, leaving the party in an embrace with one guy and showing up next morning with another. He waved a greeting to them and turned back to give his youngsters a last few minutes of a ten-a-side game. With the reserves of patience that he had learned in a decade of these training sessions, he pulled five of each side out to form a line of backs, leaving five in each pack of forwards, and Bruno himself played scrum-half for both sides, putting the ball into the scrum and then passing it out to the backs as it rolled from their heels.

'That's how he taught me to play,' Max was explaining to Jacqueline as a winded Bruno approached, his chest heaving. Ten-a-side made for a fast, exhausting game. But he had to be at the touchline to shake the hand of each of his boys as they trotted off the pitch to make way for the older players. Bruno got Max to help him move aside one of the painters' ladders that half-blocked the way to the changing rooms.

Max was already changed into the royal blue shirt and white shorts of St Denis and Jacqueline was in jeans and a sleeveless white blouse that showed her tanned shoulders to advantage. The other girls in the stand, who had all gone to school with Max, were looking at Jacqueline with guarded curiosity as she slipped her arm around his slim waist. Whatever tensions there had been between them on the previous day at the vendange were now evidently resolved.

'You look very well, Jacqueline,' Bruno said. 'Treading the grapes agrees with you.'

'You look good, too, Bruno. I see how you keep so fit,' she said, smiling. 'Max is taking me up the river to his favourite bathing spot after his practice. Then we'll have a picnic lunch before we head off to pick his grapes.' She kept her arm around Max's waist. Cresseil's grapes, in fact, thought Bruno, but the young man looked at Jacqueline with devotion in his shining eyes.

'You'd better let Max go to his practice,' said Bruno gently as the others came trotting to the field from the changing room, a rough chorus of 'Ooh-là-làs' and 'Allez, Max' at the sight of Jacqueline. With a final caress on her cheek, Max followed them and Bruno nodded amiably at

169

Jacqueline, remembering how closely she had danced with Bondino the previous evening before leaving with the American. A very sociable young woman, this Canadian. Indiscriminately sociable, Bruno thought, remembering her own instinctive flirtations with him. And she was not nearly as attached to Max as he was to her. Some half-remembered quotation came to his mind as he walked to the shower, that in affairs of the heart there is always one who kisses and one who is kissed.

As he towelled himself dry, Bruno was startled to hear a woman's brisk footsteps coming into the bathhouse. Women weren't allowed in here. Then Isabelle appeared, whom he had left with her laptop at the Gendarmerie. She was carrying his boots atop his uniform shirt and trousers and telling him to get dressed fast.

'We're heading for the Research Station. It's been attacked,' she said, bundling his sports clothes into a plastic bag. 'That's all I know.'

'Again? I'm supposed to be at a meeting at the *Mairie*,' he said, wondering what the security cameras might show this time.

'I called the Mayor. The meeting's cancelled. He's joining us at the scene.' She bustled him out of the small stadium and into her car, its blue light flashing as she raced into town. 'One of the staff went in to monitor the automatic watering systems and found the place trashed. He called his boss, who called the Gendarmerie. Paris is going to be furious about this. I called J-J to let him know and he's on the way from Périgueux with a forensics team. I also called the Brigadier and left a message. I'll have to call the Ministry as soon as we have enough to give them some kind of report.'

Bruno hadn't known what to expect, another fire or a break-in, and at first all seemed normal as they drove into the Research Station until they saw the Mayor and Petitbon and a couple of the technicians standing in front of the lines of greenhouses, their panes of glass now thoroughly drenched and covered in a thick layer of fresh white paint.

The front of the greenhouses was still spattered with red paint from the demo, but the roofs and side were now an expanse of gleaming white. Petitbon had a bottle of turpentine in his hand and a rag, and was rubbing hard at one of the panes, but making little impression beyond smearing the stuff. The main door to the greenhouses was open and Bruno could see from the darkness inside that the light had been thoroughly blocked.

'How long will your plants survive without light?' he asked Petitbon.

'A week or more, but that's not the point. We have to monitor their progress every day or our records make no sense. And this stuff isn't coming off, neither with water nor with turps. It seems to be some special kind of paint.'

'They made a hell of a job of it,' said the Mayor, staring at the splashes of red paint at his feet and around the door and the whitened sides. 'It's all round the back as well.'

Isabelle led the way inside the greenhouses, still warm but with the familiar smell of soil and fruitfulness now masked by the acrid smell of the paint. Some of the roof panes had been left open for ventilation and beneath them the white paint pooled around the rows of plants.

'That's as clever a piece of sabotage as I've seen,' she said. 'They didn't break the glass, so there was no sound. There was no break-in so no alarm sounded. But the place is destroyed, just the same.'

'Have you looked at the security cameras?' Bruno asked Petitbon.

'First thing I did. But we're not going to learn much. Come and see.'

He led the way to the front of the old house where one camera had been fixed above the door. Its lens and the stone wall behind it were covered in a spray of white paint.

'It's the same around the back,' Petitbon said. 'The only one they missed was on the chimney stack, looking over the side. I was just going to look at the tape when the Mayor turned up. Let's go and see if we got anything.'

The images were fuzzy but clear, and timed for just after two a.m. The camera showed one man dressed in painter's overalls and wearing goggles over a hood, moving with slow deliberation along

172

the side of the greenhouses. There was a large pack strapped to his back, presumably the paint reservoir, and a long nozzle in one hand that emitted a fine, spraying arc of paint on to the glass roof as he pumped a lever with the other. When he got to end of the greenhouses, he moved out of sight of the camera for a few minutes and then returned, walking in the same slow way to spray their sides.

'I couldn't identity my own wife, dressed up like that,' said the Mayor.

'That's a lot of paint,' said Bruno. 'I suppose when he disappeared he might have been refilling. He couldn't have brought all that on foot.' Nor on a motorbike, he thought to himself. 'There must have been a truck or a car somewhere very near.'

'The chain was cut on the side gates,' said Petitbon. 'The cameras don't cover that. He probably just drove straight in.'

'Check if there was anything from the other cameras before they got sprayed, just in case,' said Bruno. 'I'll take a look at the side gate.'

The chain was thin enough to have been cut with bolt-cutters, but there were two clear tyre tracks in white on the grass that faded as they led to the gate. Bruno measured the gap between the tyres and scribbled a note. It was too wide for a car. J-J's team might be able to identify the kind of truck and maybe even the tyres, although the tracks looked too smeared on the grass for easy identification. There were plenty of smudged white

173

footprints on the grass along the side of the green-houses, but nothing as clear as the imprint of a shoe. Perhaps the culprit had bags over his feet. He had left nothing else behind, not even an empty can of paint.

Isabelle was sealing a small plastic evidence bag that she had filled with a sample of the paint she had scraped off as Bruno returned to the green-house door, where the technicians were trying various products to clean the paint. None of them seemed to be working and they were muttering about some special type of cement paint. Back in the office, Petitbon had his head in his hands and a phone to his ear, muttering mournfully: '*Oui, Monsieur, oui, Monsieur . . .*'

The Mayor drew Bruno discreetly aside. 'You realise what this means? Bondino won't go ahead now. First the demo and now this. He made it clear when we met him that if there was any trouble the deal would be off.'

Bruno felt a small surge of relief. He hadn't thought of that. From the road outside he heard the sound of a police siren. That would probably be J-J. Bruno went outside to greet him, to find himself caught in the flash of Delaron's camera. *Putain*, he thought, another front-page story on the crime wave of St Denis.

'How come you're always on the scene, Philippe?' he challenged the photographer as J-J's car drew in. 'You'll be top of the suspects list if you go on like this.'

'My uncle works here,' said the young man cheerfully, focusing his camera to get J-J's hulking form against the gleaming array of what used to be greenhouses. 'He was the one who found it and called his wife, and she told my mum. You can't keep secrets in St Denis, Bruno.'

Bruno showed J-J the greenhouses and led him inside to the office where Petitbon was still on the phone and Isabelle was downloading the images from the TV camera on to her laptop.

'Think it's the same guy who set the fire?' asked J-J.

Bruno shrugged. 'Who knows? But I think I might know where he got the paint. I even think I may have paid for it.' He turned to Isabelle. 'Bring that little evidence bag you filled and let's follow my hunch. J-J, I'll leave you here to wait for your forensics boys. If I'm right, we're going to need them.'

Isabelle was on the phone to a colleague back in the Minister's office in Paris, so Bruno drove, still wondering as he parked at the rugby stadium if this was a wild goose chase. The players were still on the field, the knot of girls still watching and the painter's ladder was still there where he had left it. He took out his ring of keys and led the way to the rear door of the stadium that gave on to the kitchen and the large dining room. He didn't need his keys. The door swung open to his touch and the wood of the lock was splintered where someone had forced an entry.

A dozen large cans of paint, each about half the size of an oil drum, were stacked against the wall, with two backpacks and nozzles leaning against them. Goggles and hooded white coveralls were draped over a trestle table. He was sure the contract had said there would be three painters on the job, but he went into the office to check. Isabelle held her small exhibit bag against the newly painted stadium wall to make a comparison, but she shrugged. White was white.

He called the contractor at home. Three painters were on the stadium job, and there had been three backpacks and fourteen cans of special cement paint, brilliant white, when they packed up on Friday. Would there be any way to remove it from glass, Bruno asked. Wait for it to dry fully and then scrape it off, he was told. It should peel away easily. How long would it take to dry? Two or three days, depending on the weather. Less, if you applied a dryer. Did he have one, or better still, did he have several? He had one, but could probably round up a few more. The local Bricomarché stocked them. Bruno told him to get to the Research Station with his painters as fast as he could, along with ladders and scaffolding. Then he called the Brico manager at home and asked him to open up. Finally he called the Mayor, still back at the Research Station.

'We found where he got the paint and equipment, from the rugby stadium. Somebody broke into the dining room where the paint was stored,' he began, and then spoke over the Mayor's reply. 'Wait, there's more. The good news is that the painter says the stuff can be scraped off easily once it's dry, and we can dry it with those big industrial blowers they have at Brico. He's coming direct to the Research Station with his lads. Can you call in the *Mairie* maintenance staff with ladders and scaffolding? We can probably have the paint off by tonight if we move fast enough. I only hope that'll be fast enough to save Petitbon's research.'

'So much for the rest of our day together,' said Isabelle as he rang off.

'I'm sorry,' he said. 'You're a cop too. You know how it is.' He tried to take her in his arms, but she brushed him off.

'You're not just a cop, you're a nursemaid,' she said flatly. 'You're married to St Denis and I don't think I can compete with the whole damn town. And I heard what the Mayor said about the wine deal being off. That means you aren't going to have a fight with him and get sacked. So you'll stay, and I go.'

'Isabelle,' Bruno began, with no idea what he was going to say next.

'Don't, Bruno. Don't even start. Just get in the car and I'll take you back to the Research Station.'

CHAPTER 22

I
f there was one place where Bruno would feel
comfortable drowning his sorrows, it was the
Café de la Renaissance. He felt at home there
not just because Ivan was a friend but because it
was one of the few restaurants in the region that
were designed for the locals rather than the
tourists with their expectations of *confit de canard*
and *tarte aux noix* and other famed specialities of
Périgord. The people of St Denis had quite
enough of that at home. And it was adaptable,
with a small zinc-covered bar and elderly coffee
machine in the front room and enough space
outside for a handful of tables. In the rear was
what Ivan boasted was the smallest kitchen in
France and a dining room into which he'd
squeezed half a dozen tables. So as soon as he
heard that the *plat du jour* at Ivan's bistro was
rabbit in mustard sauce, J-J decided they should
eat there, although Bruno was in little mood for
company. And he was ready to drop with tired-
ness after his day up and down ladders and moving
the scaffolding along the greenhouses. The Research
Station was back to normal, the glass scraped clean

178

of its quick-dried paint. And Isabelle was back in Bordeaux.

Realising that there would be no long after-dinner conversation with Bruno in his current state, J-J paid the modest bill and left a generous tip for Ivan. Bruno walked him down the street to J-J's car, parked in the open ground by the Gendarmerie where a group of determined old men played boules by the light of a street lamp. J-J paused as he fished for his car key and asked Bruno if he had any suspects among the locals.

'Maybe, but I haven't got any evidence beyond a hunch,' Bruno said, yawning mightily.

'What's the Brigadier got you doing?'

'He's had me calling all the other municipal cops for miles around, about anything suspicious, if they'd seen any strangers,' said Bruno. 'Half of them thought I was mad and the other half wanted to complain about the GMO crops. The Brigadier won't find much cooperation from them. Most farmers round here think whoever burned those crops is a local hero.'

'What about you?'

'On the science, I don't know. But I can't say I'm comfortable about tampering with nature. What worries me is that as far as I can see, there's not much of a crime here.'

'How do you mean? It's arson.'

'Those crops require a series of permits before they can be grown. That's the law. They didn't have a permit from this commune nor from our

Conseil-Général. And if the crops were illegal, what exactly is the crime in destroying them?'

'What about the shed and equipment that got burned?'

'Same thing. No construction permit, no taxes paid on it, no listing of the water pipe and no water fees paid. What's the crime in destroying an illegal building?'

'You should have been a lawyer,' J-J laughed, climbing into his car. He was just closing the door when some shouts and a woman's scream and the sound of breaking glass came from the Bar des Amateurs, and a small knot of bodies erupted on to the pavement outside the bar, stumbling over the café tables and sending them flying. Trouble at this bar, run by two burly stalwarts of the town rugby team, was unheard of.

Bruno ran towards the scene, aware of J-J heaving himself out of his car and lumbering along behind. By the time he reached the bar, René the barman was holding Max firmly by one arm and a dishevelled Jacqueline was clinging to the other. Gilbert was kneeling on the chest of another man and the rest of the crowd had become so many shouting spectators.

'Silence, all of you,' shouted Bruno, and pushed his way through to René, noting the smashed plate-glass window of the bar and the stream of blood that trickled from Max's nose. 'What's going on here, René? You can't keep order in your own bar?'

'It's this bastard here who started it,' panted

Gilbert, struggling to keep hold of the flailing arms of the man he sat on. 'Just came in and started the trouble. He took a swing at Max and started dragging the girl out.'

'He hurt my arm,' said Jacqueline, her eyes blazing. 'Max saved me.'

'It's true, Bruno,' said René. 'This guy came into the bar, just punched Max in the face and he went down off his chair. Then he started pulling the girl and Max got up and began pulling her back. I tried to separate them, then he toppled backwards and broke the window.'

'That's just how it was,' came a chorus of voices from the spectators. 'The guy must be crazy.'

'Let's take a look at him and see if he's hurt,' said Bruno, and Gilbert rose carefully from the prone figure, still keeping firm hold of one arm as he grabbed the man by the lapels and hauled him on to his feet. Bruno was not greatly surprised to see that it was Bondino.

'I'm OK,' said Bondino, shaking his head to clear it and standing upright. He was clearly drunk, but hardly incapable. He pointed at Jacqueline. 'She's my girl.'

'You're going to be spending a night in the cells,' snapped Bruno. He inspected the back of Bondino's head, brushing some glinting shards of glass from his back and from his hair. He was not bleeding and his coat seemed have taken the brunt of the impact. Bruno looked at René and Gilbert. 'It's up to you to bring charges.'

'He smashed a few things, a chair and some glasses, plus the window,' said René. 'That's the big thing.'

'I'll pay,' said Bondino, reaching for his wallet and taking out a wad of the seldom-seen yellow notes of five hundred euros. He peeled off three and handed them to René. 'I'm sorry,' he said. 'If it costs more, tell me.'

'What about you?' Bruno said, turning to Max. 'Do you want to bring charges for assault?'

Holding a handkerchief to his bleeding nose, Max shook his head.

'As long as he promises to leave Jacqueline alone and stop making trouble. But if he comes at us again, don't blame me if I beat the shit out of him,' Max said.

'Right,' said Bruno. 'No charges, so we all go home. You first, Bondino. Now.' He watched as Bondino shambled off towards his hotel and then looked at Max and Jacqueline.

'You haven't asked me yet,' Jacqueline said, angrily but under control, and casting a look of pure hatred after Bondino's departing figure. 'He tried to pull me out. That's assault.'

'So it is,' said Bruno coldly, recalling the way she had danced with Bondino and left with him after Joe's party. His mild liking for the girl would disappear if she had deliberately set the two young bulls against each other.

'It seems the American thought he had a relationship with you,' he said. 'If you want to

182

bring charges, you understand that I'll have to take statements from everybody involved, and I mean everybody, to establish whether there was something that could have misled him into believing he had a relationship with you. You might want to consider that, Mademoiselle, before you make a decision. You may also want to get advice from a French lawyer, since these matters can be complicated once it becomes a formal matter.'

'I'll help you take the statements, if it's to be a criminal matter,' said J-J. 'I should introduce myself, Chief of Detectives Jalipeau of the *Police Nationale*. 'I'll start by looking at your passport, Mademoiselle.'

Jacqueline looked for a moment at Bruno and then shrugged. 'I don't want to put anyone to such trouble, so long as the bar owners are happy to let it drop,' she said, and turned to Max. 'I'd better take him back and make sure the nosebleed stops. Thanks, everybody, and I'm sorry that this happened.'

Not a bad exit, Bruno thought, as she led Max away.

CHAPTER 23

Sitting alone at the bar in Fauquet's over his morning coffee, Bruno checked his phone again. Three days now without any word from Isabelle. He had left messages and sent two emails, without reply. But then it had been the same after she had left for Paris, not a word until her sudden announcement that she was arriving. He wasn't irritated so much as mystified that she behaved this way. When she had left the first time, he had understood her silence to mean that it was over. Now he supposed it meant it was really over. Or did it? In another woman, he might have suspected crude manipulation, but not Isabelle. She was too honest for that, he told himself when his mobile rang, and with a surge of hope that surprised him he scrambled to fish it from his pouch.

'It's Pamela,' said the voice. Any disappointment he felt was extinguished by her strangely subdued tone. 'I'm afraid there's been a death. That sweet old man Cresseil. I'm at his place now, over by the Domaine. I think he's been dead for a while, but can you call the doctor? Damn, my battery's running out. I'll wait till you get here. I'm OK, I have my horse with me.'

She rang off. Tempted to head over there straight away and comfort the evidently shaken woman, Bruno knew there were duties to be done and Pamela had sounded level-headed. He first called the *pompiers*, the firemen who handled all emergencies, and then rang the medical centre who would have to certify the death. He left his office and his paperwork and put his head round the Mayor's door to let him know the news. Cresseil with his record in the Resistance had been special. Then he headed for his van, punching in the numbers for Max, who was now the next of kin. There was no reply.

Pamela always dressed smartly for her morning ride in riding boots, whipcord jodhpurs and black riding jacket, with most of her bronze-red hair tucked into her black velvet hat. On horseback, she looked magnificent. But now on foot, holding on to the bridle of her horse cropping at the grass by the small farmhouse, she appeared oddly diminished. As Bruno parked the police van at the end of the yard, he noticed that the small plot of vines had been picked.

'*Bonjour*, Pamela,' Bruno said, kissing her on both cheeks, and hugging her. 'I'm sorry you had to find him, it must have been an awful shock. Are you all right?'

She nodded, hugged him in return and then stepped back.

185

'I suppose he's in the house?'

'No, he's not,' she said in a small voice. 'He's in that barn, just where I found him. I touched nothing and called you as soon as I realised he was dead.'

'A good thing you dropped by.'

'I was really looking for Max. He wanted me to come and try some of the wine he made. He's got some idea of selling it to all the guesthouses with special labels that he can print up. He rather sold me on the idea of a Château Pamela. But there was no sign of him, nor of the old man, so I looked around.'

She hitched her horse to a fence post and they walked through the yard and down the small pathway that led to the big stone barn and the two smaller ones. She went to the farthest door, which was half-open. Inside, Bruno saw the old man, lying crumpled at the bottom of the stepladder that led up to the ancient wooden wine vat.

'I just touched his wrist to see if there was a pulse,' she said.

Bruno nodded, crouching by the body. He put the back of his hand against the old man's cheek. It was cold, showing that he had been dead for hours, but not yet stiff. The neck looked odd, twisted. Bruno looked at the rickety stepladder, its steps slippery with grape juice. Had the old fool been looking into the vat and lost his footing? Or had he suffered a heart attack or a stroke, the merciful quick end that the elderly were said to pray for? The doctors would know.

'There's nothing we can do for him now,' he said. 'We'll wait for the *pompiers* and the doctor and then get him to the funeral parlour. If you wait in the yard, I'll go into the house and see if there are any papers, a will or something.'

She nodded. 'I wonder what happened to Max. He must have been held up. But when we arranged to meet he said he'd be picking the grapes in the evening and then he'd see me here this morning. He'll be devastated, having just gone through the adoption and now this.'

'So now he's got a vineyard of his own, a nice little inheritance. All the same, I'd better go in and see if there are any papers inside. The *pompiers* will be here any minute.'

Bruno had been in a lot of homes where an elderly person lived alone, and was expecting the usual stale smells. But Cresseil's place was clean and well ordered. There was one large sitting room and kitchen on the ground floor, with a small bedroom and bathroom off to one side, and another room that looked like a study. Cresseil's legs had almost gone, so he probably spent all his time downstairs. Bruno went quickly upstairs, which contained two spartan bedrooms and no bathroom. One of the beds was made up, but the sheet and pillow were slightly creased so it looked as if it had been slept in. Perhaps Max used it when he slept over.

187

The kitchen sink was clean and empty except for two tumblers with dregs of wine. The towels in the kitchen and bathroom were fresh, the crockery all tidied away. The study was equally well ordered, with an old sofa facing the window, and a pigeon-hole desk off to the side. Most of the pigeonholes were empty except for a roll of papers held together with red ribbon, the adoption documents. In the drawers, he found bank statements and electricity bills neatly filed, an old Resistance medal and a box of photographs. Some dated from wartime, groups of smiling young men with weapons, but mainly of Annette, Cresseil's wife, and a baby, growing into boyhood and youth. At the bottom of another drawer he found the property deeds. The last transaction, dated 1949 and recording the inheritance of the Cresseil farm, carried the name of a local *notaire*, Brosseil. He was long dead, but the practice was still held by his grandson. If there were any legal papers to be found, Brosseil would have them.

Bruno turned at the sound of a heavy vehicle coming down the lane, and went out to greet the firemen. Albert stepped down, followed by Ahmed, who was driving the big truck. Pamela stayed with her horse, made nervous by the fire engine. Bruno led the way to the barn, pausing as Ahmed pulled out the resuscitation kit.

'I don't think we'll need that,' Bruno said, nodding at the gear.

'Regulations,' said Ahmed, shrugging. 'And

besides, you never know. I've seen some miracles happen with this.'

Once in the barn, Albert shook his head and sent Ahmed back.

'He's been dead for hours, poor old soul,' Albert said, and took off his helmet. 'I can't say I like the look of that neck. Do you think he fell?'

'No sign of slipping on the steps, but I wouldn't trust that ladder and I'm not half Cresseil's age,' said Bruno. 'His legs were just about gone.'

There was the beep-beep of a horn outside. The doctor had arrived. Bruno went out, to find Pamela calming her horse all over again. He grinned at her sympathetically and walked across the yard to where a young woman was pulling a doctor's case from the back of an elderly Renault 5. This must be the new doctor at the practice, the one with the Italian name. All he could see of her so far was an extremely shapely rump. She turned, and he kept his surprise under control. A large scar covered a good part of her right cheek, and she had made no attempt to cover it with make-up. While trying not to focus on it, Bruno wondered what might have caused the wound.

'I know you are Bruno, the policeman, and I am Fabiola Stern, the new doctor,' she said, smiling and holding out her hand. 'Where is the body?'

'*Mademoiselle médecin*,' he began, taking her hand. 'A pleasure, despite the circumstances. This is Madame Nelson, who found the body, and the *pompiers* you have met. And now we go this way.'

189

'Madame Nelson, a pleasure to meet you and that's a fine horse.' She turned back to Bruno. 'Lead on, and please do not call me Mademoiselle again. I'm Fabiola.'

'That neck is broken,' she said after a brief examination of the body. 'But from the pupils and the purple hands and the very pale face, the cause of death may have been a heart attack. Maybe he had a cardiac arrest and then fell. We need an autopsy.'

Putain, thought Bruno. That would both delay and complicate matters.

'Are you sure?' he asked. 'It looks like the straightforward death of a very old man.'

'Sorry,' she replied formally. 'But with different possible causes of death I have to do this by the book.'

There was no appealing the doctor's verdict. He had better get on with the notifications, starting with Max, who should be around, since who else could have picked the grapes? They must already be in the vat, which would explain why the old man had been up the stepladder in the first place. He left the barn and the body and walked into the yard, pulled out his cellphone.

'Alphonse, it's Bruno. Is Max there?'

'No, Bruno. He'll be at Cresseil's place. He was planning to pick the grapes last night and said he'd stay over. It's his organic thing, picking the grapes in the dark when it's cooler.'

'Well, they're picked all right, and I saw him in

190

town late last night but there's no sign of him here. I'm at the place now, with the *pompiers* and the doctor. Cresseil's dead, looks like a heart attack. Can you track the lad down and tell him the bad news?'

Thinking about the grapes, Bruno walked back inside the barn just as the *pompiers* were packing up to leave. Suddenly he heard the ring of a cell-phone somewhere inside the barn. Like the rest of them Bruno automatically checked his own, although the ring tone was wrong. It came from the back of the barn, where a jumble of baskets and dusty bottles and old clothes were piled on to a sagging array of rough shelves. He walked across, saw the phone and answered, noticing the pair of clean blue jeans and training shoes on which it rested.

'Hello?' he said into the phone.

'Max, is that you?'

'Alphonse, it's me, Bruno. I just answered what must be Max's phone here in Cresseil's barn.'

'What? It's not like Max to leave his phone. Is there no sign of him?'

'Hold on.' Bruno picked up the jeans and felt the pockets. There was a wallet inside, some keys and some coins. Inside the wallet was Max's library card, his university ID, and tucked behind it, he was not greatly surprised to find a five-euro phone card from France Télécom. He looked further. Over by the wall was a small red bundle. He pulled out a pencil and picked it up, conscious

191

of the eyes of Fabiola and the firemen silently following his every move. It was a pair of cotton shorts, sodden with wine.

'*Putain*,' he swore to himself. 'I never looked in the vat.'

'Alphonse, I'll call you back.' He put the phone back on the jeans and turned to the stepladder. 'Ahmed, come and hold this thing steady for me. Albert, don't pack that resuscitation gear just yet.'

He climbed up and by the fourth step he was high enough to see in. He went another step to be sure.

'Hold tight, Ahmed,' he called, and leaned into the vat, perilously far, the stepladder rocking as he plunged his hand down to the thick cap of fermenting grape juice to pluck at the head of blond hair that floated face down in the vat. It was no good, he couldn't keep a grip. He tried to grab at the shoulder but his hand slipped in the thick must of grapes. His footing seemed firm, so Bruno took a grip on the rim and vaulted in, boots, trousers and all, splashing hard through the thick must and keeping a tight hold of the rim. He kept his feet, bent down and with a great leave hauled Max's naked body out of the dense liquid and braced him against the wooden side.

'Albert, Ahmed, get another ladder and help me here. Fabiola, can you come up the stepladder?'

With one hand, he reached into Max's mouth and pulled out a froth of must and broken grapes, took a deep breath and leaned forward to plant

192

his lips firmly against the sagging lips of the boy. He blew with all his might, trying to force air into the lungs, but there was a resistance. He let go of the vat's rim, put both arms around Max's chest and squeezed hard. A gout of juice and must fountained from the throat. He took another breath and blew again hard into Max's mouth.

'That's right. You are doing the right thing,' said Fabiola, her eyes barely above the rim. 'Do that again. Keep blowing. Can I help hold him?'

With a clatter, Albert and Ahmed appeared with proper ladders and began clambering up to help. Bruno heard Pamela's voice, calling the emergency number for more help.

'Pull him out, bring him down here,' called Fabiola. 'Keep blowing, Bruno, hard as you can.'

Bruno pushing, Albert and Ahmed pulling, they hauled Max over the rim, and then Bruno held him under the shoulders as the two firemen took the weight and laid him on the ground where Fabiola took over the kiss of life. Ahmed applied the two paddles of the resuscitator to Max's chest, tapped Fabiola to let go, and the body jolted as he applied the electricity. Fabiola bent back to her work.

Breathing heavily and suddenly conscious of a sharp headache, Bruno began feeling around the vat to see if anything else was in there, but his legs were rubbery and he felt himself begin to slide. He called out something and flailed with his hand for the side of the vat.

'Albert, get Bruno out of there now,' Fabiola shouted, before turning back to the boy. 'It can kill him. Get him into the open air.'

Bruno felt a sharp pain as his fingernail tore on the wooden side. It jolted him enough to get one knee under him and suddenly Albert had grabbed the collar of his shirt and he was being hauled up. As soon as his head was over the side, Bruno took a deep breath and felt his vision start to clear. Albert kept hauling and then Pamela was below him and pulling at his flailing arm and Albert shifted his grip to Bruno's belt and tumbled him over the rim to collapse down to the ground in to Pamela's arms.

'Get him out into the open air,' shouted Fabiola. 'And then come back for the boy.'

Bruno was prone and retching, a grape-sodden Pamela sluicing him with a bucket of cold water, when Capitaine Duroc appeared. Fabiola was still giving the kiss of life to Max, and Ahmed was shaking his head sorrowfully at Albert, who was bent double, taking deep breaths of fresh air. Each one of them was purple with grape juice, thick gobbets of grape must in their hair and eyebrows and stuck to their arms.

'It's no good,' said Fabiola, leaning back, pressing her hands into the small of her back and wincing. 'The boy's been dead too long. We're lucky we didn't lose Bruno.'

'What the devil has happened here?' asked Duroc, plainly shocked.

194

'Two dead,' said Fabiola. 'Nearly three. Carbon dioxide from the fermentation of the grapes. I've heard of it though never seen it. I remember learning that the volume of carbon dioxide produced during fermentation is forty times that of the volume of the juice.'

'But it's not poisonous,' Duroc protested.

'No, but it displaces the oxygen. That's how it kills. Asphyxiation.'

Bruno looked up. His head felt clearer and the retching had stopped, He glanced at Pamela, who looked reassurance at him and squeezed his hand. She was such a sight he almost grinned.

'People die of it every year when they forget the need for ventilation,' Fabiola went on. 'Bruno was taking deep breaths inside the vat, trying to force air into this poor boy's body. He was suffocating himself.'

She looked down at the must-smeared body of a well-muscled young man, tanned brown except for the pale band of white where his shorts had been. She went inside and came back with an old blanket. Just before she laid it over the body, she bent, wiped Max's face clear, and then closed his eyelids and laid a gentle hand on his cheek.

'A fine-looking man,' she said. 'Such a waste.'

'A double tragedy,' Bruno said, standing up. 'Cresseil, possibly a heart attack, possibly a broken neck when he fell off the ladder. There will be an autopsy. And Max, Cresseil's adopted son, dead of asphyxiation in a wine vat. It looks to me like

195

natural causes or a fall for the first one, and a tragic accident for the second.' He turned to Fabiola. 'Do we need to consider an autopsy for Max?'

She shook her head, and then rubbed her eyes. 'My first week on the job, and two dead,' she said.

'You did all you could,' said Pamela.

'If it wasn't for you, we might have lost Bruno,' said Albert. 'I'd never heard of this death by fermenting wine.'

'I never heard of anybody treading grapes naked,' mused Bruno. 'I wonder why he took his shorts off? I think he must have removed them when he was in the vat and then tossed them over the side.'

'Maybe it's that organic thing he was talking about,' said Pamela.

'*Putain de merde*,' said Albert, looking at Ahmed and then down at himself. 'What a mess.'

'I'm going to clean up in the bathroom here,' declared Fabiola. 'I'm sure the late owner won't mind.' She began to walk towards the house but suddenly stopped to watch Bruno, who was poking about at the side of the barn. 'What are you looking for?'

'Cresseil's dog,' he replied, heading around the back. 'It's nearly as old as he was. Give me a shout when you're done and I'll use the bathroom myself. First, I'd better tell Alphonse.'

Bruno braced himself for a difficult conversation. The death of his chief suspect was going to

196

leave the arson case hanging. And he'd also have to tell Jacqueline about Max's death. That would not be pleasant, however much she'd been dallying with Bondino, but he was curious to see how she'd react. He pulled out his phone from its sodden leather pouch at his side. A clump of grape must obscured the buttons. He wiped them off but the phone was useless.

'*Merde*,' he muttered and stomped back into the barn to use Max's phone.

CHAPTER 24

'The important question will be who died first,' said the Mayor. Bruno, now washed and changed into a spare uniform, accepted a restorative glass of Armagnac. 'If old Cresseil died first, then Max's heir would inherit. But we don't know that he has one. He still has Alphonse formally listed as next of kin, but I'm not sure how much weight that has.'

'And if young Max died first, then Cresseil's distant cousins would inherit and that could be important for our project with Bondino. He tells me he still wants to go ahead, thanks to the way you fixed the problem at the Research Station,' the Mayor went on. 'So how do we establish who died first?'

'That decision will be made by the autopsy, which is being done by that new young doctor, Fabiola,' Bruno replied, feeling relieved that this at least was entirely beyond his control. 'But it could be very hard to tell. Time of death is never easy to establish with certainty.'

'Logic might suggest that Cresseil wondered what had happened to Max, went up the ladder

198

to see the boy lying there already dead, and the shock brought on the heart attack that killed him, or sent him reeling off the ladder so he broke his neck,' Bruno went on. 'That would mean Max died first.'

'A different logic might say that Max got into difficulties. Cresseil tried to clamber up to help, had the heart attack and died, and then in the absence of help, young Max tragically drowned,' replied the Mayor, so casually that Bruno knew the old fox was up to something. 'So the old man died first. If somebody makes the case that the boy lived long enough to inherit, we'll have a lawsuit brought by the family. It won't get settled for years and Bondino may give up in disgust. So, Bruno, how well do you know the young doctor?'

'Hardly at all. She seems a very agreeable young woman, very capable. In fact she may have saved my life,' said Bruno, starting to worry once again that his Mayor was giving so much weight to Bondino's project. He was not going to start his relationship with the new doctor by hinting that she might bend her professional verdict to suit the Mayor's scheme. 'She struck me as a person of integrity. I'm sure she'll give us an honest opinion.'

'Could you perhaps suggest the importance of this matter to her? Its importance to the future of St Denis, that is.'

'There's a further complication,' said Bruno, avoiding a direct answer. 'Earlier this week, Bondino started a fight with Max in the Bar des Amateurs, breaking a plate-glass window and assaulting a young woman. I could have arrested him, and I'm really having second thoughts about linking the future of St Denis with this young lout.'

'Strong words, Bruno.'

'Heartfelt words. I didn't feel too good about myself when I didn't arrest him.'

'Well, we were all young once. He'll grow out of it.' The Mayor paused. 'You've never liked this project, have you?'

'I like the idea a lot, in principle. But Bondino's behaviour hardly inspires confidence.'

The Mayor rose from his chair and stalked to the window. '*Merde*, Bruno, you're right of course. But what else can we do? I have to fight tooth and nail to keep the sawmill alive. I pulled a lot of strings to get the Research Station located here and now that's turned into the kind of mess that could lose me the next election. This Bondino project is the best chance we have to secure our future and I'm not going to lose it. Go and look at St Fénelon or at any other of those hollowed-out tourist towns around here, with only a couple of bistros and an estate agent and dead from September to June every year.' The Mayor went on, flourishing his hand at the window as if pointing to the ghost towns he evoked, 'No families, no schools, no jobs, no shops and most of the houses empty until the tourists come back to rent them. That's what's at stake, Bruno. We have to have those jobs for St Denis.'

The Mayor slammed a fist into the palm of his

other hand, thrust out his jaw and advanced on Bruno. 'So I don't much care if young Bondino is a drunken boor, so long as he commits that investment. You'll just have to manage him.'

'Whoa!' Bruno held up his hands and grinned. 'I'm not the council and I'm not a public meeting. Practise your speeches on me all you like, but you don't need to convince me. I like the project, but if it makes commercial sense with Bondino, it might also make commercial sense with somebody else. That's my point, and we haven't even looked at that possibility.'

'Businessmen with ten million euros to invest are hardly lining up outside my door,' grumbled the Mayor.

'But now that one is doing so, that's valuable information. Maybe there are other big companies, British or Italian, that see the same potential Bondino does. Maybe there are French investors who could be interested. If you do get the *appellation*, we can make our own deal.'

Hubert's wine shop was busy when Bruno arrived, bracing himself for the task of telling Jacqueline the bad news. Hubert was talking in English with a couple standing by the racks of vintage Armagnacs. Nathalie turned from the cash desk, where she was serving a line of customers, and greeted him sadly.

'We know about it,' she said. 'The mad English-woman came by, covered in grape juice, to tell

Jacqueline. The girl was shattered, floods of tears, so Hubert gave her the day off. The Englishwoman took her home with her, Jacqueline on the bike and the other on her horse. We're up to our eyes here, short-handed without Jacqueline and Max, and Hubert had to come in from the Sarlat office to help out. But is there anything we can do? You look OK but she told us you were hurt, too.'

'I'm fine. So Jacqueline will still be up at the Englishwoman's place?'

'Yes, she moved in a couple of days ago. Didn't you know? She said you helped arrange it.'

A tourist buying a case of Hubert's wine looked baffled at the presence of a policeman, but started tapping his credit card on the counter in impatience. Nathalie turned back to him with a tired smile and Bruno took his leave. 'We'll miss that lovely boy,' she called after him.

As Bruno opened his van door, Hubert dashed out of his *cave* and waved urgently as he trotted across the car park.

'Terrible news, a tragedy,' he said. 'But how are you? The Englishwoman told us you almost died as well.'

'I'm fine. All I needed was a shower and a change of clothes,' Bruno said, shaking his hand. 'It was that new woman doctor who saved me, once she realised what was happening. I never knew wine could be *that* dangerous.'

'Max was a fine lad,' said Hubert. 'He loved wine, and he sold a lot as well. He and Jacqueline were naturals at the wine tastings, great with the tourists, always steering them to the better bottles. I was going to offer him a job here, once he'd got his diploma.'

'I'd better go up and see Jacqueline, and you've got customers to attend to.'

'I know. But I came out to see if you wanted to postpone that dinner party of yours. The wine will keep for another evening.'

'Yes, but my *bécasses* won't,' said Bruno. 'I took them out of the freezer this morning and I don't want them to go to waste. I've never got that many in a single season before. Besides, we all need cheering up. Let's go ahead as planned.'

As Bruno drove up the lane towards Pamela's house, he regretted that Pamela had told Jacqueline of Max's death already. He'd been interested to see the girl's reaction, to judge whether Max had been just another casual dalliance or whether she'd been as attached to him as Max had clearly been to her. He doubted it, after the way he'd seen her dancing with Bondino, but maybe it was different for foreigners.

He always enjoyed the approach to Pamela's, topping the gentle slope to see her cluster of farm-house and outbuildings nestling in the cradle of the hills, with her horses cropping at the grass in the paddock. Except for the car and the swimming pool, the view could hardly have changed for two hundred years and more. He drove into the courtyard and saw Jacqueline's bike sprawled on the gravel, one of its wheels still slowly spinning. Pamela must have heard him arrive, opening the kitchen door as he closed his van door. She was still in her wine-drenched riding clothes, her hair spilling out wildly from beneath her hat.

'I'm glad to see you're well,' she began. 'I was worried about you. Are you sure you should be back at work?'

'I'm fine. I just had a bit of a headache but I took an aspirin and a glass of Armagnac. That cures most things. How's Jacqueline?'

'Not good, but we've had some tea and she's calmed down. Come in and see her. We're in the kitchen. It will give me a chance to shower and change out of these clothes – I didn't want to leave her alone.'

Jacqueline gave a hesitant half-smile as he greeted her. Eyes swollen and her nose red, a sodden handkerchief clutched in her hand, she looked shrunken and wretched. The carefree and lovely girl with her arm around Max's waist at the rugby field and the fiery young woman at the fight in the bar were hardly recognisable.

'I knew I should have stayed with him,' she said. 'Then this would never have happened.'

'We'll all miss Max,' said Bruno. There was a kind of relief in knowing that at least there would be no trial or prison, no media circus as the *écolos* tried to turn Max into a martyr.

'Such a shitty, stupid way to die, asphyxiation,' she said. 'He was here just yesterday, and the day

204

before, helping me move in. I haven't even finished unpacking yet. Some of the boxes are in the gîte, just where he left them.'

'I didn't know you'd already made contact with Pamela.'

'Right after we saw you at the rugby match,' she said, bringing the wet handkerchief to her nose. Bruno silently handed her his own clean one and she took it gratefully. 'I mentioned it to Max and he had her number on his mobile so I called and moved right in. We even talked about repainting the bedroom.' Her voice began to quaver again.

'When did you last see him?' Bruno asked. 'I thought you might have been helping him pick the grapes.'

'I was going to, but he had this organic thing about picking at night when it was cooler and I had to sort out my books.' She gave him back his handkerchief. 'Thank you for coming, but I'll be OK. Pamela has been very kind, keeping me company and giving me cups of tea and telling me to keep busy. I'll go back to work tomorrow.'

'You enjoy being at Hubert's *cave*?'

'I like it a lot. I'm learning every day and I enjoy meeting customers. Hubert has me doing a lot of their tastings,' she said, with a flicker of animation. But then her face clouded again. 'And it was great working with Max. That's how I met him. It'll be depressing being there without him, and half-expecting him to come out from the cellar or carry out some cases.'

'Well, if there's anything I can do . . .' Bruno said, running out of conversation that didn't take her back to thoughts of Max. Pamela had clearly expected him to stay with Jacqueline, so he cast around for something to say and he spotted a pile of books on the table.

'Are those all about wine?' he asked.

She rose and led him across to show them, a thick encyclopedia and several reference books in English, Hachette's *Guide des vins*, Pierre-Marie Doutrelant's classic *Les bons vins et les autres* and Moisseeff and Casamayor's *Arômes du vin*. The books seemed to revitalise her, and within moments she was almost prattling. She was showing him where she had worked in Australia in an atlas of wine when Pamela returned, smelling freshly of soap and brushing out her wet hair, and offered to see him out.

'I wanted to ask you,' she said, as she accompanied him to his van. 'Are you going ahead with the dinner you invited me to? I'd feel guilty leaving the girl on her own.'

'Bring her along,' he said, realising that Jacqueline could take the place of the absent Isabelle. 'It might help cheer her up, and she knows her wines so she'll appreciate it.'

CHAPTER 25

There were not many car parks in St Denis but Bruno dutifully visited each one, looking for the types of small truck that J-J's team had listed as having the track width to match those in the grass at the Research Station. Each time he found one, he examined the tyres minutely for signs of white paint. Having exhausted the school, the supermarkets and the garages, he set off in his van for the builders' yard and the post office. Bruno had only a handful of potential trucks remaining in St Denis. The one he particularly wanted to see, the very old Renault that Alphonse used for his cheeses, was delivering to shops all across the region and would not be back before night. By which time any tell-tale sign of paint would have been worn away by country roads, Bruno thought glumly.

He turned through a pair of imposing iron gates into one of the last possibilities, short of visiting every single farm, and he'd see most of those trucks on market day. It was Julien's Domaine de la Vézère, hotel and vineyard, the crown jewel of Bondino's ambition. The long drive was fringed first by woods and then by the formal gardens of the undistinguished château that was the heart of the property. A clumsy nineteenth-century restoration of a late Renaissance manor house, it had been adorned with circular turrents with pointed roofs at each corner, a crenellated wing that looked solid enough to stop artillery, and a grandiose terrace with wide steps leading down to the garden. The lawn was broken into geometric designs by gravel paths and dotted with unlikely topiary. To one side stood a large swimming pool, protected by hedges with more topiary, from which came the sound of children gleefully splashing and diving. To the other side, beyond the vast wing that had been turned into a restaurant, was a large modern barn, expensively covered with wood to look suitably antique, which housed the winery and a large yard for delivery trucks. The ones he saw were too big for his inquiry, so he set off to look for Julien, who might also have something useful to say about Bondino.

Bruno started his search at the winery, where the elderly cellar-master Baptiste was supervising a gang of seasonal workers who were cleaning the vats ready for this year's harvest. He nodded at two *Mairie* employees doing some moonlighting. Baptiste said he had not seen Julien all day and suggested he try the main office. That was odd. It was not like him to be away from the winery for an hour at this time of year, let alone all day. The winery office was empty, so Bruno went round to the front of the château, threading his way past the rows of vines heavy with fruit, through the car park and up the steps to the main entrance of what was now the hotel. There was nobody at reception, so he looked in the small office behind the front desk and Marie-Hélène was there, as she had been for years ever since she had retired from teaching at the nursery school. Surrounded by a thick scent of lavender, she was tapping away angrily at a computer as if she had a personal vendetta against it.

'*Bonjour*, Bruno. I hate this thing worse than the telephone. Why does nobody write letters any more? I have to print out everything so I can file it properly or I'd never find another reservation.'

'They're supposed to make your life easier, Marie-Hélène,' he said, bending to kiss her on both heavily powdered cheeks. 'Is Julien around?'

'Who knows, these days?' she snorted. 'I hardly ever see him, and when I do his mind's elsewhere. If I didn't have this place running like clockwork, I don't know where we'd be. I tell you, Bruno, I'm worried about him. And did you know Mirabelle has been in hospital?'

'That was back in the summer. Some woman's thing, Julien said.'

'Well, she went back, all the way to Bordeaux. She was there over three weeks, and Julien drove there every day. He told us not to tell anyone. He just brought her back two days ago and he hasn't even let me see her. I think it's really serious, but

209

Julien doesn't want us to say anything. He says it'll be bad for business.'

'It's almost time to pick the grapes,' said Bruno.

'Bunch of layabouts have turned up already, I'm running out of space in the barn to put them all up. But the old fool still hasn't given the green light to start picking and they're eating their heads off. You'll probably find him in the family quarters round the back.'

Bruno walked through the ornate salon that contained the château's best feature, an original sixteenth-century fireplace that was large enough to roast an ox. Bruno had once been in attendance at the roasting of a wild boar that seemed almost dwarfed by the great hearth. Various assemblies of furniture were dotted around the giant room, some Louis XVI chairs around a card table, two vast Napoleon III sofas squared off against one another across a marble-topped table. An Empire couch perched against one wall with a decent copy of David's *Madame Récamier* hanging above it, and two rather battered Empire chairs on either side. A large Restoration writing desk, bearing an ormolu clock, was placed against the row of French windows, and the rear wall was graced by two lovely English bookcases. No scholar of antiques, Bruno identified all these because Julien or more likely his wife had thoughtfully placed small handwritten cards on the respective tables, identifying them as '*Coin Empire*' or '*Coin Louis XVI*'.

Not sure whether this said more about Julien or his clients, Bruno went through the French windows and along the terrace to the wing adjoining the swimming pool, and knocked on the discreet door that led to Julien's apartment. No reply. He knocked again, more firmly. The door was quickly flung open and an angry Julien began saying: 'I told you not to disturb . . . Oh, it's you, Bruno. Sorry, but the staff never leave me a moment's peace. What can I do for you?'

'*Bonjour*, Julien, I'm sorry if this is inconvenient.'

It looked very inconvenient indeed. The usually immaculate Julien was wearing stained trousers, carpet slippers and an old denim shirt that looked as it had been used to polish a car. His hair was uncombed, his jaw unshaven and his breath stank of alcohol.

'No, no, come in. It's a relief to see somebody who doesn't want something from me. Sorry, Bruno, but I'm having a few problems just now.'

'Anything I can do to help?'

Julien nodded, and led the way into what was normally a carefully kept and welcoming sitting room, with even better furniture than the assortment in the hotel's salon. But there were papers all over the chairs, empty wine bottles and even a couple of dirty plates on the floor.

'How's Mirabelle?' Bruno asked, wondering if Julien's wife had left him.

'In bed. Not well. *Putain de merde*, I can't keep it bottled up. It's shit, Bruno. Complete and utter.

Cancer of the liver. She won't live out the year, and I've got the grapes to be picked, the wine to be made, the hotel to manage and the staff. The chef left and I'm making do with a temp with some fancy diploma from a job-training centre who doesn't know a *roux* from a *rillette*. I'm overstretched on a loan and business is not good. Christ, it seems for ever since I saw a friendly face. I'm glad you came, Bruno.'

'I'm really sorry about Mirabelle. Can I see her? Is she well enough?'

'Maybe. Poor thing can't get any sleep with those damn kids in the pool. She's seen nobody so far. We came back from the specialist in Bordeaux and she just took to her bed. She doesn't even want to see Father Sentout.' Julien turned and went down the corridor to the final door, opened it softly and peered in. Bruno heard a gentle murmuring, and then Julien turned and beckoned him to come forward. Bruno stopped by the door and took Julien's arm.

'Listen, leave her to me for a bit and you go and take a shower and a shave and get changed into clean clothes,' he said firmly. 'You stink like an old goat, and that won't do Mirabelle any good. Now off you go, or I'll toss you in the pool myself.'

Leaving Julien in the corridor, Bruno went into the darkened room, the shouts of the children in the pool very close although the windows were firmly closed and the room felt hot and stale. Mirabelle made a small mewing sound and said: 'Is that really you, Bruno?'

'Yes, my sweet, it's me.' He came forward and kissed her gently on the cheek and took a clammy hand. Too tired to even think of her hair or the matted bedclothes around her, her head was covered in a small skull cap. 'Julien told me the news. I'm sorry to hear it, but we'll soon have you dancing again. Remember that song you loved, "*Je Suis Seule Ce Soir*?" You used to sing it as you danced.'

'Ah, Bruno, I don't think I'll be dancing again. But listen, take care of Julien. He's been knocked out by this and everything's going to pot.'

'Did the doctor say you should stay in bed?'

'Yes, well sort of. He said I'd be getting very tired all the time and not to exert myself. They gave me radiation and then some chemotherapy that makes me sick and all my hair fell out. I can't go out like this.'

Bruno went over to the window, threw back the curtains and opened the French windows. Somehow the kids had disappeared. He looked out into a small walled and private garden, bathed in sunshine. He looked at the chaise longue at the foot of the bed, walked back and picked it up and took it out into the fresh air. Then he returned to the bed, scooped up Mirabelle, bedclothes and all, and carried her out into the sunlight, her eyes squinting against the glare. He laid her on the chaise longue, took his sunglasses from his shirt pocket and put them on her face.

'It's beautiful out here, Mirabelle. Smell the air.'

'Oh Bruno, I can't. I can't smell, I can't taste. I can't eat.'

'You will, though. Try it. Keep your eyes closed and breathe with me, come on, a deep breath out and then breathe in through your nose. Can you feel that gentle breeze on your cheek?' She shook her head. He put his hand to his mouth and wet his finger, and then gently removed the sunglasses and stroked his moist finger on her closed eyelids. 'Now can you feel the breeze on your eyes?'

'Yes, yes, I can,' she said breathlessly. He put the sunglasses back.

'Julien's such an old fool,' she said, the tenderness in her voice belying the words. 'He wants to sell up everything, you know, take me to some place in Switzerland he found on the internet that claims to do miracle cures. The doctors in Bordeaux warned me about places like that. They'll just take all his money and leave him with nothing. I just want to stay here, Bruno, to keep it all as it's always been, like it used to be.'

Her voice trailed off. 'You'll take care of him, Bruno?' Then her body relaxed into sleep, her mouth slightly open, her face waxen and yellow. Bruno sat with her until Julien came into the garden, clean-shaven and neatly dressed.

'That looks more like you,' Bruno said. 'She's asleep.'

'She sleeps a lot. She never wanted to be in the garden before.'

'I didn't ask her, just carried her here. She was glad to be in the open air. I think she just didn't want to trouble you.'

'Trouble me? God, she's no trouble, my lovely Mirabelle. Thirty-six years married, Bruno, and I don't know what I'll do without her. I just want to make her comfortable, to try everything, even if there's no hope.'

'There's always hope, Julien, but the living have their own needs. Mirabelle wouldn't want to see you let yourself go. You have to be strong for her, and for your business, all the people here at the Domaine who depend on you.'

'I'm thinking of giving it all up.'

'That's why I dropped by, to talk about that,' said Bruno. 'Come over here by the wall where we can talk quietly without disturbing her.' He led the way to two metal chairs, painted green with wooden slats for seats. They looked flimsy, but chairs like them had taken the weight of generations of customers on the terraces of French cafés.

'I shouldn't be surprised that you heard something, but I am. I thought it was a very discreet negotiation.'

'I'm sure it was, until the guy who bought your option came to see the Mayor and talked about a big expansion. That's how we heard.'

'Dupuy? An expansion? He's just a Paris businessman, a property dealer I assumed.'

'Maybe he is. But he's acting for a very big fish indeed. Bondino wines of California. They're the ones talking about expansion and buying up more land here.'

'You'd need a lot of money to do it right. I thought of doing it myself, raised a bank loan I couldn't really afford, but you need deeper pockets than mine. The potential is there, the land and the climate. Did you know we used to produce more wine than the whole of Bordeaux before phylloxera? Those river boats you see, the flat-bottomed *gabares* they build for tourist trips? They used to take the wine barrels along the Vézère and the Dordogne in the old days, down to Bordeaux where they'd sell the wine and then sell the wood from the boats and walk back up here.'

'Really?' Bruno knew the old story well, but he was pleased that Julien sounded again like the man Bruno had long known, alert and talkative.

'So I always thought of making wine here, and made a good business from selling it at the restaurant, but then I started expanding and things became tight. The loan is guaranteed by the hotel so the bank isn't worried, but the interest payments have been hurting, and then Mirabelle got her diagnosis and it all became too much. So when Dupuy came along with fifty thousand euros for the option, it seemed like the right solution. That pays all the bills, and then when I sell the place there's more than enough left over for me to retire on. There's not much point carrying on here without Mirabelle.'

'Don't be a fool, Julien,' came a small but firm voice from the chaise longue. 'You're not even sixty yet, you've got a good ten years to build up something to be proud of. My life insurance will give you the working capital. If you just waste away when I'm gone, I swear I'll come back and haunt you.'

There was a twinkle in Julien's eye as he looked at Bruno and then rose and moved across to his wife, knelt on the grass at her side and took her hand.

'You're awake, my love. Shouldn't you get some more rest?'

'Why should I rest when you're throwing your life away? One thing I know from this damn cancer is that life's far too precious to waste while you've got it. You need a goal in your life, Julien. And you probably need another wife as well, just to ginger you up!'

Bruno rose, half-smiling, and went across to kiss her and pat Julien on the shoulder and take his leave.

'She talks a lot of sense, your Mirabelle,' he said.

'She always did,' Julien replied, gazing at his wife with deep affection. He rose. 'I'll walk out with you.' He bent and kissed Mirabelle. 'Back in a moment.'

When they got to the salon, Julien stopped. 'It's not possible, you know. That option I signed is very clear. If they want to proceed by the end of the year, I have no choice, I have to sell.'

'What? Even if you paid back the fifty thousand euros?'

'Well, no. That would cancel the deal. But I've already paid some of it out to the bank and on wages, and then there was a second specialist I consulted. And I'd probably be liable for legal fees. I can't do anything about it now, Bruno. The Domaine is going to be sold by the end of the year. They want it as a going concern, along with the furniture and all the wine in the cellars and this year's wine as well. That's probably why I can't summon the enthusiasm to work at it. It's all for nothing.'

'Maybe, maybe not. If the doctors are right about Mirabelle, there's her life insurance. And if she recovers, you could always cash it in. But whatever happens, she's right. You're an active man. You'd get bored stiff with nothing to do. Life goes on, Julien. And it's probably time you walked along the vines and tasted a few to see whether it's time to pick. Your picking crew is here and they're already picking elsewhere. I just called at the *cave* and Hubert was out at the vineyard. You don't want to leave it too late.'

'You're right. Do me a favour and come with me, keep me company. And keep me up to the mark. Besides, I always like a second opinion on whether it's time to pick. And then we might have a bit of lunch.'

CHAPTER 26

Pamela was the first to arrive for Bruno's dinner, wearing a pale blue summer dress that left her tanned shoulders bare, and Gigi raced barking to the parking place at the end of the lane to greet the clattering arrival of her Citroën *deux-chevaux*. Putting his head out of the kitchen window, Bruno waved, checked that all his prepared dishes were covered with cloths and went out with a bottle of champagne. She had a white jacket under her arm and a large jar in her hand which she handed to him. Gigi stood at her heels, sniffing.

'I know you have all the jam in the world from your black-currants and strawberries and apricots,' she said. 'But I don't think you will have tried this. Rose-hip jam, from my grandmother's recipe.'

'My thanks, and Gigi's. This will enliven our breakfasts. I never even heard of it. Come and have a glass of champagne. You didn't bring Jacqueline?'

'She's coming with Hubert and Nathalie and she's already paid her first rent in advance,'

219

Pamela said. 'She's young and resilient so I think she'll be fine.'

'She may be rather sad company but perhaps we can cheer her up. Now, hold your glass ready, or do you want some cassis in there first?'

'No, just the champagne on a lovely warm evening like this.' She turned, taking in the wide view of the ridge and the rolling hills from Bruno's garden, and then the rows of truffle oaks and fruit trees, the vegetable garden and the hen-coop, the garden table with its array of glasses.

'It's a lot bigger than the cottage you told me to expect. Either you've got a secret family hidden away here or you'll be going into competition with me.'

'I don't think many holidaymakers would like to rent a room in a policeman's house,' Bruno said, handing her a glass. 'It might stop them from relaxing. Besides, they only want a place with a swimming pool.'

They turned at the sound of another engine labouring up the steep lane, and the Baron's old Citroën DS rolled into view. It set Gigi off barking a new welcome, which redoubled when the Baron opened the rear door and his own dog jumped out, a giant Bordeaux hound named Général. Old friends and hunting partners, the two dogs sniffed one another politely and then raced off towards the woods.

The Baron handed over a bottle wrapped in the

distinctive brown paper and wax seal of Hubert de Montignac's *cave*.

'I saw Hubert, who told me he was bringing your St Estèphe,' the Baron announced in his deep, rolling tones. 'I thought I'd bring a good Beaune so we can make the comparison and settle the old argument. It will help take our minds off the sad events.'

Hubert's white Mercedes, its hood down, rounded the corner, Nathalie in headscarf and sunglasses beside the driver and Jacqueline waving rather more cheerfully than he'd expected from the rear seat, her hair spread out in a vast fan from the wind over the open car.

'*Mon Dieu*, that's a pretty one,' the Baron said. 'An evening to be graced by three beautiful women. This will cheer us all up.'

Nathalie handed Bruno a cold bottle of Krug, while Jacqueline placed a bottle of Monbazillac on the table, and Hubert bowed solemnly as he placed the St Estèphe in Bruno's hands. Bruno glanced at Jacqueline, who seemed to be wearing more makeup than usual, perhaps to cover the effects of her crying. He left them all chatting as he went to his barbecue, thrust in an armful of dried vine branches on top of the crumpled pages of the previous day's *Sud-Ouest* and lit the fire. He waited until the twigs flared and then tossed on four handfuls of charcoal and headed for the kitchen to wash his hands and bring out the sliced baguette and the *bécasses*.

'That's unbelievable,' said Hubert. 'Six *bécasses*. My dear Bruno, your luck must have been magnificent this year. I never managed more than two in a season, and I was pretty proud of that.'

As Bruno went back into his kitchen to prepare his omelette, Hubert joined him, bringing the St Estèphe and the Baron's Beaune to be decanted. Hubert knew the house well, found the corkscrew in the kitchen drawer and the decanters in the dining room and set to work. The other guests gathered at the wide kitchen window, looking in as Bruno took a pebble-sized truffle from the jar filled with walnut oil and began to slice it very thin with the knife from his belt.

'Is that all you need?' asked Pamela. 'I've never made a truffle omelette so I need to learn.'

'It would suffice, Madame, and that is more truffle than you would get in any restaurant,' said the Baron. 'But I know Bruno's cooking and I can assure you that another truffle even larger than that one has been steeping in his bowl of eggs in the refrigerator since yesterday evening.'

'Almost right,' said Bruno. 'I never make an omelette with cold eggs. They have been in the pantry for the last hour.'

'Might I smell a piece?' asked Jacqueline. Pleased that it seemed to have distracted her, Bruno handed her a slice on the flat of the knife. Cautiously, she sniffed at the dark brown truffle. 'It smells of the woods. Might I taste it, or do you need it all?' Bruno nodded and she crumbled off half the slice and put it in her mouth, her face screwed up and eyes closed in concentration.

'Not as gritty as I'd have expected, and very delicate,' she judged. Bruno glanced out at the barbecue, starting to glow nicely, and tossed a large lump of duck fat into his huge frying pan. When it was hot enough, he used a small press to add the juice of two cloves of garlic, poured in the eggs and began to twirl the pan from one flaming gas ring to the next.

'A master at work,' said Pamela, raising her glass to him through the window. Keeping his eyes on the eggs, Bruno took his own glass from the counter, raised it in return and drank more champagne before taking up his spatula, dark with age and many meals, and beginning to push the eggs away from the sides of the pan.

'When it's done we let it rest a moment while you take your seats at table,' said Bruno, and darted out to the barbecue to prepare the next course. He was back within the minute, bearing the golden-yellow omelette, rolled into the shape of a baguette and sprinkled with flat-headed parsley, and sliced and served it at the table.

'My first *omelette aux truffes*,' said Jacqueline, her eyes shining. 'Thank you, Bruno.'

'Both eggs and truffles come from within a few footsteps from this table,' said the Baron, and leaned forward to pick up the bottle of white wine. 'New Zealand? What surprise is this?'

'Try it with the omelette. You'll be very pleasantly

surprised,' said Nathalie. 'One of Bruno's finds. Hubert wants to see if he can make a Sauvignon Blanc like it in the new vineyard.'

'New vineyard?' queried the Baron. 'This is a fine omelette, Bruno, by the way. Your truffles are coming on splendidly. But Hubert, I want to hear your plans.'

'Well, since we're among friends, and this should go no further, I bought old Philibert's place by the Domaine as an investment, but I'll plant vines on the land in November and Nathalie's right. I'm going to experiment with Sauvignon Blanc. I think the grapes could do well there.'

'I thought that grape was mainly grown in the Loire for Pouilly-Fumé,' said Jacqueline. 'Is that not right?' Bruno was pleased to see she was coming out of her shell, her mood lifting.

'So it is, but it is also grown in the Bordeaux, and some of the best whites from Graves are Sauvignon,' said Hubert. 'But I'm with the Baron. The omelette is perfect, and now let me try your experiment, Bruno.' He sipped, and the rest of the table followed. They all waited in silence for Hubert's verdict. 'I think it's a really good combination, as creamy as your eggs and sharp enough to balance the truffles,' said the vintner.

'Now, Jacqueline, you must tell the rest of the table about your family's wines,' Hubert went on. 'It will come as a surprise to most of them to hear that a country as far north as Canada makes excellent wine.'

'Well, it may be north, but near the Niagara Falls we have a micro-climate that lets us grow ice wine, picked very late when the grapes have shrivelled and frozen, and it makes a wonderful dessert wine. It's very concentrated so we sell it in small bottles. Hubert knows it, but not much gets exported except to the States.'

'I tasted an Inniskillen, thought it was marvellous and was able to get some cases. But I never tried the Duplessis, that's Jacqueline's family, until she brought me a bottle. So as you can tell, I have employed someone with wine in her veins. And the New Zealand wine with Bruno's omelette is a marriage made in heaven. No question. You must tell us how you came upon it, Bruno. I was surprised when you asked me to find some for you.'

'It's a long story,' said Bruno. 'I first tasted it in Bosnia, thanks to the quartermasters of the French army, who have my deep admiration since they always managed to track down something that might be called wine for us, whether in the jungles of Côte d'Ivoire and Madagascar or the deserts of Tchad. But Sarajevo had been difficult until they reached an arrangement with the NATO base in Italy, then a strange assortment of Californian Zinfandels and Australian Shiraz and Chilean wines found its way to our commissary. And on one memorable evening I drank a white wine of such remarkable freshness and style that I vowed to track it down again some day. It was named after the English General, Milord Marlborough. And I'm delighted that you all approve.'

Bruno stood and bowed, winning a brief round of applause, took out the empty serving plate, and went out to his barbecue.

'Bruno and I are of the old school,' he heard the Baron begin. 'We always use the same plates, cleaning them off each time with some bread to cleanse the palate. I suggest you follow my example, since the taste of the *bécasse* that is to follow will be particularly fine.'

Back in the kitchen with the birds, Bruno put more duck fat and garlic into the frying pan and tossed in the sliced waxy potatoes known as *rats* that he had parboiled and dried earlier. More parsley, more garlic, and he began stirring with the spatula as Pamela came in carrying two glasses of wine, and handed one to him.

'It's a magnificent dinner, Bruno. Just what we all needed. So kind of you.'

Six shining plates, still warm from the omelette, greeted Bruno as he returned with another great platter, the six grilled *bécasses* neatly arrayed. Their heads and long beaks were still attached, but each bird had been split down the middle, and six slices of freshly grilled baguette lined up beside them.

'This is for Jacqueline and Pamela, who have never tasted this delicacy,' Bruno announced, standing at the head of the table. 'Hubert, if you would begin by pouring the St Estèphe, for which we are all most grateful. You should all know that the *bécasse* has a peculiar characteristic. When it is startled and flies from the ground, it evacuates its bowel. This is very easy since it has a very simple digestion, just a single stomach which is completely emptied when it takes flight. This delicacy is that tube, which softens when cooked into a most delicious and creamy consistency, which we spread on the grilled bread.'

He took a long spoon, and scraped from the inside of each of the grilled birds a white tube, perhaps half an inch wide and less than two inches long. He placed each one on a tranche of bread, spread it with the back of the spoon, and then handed out one to each of his guests, and then served the bird itself.

Hubert then stood, and raised his glass of wine. 'A toast to our chef, my dear friend, but also to the memory of our young friend Max, whom we all miss, and let us hope they serve wine as good as this in heaven.'

'And let's not forget Cresseil, a Resistance fighter who then joined the army to chase the invader back into Germany,' added the Baron. 'We honour a brave son of France and this is a fitting wine to drink to him.'

That was cleverly timed, thought Bruno, as they each raised a glass in salute, and then savoured the St Estèphe. Even Jacqueline joined in the murmurs of appeciation as they all addressed themselves to the food.

'But I want to hear more of your vineyard plans,' the Baron went on. 'I have never been much impressed with Julien's wine. You think you can do better?'

'I know he can,' said Nathalie. 'The land is good, the drainage excellent, and some of Julien's most recent wines promise well. Obviously we are not suggesting that we can make a new St Estèphe, but I think we can match the best of Bergerac. Anyway, we're going to try. But first, I'm going to try this. It's always my favourite part of the *bécasse*, Bruno.'

She neatly severed the charred head of the bird from the remains of its body, and then picked it up by the beak. She put the head of the bird into her mouth and cracked the thin skull, tossed the beak back into the plate and chewed with evident pleasure. The other French people at the table followed her example. Jacqueline and Pamela stared.

'I don't believe I'm doing this,' said Jacqueline, but followed suit. Very gingerly, Pamela did the same.

'But that's delicious,' said Pamela, in tones of considerable surprise. 'I thought it would be all bone.'

'The secret of French cooking,' said the Baron, 'is never to let anything go to waste.'

Hubert began talking enthusiastically of the blend of Cabernet Sauvignon and Merlot and Cabernet Franc that he thought would best suit the land around the Domaine. Jacqueline sat with her chin on her hands, taking in every word, her eyes fixed on Hubert's animated face while Nathalie wiped her plate clean with bread and observed her coolly. Aha, thought Bruno, a little tension seems to be developing. He looked across at Pamela, who glanced at Nathalie and returned an amused glance at him. Time to change the tempo.

'Is it time for the Baron's Beaune, Hubert?' he asked.

'Ah yes, excuse me,' said Hubert, picking up the second decanter and pouring into the fresh glasses. Bruno might prefer to use the same plates for his dishes, but he always offered different glasses for different wines.

'Well, if you think there's real potential there, that could be interesting to me,' the Baron said. 'You know I own some of that land by the Domaine and I had an interesting offer for it just the other day from some Parisian. He wanted to pay me for an option to buy it by the end of the year, but he was a bit too cagey about his plans for me to bite.'

'What did he offer?' Hubert asked, rather too innocently. 'You know some of that land has been going for four thousand euros a hectare and more.'

The Baron looked across the table at Hubert, weighing whether to answer or to concentrate on his food and drink. Courtesy won the day. 'He offered more for the barns and buildings. I was quite surprised.'

'You turned him down?' asked Nathalie.

'No, we'll be meeting again. But I need to make some inquiries about land values and what it might cost me to restore the buildings.'

'Houses and land, you should ask at least six hundred thousand,' said Hubert.

'His offer was short of that. We'll see what happens when we meet again.'

'You should hold out for a lot more,' said Jacqueline. 'Did you know that the real buyer is Bondino, the big American company? Max told me they're trying to buy up all the land, including Cresseil's.'

Hubert threw her a frosty glance, as if he'd rather this information had not been revealed. But her remark made Bruno pensive. That might explain why she spent time with Bondino. Max might have asked her to find out more about Bondino's plans.

'Bondino? That's very interesting,' said the Baron, finishing his Beaune with a satisfied smack of his lips. 'I must make more inquiries. Thank you, Mademoiselle.' He glanced at his watch. 'No more for me, Bruno. No dessert, none of your Monbazillac, just in case the Gendarmes are out tonight.'

'I couldn't manage another thing,' said Nathalie. 'Not a bite and not a drop. It was lovely, Bruno, a dinner to remember, despite everything that's happened.'

'It was your wine that made it,' smiled Bruno. 'But no Monbazillac? No coffee? No little *digestif*?'

he asked, to a chorus of Noes and much patting of full stomachs.

'So it seems there is a choice to be made, Hubert. Either you will bring our valley back to its wine-growing tradition, or the Americans will. We should discuss this further,' said the Baron, strolling out to the garden where the two dogs waited hungrily by the still glowing barbecue.

CHAPTER 27

Bruno was just piling dishes beside his sink when he heard the rattling of Pamela's starter motor, trying to fire up her *deux-chevaux*. Leaving the dishes, but still wearing the old towel around his waist that he used as an apron, he walked to the head of the lane.

'The car likes to tease me,' said Pamela. 'It usually starts first time. But it can be moody.' She tried again, and this time Bruno heard the slowing of the starter motor as the battery began to fade. 'Oh God, it's dying on me. I knew it was time for a new one.'

'I'll drive you both back, but Jacqueline will have to ride in the back,' Bruno said, feeling responsible for his guests. 'I have a charger for the battery in my barn. I'll attach it overnight and it'll be fine tomorrow.'

Bruno quickly cleared some of the jumble in the back of his van and turned his sports bag into a makeshift seat. Then he rang the duty sergeant at the Gendarmerie to find out if the patrols were out. He'd have to drive through town and over the bridge and the last thing he needed was to try to talk himself out of a breath test. His old friend Jules answered the phone sleepily and told him all was quiet, and Bruno drove down to the head of the lane to pick up Pamela.

'That was an amazing dinner, Bruno. Really, I can't think when I ever dined like that,' said Jacqueline from the back.

'And those wines were heavenly,' added Pamela.

'Sadly, I can't afford to drink like that often,' he said.

At the Bar des Amateurs, Jacqueline asked to be dropped off, saying she had to meet someone for a nightcap. Raising his eyebrows slightly, Bruno pulled over and let her out. She thanked him again before running into the bar. He drove through town.

'I'll see if your car starts in the morning and if it does, I'll drive it over to pick you up,' he told Pamela. 'Then you can drive me back to my house to pick up my van.'

'I'll have some coffee ready for you. About eight?'

'Fine. I'll bring some croissants.' They drove on in companionable silence over the bridge when she turned to him.

'That girl's not going to be your latest, is she?' Pamela said, with a not very convincing laugh. 'Now she's moved to my place, should I expect to hear your little van coming down the road for a romantic rendezvous?'

'No,' he said firmly. 'She's still a child in many

ways. But also I think she's a very calculating one and that's not a combination that appeals to me. I honestly wondered if she'd come tonight. I thought she'd be too upset. How's she going to get back to your place?'

'I know she left her bike at the *cave*. She came straight to your dinner from work with Hubert and Nathalie.'

'Did you notice her showing off about wine to Hubert over dinner?'

'Who could have missed it?' she laughed. 'Nathalie was looking daggers at her. It's just the way she is, realising how attractive she is to men and trying out her powers. She'll grow out of it.'

'You haven't grown out of it,' he grinned in the darkness, his eyes on the narrow road ahead. 'Not many women do, thanks to *le bon Dieu*.'

'I hope I can be more subtle than that. She's in her early twenties, finished university. You'd have thought she'd have matured by now,' said Pamela, staring ahead. Bruno felt comfortable with her in the strange mix of intimacy of space and anonymity that came with driving together at night, almost like a confessional.

'Tell me what brought you here to St Denis.'

'A divorce. I married far too young, almost straight out of university, and my husband was in banking, working very long hours in the city. It was the usual story. He fell in love with his secretary. Well, he probably fell in love with the money but she happened to be around and available.

I was teaching, which I quite enjoyed but not enough to devote my life to. I'd always loved France, so when we sold the house and divided the property it was the opportunity to come here and have some horses. It worked out very well for me, but he's divorced again, poor man.'

'What did you teach?' He'd always been curious about Pamela's past. But what did that mean, when she called her former husband 'poor man'? Was she still attached to him?

'History and French, to children between the ages of twelve and sixteen who were always getting lost on school trips to Paris. Thanks to them I've been up the Eiffel Tower three times and seen the *Mona Lisa* and the Sacré Coeur four times each. The fourth time I should have been going up the Eiffel Tower I was looking for a child we'd lost at Napoleon's tomb in the Invalides. Knowing the girl in question, I was sure she was plotting to steal the body. A little devil.'

'Maybe Jacqueline was like that when she was a child,' Bruno said.

'Maybe. I'm going to feel like an old chaperone if she comes to lodge at my place. I should have asked her if she likes horses. I'd be glad to have someone help exercise them. That new doctor, Fabiola, says she likes horses.'

'Maybe you could teach me to ride some day,' said Bruno. 'Properly, I mean. I remember seeing you and your friend Christine in the summer galloping through the field. It was a marvellous sight and made me envious.'

'Riding with me would certainly get the town gossips talking. But yes, I'd love to teach you, but you'll have to be patient.'

'Well, there's a project for the winter,' he said, a little surprised at how much he was looking forward to the idea, and not only because of the riding.

'I don't think I'd want to try to teach the Baron, though, nor Hubert. I don't think they'd take easily to being instructed by a woman.'

'Ah, but you're English so it doesn't count,' he laughed, and she poked him in the ribs as they took the rough track up to her house.

'This is one of my favourite buildings in the neighbourhood,' he told her. 'I remember when I first saw it in the sunshine, warm and welcoming with the flowers in the courtyard and settling so contentedly into its hillside.'

'It's the stables you'll get to know from now on, Bruno. We'll see how welcoming they feel after I get you to clean them out.' He pulled up at the entrance to her courtyard, the old stone buildings glowing brightly in his headlamps. He set the brake and walked round to open her door.

'Thank you, Bruno, for everything, and I'll have the coffee ready at eight.' She turned to kiss him goodnight but somehow they turned their heads the wrong way, or not quite enough, and Bruno felt himself kissing her mouth and realising that her lips were relaxing against his own. Uncertain, he moved his head and kissed her on the cheek and broke away.

'Goodness, that was a nice surprise,' she said, flustered. 'Now, where's my key? Foolish me, of course I didn't lock the door.' She opened it, and went in, half closed the door behind her, and then peered around the side to say: 'Goodnight, until tomorrow,' before closing the door.

He stood watching her a moment, wondering just what had taken place, and remembering the frisson of pleasure that had run through him when he realised he was kissing her lips. But remember your rule, he told himself. Not on your own doorstep. Maybe he should bend the rule this once, after Isabelle's silence. But he'd thought it was over before, and then she came back. God, it was hard sometimes. He went back to his car, forcing himself to think about the pile of washing up that awaited him, but knowing that he really wanted to anticipate the riding lessons with Pamela that lay ahead.

As he crossed the bridge and turned into the main street of St Denis, the *Mairie* was dark and he saw Ivan placing the chairs on the tables of his Café de la Renaissance. The blue neon light of the Bar des Amateurs at the end of the street was still glowing. Not everything was closed. Suddenly, by the light from the wide window of an estate agency, he noted a quick blur of movement and slowed to see two figures scuffling in the small alley beside the Maison de la Presse. Slowing the van, he pulled in beside a darkened pharmacy and stepped out, feeling slightly ridiculous as he realised he was still wearing the old towel around his waist. He whipped it off, tossed it into the van, and began to run when he heard the sound of a slap and a woman's cry, the growl of a male voice.

'Good evening,' he called loudly and the scuffling figures broke apart. 'This is the police. Might I be of assistance. Mademoiselle?'

'It's nothing, friends, argument,' said the male voice in accented French, the words slurred with drink. Bruno recognised Bondino.

'Hello again, Bruno,' said Jacqueline. 'It's OK. This man is just leaving.'

'I heard a blow, a slap,' Bruno said. 'That didn't sound friendly to me. Are you sure, Jacqueline?'

'Yes, yes. He just wanted to take me for a last drink, a nightcap. I can handle this, Bruno.'

'Step forward, Monsieur, if you please, and show me your papers. We like to treat women with respect in this town. I thought you were staying in Les Eyzies? You're in no condition to drive back there tonight.'

'He's moved to the Manoir, here in town,' said Jacqueline. 'Listen, it's OK, really. I'll see he gets back all right. He's just drunk.'

'Did you slap him?'

'Yes, just to sober him up. It's not a problem.

I'm sorry, Bruno. When I got to the bar I didn't realise how drunk he was.'

'I think you'd better go back to your bike and go home, Jacqueline. I'll see Bondino gets back to the Manoir.'

Jacqueline shrugged and turned, and began walking slowly down the street that led to the *cave*, while Bruno scrutinised the young man slouched against the wall. 'Thanks again, Bruno, for everything,' Jacqueline called, too loudly for so late at night. He waved at her vaguely and repeated to Bondino: 'Your papers, please.'

Bondino handed over an American passport. In the light of the estate agency, Bruno read the name, Fernando Xavier Bondino, born in San Francisco, just turned twenty-eight. He handed it back.

'Come on, you young fool. Let's get you back to your hotel.' He took Bondino's arm and began leading the shambling figure to his van. Bondino jerked out of Bruno's grip and lurched off after Jacqueline, swinging an aimless arm as if to sweep Bruno out of the way and catching him painfully in the eye.

Bruno had dealt with violent drunks before. He grabbed the flailing arm, twisted it up behind Bondino's back and slammed him hard against the front of the police van, bending him double. Then he pulled on Bondino's collar, turned him and forced him to his knees in the gutter and stepped back as the lad retched and a gush of vomit flooded from his mouth and nose. Bruno stood waiting until Bondino finished, and then went to the back of his van and took a bottle of water from his sports bag.

'Here,' he said, handing over the bottle. Bondino mumbled something that sounded like thanks and rinsed out his mouth, retched drily, and then began to drink.

'Keep it,' said Bruno and hauled him to his feet and pushed him into the passenger seat of the van. It was less than two hundred yards to the Manoir, a small and expensive private hotel that was darkened and its main gate on to the street already closed at this time of night. Bruno sighed. He could ring the bell and wake everybody, or call the private number of the owners, doubtless asleep at this hour. And then the word would go around that the drunken young man who was probably going to be important to the future of St Denis had been dragged back to his hotel by the cops. The tale would lose nothing in the telling, Bruno knew, and that would colour the town's relationship with Bondino for ever.

He turned his van around and with Bondino now snoring beside him drove up the hill to his home and to the pile of dishes that awaited him, and saw Gigi still standing patiently by the cold barbecue and wondering where his portion of the meal might be.

CHAPTER 28

Bruno awoke just as the dawn was leaking pink streaks into the sky to the east and the cockerel in his hen-coop greeted the new day. He lay quietly a moment, his eyes closed, thinking of the difference between waking with Isabelle beside him and waking alone. His thoughts drifted to Pamela, and he snapped his eyes open and scolded himself for self-indulgence. There was work to be done and it promised to be a busy day. He had to visit Alphonse and check the tyres on his truck. And he still hadn't found out what had happened to Cresseil's dog, so he'd better look in at the farm.

He did his exercises, showered and donned his uniform, then looked for his dog to feed it. That was unusual. He strolled to the hen-coop, but no Gigi, and then to the top of the lane. Finally he went to the back of his house, to the large court-yard with the barn and outbuildings, and saw his dog sitting patiently at the foot of the sagging sunbed in the barn. Bondino lay there asleep, an old blanket thrown over him, where Bruno had left him. Bruno did not mind taking care of the young man, but drew the line at his being sick in the spare room he used as a study. There was a small pool of vomit by the sunbed. Gigi turned to look at his master and ran across to be patted, but then scampered back to the stranger asleep on the sunbed.

Bruno fed his chickens, collected some eggs for Pamela and went back into the kitchen, where he put on some water to boil for coffee and listened to the news on Radio Périgord. He went back to the barn and unhooked Pamela's battery from the trickle-charger and took it to her car, replaced the cables and tried the motor. It started first go. He left the engine running and went back into the house. The coffee was ready. From the bathroom he took a large sponge, and put the coffee and two cups on a tray. From the courtyard tap he soaked the sponge, and then held it over the sleeping face of the young man and squeezed. It took a moment for the cold water to register, then Bondino sat straight upright, dashed water from his eyes and looked wildly about him before his gaze fixed on the silhouette of a policeman standing over him against the strengthening early morning light.

'Coffee,' said Bruno, handing him a cup and then sipping at his own.

'Er, good morning.' Bondino stared around at the barn, the dog, the courtyard. Looking at Gigi, he smiled, bent and put out his fist to be sniffed, and then stroked the dog's head. Gigi submitted to this with pleasure and then rolled his head against Bondino's leg. Bruno noted this with interest. Gigi was one of the finest judges of human character he knew. If his dog liked this American, there was probably more to the young man than the dishevelled sight that met the eye.

'You brought me here yesterday night?' he asked.

Bruno nodded. 'Drunk.'

'I'm sorry.'

Bruno shrugged. 'You were fighting with a woman. You should apologise to her.'

Bondino felt his forehead, groaned and took a sip of coffee.

'And you fought me,' Bruno went on relentlessly. Bondino closed his eyes and hunched forward. Gigi began snuffling around Bruno's feet so he took the dog inside and fed him, finished his coffee and went back outside. Bondino was holding a silver flask over his coffee, letting the last drips fall out.

'Hair of the dog,' Bondino said in English. Bruno nodded. It was a phrase he remembered from the British troops he had known in Bosnia.

'Your dog is magnificent,' he said, pointing at Gigi and smiling. It was a pleasant smile, the first Bruno had seen on the face of this young man he had instinctively disliked, and it appeared genuine. And Gigi liked him. Bruno resolved to reserve judgement.

'I'll drop you at your hotel,' Bruno said. 'But first, you clean that up.' He pointed at the pool of vomit, pulled the young man to his feet and showed Bondino the hosepipe and the broom. Then he drove the van up to where Bondino was working, pointed to the streaks of vomit on the side, and told him to clean them.

Once inside Pamela's Citroën Bondino stank like a brewery. Bruno started the engine and drove into town in complete silence. He stopped at the wrought-iron gates that guarded the entrance to the Manoir. They were open. He turned to Bondino.

'No more fighting, understand? Next time, I'll arrest you. And stop drinking so much.' He pushed Bondino out, and drove on through the town, still too early for many people to be stirring, parked in front of the *Mairie* and went into Fauquet's, where the air smelled of warm bread and coffee and the espresso machine busily bubbled steam into a large jug of milk. He looked briefly at that morning's *Sud-Ouest*, checking the front page, the sports scores and the local news, greeted Fauquet and kissed his wife and little Hélène, who had just left school and used to be in his tennis class. He shook hands with the knot of men from the Public Works Department in their bright yellow worksuits and nodded affably to Mr Simpson, the retired Englishman who had taken enthusiastically to the local custom of a small glass of red wine for breakfast. Protocol satisfied, he bought his croissants and a baguette, went back to the car and drove out on the long road past the supermarket toward St Cyprien.

Pamela was already in her courtyard, wearing her riding jodhpurs and a white shirt, and watering her geraniums when he parked. He took off his peaked cap and strolled toward her. Arms outstretched and smiling, he held out the bag of croissants and fresh eggs in one hand and the baguette in the other, and took such good care to kiss only her cheeks that he almost pecked at her ear.

'This is very kind of you, Bruno,' she said, leading the way into her kitchen, where two places were laid at a small table, with a bowl of fresh-picked berries at each place, bowls of yogurt and cereal and a large jug of orange juice. He put the croissants and bread on the table, and watched Pamela move to put the table between them and make herself look busy although the breakfast had already been prepared. These are the signals a woman sends when she does not want to suggest that she is available, Bruno thought. He wondered if she regretted the half-kiss they had shared, but looking again at this handsome woman, he realised that he didn't regret it in the least. He took his seat, deciding not to make some foolish joke about breakfasting with a woman with whom he had not spent the night.

'The real drama of last night took place after I left you,' he said, and described the scuffle, the slap, Jacqueline's protests that all was well, and the drunken attempt to punch him. Pamela's eyes opened ever more widely as he recounted the nausea, the closed hotel, the need for precaution against scandal, and the young man's night in the barn with a blanket that smelled very strongly of Gigi.

'Is the girl all right?' Pamela asked. 'She left for work not long before you arrived.'

'She was fine. Bondino was too drunk to be anything more than a nuisance. Maybe she'd flirted once too often. Maybe I'll have to make some inquiries at the bar. I don't like the thought of their serving someone as drunk as he was. But he had a flask with him. Maybe he was drinking from that.'

'Maybe.'

'The good news,' he concluded as he dug his spoon into the bowl of berries, 'is that your battery's fixed and your car started at once. But there's something else. Do you remember the conversation last night over dinner about the value of the land and the houses? I need to understand the economics of this. Say you buy an old house with a barn and a few hectares for a hundred thousand, and you spend another forty thousand to fix it up, install water and electricity. What can you make out of that, as a *gîte*?'

'Add another ten thousand to furnish it and twenty thousand for a swimming pool. That's a necessity. Say you have three bedrooms in the house and put two more in the barn. Five bedrooms at around sixty euros per night each, say two thousand euros a week for the twelve weeks of the season, a bit less in May and September. You should get thirty thousand a year, less the cleaning costs and linens, replacement of furniture, repairs and don't forget taxes. Maybe twenty thousand a year, total.'

'More than enough to pay off a loan from the bank, I think,' Bruno said, scribbling in his notebook.

'If you get full occupancy, which means marketing costs,' she said. 'But that's with the owner doing all the admin, the bookings and tax forms and accounting. If I had to pay someone else to do that, it would take half the profit. Why the questions? You thinking of going into business?'

'Not me, but there's a proposal before the council where knowing these figures could come in useful.' Bruno checked his watch. 'Wonderful breakfast, Pamela, thank you. I suppose we'd better go. I've got a meeting at the *Mairie*.'

'Is this to do with that scheme you were talking about last night over dinner, Hubert's new vineyard by the Domaine?' she asked, as they drove into St Denis.

'In a way.'

'You realise that you don't have to rent out the buildings as *gîtes*,' she said. 'You can always restore them first and then sell them, each with a small garden, which is all that's wanted by most of the people who buy second homes. So you take your profit and still keep the rest of the land.'

'It sounds too good to be true.'

'As long as people from England and northern Europe want to come down here to retire or just to buy second homes, it works fine. But if there's a recession, or if those people fear that the value of their property might stop going up, it could all come to a screeching halt. That's why I don't do it. I'm not businesswoman and besides, I like having my land. I couldn't keep my horses without it.'

Isabelle was still keeping radio silence, thought Bruno, as he scanned his emails and phone messages again. Did that mean it was really over this time? He didn't know, just as he wasn't sure how he felt about that. What was different was that the first time they had parted when she left for Paris, they had been sad but loving and somehow resigned to the end of their affair. This time when she left, she was angry but didn't seem at all resigned, and she'd made it clear that she wanted more than a long-distance affair. Isabelle wanted him in her apartment, in her profession in Paris and in her life. And he didn't know what he wanted, except that he hadn't the slightest wish to live in Paris, or any big city.

The phone broke into his thoughts.

'*Monsieur le Chef de Police?*' came the smooth voice on his phone. 'Dupuy here, with the Bondino project. Fernando asked me to call and express his personal thanks to you for last night, along with his deep regrets. Apparently you took him home and looked after him when he was somewhat the worse for drink.'

'Did he tell you he took a slug at me in the street?'

'He didn't go into any details. But he said that your behaviour was above and beyond the call of duty and he wanted to thank you personally, but you were in a hurry when you dropped him. And of course I would like to add my own thanks for your kindness and forbearance.'

'He'd better not make a habit of it. He was scuffling with a very unwilling young woman when I found him. And before that he was in a nasty fight in a bar where some windows got broken. That's not the kind of behaviour we tolerate here. I hope he understands that.'

'Most certainly.'

'If it does it again, he'll spend the night in the cells at the Gendarmerie, and not at my place, whatever that may mean for St Denis. Please impress that upon him very forcibly.'

'I don't think that'll be necessary, and please remember that this project is not committed to St Denis, not by any means.'

'I hope that's not a threat, Monsieur Dupuy. I have yet to talk to the young lady whom young Bondino attacked last night about whether or not she might wish to lay a formal complaint. If she does, the law would take its course.'

'I know that we can count on you, my dear *chef de police*, to uphold the law and to handle these matters in the best interests of St Denis. But again, please accept the young man's thanks and my own. I should add that he has written a formal letter of apology along with his heartfelt thanks to you, with a copy to your Mayor. *Au revoir*, Monsieur.'

As soon as Bruno rang off, his phone rang again. This time the summons wasn't even polite. 'Bruno, it's the Brigadier. I need you at the Gendarmerie right now. There's a break in the arson case. Duroc has made an arrest. A friend of yours, I gather.'

CHAPTER 29

From his perch on the window ledge, Duroc looked triumphant as Bruno was shown into his office. Always polite, the Brigadier rose from behind Duroc's desk to shake Bruno's hand.

'So who's been arrested?' Bruno asked. 'And where is this friend of mine now?'

'In one of the cells below,' said Duroc. 'He's one of the gardening staff employed at the research station that you and the *Police Nationale* were supposed to have checked out. On information received, I now know one of them was lying about being at home that night. Apparently he knows you from the hunting club. We offered him a lawyer and he asked for you instead. His name's Thiviers, Gaston Thiviers. No previous record but I had him brought in.'

'He's certainly a hunter, and a good one. But Gaston is definitely not a Green,' said Bruno. 'He's a strong supporter of the Chasse-Pêche party, stood for them at the last election. He was nearly elected councillor. What's the evidence against him? And when you say information received, do you mean an anonymous letter?'

'I can't talk about my informants,' Duroc said, turning directly to the Brigader and looking smug. 'But I got his wife to confess that she'd lied to the police and he wasn't home on the night in question.'

Bruno closed his eyes and winced. Damn Duroc, going at things like a bull in a china shop. When he looked up, the Brigadier was looking at him curiously. 'You have something to add?'

'Yes, Sir. Full marks to Capitaine Duroc for initiative, but I think you'll find that if we check with Madame Geneviève Vuillard at the bank, Gaston will still have an alibi.' He turned to Duroc. 'You noticed, I'm sure, that Madame Thiviers was in a wheelchair?' Duroc nodded.

'Her maiden name was Vuillard and she was crippled in a car crash about five years ago when her brother was driving,' Bruno went on. 'He was killed in the crash, leaving a widow. So what you've stumbled on is a very discreet family arrangement. Gaston's a good man, a devoted husband, and he takes wonderful care of her. But because of her injuries, Gabrielle can't be a wife to him. So he spends a couple of nights a week with his widowed sister-in-law. They all know about it, they go on holiday together and they're all three happy.'

'Madame Thiviers said nothing about that,' protested Duroc crossly. 'Under questioning, she finally confirmed that her husband hadn't spent the night with her. She lied in her statement to

252

the police. I warned her she could be prosecuted. He also lied in the statement the police took at the research station.'

Bruno started up angrily but controlled himself. Whatever brief satisfaction he would enjoy by telling Duroc he was a fool would be paid for in bad relations for months to come. 'She probably felt humiliated at confessing to a stranger that her husband was elsewhere overnight,' Bruno said, forcing himself to sound reasonable. 'Now she'll be terrified of getting him into trouble and being in trouble herself. I just wish you'd asked me about this earlier so I could have explained the background. I told J-J, which is why the *Police Nationale* didn't pursue it. In fact, I believe J-J made a very discreet check with Madame Vuillard.'

The Brigadier was grinning openly, whether at the marital arrangements of the Thiviers-Vuillards or at Duroc's discomfiture was not clear. 'Anonymous letter, was it?' the Brigadier asked Duroc.

'Yes, Sir.'

'Don't tell me,' Bruno said. 'It wasn't posted but hand-delivered to the Gendarmerie early in the morning. Mauve notepaper, handwritten in the old-fashioned way they used to teach and with lots of words underlined.'

Duroc blushed, but nodded reluctantly when the Brigadier gave him a keen glance.

'It's old Virginie Mercier from the retirement home,' said Bruno wearily. 'She's been a bit funny that way for years. She spent over fifty years

253

working as a maid in the priest's house before
Father Sentout sent her off into retirement. The
time she doesn't spend in church she spends
spying on what she calls immoral behaviour and
sends off letters denouncing it. This won't be the
first you've had from her, I'm sure. I get one a
week, regular as the town clock. I think one of
them was about you, *mon Capitaine.*'

'I've had several complaining that you and the
Mayor are suppressing the evidence she gave you,'
Duroc said stiffly. 'This is the first one she sent
with any information we could act on.'

'You didn't ask any of your Gendarmes here
about it first?' Bruno asked. If the man didn't
consult his own team, he was even more of a fool
than Bruno feared. 'Your sergeant would certainly
know about Gaston's little arrangement. He and
Gaston go hunting together.'

'Sergeant Jules is off today,' Duroc said, swal-
lowing hard. Bloody liar, thought Bruno, who had
seen Jules in his usual place at the desk when he
walked in.

'Well, this will obviously have to be looked into,
and it confirms the importance of local knowledge,' said the Brigadier, whose eyelid seemed to
droop a little at Bruno as he maintained a solemn
face. 'If Madame Vuillard confirms that Gaston
was with her on the night in question, his alibi
holds and we have no reason to detain him, nor
to trouble his unfortunate wife further.'

On his way out, Bruno stopped for a word with

Jules at the desk to tell him Gaston was in the clear. 'And another thing. Cresseil's old dog's has gone missing. You remember, that Porcelaine. Can you put out a call to the Gendarmes and municipal cops downstream, in case it went into the river.'

The Bar des Amateurs had become a remarkable success despite its location at the far end of the Rue de Paris, opposite the Gendarmerie. It boasted a large TV screen for sports and stayed open late. The formidable size of the owners, whose wives prepared the *crêpes* and pizza and the occasional *croque-monsieur*, guaranteed that its customers seldom dared to disturb the late-night peace of the town. So they needed little prompting to answer Bruno's question about the drunken young American and the pretty Canadian girl.

'He'd been in most of the evening off and on, going out to walk along the street and then back,' said Gilbert, a tall man with a hooked nose who jumped high enough to dominate the lineouts. 'He said he was waiting for somebody, and had another drink each time he came back.'

'Vodka tonic, he was drinking,' chimed in his partner René, a squat and powerful prop forward.

'Then about eleven he came back in with the girl and they sat talking, quietly enough, no trouble until she got up to leave and he grabbed her arm,' Gilbert went on. 'I walked over, very polite, asked if everything was OK and she said it was fine. He asked for another drink but we wouldn't serve him. He'd had more than enough, but the girl said she'd see him back to his hotel.'

'Why did you still serve him after he smashed your window?'

'He paid up fast enough. And it's only a couple of evenings they've been in, usually pretty late, as if they'd come from dinner. She used to come in with Max but then she seemed to switch to the American. I thought they'd only got together very recently from the way they'd always be talking, like strangers discovering things about each other. Not like a regular couple who've been through all that.'

'I heard that,' called his wife through the hatch from the small kitchen.

'Not you, my love. There's always something new and mysterious about you,' René called back, winking at Bruno. He leaned forward, dropping his voice. 'You couldn't help but look at her, a real stunner that Canadian girl.'

'I heard that too,' came the voice from the hatch. Gilbert rolled his eyes and Bruno grinned and took his leave. As he strolled up the Rue de Paris towards his office he passed the most modest of the town's three hotels and remembered another small detail he was supposed to check. The hotels of St Denis were each well-tailored to the range of visitors; the Manoir was for the wealthy, the much larger Royale was for

256

the package tours and the Hôtel St Denis was cheaper, much more old-fashioned and in Bruno's eyes far more agreeable.

It had been a rather grand townhouse with its own large courtyard and stables, and only the best rooms had their own bathrooms. In the communal bathrooms on each floor, the plumbing was ancient and the scale of the baths magnificent. On market days and in the tourist season, the courtyard was constantly filled with tables and customers and in winter the hotel seemed reserved for commercial travellers and morose fishermen. It served breakfasts and snack lunches but had no restaurant, no conference rooms and no internet. It was as French provincial hotels used to be, which was why Bruno felt warm towards it, and its owner-manager was the long-standing chairman of Bruno's hunting club.

'*Salut*, Mauricette,' he greeted the owner's wife who ran the café, kissing the formidable woman with steel-grey hair. 'Is Christophe around? Or maybe you can help. I need to check the reception book.'

She led him round to the small reception desk with its telephone and registration book.

'It's one of your guests, Mademoiselle Duplessis, Canadian passport. Do you have her details?'

'That Jacqueline?' Mauricette sniffed. She leafed back through the pages of the massive book. 'Mid-August she arrived. Here it is, on the nineteenth, not long before that big fire.'

'Are you sure? I thought she told me she'd arrived in town later than that.'

'Well, I hardly saw her in the day, she was always out and about. A different story in the evenings, mind. In and out, constantly changing her clothes, always a different beau in tow, and some of them didn't leave when they should have done. No better than she ought to be, that girl.'

'You mean she had men in her room? I thought you didn't allow that.'

'We don't, in principle, but there's not much you can do these days. We can't afford a night porter after the end of August and guests get a key so they can come and go as they please. But I know what was going on up there because I'm the one that changes the sheets.'

'Who was the lucky man? Did you know him?'

'It wasn't just a him, it was them. At least two, anyway.'

Bruno's eyes widened. He had been a policeman too long to be shocked by anything in the sexual habits of others, but he had not thought of Jacqueline as quite so cavalier in her ways. Inwardly he shrugged, recalling that his own life had on occasion been complicated by the challenge of managing two simultaneous liaisons. Indeed, the errant thought struck him, this might happen again.

'There was a young American, and then also one of our own youngsters from the rugby team.

258

I don't know his name but you see him in the market selling goat cheese.'

'You mean Max, from the commune. You know, the young man who died, you'd have seen him at the market stall with Alphonse, the older man with the long grey pigtail.'

'That's the one, but like I said, I don't know his name, poor boy. Terrible way to die. The American was a stranger to me, except he's been in here at lunchtime for a *croque-monsieur* and spoke decent French. We got talking, so I learned he was from California. A plumpish sort of chap but very well dressed. Not nearly as good-looking as our French boy.'

'Did you ever get talking to Jacqueline?' Bruno never underestimated the amount of information that could be elicited by a hotelkeeper, and Mauricette was a born gossip.

'Oh yes, she told me all about her job down at Hubert's *cave* and her own family's wines. I never knew they could make wine in Canada. She's a pleasant young person, apart from her love life. She checked out a few days ago, all paid up. That local lad helped her with her suitcases. Full of wine books, one of them. She used to have them all piled up on the desk in her room. Not that she can have had much time to study them, given the boyfriends.'

'How did she pay her bill?'

'Credit card, a Visa. It all went through with no problem.' Mauricette turned the register toward him, and pointed to the final column where she had written down the number of the credit card. Bruno copied it again into his own notebook.

'What's your interest in the girl, Bruno? She in trouble?'

'No, it's just that we've got a team of detectives looking into that fire and they asked me to get the details of any strangers staying in town, beyond the usual tourists. It's just routine. Thanks, Mauricette.'

Back in his office, morosely opening his emails and assuming that once again there'd be nothing from Isabelle, Bruno sat up straight when he saw the message from her private address on Hotmail, not her official one: 'Sorry for silence. Suddenly reassigned to Luxembourg. Same case, new direction. I'll call when I can. Maybe. Don't use my other email. Kisses, Isabelle.'

What on earth did she mean by that, except to keep him guessing and uncertain? She'd call, *maybe*. And to sign off 'Kisses' was the way you might end a note to an old boyfriend from schooldays, or a family member, a usefully vague word for Isabelle to deploy. There was a hint of conspiracy in asking him to avoid her official email, and what on earth could be taking the case to Luxembourg? It was a message calculated to raise more questions than answers, which was probably what she intended. I am being kept on the hook, Bruno concluded, while carefully timed silences and even more carefully worded messages send my spirits down and then up and then not quite knowing where they are.

And I am, Bruno told himself as the ringing phone brought him back to the real world, a little old for such games. It was the funeral parlour calling. Could he come at once?

CHAPTER 30

François Cheyrou had inherited the St Denis funeral business from his father and grand-father, and Bruno expected that Francois's teenage son Félix would probably bury him one day. Since Bruno was responsible for all the registration of deaths in the commune, he knew François well and was a frequent caller at the discreet building that was tucked away behind the municipal campground. There was a large parking area, shaded by trees, and then a row of rooms where the dead could be laid out for viewing. The rooms were furnished with simple dignity, a bed, two prayer-stools, vases for flowers and a small table that carried the condolence book for visitors to sign. Behind the viewing rooms was an office and waiting room and a garage for the hearses. Further back, well out of earshot, was the large workshop where the coffins were made. To one side stretched some smaller rooms for embalming and others for the dressing of the dead and the cosmetics that could repair the ravages of death before they were subjected to public view.

It was to one of these smaller rooms that

François led Bruno, where Max's washed and naked body lay on a long metal table that had two taps at one end and a drain at the other.

'I was trying to comb out the hair when I found it,' said François, and lifted Max's head so Bruno could see the gash at the side of the scalp. He bent down to peer. It was less a wound than a bad scrape, but the skin had broken and the flesh was swollen. Bruno remembered that Max's body had spent hours soaking in wine, and was then hosed down by Fabiola before being washed again here at the funeral parlour. Heaven alone knew what effect that had on a wound.

The ash on the end of the cigarette François kept in his mouth curved down at an improbable length. Automatically, Francois turned his head and blew. Ash tumbled to the floor. 'Sorry. Stops me smelling the corpses. Get a bit ripe, some of them, till I do the embalming. Anyway, look at the size of that bump. I don't think he got that by accident.'

Bruno nodded, agreeing. 'Have you called a doctor?'

'You know the law. Anything suspicious on a body and we call the police first and then a doctor.' He took out the dead Disque Bleu from his lips and instantly lit a fresh one. 'I called the medical centre and asked for that new one, Fabiola. She signed the initial death certificate so she has to be called in. It was marked as a non-suspicious death. She was the one who told me to try that

263

number I reached you on. Your own cellphone isn't working. Have you changed it?'

'It's a long story. Use the new number for the moment. It was a non-suspicious death when we found the body, but it's certainly suspicious now,' said Bruno. 'What do you make of it? Could he get that kind of wound from just falling and hitting his head on something?'

'If he fell from a height, yes. But the way it's supposed to have happened, collapsing in a wine vat, I can't see how he'd have got this bump. It's not the usual kind of wound you get from a club or anything like that. I can't say much more because I don't have the kind of equipment that forensics staff have, but it just looks odd to me.'

'Could it have been inflicted after death?' Bruno pressed. 'I wasn't being gentle when I pulled him out of the vat and threw him over the side. Maybe he could have got that when he landed.'

'Don't ask me.' François shrugged. 'You need a forensic specialist.'

Bruno was already on the phone to J-J when Fabiola arrived, pulling on surgical gloves and a facemask, wrinkling her nose at the smell from François's cigarette. With her scar covered, Bruno noticed that her eyes were magnificent, large and dark and fringed with very long eyelashes. She took plastic bags from her briefcase and put them on the corpse's hands, and then pulled out a magnifying glass and began to peer at the wound.

'The doctor is looking at him now, J-J. What

time should I expect you? OK, within the hour. Call me when you get to St Denis because I'll be at the old farmhouse where it happened, sealing off the place. You'd never find it.'

'There are wood splinters in this gash in the head,' said Fabiola as Bruno closed his phone. 'I'll leave them there, but make a note, please, while I continue the examination.'

'The forensics experts from Bergerac . . .' Bruno began.

'I know,' she said briskly. 'Don't worry, I won't do anything to affect what clues may be left. But write down what I said about the wood splinters. I'm pretty sure that blow to the head wouldn't have been fatal and I'm going to stick with my initial opinion of asphyxiation as the cause of death, but he may have been knocked unconscious.'

'Could that have been accidental?' Bruno asked.

'I don't know. Head wounds are funny things.' She pulled back the eyelids, peered into the mouth and nostrils and then began to examine the rest of the body more closely.

'Have you noticed the penis?' asked François. 'If you ask me, this guy had sex not long before death. You might want to tell the forensics to check the seminal vesicles.'

Fabiola nodded and took her magnifying glass to the groin area.

'I think you're right, make a note of that too,' she said, and took another plastic bag and placed it carefully around the boy's genitals. She parted the legs and peered closely. 'No sign of anal penetration.' Then she began to look at the hands through the thin plastic film, paying particular attention to the nails. 'Left hand, foreign matter in the nails of index and middle finger. Hair, possibly pubic.'

Her inspection completed, Fabiola took a large plastic bag and wrapped it around Max's head. 'Short of cutting him open, that's the best I can do, but make sure the forensic team gets my note, and give them my card. Since this looks like it's going to be a police inquiry, I'll type out a statement for you, Bruno. I can't rule out the possibility that he fell awkwardly and hurt his head that way but I'd say it was unlikely. I think somebody hit him or pushed him.'

'It could have been me, when I got him out the vat,' said Bruno. 'You remember helping me hold him up when we tried to breathe air into him before I pushed him out?'

Fabiola nodded. 'You're right. But we might be able to exclude that if we can establish an accurate time of death. It won't be easy after he was in the wine so long. It works on the tissues. There's also signs of recent bleeding from the nose and bruising, but it looks two or three days old. Could be a rugby injury or maybe he was hit on the nose.'

That must have been the bar fight, thought Bruno. 'Anything else?' he asked, scribbling quickly in his notebook as she took off her face mask and peeled off the surgical gloves.

'Yes, there's something the forensic team should look at carefully. I think François is right about the boy having sex, and quite rough sex at that. It could have been masturbation, or possibly sex under water reducing the natural lubrication. But I think there was a partner because of those scratches on his buttocks.'

'Any sign of whether he died before Cresseil, or was it the other way round?' Bruno asked, remembering the Mayor's concern. 'The lawyers will want to know for the inheritance.'

'They both died in the same time frame, but perhaps the Bergerac lab can narrow it down.' She turned to François. 'You're good,' she said. 'Not many people would have noticed that inflammation. Did you have any medical training?'

'In the navy,' he said, lighting another cigarette. 'Military service. I was an orderly. But I see a lot of bodies. Amazing what you can tell from them.'

'You'll be a dead body yourself if you go on smoking like that,' she said. 'But while you're at it, pass me one. I haven't had a Disque Bleu in years.'

CHAPTER 31

Bruno sighed as he looked around the barn that still stank of the wine that had splashed out when he'd pushed Max's body from the vat. Alongside heaps of junk that looked as if it had been there since before the war, dusty shelves and dustier bottles were stacked along the back wall. Two members of the scene-of-crime team, dressed in white coveralls, were poking gingerly through it.

'They'll have their work cut out in here, but the house is tidy enough,' J-J went on. 'Forensics in Bergerac agree with your doctor. Somebody gave that boy a crack on the head, even if he did die from carbon whatever it was. So if it's not murder, it's aggravated manslaughter. Anyway, as far as I'm concerned it's a good excuse to get away from being at the beck and call of that Brigadier. Murder trumps arson. Who are our suspects, beyond that American we saw him fighting with? He's got to be number one.'

Bruno shrugged. 'We'll want to talk to Jacqueline, that was the girl with him. She should know his movements, and if he was having sex

268

not long before he died it was probably with her. We should also talk to Dominique, and then we'll have to ask Alphonse what he knows of Max's movements in the last few days and check the tyres on his truck. Then there were those glasses in Cresseil's kitchen. There may be fingerprints.'

'So the dead youngster could have been mixed up in that fire? And that Dominique comes up again. Could there be a connection, do you think?'

'Maybe, but there's no evidence of that,' said Bruno. 'I thought the leads would be coming from your *écolo* network in Bordeaux.'

'I wanted to talk to you about that. Where can we go that's private?'

'Down the garden. They'll want to fingerprint the house. What's so private?' Bruno guided J-J out past the forensics team and led the way past the house and the vegetable garden down towards the river before J-J spoke.

'There's almost no sign on any of the *écolo* websites that anybody knew much about this research station. It doesn't come up, no rumours, nothing except for one posting by your Alphonse asking if anybody had information about it. Usually before there's an attack or a demonstration, the websites will be full of information about the particular farm or the company, like whipping up a campaign about it. Before they attacked that McDonald's, the websites and the left-wing press and the newsletters were all full of material. It was the same when they hit that experimental rapeseed crop down near Foix. But not this time. The fire came out of nowhere, and that's odd.'

'So what does that mean, a lone arsonist, with no connection to the movement?'

'Did you ever read Sherlock Holmes?' J-J asked suddenly.

Bruno looked at him quizzically. Where had that come from? 'Years ago at school. I saw an old film about him once. I remember that funny cap he wore and lots of London fog, and that he could identify hundreds of different kinds of cigars from their ashes.'

'He has a story about the dog that failed to bark in the night. The point was, it should have barked but it didn't, so it probably knew the intruder. On this arson case, the usual dogs among all the activists didn't bark at all, so I'm beginning to think this wasn't the *écolos* but something else altogether, maybe someone with a grudge against that scientist who runs the research place.'

'Have you talked to the Brigadier about this dog that didn't bark?' Bruno asked.

'He's the one that explained the strange silence of the *écolos*. You and me, we're just the errand boys, the local help he expects to do the footwork for him. But his real interest in this case is using it to build up a database on all the *écolo* movements. He's taking the opportunity to trawl up computer hard disks all over the region. That's what they do in the R-G. So we're supposed to solve it on our own, because once he realised this

270

wasn't some big *écolo* conspiracy his level of interest dropped right off.'

'So you want to start looking into local feuds around the research station? Nothing much comes to mind. That director you met, Petitbon, lives a very quiet life, except that he's passionate about cycling.'

'Where else do we start to look?'

'There's some things I ought to check on, like when Max picked the grapes, and if anybody has found Cresseil's dog. I've also got to see if my phone can be repaired. You'll need some place to work and set up a squad room. I'll take care of that, but it can't be till tomorrow.'

'That's OK, I've got the new mobile incident centre coming down now we've got a suspicious death. It's just a caravan but I can work out of there and three of my squad will be coming with it. As soon as they get here, I'll get the Gendarmes to start bringing in the witnesses. We can set up here in the courtyard. I'd better stay here and wait for them, poke around a bit, see what's in the house and the other outbuildings.'

'That reminds me,' said Bruno. 'I haven't seen Max's bike, some antique that he managed to get running again. It's probably in that shed.'

Bruno looked around the outbuildings and the back of Cresseil's cottage. He found an ancient Somua tractor that hadn't been moved for decades and a wooden dogcart that someone had sanded down and started to repaint, but no motorbike.

There was little doubt where it had been, from the pool of old oil on the floor of the small barn and cans of oil and tools on a bench beside it. There were some oil-stained rags and motorcycle magazines and a mechanics manual on a shelf above. And then a gap. Bruno pondered that gap, and on an impulse, hauled up an old crate, stood on it and looked at the gap on the wooden shelf. He saw a stain of regular shape, an oblong with rounded corners. It could have been the shape of a petrol can. He pulled out his tape measure and scribbled down the dimensions and then looked at the slip of paper that marked a place in the manual's oily pages. It was a receipt from Lespinasse's garage for *mélange*, the oil and petrol mix that old bikes required.

Armed with the shape of the oil stain traced on to a sheet of paper, Bruno parked his van on the forecourt of the Total garage on the Bergerac road. Lespinasse's sister was dealing with a tourist who had stopped to fill his tank. Most of the locals went to the pumps at the supermarket where the price was three centimes less per litre, which saved more than a euro on a full tank. But Lespinasse had always made more as a mechanic than he ever had from selling petrol, and his son Edouard had inherited his father's skill with engines. Before he went through to the large garage at the rear where they kept the old Citroëns they loved to work on and restore, Bruno stopped in the small showroom attached to the office and looked at the *bidons*, the small petrol cans. He saw two models in plastic and one in metal. He tried each of them on the traced outline on his sheet of paper and the metal one was a perfect fit.

With a tinny radio blaring out a call-in show from France-Inter, father and son were working on a stripped-down *traction-avant*, a classic Citroën that dated from the 1930s and had been the staple of the old *policier* films that Bruno loved. Lespinasse was beneath the engine and young Edouard leaned perilously in from above, one foot on the running board and the other waving in the air to the sound of clanging metal and muffled curses. Rather than disturb them, Bruno looked around the cavernous space, the array of bicycles they rented out to tourists, the Renaults and Peugeots waiting for their inspections and maintenance. One of the commune trucks up high on the hydraulic lift bared its underparts to Bruno's curious gaze. Beyond it three trail bikes stood in a row looking wickedly fast with their knobbly tyres and high mudguards, and at the end of the line with a large and almost overflowing drip pan beneath its leaking engine lurked Cresseil's venerable bike.

'*Putain,*' came a roar from the old Citroën, and Lespinasse heaved himself from beneath the car, sucking on a barked knuckle and waving a large spanner in a vague greeting. '*Ça va, Bruno?*'

'Have you got a moment?' asked Bruno, shaking

the forearm Lespinasse proffered rather than the oily hand, and Edouard came forward to brush cheeks.

'Cresseil's old bike. How long have you had that in here?'

'Well, it was Max's really. He and I worked on it to get it going again,' said Edouard, 'but we couldn't get the right parts. We tried machining some different parts to fit and it sort of ran but lost a lot of oil. We were going to put some new piston rings in, but I don't suppose I'll bother now that Max is dead. I can't believe it, Bruno. We went all through school together.'

'Tragic, what happened. I never knew you could die that way and I liked Max,' said his father. He turned to Edouard. 'I suppose he's still got that old trail bike of yours that you lent him. Don't forget to bring that back.'

'Max has been using a trail bike?' Bruno asked, suddenly alert.

'My old Kawasaki,' said Edouard. 'It was a bit small for him, really, but when the old bike started dying he needed it to get about.'

'When did you first lend it to him?'

'Couple of weeks ago, this time. But he used it whenever he wanted. We were always good mates.'

'Can you remember exactly?'

'Well, that weekend before the fire, he and I were trying out that motocross course by the go-kart track on the way to Périgueux. He kept it after that. It was OK, all insured through the garage.'

274

'Did he buy his petrol here?'

'Well,' said Edouard, with a nervous glance at his father. 'We usually filled up together, so it was my bike. I mean, he didn't always pay, except for the parts of the old bike. I didn't charge my time because it was after hours. He paid the full amount for everything else, for his helmet and the oil and that petrol can he bought.'

'When did he buy that?'

'That same weekend we tried the motocross course. He said he might need some more for himself because he wanted to try that other motocross place on the Bergerac road. So he bought the can and ten litres. He paid for that, though. He did, Dad. Honest. It's in the book.'

CHAPTER 32

Sitting in the passenger seat of J-J's car, with Félix Jarreau, the retired postman from Coux, in the back seat, Bruno tried not to listen to J-J's curses as his big Peugeot wallowed its way down the narrow lane to Alphonse's commune. He was waiting for the look on J-J's face when he first saw the geodesic dome and the house dug into the growing hillside.

In the event it was the postman who first spoke.

'This place has changed and haven't they done well?' he said. 'I delivered here years ago when I had to take over this route during holidays. They used to tell me their plans but I never thought they'd stick it out.'

Bruno headed directly for the dome, the place he thought he was most likely to find Alphonse. J-J simply leaned into his car and started blaring the horn. Goats began moving amiably in his direction and a toddler appeared wearing a vest and waddling towards J-J with a large smile. Edouard's trail bike, with a helmet perched on the handlebars, was parked under a lean-to at the back of the dome. An old Renault flatbed truck was parked just beyond it, and even without a magnifying glass Bruno could see a trace of white paint on the side of a tyre. He walked across and scraped a fleck of it into an evidence bag and then beckoned the old postman to join him. J-J's horn stopped, and he heard Alphonse shouting 'In here' from somewhere inside the cheese barn.

'Does that bike resemble the one you saw at the phone booth?' Bruno asked the postman.

'Yes, it does. But they all look the same, those motocross bikes. It seems the same but nobody could be sure. But that's the helmet, I'm sure of that. I never saw one like that before with the built-in chin, but that's what the chap was wearing who made the phone call. And it's the same light colour.'

'What about this?' said Bruno. The key was in the ignition so he turned it on and kick-started the engine into life, revved it a few times before turning it off.

'Does that sound familiar?'

'Yes, but they tend to sound the same. It's the helmet that stuck in my mind.'

'Thank you for that, Monsieur,' said J-J. 'Now perhaps you'll go back to the car and wait till we finish up here.'

The old postman turned to leave as Alphonse joined them, wiping his hands on a cloth and wearing the kind of brown woolly hat that Bruno recalled seeing on TV news shots of Afghan mujahedin.

'What's all this noise?' he demanded crossly, and then his face broke into a sad half-smile when he saw Bruno and the postman and he hurried forward to shake hands. 'Welcome, Bruno. I was going to call you. We'll be having a ceremony for Max up here tomorrow evening, light a fire for him and drink to his memory. I'd like you to be there and I know Max would have wanted that.'

'I'm supposed to go,' said the postman. 'I'm sorry for your trouble.' He went back to the car, and Bruno waited until he was out of earshot before speaking again.

'It's a bit difficult, Alphonse. Félix is pretty sure that this was the bike and the helmet of the person who made the phone call from Coux about the fire. We know that Max bought petrol and a petrol can just before the fire. And I'm pretty sure that white paint on the tyres of your truck is going to match the stuff that was sprayed on the research station. It was Max who burned down those crops.'

Alphonse looked at them sharply, scanning Bruno's face, as if about to protest, but then his shoulders seemed to slump and he sighed and shrugged. 'I think you're probably right. But since he's dead, poor lad, it hardly matters now.'

'Well, it means we can stop wasting police time looking for another arsonist,' growled J-J. 'It might mean we can put more resources into finding out who killed your boy.'

'What do you mean, killed?' Alphonse's hands

278

fell to his sides and the cloth fluttered to the ground. He turned to Bruno, dismay giving way to anger. 'Bruno, you told me it was an accident, asphyxiation. What is this about him being killed?'

'We found a bruise and a gash under the hair-line. It looks as if he'd fallen or he could have been hit, but as yet we don't know when or how. The doctor still says the cause of death was asphyxiation. But tell me, Alphonse, why do you think it was Max who burned those crops?'

'From his computer. When that Brigadier of yours took mine away, I had to use Max's laptop to get on the internet and keep up with our orders. Max had left it at Cresseil's place so the Gendarmes missed it when they searched here. I told you, Bruno, that we sell more and more cheese on the internet. Max set that up for us.'

I missed it too, thought Bruno. I should have thought Max would have a laptop of his own. 'So what was on his computer?'

'A poem he was writing about it, or maybe a song,' said Alphonse, half-smiling at the memory. 'There's a lot more that's encrypted but the poem was up on the screen as a separate Word docu-ment. I can show you, if you like. It's not finished, but it's a good poem about the fire cleansing the poison, but how hard it was to wash away the smell of the petrol. There is another big file on GMOs. I just put two and two together. I was planning to tell you when you came up tomorrow for his wake.'

'I'm afraid we're going to have to take that computer as well,' said J-J. 'And we could have saved a lot of time if you'd told us of this second computer when we first called you in.'

'But I didn't read any of his stuff until this afternoon.' Alphonse snapped, more fiercely than Bruno had ever heard him. 'I just used his laptop to log on to our email. Max was entitled to his privacy.'

'It's a sad day, so we'll just leave it at that,' said Bruno, laying a hand on J-J's arm as the older policeman braced himself for an angry retort. 'I'm sorry for your loss, Alphonse. You raised a fine lad and we'll miss him. If you could let us have that laptop, we'll be off.'

'But I need it for the email.'

'I understand. Come into the *Mairie* any time and use mine in the office until we can get one of your computers back to you. Just type in Bruno to start it up and then my cellphone number is the password.'

'Don't you need a court order or something to take it?'

'No, we don't,' said Bruno reasonably. 'But the alternative is that I stay here until J-J here comes back with a carload of Gendarmes and a couple of magistrates and every piece of paperwork you might need, and then they'll hunt through everything and tear up your houses and take the lot. You know that, Alphonse. Arson is a serious crime. Let's not make this worse than it is.'

'You're right,' Alphonse sighed, went into the dome and came back with the laptop. 'You're still welcome at the wake for him tomorrow, Bruno. Max thought the world of you.'

'And I thought the world of him. Thanks for the invitation, and I'll be here tomorrow. Keep your spirits up, and call me on Max's phone if you need anything. It's the only one I've got, after the last one went into the wine vat with me when we pulled him out.'

'That's fine. He'd have wanted you to have it if you needed it. Bye, Bruno.' Alphonse came forward to embrace him, and then turned and walked slowly back into the cheese barn.

'A strange kind of policeman you are,' said J-J as they walked back to his car. 'It's just as well there was none of my recruits here to see that. Giving away your computer password. It would put their training back years.'

'Maybe it's exactly what they need. It would do them all good to spend a year as a village copper. You've hinted as much yourself, J-J, more than once.'

'I'd probably had a drink or two when I said that. Still, if you've got your old phone, I've got a lad on my team who can do wonders with phones. If he can't fix it, he'll transfer all your phone numbers into that new one in a couple of minutes with his laptop. And I think we've got a couple of spares in the mobile unit. You deserve one for solving this case.'

'But now we've got a bigger one to tackle.'

'Crime never sleeps,' said J-J, starting his car and driving off up the bumpy narrow lane. Branches scratched the sides of his Peugeot. '*Putain, putain, putain.* I knew we should have taken your van.'

'We needed your car to bring Monsieur Jarreau. My van only has two seats,' said Bruno. 'One thing a village copper knows is never to leave a co-operative witness stranded miles from anywhere. I'm surprised you don't teach the recruits that in the *Police Nationale*.'

CHAPTER 33

Bruno was a fatalist, like most soldiers who have been shot at and lived. The bullet would either get you or it wouldn't. So while he admired people who prepared their meetings and their conversations in advance, he could never do it himself. Even if he was making official inquiries or involved in an interrogation, whatever line he'd planned to pursue was soon diverted into unexpected directions. On the whole Bruno thought these tended to be more rewarding than his intended approaches. Rather like being forced to take a detour when travelling, the surprises were more interesting than the planned routes. So as he headed for Hubert's *cave*, he thought he would just ask Jacqueline the simple questions: when and where she had last seen Max, where they had planned to meet next and whether she had heard any more from young Bondino. That should cover it, he thought, as he greeted Nathalie and looked at Hubert's latest special offer. With the tourist season over and soon needing some space for the first of the Beaujolais and the new deliveries, this was the time when Hubert started selling off some stock cheaply.

'*Salut*, Bruno, I was just closing. Have you come in for that Gigondas?' she asked. 'Word's getting around and it's going very fast. It's an amazing buy at four euros. He must have been in a bad mood when he tasted it.'

'I was looking for Jacqueline, but I'll take three bottles if it's that good.' He handed over a twenty-euro note.

'You just missed her. We had a long day stock taking so I said she could go when I started to lock up. Since it's you, I've got half a case left of that Gigondas that you can have for that twenty.'

With the half-case of wine cushioned by his sports bag, Bruno took the familiar road past the railway bridge and along the lane to Pamela's home. It was one of his favourite spots in the region, the familiar mixture of the honey-coloured stone and the dark red roof tiles, the crushed chalk *castine* of the courtyard and the lush greens of garden and countryside had come together here in a particularly satisfying harmony. Perhaps it was the way the hill curled down to nestle the property like a jewel into its setting, or the contrast between the shielding stand of tall poplars and the lower cluster of buildings. There was something comforting and fitting in the way that it still had the appearance of a working farm, with its large vegetable garden and the two horses idly cropping grass, the placid cows on the hill that she leased out to a neighbouring farmer. And his own fondness for the owner and the life that she had built probably also played a part, he told himself. But apart from his own cottage, for which he had the fierce affection that came from building so much of it with his own hands, there was no other house in his district that made him feel quite so content.

'I tried to call you, but your mobile's still dead,' said Pamela, coming out to greet him in the court-yard. He was careful to kiss her cheeks, but he could not disguise his smile of pleasure at the sight of her, dressed for gardening in green gumboots, a wide floral skirt and what looked like a man's old white shirt, all topped with a large straw hat. She carried a large hoe. 'I was just going to weed the vegetables. Did you want to see Jacqueline? She's in her gîte. I just took her a cup of tea.'

Bruno smiled at the Englishness of it, the firm belief that tea was the answer to everything. He enjoyed the way that Pamela fulfilled so many of the beliefs the French held about their neighbours across the Channel, from her perfect complexion and love of horses to her belief in the healing powers of tea.

'Yes, to ask her some routine questions.' Bruno reminded himself that the knowledge that Max's death had become a murder inquiry was restricted. For Pamela, and presumably for Jacqueline, it was still a tragic accident. 'How about you? You look like you're over the shock.'

'Life goes on, the weeds keep growing, the horses must be seen to,' she said. 'I find that routine tasks can be rather soothing in difficult times. And you're the one who almost died in that horrid vat. Would you like some tea, or coffee, or a *petit apéro*? It's quite late enough for one and you must have been very busy.'

'Nothing just now, thanks, and yes, we have been busy. We solved the first crime, of the fire. Keep it to yourself but we now know it was Max, and we know when and where he bought the petrol, how he got there. There's no doubt about it. So if he hadn't died, he might well have been heading to prison. That's what I did today.'

'Heavens, that foolish boy,' she exclaimed. 'I'll make some coffee. You look as though you need it. Come on into the kitchen.'

She put down the hoe and took his hand and almost pulled him inside, sat him down at the table and began bustling at the stove with kettle and filter paper and pouring the beans into an old hand grinder that was attached to the kitchen counter.

'Have you eaten today?' she went on.

He shook his head. 'I'll get a pizza later, probably with J-J, the big detective from Périgueux I worked with on that murder of the old soldier from Algeria. He's going to have to stay here for a day or two for Max's case.'

'I'd rather like to meet your J-J, from what you've told me about him,' she said, piling cups and sugar on to the tray as the familiar smell of fresh coffee reached Bruno's nose. 'There aren't many men you admire, but you certainly think highly of him. Bring him here for a meal this evening, rather than make do with pizza.'

'Well, thank you. That would be something to look forward to. And I can provide some very nice wine, a Gigondas I just bought from Hubert's place.'

'The stuff on special offer at four euros a bottle?' she laughed. 'If you hesitate, Nathalie will let you have half a case for twenty. There's my six bottles over there, I haven't put them away yet.'

'You bought some too? She's a good sales-woman, is Nathalie. And you make good coffee, Pamela, thanks.'

'Yes, but I'm sorry we won't have the chance to enjoy Max's wine. I think he was going to be a rather special young man, despite what you say about the fire.'

'That reminds me, what time did Jacqueline get back that night, the day before you found Cresseil?'

'Late. I was still reading in bed after midnight, and I didn't fall asleep straight away. You know how it is when your thoughts start churning. So she didn't get back before one, maybe even later. And she can't have been with Max, I'd have heard the motorbike.'

'Did she ever say what she was doing that night?'

'No, except that she was planning to help Max

287

pick his grapes. She said something about him wanting to pick them at night, after the heat of the day. I didn't pay much attention.'

'But you're sure that she wasn't back here before one in the morning.'

'Well, almost sure. It's possible that I may have dropped off and I didn't notice her return.'

'And when did she leave that morning?'

'Usual time, not long after eight-thirty. The *cave* opens at ten but Hubert wants the staff there before nine for stocktaking and so on. That's what she said.'

'Do you like her?'

'I'm not sure. She hasn't been here long.'

'You must have formed an impression.'

'Hmmm. Do I like her? It's too soon to say, our dealings have been very matter-of-fact. We haven't had the kinds of conversation that lead to intimacy or friendship, and I rather doubt we will. I suspect she's one of those girls whose behaviour is very different with men from the way it is with women.'

'I think you're right,' said Bruno. 'Maybe that's how it has to be for pretty girls, accustomed to getting so much attention from men. You'd know that, Pamela.'

'I think you just paid me a compliment, so thank you. But no, even when I was younger I don't think I was that different when I was with men or women. It's just the way Jacqueline is. Some women are like that.'

288

'Did you ever come across any other boyfriends of hers, apart from Max?'

'She's hardly had time for other suitors, has she?'

'Remember I told you about the American, the drunk who was pestering her in the street? He had a fight with Max in the bar over Jacqueline. He seemed to think he had prior rights.'

'I never saw him here. Max seemed to be her regular. Rather good taste on her part, I thought.'

CHAPTER 34

Wearing jeans and a T-shirt when she opened the door to his knock, Jacqueline smiled a welcome and invited him in. She was made up and wearing fresh lipstick, which to Bruno suggested that she had her emotions well under control. Her laptop was open and running and one of her big wine books was open beside it with a stack of manila files to one side. Perhaps the affair with Max had been just a casual thing, like that dalliance with Bondino. Bruno reminded himself that he rather liked this young woman, even if he wasn't quite sure that he approved of her.

'I'm sorry to bother you at this time, Jacqueline, because I know you were close to him, but I have to ask some questions about Max. It's just routine, when there's a death.'

'That's OK. I understand. And I wanted to thank you for dinner. I should have sent a note.' She sat down in an armchair and gestured to him to take a seat on a chaise longue opposite her. 'I liked him a lot and it might have grown into something more. He was so young and full of life.'

'A few years younger than you, I think.'

'Well, so what? He was mature for his age. And he could talk about things other than sport.' Unlike most men, she seemed to be adding under her breath as she looked almost angrily at him. Then she seemed to take hold of herself and sat forward, fumbling for a tissue from a box on the low table beside her and holding it to her eyes.

'When did you last see him alive?' Bruno pressed on. He had observed many people under police questioning, had noted their shifts of mood and posture and manner, their varying attempts to exert some attempt at control of a process where the police always had the initiative.

'Not long after we saw you, after that scene at the café. We walked back to where I'd left my bike and said goodnight.'

'So you left Max what, five minutes after you saw me outside the café?'

'Maybe ten minutes, not much more.' She gave a timorous smile and put her hand to her cheek, as if remembering a tender moment.

'And you came straight home, back here?'

'Yes.'

Bruno sat back, looking at her. She seemed to straighten her back under his gaze. She was certainly acting, but why was she lying? Pamela had been sure she had not returned before one in the morning, and the fight at the bar had been before eleven. And what about Max having sex before he died? He took out his notebook and

291

pen, and began writing, aware that she was reaching for another tissue. He continued to write, letting the silence build, the oldest trick in the interrogator's book.

'I really liked Max, you know,' she said into the silence. 'It was a relationship that kept getting better. Most young men are static. What you see when you meet them is all there is. It was like Max was older, more mature, he had the depth of an older man.'

Bruno glanced up from his notebook. She was looking at him with wide eyes, her mouth a little open, her arms to her sides and pressing her breasts forward. It was, he knew no other word for it, a flirtatious pose. He looked back down at his book and kept his pen at the ready as he asked his next question in a flat, almost bored tone of voice.

'Was Max in good health when you left him that night? Did he seem normal or depressed?'

'Yes, completely normal. In good spirits.'

'You're sure you didn't go to Cresseil's place with Max after the bar? He didn't ask you to tread the grapes with him?'

'He asked me to go back with him, but I was tired. I'd been working all day and we'd been picking grapes all evening. I needed to rest.'

'When you said goodnight to him, was it affectionate, a long embrace?'

'He was my boyfriend,' she smiled. 'We kissed goodnight for a while.'

'Did you make love?'

'Dammit, Bruno,' she said, jumping up and glaring at him. 'This is none of your business. No, we didn't, but what has that got to do with his death?'

'Because from the autopsy we know that Max had sex shortly before he died. If not with you, then we need to find out who the partner might have been. This is not about you, Jacqueline, it's about him.'

'Well, yes, we did make love,' she said defiantly, as though daring him to disapprove. She went to the dresser and lit a cigarette and began smoking as she spoke. 'In the field by the caravan park on the other side of the river. We liked to make love in the open air. And then I came back here.'

'And Max? Where did he go?'

'I don't know for sure. To Cresseil's place, I guess.'

'He was alone when he left?'

'Of course. We'd just made love.' This time, she said it almost proudly, a kind of arrogance about her as she began to stride back and forth across the room. It felt somehow false to Bruno.

'How did he leave, on his motorbike?'

'No, on foot. I don't know where his bike was.'

'Did you talk about the fight at the bar?'

'A bit, just saying that the American guy was crazy. That's all.'

'You didn't see the American again last night?'

'No. Not after the fight and after you came.'

'Max didn't ask you why the American seemed so persistent?'

'No. He was just angry that he wouldn't take no for an answer.' She sounded bored as she said it, and stubbed out her cigarette with three savage jabs. Bruno had the impression that in her different moods she was copying the mannerisms of some actresses she had seen, as though trying to invent emotions like anger and boredom that she would be expected to display. None of it seemed to come from her. Perhaps it was time to jolt her.

'Had you always said no to the American?'

At that, she stopped her pacing and looked down at him with real surprise. Then she put her hands on her hips, tightened her mouth and released what seemed to be some genuine anger, or perhaps another emotion.

'Bruno, this is very hostile questioning into my personal life, and I don't see any relevance when it comes down to Max's accidental death. If you want to ask any more of these dirty old man questions, I'm going to call a lawyer.'

'That's up to you, Jacqueline,' he said calmly, scribbling in his notebook and avoiding her eye. 'We can always continue the questioning at the Gendarmerie, but you'd have to stay in the cells under what we call *garde à vue* and I doubt you'd get to see a lawyer for some time. In any event, this is France and we can hold you for questioning for three days. I repeat, had you

294

always said no to the American? I'm trying to understand why he felt he had some claim on you and why that should lead to a fight with Max.'

She turned her back on him. 'I got drunk one night and let the American into my room. It was a bad mistake. I'm not usually like that. It made me feel like a slut.'

'Thank you for telling the truth. Had you lied, I would have known because I've already talked to the hotel about this. You may stop answering my questions at any time and call a lawyer, but I and the magistrate making the formal inquiry into Max's death would draw the appropriate conclusions. And as far as we know, you were the last person to see Max alive. That makes your testimony very important.'

'That's what feels so strange about this,' she said. 'He was fine, happy and affectionate when we parted. And the next thing I know, he'd dead in this bizarre way. It's a shock. You don't expect someone young and healthy to die just like that.'

'You have no reason to believe that his death was anything other than an accident?'

'What do you mean? Of course not. An accident is what I heard. If you know any different, tell me. He was my boyfriend, dammit. I have a right to know.'

'The precise cause of death has not yet been established, Jacqueline. And it was clearly an unusual death, so we have to make full inquiries.

Moreover, it seems that Max may have been involved in another matter we are investigating. Did he ever talk to you about that fire up in the hills a couple of weeks ago?'

'Not specifically. People were talking about it in the *cave* and at the bar in the evenings. Most people seemed to approve of it, I mean, to applaud whoever it was who burned the GMO crops. They're not too popular around here.'

'Max never talked about GMO crops with you?'

'Sure. When the topic came up in the bar, he was against them. He was very green-minded, organic wines . . .' She smiled, and for the first time Bruno felt she was showing a genuine emotion.

He did not return her smile and rose. 'I'm sorry about this, but it's my job. I'll type this up as a statement and then you may correct it before signing it. I should warn you that under French law, a signed statement is a very serious document. Any lies or misrepresentations in it can lead to prison or other serious consequences.'

He turned as if to go. 'Oh, one more thing. May I check your passport?'

She fished in her bag and handed it to him. He flicked to the back page to check the photo, and then took out his notebook and scribbled down the details. He listed the date and place of birth, the passport number and next of kin and the date of the French entry stamp, August 15th. He handed it back.

'My condolences on the death of your boyfriend, Jacqueline. You may be needed as a witness as inquiries progress. Please do not leave St Denis without informing me.'

CHAPTER 35

Bruno didn't recognise anyone at the mobile police station parked in Cresseil's court-yard, but a prematurely bald young man introduced himself as Yves, one of J-J's team, and asked for Bruno's old phone that had been wrecked in the vat.

'J-J has gone to the Manoir to see the young American,' he said. 'But he told me to replace your phone. He said you got a good result on the arson.'

Bruno handed over both his and Max's phones. Yves attached various wires to the old phones and then plucked a new one from a shelf in the van. He plugged them all into his laptop, and then his fingers started dancing over the keys.

'You had a lot of calls,' he said. 'The phone is finished but the memory's OK. What about this second phone, is that yours?'

'No, it belonged to the man who died. I was using it while mine was dead, but I thought you might want to see if you can learn anything from it.'

'Thanks, I'll get on to it. Any developments from your talk with the girlfriend?'

298

'I'm not sure I believe her, but there's nothing hard to go on. She says they made love after the fight in the café and then she left to go home, but the other woman who lives there is pretty sure she didn't get home for a couple of hours after that. Maybe the romantic interlude lasted longer than she thought.'

'Could be. Time goes faster when you're enjoying yourself. Here's your new phone, all loaded with your old numbers and messages, courtesy of the *Police Nationale*. Give me a shout if you need anything.'

Yves ducked back inside the mobile unit and Bruno started going through his messages and returning calls. There was one he recognised from Jacques, his fellow policeman in the next commune down the river, and he returned the call. A white dog had washed ashore that afternoon. He put his head around the back of the mobile and said to Yves: 'If J-J gets back, I've gone to check out Cresseil's dog.'

Jacques was waiting for him at the foot of the bridge where the River Vézère flowed into the Dordogne, a spot Bruno knew well. It was one of the prettiest rugby fields in the valley, a site usually worth three points to the local team as visiting players became distracted by the charming setting with the curve of the river and handsome bridge and the château on the bluff above. They shook hands, and Jacques said curtly: 'It's not pretty.'

'Bodies in the water seldom are.'

'It's not that. Just wait till you see.' He led the way across a sward of turf and through a glade of trees with picnic tables. Stalls to rent canoes were still open for what was left of the season. A smell of roasting meat hung in the air from two families with barbecues. Beyond them was the pebbled beach leading to the shallows where the river took its lazy curve. The dog lay on the pebbles, as yet unswollen by death or immersion, but the fine head of the Porcelaine had been crushed into a lumpy, distorted ugliness. The blood had been washed away, but the broken bones of the animal's skull showed through the torn skin.

'That's a terrible thing to do to a dog,' said Jacques.

'He was old, but he was a great hunting dog in his time,' said Bruno. He knelt to take a closer look. The skull was caved in over a wide area, smashed by something much bigger than a club, probably a large stone. 'Any idea how long it might take for a dead dog like this to drift down from St Denis?'

'We seem to get cats mostly. It can take anything from twelve hours to a few days, depending on the current or if it gets caught in the reeds. Sometimes the pike have a go at them. Bodies tend to come ashore here because the flow round the bend brings them to the shallows. What do you want me to do with it?'

'I'll take him with me, let the forensics lads see if they can find anything. Then I'll probably bury him in Cresseil's garden. He was a good dog and the old boy was very fond of him. Can I get the van down here or shall I just bring a tarpaulin so we can carry it up?'

'Easier to carry it,' said Jacques. 'I thought you might want to take it so I got some tarpaulin ready. It's significant then?'

'Very significant. I'm now sure we've got a murder on our hands. Did you ever read Sherlock Holmes?'

Bruno parked his van beside the mobile unit, went to the back and came out with the tarpaulin-wrapped body of the dog in his arms. The Brigadier and J-J fell silent as he laid it gently at J-J's feet and unwrapped the covering to expose the shattered head.

'One of the finest hunting dogs in the valley,' Bruno said. 'Your dog that didn't bark. Or maybe it barked too much. Maybe your boys can find something from the bones. Somebody, almost certainly the murderer, killed him on the night Cresseil died and then tossed him in the river. He washed ashore today.'

'You're more angry about that dog than you were about the fire,' the Brigadier said. 'Well, I'll leave you to your new case. I just came up to give you my congratulations and to say thanks for solving the arson case. The laptop you brought back and that paint from the truck tyre pretty much confirm that the boy did it, all on his own. No big conspiracy, but a lot of fallout. You won't have seen today's *Le Monde* but I got an email. There's a big story about this Agricolae group breaking all the rules in the book about GMO plantings, and then there's the mystery of who owns it. It seems it's owned by a holding company that's registered in Luxembourg, and that's where the trail stops for the moment. I've had Isabelle and two more of my people there for a day or two already. But I wouldn't be surprised to see the list of shareholders emerge some day. And I'll be even less surprised to find it includes the name of the odd son-in-law and cousin of some of our politicians.'

'Is that going to be a problem for you?' asked J-J.

The Brigadier shrugged. 'The ministers and the politicians come and go, but we go on for ever. They gave me a case to solve. Thanks to you two, it's solved. You'll get full credit in my report. I left all the computers in the mobile unit, by the way. We've taken all we needed so you can hand them back to their owners. And I wanted to say thanks in a more personal way.'

He went over to his large black car and brought out a bottle and three small shot glasses from a cabinet that had been built into the back of the front seats.

'A British colleague introduced me to this when I was over in London on a liaison course. One of their special whiskies, Balvenie. I was in that famous *cave* of yours earlier and saw that they had some, so it seemed right to share it.' He poured out three glasses, raised his own to J-J and Bruno and the three men sipped.

'Tastes of smoke and the sea,' said Bruno. 'A fine drink for winter, and for a last toast to a good hunting dog.'

'If you ever need a favour from the R-G, here's my card with my direct line and email. And if you one day fancy a change of pace from this charming little valley of yours, Bruno, we can always use a good man.'

'You're not the first to try to lure him away,' said J-J. 'Forget it, he won't come.'

Probably not, thought Bruno. But it would certainly make Isabelle's invitation to Paris look like a workable idea. Perhaps she had planted the idea in the Brigadier's mind. It wouldn't surprise him. But if Isabelle thought he'd ever want to work for the shadowy R-G she didn't know him at all.

'Any news on the murder case?' asked Bruno.

'The boys found a couple of prints we can't identify on a glass in the kitchen,' said J-J. 'The strands of hair in Max's fingernails are from someone's head, not pubic. It'll need DNA analysis if we ever get a suspect. The American is still at the Manoir. He came back from a trip to Nevers, said he'd been looking for oak for wine barrels. We checked it out and he was there all right. He said he went straight to bed on the night after the fight and got up early for a meeting with some wine *négociant* in Bordeaux. That also checked out. The hotel staff said they gave him a wake-up call at six with coffee and he was out of the door by twenty past. He volunteered to give us his fingerprints, so I don't think he's our man.'

'Did you check whether he had a key to the hotel?' Bruno asked. 'He could have come and gone through the night without alerting the staff.'

'Yes, he has a key. A very good customer, they tell me. Messy in his habits but tips well.'

'Well, good luck with this new case and I'll hope to see you two again sometime in happier circumstances,' said the Brigadier, shaking hands and heading for his car. 'If you're coming to Paris, give me a call. I know you're all rugby-crazy down here so I'll see if I can get you some tickets for the next international.' He climbed into the back seat and then lowered the window. 'And take a look inside the mobile unit, in the evidence case. There's a couple of bottles of that whisky, one each, with my thanks.'

As the Brigadier was driven away, J-J said: 'I hope you're not tempted to take up his offer. The R-G is quite dangerous enough without you joining their ranks. Besides, you'd shake my faith in human nature. If you leave, how could I hang on to my little fantasy of giving up all this *merde* and enjoying the nice quiet life of a country copper, inquiring into stolen apples and dead dogs?'

'Amazing where dead dogs can take you, here in the nice quiet country,' said Bruno, looking at his watch. 'You've just got time for a quick wash at the hotel in town. We're invited to dinner with a charming lady who thinks we need a good home-cooked meal after all our hard work.'

'I was wondering who you'd taken up with after that lovely inspector of mine went off to Paris.'

'I haven't taken up with anyone,' said Bruno, grinning. 'I'm just a battered old romantic nursing a broken heart.'

'Can we take my car or is it another one of your country lanes that like to wreck my suspension?'

'She drives her old Citroën back and forth with no trouble and my van takes the lane just fine.'

'Right, we'll take your van, unless you're planning on staying the night and we need two cars.'

'We'll just need the van.'

'Fine, you can tell me about our hostess on the way. Do we have time to buy her some flowers?'

'She grows her own flowers and I've already got some wine. You could always give her your bottle of whisky.'

'A word of advice to you, young Bruno, from an older and wiser man with the experience of many years of marriage,' said J-J, putting an avuncular arm around Bruno's shoulders. 'Never let your women get accustomed to really expensive presents. You don't want to spoil them.'

'Particularly if you want to keep the whisky to yourself,' said Bruno.

As they climbed into Bruno's van, J-J's phone rang and after a moment he put his hand out to stop

Bruno reaching for the starter. He listened a little more, his eyes on Bruno's face, and then he said: 'Pick him up and take him to the Gendarmerie. I'll interrogate him in the cells there.'

He closed the phone. 'No dinner for us. You'd better call your friend and tell her something came up. And let's get moving. You know I told you we'd taken the American's fingerprints, just a routine? We've found his thumbprint on one of the glasses that were in Cresseil's sink.'

CHAPTER 36

Capitaine Duroc had done them proud. He had moved a small table and two hard-backed chairs into one of the cramped basement cells and put a dirty blanket over the ancient horsehair mattress atop the iron bed frame. Bruno leant against the iron door as J-J faced Bondino across the table. The cell stank of ancient sweat and black tobacco, with the distant memory of disinfectant failing to overcome decades of drunks' vomit. It was a most unpleasant place to be for a man as used to luxury as Bondino. He was dressed in a cream silk shirt, open halfway down his plump chest to reveal two gold chains with various medallions, his usual slipper-like shoes and a matching black leather jacket. Unlike his usual sprawling pose, he kept his arms and legs tucked in, as if nervous of contamination by the grimy cell. But his face was calm and his gaze level.

'We know you're lying. We can prove you were in that house,' said J-J. 'We've got the fingerprints to prove it.'

Bondino shook his head. 'I only went to that

farm once, with Dupuy. I never went inside. I never took a drink of wine or anything else. He was there.' He nodded at Bruno. 'He saw me leave. I want a lawyer and I want the American Embassy.'

'This is France, not the USA. You're under *garde à vue*. That means you answer my questions until you're charged or I'm satisfied. So let's go through this again. With my own eyes I saw you fighting with a young Frenchman over a girl. I saw him bleeding. I saw you restrained by the bar owner whose window you had broken. I saw your enemy go off with the girl you thought was yours. This was more than just a barroom scuffle. This was personal and it was vicious. You went in and hit him, and the guy later turns up dead and you tell me you had nothing to do with it?'

'I know nothing about it. I want to contact my Embassy.'

'What really upsets me about this is why you had to kill the old dog,' J-J went on, speaking over him, but this remark about the dog drew a reaction. Bondino began shaking his head angrily. 'We found the rock you used, bits of the poor animal's blood still on it. We're going to find your fingerprints on that as well.'

'I have never killed a dog. I would never kill a dog,' Bondino said. 'I like dogs and I want to speak to my Embassy.' He nodded at Bruno again. 'He knows I like dogs.'

Bruno took the opportunity to intervene. 'You don't need to be ashamed of anything. You had a fight over a girl. Happens all the time. We understand that in France.' Bruno kept his voice almost friendly. He and J-J had played the hard-cop soft-cop roles before.

'We call it a *crime passionnel* and we've got a special law for dealing with such matters. It gets a lesser punishment, did you know that? A guy gets home early from hunting, finds his wife in bed with another man. Blam-blam, he lets them have it, both barrels. *Crime passionnel*, he walks free. And that's what it was here, a *crime passionnel*, inflamed with jealousy against this rival who had stolen your girl. We're all guys here, we understand that kind of thing. Was that how it was?'

'I'll say nothing more until I talk to the US Embassy.' Bondino set his shoulders as he looked at Bruno in a way that seemed more confident than defiant. Perhaps it was the manner of a rich and privileged youth who knew that expensive lawyers and political influence were at hand. But that kind of protective shell didn't usually last long under interrogation, so Bruno found his curiosity growing. They seldom had people looking as calm as Bondino in a police cell.

'You can talk to the President of the United States if you want, but even he can't explain away your fingerprints in that farm-house,' Bruno said.

'I have nothing more to say.' This time Bondino gave Bruno an almost casual nod. The young man was in complete control of himself. Maybe it was an American thing, a national arrogance, or

309

perhaps the confidence that came from some schoolroom lecture about inalienable rights.

'Your body does. It will have a lot to say, just like your fingerprints,' said J-J. He leaned down into his briefcase and pulled out a plastic evidence bag and held it against Bondino's head.

'It looks like a match to me,' he said. 'We pulled these hairs out of the fingernails of the murdered boy. I say they're yours, and they're going to convict you of murder.'

'They can't be mine,' Bondino said levelly. 'He didn't even get to touch me in that fight we had in the bar. I hit him, he went down and then the barman pushed me through the window. There must be a mistake.'

'We haven't laid a hand on you yet, so we didn't pull any of your hairs out, so don't even think about saying we planted them. But there's an easy way to settle this, although it does mean you'll be enjoying my company for some days to come.' J-J turned to Bruno.

'Send me down a couple of gendarmes to hold this prisoner down while we take a sample of his hair and a swab of his mouth.' He turned back to Bondino. 'Maybe you thought us simple French people didn't know about DNA evidence? You're about to learn different.'

'You have no right to do this without letting me talk to my Embassy.'

'This is a French police station under French law and I'll do what I damn well want,' shouted

J-J, who seemed to be getting more excited by the interrogation than Bondino.

Bruno heard J-J's intimidating voice echoing from the cells as he mounted the stairs, relieved to be out of that atmosphere and even more relieved for the opportunity to make some vital phone calls. He told Jules at the desk to send down two gendarmes and a DNA kit and then stepped outside into the cool of the evening and pulled out his phone.

'*Monsieur le Maire?* It's Bruno. We have a real problem. Bondino has been arrested on suspicion of Max's murder. We found his fingerprints at Cresseil's place. He's under *garde à vue* at the Gendarmerie, being interrogated now. He's asking for a lawyer and the US Embassy. If we want to salvage anything from this Bondino project, we'd better get him a lawyer and inform the Embassy.'

'Is he guilty? How long can he be held?' the Mayor demanded.

'I don't know if he's guilty, but the evidence is very strong. He denies being at Cresseil's place but the fingerprints prove he's lying. There may also be DNA evidence but that will take some days. He can be held for three days under *garde à vue* without being charged, but then he'll go before a *juge d'instruction* where he can be defended by a lawyer. But with some heavy pressure, we can probably get a lawyer in to see him before that. I could call Dupuy and get him involved. He can contact the Embassy . . . No,

311

please wait and don't interrupt, Sir. That is what we can do, but we need to decide whether we should intervene in this way. The evidence against him is quite strong, and in my view, the very fact of his being detained means the Bondino deal is dead even if he turns out to be innocent.'

'Where are you now, Bruno?'

'Outside the Gendarmerie, where Bondino is being questioned in the cells.'

'Do you have time to meet me?'

'If we make it quick.'

'I'll be there in five minutes. Make that three. Meet me at the rugbymen's bar.'

Bruno went back into the Gendarmerie and told the desk sergeant that if J-J wanted him, Bruno had to see the Mayor on some local business. Old Jules shrugged, and Bruno left for the Bar des Amateurs. A large sheet of plywood still covered the broken window. He took a table outside, far from the only other occupied table. His glass of *pression* arrived at the same time as the Baron's big Citroën DS drew up outside the bar and he and the Mayor climbed out. Bruno wasn't surprised. The two men had been at primary school together.

'*Bonsoir*, Bruno.' The Baron shook his hand. 'I was dining with the Mayor and he wanted me to come along.'

'We weren't just dining, we were planning,' the Mayor said, rubbing his hands together in that way Bruno recognised. Bruno felt his antennae quiver. The Mayor was up to something. He'd expected his boss to be in despair at the prospect of losing the Bondino project.

'That point you made about other businessmen possibly being interested in the vineyard project, it got me thinking,' the Mayor said. 'So the Baron and I put our heads together and maybe we can make a modest version of this scheme work, even if Bondino pulls out.'

'I don't see him wanting to stay involved with St Denis after this,' said Bruno. 'When I left the cell they were just about to hold him down and take DNA samples by force.'

'Is he guilty?' asked the Baron.

'I don't know. He could be. His fingerprints show he lied about not being there. He's an arrogant young pup, thinks he can get away with anything with his money. But I can't quite see it. He's not a big lad and he's out of condition. Max was bigger, stronger and in peak condition. You've seen him play rugby, Max was hard as nails. I wouldn't have thought Bondino would have had the *couilles* to tackle him, but then he did just that one night at the Bar here. That's how the window got broken. If he took Max by surprise, or found him passed out in the vat, then it's possible.'

'If we just let the law take its course, what happens?' asked the Mayor.

'He can be held until J-J brings in a *juge d'instruction* and the story probably won't reach the media until then. With the finger-prints, there's enough evidence for the magistrate to hold him after that, at least until the DNA evidence comes back. But by that time, we'll have an international incident on our hands and half the foreign press corps camped out at the bar here. American wine tycoon's son held on murder charge after a body found in a wine vat. You can imagine the headlines.'

'Would they keep him here for the three days?' the Mayor asked.

'More likely they'll move him to Périgueux. But the TV cameras will all descend on us anyway to get pictures of the wine vat, photos of Max on the rugby field, interviews with Jacqueline when they learn about the bar fight. Still, the main focus would be Périgueux, and the sooner Dupuy and the Embassy get involved, the sooner they'll move him and bring in the lawyers.'

'That settles it,' said the Mayor. 'You call Dupuy. I'll call a man I know at the Quai d'Orsay.'

The Baron got to his feet. 'I'll go and see Julien at the Domaine and set up a meeting for tomorrow morning. I think Bruno should be there, along with Xavier and Hubert and the bank manager. Perhaps I'll bring one or two more. Ten tomorrow, Bruno, at the Domaine. Let's see what we can save from this mess.'

The Baron climbed into his car and Bruno and the Mayor began working their phones. Bruno had just got through to Dupuy, dining in a restaurant from the sound of it, when he saw J-J come out of the main door of the Gendarmerie. He put his hands on his hips and glowered in Bruno's direction. Bruno held up a restraining hand when J-J started heading towards him. He spoke urgently.

'Monsieur Dupuy, this is Chief of Police Courrèges in St Denis. Bondino has been arrested on suspicion of murder. He's under *garde à vue* at the St Denis Gendarmerie. You need to alert his Embassy and get a lawyer fast. The arresting officer is Commissaire Jalipeau of the *Police Nationale* in Pèrigueux. I'll call you back when I can.'

He closed his phone and stood up. J-J was steaming up like a battleship, angrier than Bruno had ever seen him.

'If you're interfering in my case I'll have you in that damn cell, Bruno, you know that.'

His voice was so loud that people peered out of the bar at the scene on the terrace. The Mayor turned and wagged his finger at J-J, went 'Sssssh' and turned back to his phone call.

'Your suspect is absolutely within his rights to refuse to say anything to you until he has been allowed to contact his Embassy and take legal advice,' Bruno said quietly. 'It's the law.'

'Don't tell me about the law,' J-J shouted. 'I live the law. I am the law. And what kind of cop do you call yourself?'

'I'm a cop who obeys the rules. You know them as well as I do.'

'Dammit, Bruno, I've got a murderer in there.'

'No, you haven't. You've got a suspect. And now

you've shouted that allegation to the whole town. Can't you control yourself, J-J? This is not a conversation to be having on the street.'

'*Putain de merde*, you're meant to be on the side of the law, Bruno,' J-J said, more quietly now. 'I suppose this is another time when your St Denis comes first. Well, I don't get it, because you've got one of your own St Denis boys lying dead and cold and you're trying to protect some fat foreigner who killed him.'

'Oh, sit down and have a drink, J-J. And say hello to my boss.' Having noticed that the Mayor had just finished his phone call, Bruno was relieved to change the subject.

'*Monsieur le Maire*,' grumbled J-J, forced to shake hands and accede to the etiquette of the occasion.

'Well, I'm glad you've stopped shouting, J-J. For a moment there I thought you were going to have a heart attack and that would have been very embarrassing for St Denis, and very sad for you and a great loss to the *Police Nationale*,' said the Mayor. He was hanging on to J-J's hand and shaking it slowly and repeatedly as he rambled deliberately on. Bruno realised that J-J's anger was being diluted with every emollient phrase.

'It's a pleasure to see you again, J-J. I well remember that excellent work you and Bruno did together on that bank robbery we had, and again on that dead Arab. I always thought that the two of you represented a model of what good relations should be between the various arms of the law here in our little part of the world. Now do as Bruno says and sit down and let's have a drink. Cognac for me. And you, J-J?'

J-J looked at the Mayor, who still clung to his hand, looked at Bruno who was beaming innocently at him, glowered briefly at the small knot of spectators in the doorway of the bar, let out an enormous sigh and sat down.

'Scotch whisky,' he said, and turned his face up to the evening sky. 'Thirty-six thousand, five hundred and sixty-five communes in France, so why do I always have to end up in this one?'

'Because we make you so welcome,' said Bruno from the doorway where he was calling to the barman. 'Cognac for the Mayor and two large Glenfiddichs from your special bottle.'

'Now that you're here,' he went on, returning to the table, 'let me tell you why it might be a good idea to release Bondino overnight and let him sleep in his hotel just down the road. He won't be going anywhere. You'll have his passport and you can take his car keys and wallet, and I can stay in the suite with him if you want.'

'I'll take some convincing,' said J-J, as René brought the drinks.

'Your big problem is that so far you don't have a formal statement of unlawful death from the pathologist. Until you get that, you don't have a crime. That's the first thing the *juge d'instruction* will want to see, and as soon as Bondino gets a

317

high-price lawyer on to this case that's the first thing he is going to demand.'

'I'll have it tomorrow,' J-J said.

'Even if you do, any smart lawyer would file a complaint against you for keeping him in cells overnight before you have it. Let him out into my custody and you're covered.'

J-J took a thoughtful sip of his drink and Bruno pressed home his argument.

'Look, J-J, you haven't got a *juge d'instruction* on this case yet, so right now it's your head on the block and only yours. If the *juge* decides to detain him, it's no longer your responsibility. And you can still have Bondino to interrogate all day tomorrow if you want.'

'Bruno's right,' the Mayor chimed in. A long silence ensured, while J-J sipped at his whisky.

'If I transfer him to your custody and you sign the receipt, it's your head if he goes missing.'

'And mine,' said the Mayor. 'Bruno works for me and I authorise this.'

'OK,' J-J nodded. 'I want him back at the Gendarmerie at eight a.m. sharp and I'll take him to HQ in Périgueux.'

'You'll probably find the American Ambassador and a small army of very expensive and bilingual lawyers in your office by midday,' the Mayor said, slipping a banknote under his glass to pay the bill.

'Come on, let's get him out of there,' said Bruno, finishing his drink and rising to his feet.

CHAPTER 37

His shoulders bowed and his eyes blank, Bondino was silent as Bruno led him up the stairs of the Gendarmerie. When Bruno opened the passenger door of his van and gestured him to enter he looked startled but complied. As Bruno drove off, Bondino asked: 'Where are we going?' and Bruno simply said: 'My house. Again.' Then the American fell silent, eyes fixed on the dark country road ahead. The passing tree trunks flared and faded in the yellow light of Bruno's headlamps, and then they were on the bumpy lane up to his cottage.

Gigi welcomed them with a single bark of greeting and sniffed at Bondino's trousers, probably trying to decipher the rich mix of scents picked up in the cell, then gave his ear a lick of sympathy as Bondino kneeled down to fondle him. Almost at once the American found all of Gigi's favourite places, the two spots on either side of his backbone, the place on the side of his belly that made Gigi pump a rear leg in ecstasy. Bondino was smiling and murmuring softly, and Gigi jumped up to rest his paws on the American's

319

chest. He liked dogs, that was clear, and had a way with them, and dogs liked him. Bruno could not see him killing one.

'Tonight, you're in my custody. You can choose to stay in your hotel or here. But I must stay with you. Now, I have to feed my dog.'

Bondino and Gigi followed him into the kitchen, where he took some leftover soup from the refrigerator and warmed it on the stove, and then poured it over crumbled dog biscuits. The American looked around curiously at the shelves of home-canned preserves, the rope of garlic, the framed photo on the wall of Bruno and Stéphane in hunting gear. A dead deer was slung on a long pole between them, Gigi standing proudly by Bruno's feet, his head cocked and his tail high. Bruno refilled Gigi's water bowl and then showed Bondino the spare room.

'Here or the hotel?' he asked.

'Here,' said Bondino. 'I like your dog.' And then; 'What happens tomorrow?'

'Tomorrow, more police and more questions,' said Bruno. 'Now, you need the bathroom.' He handed Bondino a fresh towel from the cupboard. Once the American closed the door behind him, Bruno went to double-check that his guns were locked away and the ammunition locked in its separate case.

'You want a drink?' he asked as Bondino came out, looking much fresher. 'Coffee, beer, wine?'

'Wine, please.'

Bruno opened one of his unlabelled Pomerols and poured them each a glass. He sat in his armchair by the chimney and Bondino took the sofa, a coffee table between them that carried a booklet on amendments to the law that Bruno was supposed to study, a historical novel by Brigitte le Varlet from the St Denis library that he much preferred to read, and the latest well-thumbed copy of *Chasseur* magazine with a photograph of a stag on the cover.

'Very good Bordeaux,' said Bondino. 'Merlot, very little Cabernet. A Pomerol?'

Bruno nodded, impressed.

'Why are you kind to me?' Bondino asked.

'My dog likes you.'

'You think I'm a killer?'

Bruno shrugged. 'I know you can be violent. You attacked me when drunk. You attacked Max in the bar. And your fingerprints are on a glass that was found near the body.'

'Somebody must have put that glass there deliberately.'

'And you and Max were rivals for the same woman,' Bruno went on.

'Jacqueline is very beautiful. She makes me crazy,' Bondino grinned wryly. He raised his glass to Bruno and said: 'Love.'

Bruno nodded, and drank in turn.

'When I first saw her, in California, I felt it here.' Bondino tapped ruefully at his heart.

'Calfornia?' asked Bruno, suddenly alert. 'I thought you met here in St Denis.'

'No, at university, she was a student of a professor I know. My family gave money for a Bondino chair of global wine studies. I was asking the professor about France, where I should look if we wanted to buy. Jacqueline came into his office when I was there. It was the only time I saw her until here, just two minutes, but I didn't forget her.'

'What did your professor say?'

'He said there were very good possibilities here in Dordogne and he said to see Hubert de Montignac and his *cave*. The professor wrote us a report on the history and prospects of wine around this valley. That's when I got in touch with our Embassy in Paris and they recommended Dupuy. Apparently he used to work for President Mitterrand and he's well connected.'

Bruno nodded, and sipped at his wine. So Jacqueline knew that Bondino was coming to St Denis and she must have had some motive for making the same journey. He needed to find out exactly when she'd arranged to get her job at Hubert's *cave*.

'Do you love someone? There's no woman here.'

'No woman just now,' said Bruno. He stopped. Bondino looked at him expectantly. Bruno shrugged. 'In the past, I've loved very much. Perhaps I will again. I hope so.'

'I hope so too,' said Bondino, raising his glass. This was a strange conversation to be having with a suspected murderer. Bruno refilled the glasses, pulled out his phone and rang Dupuy again.

'Chief of Police Courrèges. This time I'm calling from home and we can speak now. I have Bondino with me, in my personal custody but at least he's out of the cells.'

'So he hasn't been formally charged?'

'Not yet. The police will start questioning him again tomorrow.'

'Is he all right, not too shaken up?'

'He's fine, enjoying a glass of wine and stroking my dog. You want to speak to him?' He handed his phone across to Bondino, saying: 'Your man Dupuy.'

A long conversation in English ensured, too fast for Bruno to follow, and Bondino's eyes kept returning to Bruno as his free hand stroked the dog. He handed the phone back.

'I cannot thank you enough,' Dupuy began. 'Bondino's father is getting a plane from California to Paris and then a charter that will land him at Bergerac airport sometime tomorrow afternoon. I'll meet him there with *Maître* Bloch from Bordeaux, the best lawyer I could find at this hour. The Embassy is also sending someone. We'll come direct to St Denis.'

'By then, he'll probably be at the *Police Nationale* HQ in Périgueux. That's where they're planning to take him.'

'Might I ask why you're sticking your neck out like this?'

'It's not just me, it's the Mayor as well. But Bondino has a right to contact his Embassy and to see a lawyer. And I wouldn't keep a dog in those Gendarmerie cells.'

'I won't forget this, and I'll make sure the Bondinos understand what you're doing. I'll call you tomorrow when I've talked to the lawyer and the father. Will that be OK?'

'That'll be fine. We'll stay in touch.' Bruno rang off, and filled the glasses again, the bottle now close to empty. 'Tomorrow, you'll have your father and lawyers.'

'Thanks to you.'

'Did you kill Max?'

'No!' Bondino shook his head. 'No.'

They drank in silence, studying one another, Bruno's dog lying comfortably between them, his head on Bruno's foot, his rump against Bondino's leg.

But if *he* didn't, thought Bruno, who did? And who killed Cresseil's dog?

CHAPTER 38

Just after eight the next morning, his prisoner safely deposited back at the Gendarmerie, Bruno took his dog along the river-bank for the long stroll to Fauquet's café. He had to call at the *Mairie* to pick up his notes on land and vineyard prices and his research file on the Bondino project ahead of the meeting at the Domaine, but for the moment there was time to enjoy the beginning of a perfect September day. Gigi loved the river, darting in and out of the shallows to chase the ducks and splashing through the shaded waters where the willows hung low, and then looking back to see that his master was properly admiring his feats. As they rounded the bend past the old manor house, now converted into a tourist information centre, Bruno's favourite view of his town unfolded, the three arches of the great stone bridge flanked by the *Mairie* and the church's bell tower and directly ahead of him the wide stone steps that led up from the river to the market square. He walked on through the bridge to greet Pierrot, sitting by the base of one of the great arches with his rod in his hand and two small trout already in his bucket.

Gigi raced ahead, and then stopped on a small rise, standing like a pointer with one front paw raised, his head and tail high, watching the curl of the river where he sensed something was about to appear. Squinting against the glare of the morning sun on the river, Bruno saw the silhouettes of two riders appear on horseback, picking their way across the shallow waters of the late summer. Gigi barked and raced up the riverbank to greet them, Bruno following until Pamela and Fabiola reached him and swung down from their horses to greet him.

'I'm having a wonderful day,' Fabiola began. 'I have a horse to ride and a house to live in. I'm going to rent one of Pamela's *gîtes* until next season.'

'With Jacqueline that makes three lovely women together in one property. You'll have an endless parade of admirers,' said Bruno, kissing each of them. 'But will one of the horses ever be free for me to learn to ride?'

'Don't worry about that. You can have her whenever I'm working,' said Fabiola, bending to make friends with Gigi. 'Pamela told me about him. I can't believe he's a hunting dog with these funny long ears and short legs. How can he run fast enough?'

'He doesn't have to. He just plods along relentlessly all day after the scent until the prey is exhausted.'

'Do you use him to hunt criminals?'

Bruno shook his head, grinning. 'Never had to, but he did once find a little boy who'd strolled away from a family picnic and got lost in the woods.'

'Come and get to know the horses,' said Pamela. 'This chestnut is called Bess, after Good Queen Bess, and Fabiola's grey is called Victoria.'

'She couldn't be easier to ride, very patient and stately,' said Fabiola. She fished into a pocket of her jeans, pulled out a bag of small carrots and handed one to Bruno. 'Here. Give her this and pat her neck so she'll know you're a friend. She'll remember you.'

'That's the difference between Fabiola and me,' Pamela grinned, bringing some sugar lumps from her pocket. 'As a doctor, she offers healthy carrots and I give them these. Here, give one to Bess, she loves them.'

'Do they like apples?' Bruno asked, gingerly holding his palm forward, the carrot perched on top. Victoria delicately snuffled it from his hand, and he felt only the warmth of the horse's breath and the touch of a very soft muzzle. Then he gave Bess her sugar lump, keeping a wary eye on her teeth.

'They adore apples. Bring a few of them and they'll be your friends for life.'

'By the way, I have some news for you,' said Fabiola. 'The pathologist at Bergerac is a friend, we did our training together in Marseille. He and

I both agree that old Cresseil had a heart attack that would certainly have killed him if he hadn't broken his neck first. He was dying when he fell, if not dead.'

'Does that mean he died before young Max?'

'Only *le bon Dieu* could tell you that. They died in the same time period, within an hour or so of each other, but that is as much as medicine can say.' Fabiola shrugged. 'One thing we know is that Max died of asphyxiation, not of drowning. There was no grape juice in his lungs.'

'And that wound to the head?'

'Not hard enough to crack the skull so it probably didn't kill him, and my friend in Bergerac is still trying to establish when exactly it happened. With the grape juice washing away the blood, and then sluicing his body clean with water, it's not easy to see how much he bled. He's calling in his chief pathologist who'll do his own examination later today. But we're sure Max wasn't hit with any kind of weapon. The wood splinters in the wound came from the vat itself.'

'So the pathologist has not issued a formal statement of unlawful death?'

'Not yet. It's a delicate matter, and we're under a lot of pressure from the police. My friend in Bergerac said some Commissaire was calling the pathology lab every few hours, demanding the *attestation*. Maybe this afternoon. He'll let me know.'

'I suppose the adoption makes it important to decide which of them died first,' said Pamela.

Bruno nodded. 'There are some cousins who stand to inherit if it's clear that Max died first. If not, it could mean a lawsuit. And I meant to tell you, there's a ceremony for Max up at the commune this evening, like an Irish wake. A lot of people will be there, the rugby team, his school friends. Would the two of you like to come with me?'

'I would. Having been a witness at the boy's adoption, I feel very much involved. I assume Jacqueline will be going as well. You should come too, Fabiola. It will be your chance to meet half the town. They're not all hypochondriacs.'

'Which of Pamela's places are you taking?' Bruno asked.

'The one beside the stables. It's lovely, light and airy and Pamela has decorated it very simply, just as I like it. It's probably a bit big for me but Jacqueline has the smaller one.'

'Have you met her yet?'

'Just briefly this morning when we saddled the horses. Poor girl, she looked very tired. Perhaps I should have offered her some sleeping pills.'

'Can you tell her about the event at the commune this evening?' Bruno said. 'I'd offer to pick you up but my van would hardly take you all. But I can come by at about seven and then lead the way. You'd never find the place otherwise. Now I'm heading for Fauquet's for some breakfast. Would you like to join me?'

'With pleasure,' Pamela smiled. 'That's what we

were planning to do. Fauquet loves it when I hitch the horse outside the café. He says it brings in customers. Did you know he keeps a small shovel just inside the garden gate for the droppings? He puts them straight on to those roses he's so proud of.'

'They win him prizes.' Bruno nodded. 'You'll see the diploma he got from the fair at Bergerac up on the wall of the café in its own frame, right beside his certificate as a *maître pâtissier*. But your own roses are just as good, Pamela. Maybe you should exhibit yours next year and give Fauquet some competition.'

'But if I won, he would never forgive me,' she laughed. 'And then I'd worry that my coffee would be muddy and my croissants burnt and he'd only give me the baguettes with the misshaped ends. Life wouldn't be worth living.'

Fortified by his breakfast, Bruno arrived early at the Domaine and was heartened to see the winery busy and Julien bustling around the vats with his long thermometer, scribbling figures into his note-book as Baptiste stood patiently by. The aged foreman carried a long glass pipette to take his samples, and both men beamed with pleasure at Bruno's arrival.

'It's not time for the meeting yet,' said Julien, glancing at his watch. He was freshly shaved and his jeans and shirt were clean. He looked a different man from the unkempt figure who had greeted Bruno on his last visit. 'I've still got work to do here.'

'No, I just wanted to say hello to you and Mirabelle first, if she's here,' said Bruno. 'I'm glad to see you busy, but I thought this was the time when nature took its course with the wine.'

'I'm trying something new that Baptiste suggested,' said Julien. 'There's a technique to get the maximum fruit flavour through maximum skin contact, leaving the grapes in the vat for six hours before we started the pressing. We did it with the one vat only as an experiment and we're just seeing how it's going.'

'What's the verdict?'

'Promising, but too early to be sure. I was worried it might produce some bitterness, too many tannins, but the fermentation temperature is normal and there's no bitterness in the taste.'

'You worry too much,' said Baptiste, holding the pipette over a wine glass and lifting his thumb from the end to let the young wine drain in. He handed the glass to Bruno. 'Try it.'

'Tastes like grape juice, but very fruity,' he said. 'Not bitter at all.'

'Mirabelle is at home and the door's open. You can let yourself in,' said Julien. 'Go and say hello and I'll join you in the salon at ten.'

Mirabelle was up and dressed in a flowing kaftan, a turban on her head and her face made up with rouge and lipstick so that she looked almost healthy until Bruno noted the hollowness

331

of the flesh around her eyes. She raised her cheek to be kissed and Bruno recognised the scent of Chanel Number 5.

'I'm determined to be at this meeting,' she said. 'I've put too much of my life into this Domaine for Julien to abandon it now.'

'I'm happy to see you looking so much better.'

'It's one of my good days. I was determined it would be,' she said firmly. 'Julien has been a lot better since you came, his old bouncy self again. Listen, the important thing to ensure at this meeting is that Julien buys back the option to sell the Domaine. It means raising fifty thousand euros one way or another because if he doesn't have this place to fill his time when I'm gone, he'll just fall apart again. I know him.'

'Is that the only way, Mirabelle? What if he were to run the winery but let somebody else manage the hotel and restaurant like you've been doing? That's not his strong point.'

'But they need to be under a single ownership. That's how we make our profit, by selling our own wine at restaurant prices. If he just makes wine, the *négociants* will screw him down on pricing like they do with all the small producers. Now will you help me across to the salon so I can greet our guests.'

As Bruno helped Mirabelle up the steps, the Mayor and the Baron arrived together in the Baron's old Citroën with Vauclos, the local bank manager. Then came Hubert in his Mercedes with

Jacques Lesvignes, who ran the largest of the town's small building firms. Xavier's Renault followed, and the young *Maire-adjoint* came out with his father the local Renault dealer and his father-in-law who owned the sawmill. As Julien bustled in from the winery, an old Jaguar appeared, and Dougal the Scotsman joined them. Having come to St Denis to retire, Dougal had found himself bored and started a company called Delightful Dordogne that specialised in renting the local *gîtes* and houses to tourists. With the handymen and cleaners he hired, Dougal had become an important local employer. Bruno smiled to himself in admiration at the Mayor's planning; the main businessmen of St Denis were now assembled. Julien shook hands all round and steered them to the corner of the salon that Mirabelle had chosen, seated under the painting of Madame Récamier.

'I think we have to presume that the American venture is dead,' the Mayor began. 'The son is under arrest. Even without that, many of us have doubts about the desirability of the big Bondino company as a partner for our little town. But there's been one important benefit for us, which is that we can be confident of getting *appellation contrôlée* status for our wines. The heart of this venture has to be the Domaine, so the first question has to be, what are your intentions, Julien?'

'I have two problems. The first is the option to buy the Domaine. I could buy it back for fifty thousand euros, but I don't have the money. The second is that I timed my expansion wrong. There's a wine glut, so prices are low, and I'm already making more wine than I can sell through the hotel and restaurant. What's worse is that I don't have the working capital for a proper marketing campaign.'

'We have put together a proposal for you that has the backing of everyone here,' said the Mayor. He went on to describe the initial investment that each man at the meeting had agreed to put into the new company, Vignerons de St Denis-sur-Vézère, before offering to sell shares to all the citizens of St Denis. The new company would buy back Julien's option to sell the Domaine so he'd keep the hotel and vineyard. Hubert would market the wine Julien couldn't sell.

'We've also decided that the company should see if it can acquire Cresseil's farm cheaply,' said the Baron, explaining the problem with the inheritance. The Mayor had tracked down his relatives, distant cousins in Tulle, who would be at the next day's funeral. They might have been hoping for a windfall from the farm but instead would discover that they faced a long lawsuit.

'So we're going to propose that we buy their claim to the property for fifty thousand in cash. I'm prepared to go a bit higher, but that should tempt them,' the Baron went on. 'We may have to offer the same to Alphonse, but even then we'll be buying it for less than half what it's worth. And if we have both claims, there'll be no lawsuit.'

Bruno watched fascinated as the meeting progressed, remarkably smoothly, he thought, given the different interests involved. The Mayor was at his most articulate and persuasive, and his explanations were backed by the hard-headed business sense of the Baron. Wily old politicians, the pair of them. Years of practice, he supposed.

The Mayor described the plan to restore the barns on the various properties into *gîtes*, which meant lots of work for Lesvigne's building firm, which in turn meant jobs for the town's school leavers as apprentice plumbers and electricians. Xavier described the state grants available to pay for their training and salaries while they worked and learned their trade. Dougal said he'd been planning to expand anyway, and would rent the new properties to tourists.

'This sounds like a property company,' said Julien. 'What about the wine?'

Hubert expained that the land would remain the property of the existing owners. But it would be leased to the new company which would make wine under his and Julien's direction. On a rough calculation, the new company would have at least twenty hectares of vines and that should produce a hundred thousand litres a year or more.

'Right now, I only sell about a thousand cases a year through the hotel and restaurant. That's twelve thousand bottles,' said Julien. 'How do we find a market for the rest?'

'I get over five hundred tenants a year,' said

Dougal. 'We give them each a free wine tour and tasting at the Domaine and a discount price and I'll be surprised if we don't sell another five hundred cases.'

'I'll sell the wine at my *cave* here, and also offer it to all the local restaurants who are already my clients,' said Hubert. 'I also offer it to all my other customers who buy my Bergerac blends. Since I'll be the *négociant*, in a company in which I'm a major shareholder, we save the usual middleman's profit. I've already talked to Duhamel at the supermarket, and he'll take five hundred cases. That means we already have a market for all the wine your Domaine makes now, and quite a bit more. We won't be selling the wine from the new vines we have to plant for another three or four years at least, and by then we should have built up a reputation. That's our challenge. You and I are going to have to make wines that win prizes.'

'We also have to build a proper visitors' centre at the Domaine,' said the Mayor.

'I'm certainly prepared to make a loan for that and provide working capital for the company. Indeed, I'm putting fifty thousand of my own money into shares in the company,' said Vauclos, the plump-faced and genial Gascon who ran the town's Crédit Agricole.

Bruno smiled inwardly. The *Mairie* was the bank's main client. All the *Mairie*'s salaries and the town's taxes went through its books and the handful of men in Julien's salon accounted for most of the town's business. It would be a foolish bank manager who did not support a venture with such backing. And then Bruno began thinking of his own modest savings and how many shares he might be able to afford.

'When you suggested offering shares to the citizens of St Denis, how would that work?' he asked.

'We price each share at a hundred euros, but any local taxpayer can buy a share for a discount, say ninety euros,' said Xavier. 'And of course every shareholder will have the right to buy the wine at a special discount. We have nearly a thousand households here in St Denis. If they each buy a case a year, that's twelve thousand bottles.'

'So what we are planning to do is to take Bondino's idea, and do it all ourselves without Bondino and on a slightly smaller scale,' Bruno mused.

'Well, I'm convinced,' said Mirabelle, who had been following the proceedings closely. With an obvious effort of will, she sat upright and fixed her eyes on Julien. 'This is the best way for Julien, for the Domaine and for St Denis. We accept.'

'What if the citizens don't go for it and you don't sell all the shares?' Bruno asked quietly.

'Then the *Mairie* buys the remainder on behalf of the commune as a whole,' said the Mayor. 'We'll use the profits to build that indoor sports centre you're always nagging me about, Bruno.'

'All right,' said Bruno. 'If Julien and Mirabelle and you all are agreed, I'm prepared to join in.

The shares are a hundred euros each, right? So with my discount, I can get a hundred shares for nine thousand euros. But I warn you all, I'm going to be a very active shareholder. These are my life savings I'm investing.'

'My dear Bruno,' said the Mayor. 'Why do you think you're here? All this was your idea. You were the one who said that if this made sense for the Bondinos, it would make sense for French investors as well. And here we are. So you're already getting an allocation of two hundred shares as the initiator of the project and we all want you on the board of directors. But of course we're delighted to have your nine thousand euros as well.'

CHAPTER 39

Bruno parked his van beside a score of others in the paddock off the narrow lane that led to Alphonse's commune, and Fabiola pulled her Twingo in neatly beside him. He opened the door for the women, took the pannier with wine and food from Pamela and led them across the field. Fabiola clapped her hands with glee at the sight of the dome. Pamela pointed out the turf-covered house, the log cabin and the wind-mill to Jacqueline, who stared as if mystified. Bruno wondered, had Max never brought her here?

'I should warn you,' Bruno said. 'This is not a funeral and if I know Alphonse, it'll be more like a celebration of Max than a traditional wake.'

There must have been fifty people assembled already, mostly young and from the rugby club or Max's school friends, but Fat Jeanne and Madame Vignier and Fabrice and Raoul and Stéphane were there from the market. A small cheer went up from the rugby players when Bruno arrived with the three women and soon they were overwhelmed with greetings and introductions, and Fabiola was

339

waltzed away by Bertrand and young Edouard from the garage to join the dancers in front of the cheese barn. A sound system was playing the Rolling Stones and rows of tables offered paper plates and the commune's breads and cheeses, and dozens of bottles and pâtés and hams and *tartes* brought by the guests. On a table to themselves stood four magnificent cakes, being eyed with longing by three of Alphonse's goats and two of his toddlers who kept pushing the goats away, so Fauquet must be here somewhere.

Behind the tables, two of the year's spring lambs were roasting over a deep pit above the heaped and glowing ashes of a fire that must have been lit before midday. Their limbs wired to a long spit, the carcasses dripped fat into the ashes which flared briefly at each new drop. The skins were brown and glistening with the marinade that one of Max's schoolmates was applying from a bucket with a long brush made of the branches of a bay tree fixed to a broom handle. Bruno asked him about the marinade: olive oil, honey and *vin de noix*. He nodded approvingly. The bellies of the lambs had been stuffed with rosemary and bay and then sewn closed with baling wire. The scent of roasting meat drifted enticingly into the beginnings of twilight.

Standing by the table with the bottles, and pouring wine from a large jug into rows of small glasses, Alphonse looked up at Bruno's approach, put down the jug and embraced him. He looked both odd and magnificent, wearing an embroidered jacket from India in reds and golds, bright blue trousers and a tall red fez. A strong scent of patchouli hung almost visibly around him and Céline appeared beside him in a great green tent of a robe, her hair glowing with fresh henna and a large joint in her hand. Bruno pretended not to notice.

'I'm making sure everyone gets at least a glass of Max's wine for when I start the bonfire,' said Alphonse. 'So we'll have that to remember him by. I just hope we have enough, so many of his friends have come. And I'm delighted to see you again,' he went on, turning to Jacqueline. 'He was very much in love with you, and very happy in those last days.'

Jacqueline managed a small smile, the first sign of animation on her face since Bruno had arrived at Pamela's place to collect the three women. She embraced Alphonse, and then almost disappeared into Céline's billowing dress as she was embraced again. Then Pamela was embraced and hailed as an honorary godmother for being a witness at Max's adoption. Dominique, wearing an apron and brandishing a large knife, came from the table where she had been helping Marie prepare great bowls of salad, to kiss Bruno and exchange a cool, appraising handshake with Jacqueline.

'It's a reunion,' said Alphonse, handing out glasses of Max's wine. 'All the originals of the commune have come down from Paris for this

341

and one even flew in from London. Max was like a son to all of us. And the children have come back, from Bordeaux and Marseille and everywhere.'

'We wanted to have his ashes scattered here tonight, when everyone was with us, but they won't release the body,' said Céline. 'I don't understand why not. You must know, Bruno, what is it?'

'I think there is some concern about whether Max died first or old Cresseil, and that will affect the inheritance,' said Bruno. He changed the subject. 'What time do you light the fire?'

'Any time now, when it's really dusk. But first I think I should dance with Jacqueline, the last woman who held our dear boy and made him happy.' He took her hand, turned to take a long puff from Céline's joint, and led Jacqueline away.

'I'm glad you didn't notice that,' smiled Pamela. 'It would be awful to ruin the evening by arresting the host.'

'Live and let live,' said Bruno. 'Would you like to dance?'

They strolled through the throng, pausing to greet new arrivals, dodging around goats and children, and arrived at the terrace that had become a dance floor, to see all the dancers standing in a ring and grinning as Alphonse performed one of his extraordinary dances to Jefferson Airplane's 'White Rabbit'. Jacqueline looked bewildered as she tried to keep in something like step as Alphonse jerked and bounced happily around her,

342

his elbows jerking out from side to side, his fingers snapping and his head rocking as he belted out the words of the song.

'Did people use to dance like that, back in the old days?' asked Pamela.

'They must have done,' said Bruno. 'Look at the new arrivals.'

For now Céline had taken the floor, twirling around with her arms outstretched, her green robe billowing like a mainsail as the smoke from her joint drifted into the air. Another of the commune originals, tall and gaunt and completely bald and wearing a suit of black velvet, joined her and began to sway. An even older couple with white hair stepped onto the floor and began to jive.

'I'm not sure I can do any of those dances,' said Pamela. 'But let's try.'

The last echoes of 'Feed your head' were fading, to be replaced by Eric Clapton's 'Leyla' as Bruno and Pamela stepped forward. Bruno encouraged others in the surrounding crowd to join them, and soon it seemed everyone was dancing, including the Mayor and Xavier and René and Gilbert from the bar with their wives. The Mayor cut in on Bruno, took Pamela in his arms and began what looked like a slow foxtrot, leaving Bruno to join Jacqueline just a moment before half the rugby team descended on her.

'Alphonse said he had to light the fire,' she said. 'Isn't he bizarre? You wonder how Max grew up so normal in a place like this.'

The music faded and the boom of a great gong sounded. People turned to see Alphonse standing by the bonfire, holding up a large brass disc and beating it again so that the sound echoed back and forth across the hollow. Even the goats stopped their chewing and stared. Céline walked down to stand beside him. Alphonse laid down the gong and picked up a large stick, its tip black and sticky with oil.

'Friends and family, everyone here, we are all here because of Max, and in this commune we do not grieve the passing, we celebrate the life. So we dance and sing and feast in his honour. I raised Max and I loved him, and his memory will always be with me, as it will be with you, and I'm grateful for the warmth he brought to all our lives. Now I'd like all the family of our commune to come down here and join me.'

They came to stand with Alphonse and Céline as the darkness gathered and Alphonse lit his torch. Céline bent to the floor by the bonfire and pulled out a sheaf of similar torches, handing each one to a member of the family, and they all held them against Alphonse's flame until half a dozen were flaring against the darkening sky, casting red glows that flickered over the faces of the family while the heady scent of roasting meat drifted across the crowd. It felt pagan, almost barbaric, but somehow deeply familiar to Bruno, as though this was how all celebrations and events must have been in the past, centuries of roasted lambs and fires and wine, before the age of electricity, when there was only fire to light the darkness.

Alphonse and Céline thrust their brands into the base of the bonfire, and then one after the other the rest of the family followed suit. Hesitantly at first but then with growing vigour the fire began to rise up the tall sticks, delicate blue flickerings at first and then flaring into yellow and then into thrusting, eager red flames four metres high, towering above the heads of the family who stepped steadily further and further back.

'Farewell, Max,' called Alphonse, and turned to embrace Céline, and then all his children and family, and led them back to the wine and the roasting lambs and the throng of friends, all lit by the raging fire.

Stéphane and Raoul were the carvers, neatly severing the heads and legs by the light of oil lamps and the distant bonfire, before slicing the meat into hearty portions. Alphonse was brandishing a massive ladle, serving cous-cous from a giant *fait-tout* cauldron, and Bruno had been recruited to help Xavier open the massed ranks of wine bottles the guests had brought. Pamela was at the next table, tossing vast bowls of salad with olive oil and the commune's own wine vinegar. Fabiola was bandaging the skinned knee of a weeping small boy who had tripped over one of the young goats, and Jacqueline was still dancing.

When the crowds were all served, and Bruno

and Pamela and the other servers began to feed themselves, the few available chairs were all taken. Bruno tucked a bottle of wine under each arm, his plate in one hand and a stack of plastic glasses in the other, and joined Dominique and Stéphane sitting on the grass. Pamela brought her plate atop a large bowl of salad with one of Alphonse's loaves under one arm and a roll of paper towels under the other. Alphonse had turned down the volume so the Beatles' White Album was a distant backdrop.

'This is a wonderful way to eat but I feel I'm back in the Middle Ages,' said Pamela, giving up on the feeble plastic forks and starting to eat with her fingers. Bruno handed her his knife, knowing it would make little difference. He had been to such events before, and reached into a side pocket of his cargo pants and brought out a fistful of foil packets, emblazoned with a lobster and each containing a moistened towel.

'I get these by the box at the start of every summer and never go to a picnic without them,' he said. 'The Middle Ages might have been different if they'd had them. But I know what you mean, feeling that we're going back in time at a feast like this, feeling that this is how it must have been for our ancestors. Maybe that's why we enjoy it.'

Looking out over Alphonse's strange property, he saw Fabiola and Jacqueline squeezed into benches at the same table with the rugby team, laughing and chatting. The Mayor was at a table with Alphonse and Céline and some of the original commune members.

'You're like a mother hen,' grinned Pamela. 'Don't worry, all your chickens are happily taken care of and enjoying themselves. The guardian of St Denis can relax for once.'

'I was just a bit worried about Fabiola, but she seems to be fitting in fine and meeting people.'

'She's a pretty girl, despite that scar, and since she doesn't pay much attention to it, other people don't get embarrassed and after a while you forget about it. It's like having red hair. I hated it when I was a girl and thought everybody was looking at me all the time, but then you realise they aren't, and if they are it doesn't matter.'

'Really?' Bruno asked. 'I thought your hair must always have been that glorious auburn-bronze colour.'

'It was brighter when I was little. Carrot-top they called me, and sometimes Ginger. I had an uncle who used to pretend to light his cigarette from it.'

'They used to call me "dwarf" and "shorty" and other names because I didn't really grow until I was fifteen,' said Dominique. 'Except Max. He never called me names and never let other people do so, not when he was around.'

'You know you had me worried for a while, when you went off to the *lycée*,' said Stéphane. 'I thought you and Max were getting far too serious for your age.'

'Silly old dad,' she smiled, putting a fond hand on his knee. 'It was never like that with Max. He was much more like a brother.'

'So you didn't mind when Max took up with Jacqueline?' Bruno asked.

'Not like you think. But I can't say I was happy about it. She was quite cruel to him at first, dating that other guy, the American. Max used to confide in me and I didn't like what I heard at first.'

'She seems to be over it now,' Pamela said in a low voice, gesturing over to the dome where Jacqueline was laughing at her table. 'But I think she was upset. She's been throwing herself into her work. I took her some coffee earlier today and she was upstairs asleep, but the table was full of work, all her wine books and thick files about vineyards and companies. There was lots on that Bondino group, the one with the young American. Since she wants to be in the wine business, I'm surprised she dropped him.'

Bruno looked sharply at Pamela. 'When you say she had lots on the Bondinos, how do you mean?'

'Well, I didn't really look, but annual reports, files of press clippings, lots of loose photos of the family. There were a couple of really thick files as well as the one that was open. I suppose she got them all from the internet, doing some research when she started dating him.'

'Is that something you ever did, research someone you were seeing?'

'That was before the internet and the age of Google,' she smiled. 'But yes, you ask around your friends, try and find out something about someone who could be important to you. It's human nature.'

'What you describe sounds a lot more than that. Family photos, thick files.'

'Yes, I was surprised. It struck me as being like a special research project. Real photos, not just portraits but groups of people, like family snaps, some quite old from what looked like the Thirties and Forties. But I think you can get real photos made from computer images these days.'

Bruno nodded. It was more than strange for Jacqueline to go to that much trouble for a guy she'd dated briefly and then dropped. But he was rich. Maybe that was it. Despite her affair with Max, she was thinking of Bondino and his money. Or perhaps she was hoping to make her career in the Bondino firm. That would make sense. But all these photos suggested something different, more personal than just researching a company for a job prospect. Even beyond her manipulative ways there was something about Jacqueline that troubled him. He'd have to question her again, maybe get a look at those files.

Dominique was gathering up the used paper plates and putting them into a big black plastic bag. Stéphane hauled Pamela to her feet and back to the dance floor where the music was now Beach Boys surfing songs. Alphonse's collection seemed to stop at about the time he moved down to start the commune. Dominique gave her hand to Bruno and they went off to join the dancers where Alphonse and Céline once more held the floor.

'Max would have loved this,' said Dominique. 'It's just his kind of party.'

The music changed to Françoise Hardy, *Tous les Garçons et les Filles*, and as Alphonse cut in to dance with Dominique, Bruno found Pamela and took her in his arms.

'This is rather more my kind of music,' Pamela said. 'I never really enjoyed the bouncy stuff.'

'Just wait,' he said. 'I know Alphonse's music. Next it will be Charles Trenet from the 1940s and then some slow numbers from Juliette Gréco and Yves Montand.'

'Better still,' she said, and spun away, still holding his hand, to turn a stately pirouette before coming back into his arms. In the firelight with her fine skin and clear complexion, she looked impossibly young and Bruno felt the supple play of a horsewoman's lithe muscles under the light touch of his hands.

'I never thought of you as a dancer, with all that energetic rugby and tennis,' she said.

'You forget the hunting,' he said. 'The patience, the silence of the woods, the long slow stalking.'

'Oh no, Bruno. I'd never forget the hunting,' she replied. She was smiling and moved in towards him, her cheek close to his. He shifted his head a fraction to nestle his cheek against hers, and he felt the slightest tremble under his hands. Yves Montand was singing *Feuilles Mortes*. He heard Pamela singing along quietly in English. 'The autumn leaves of red and gold . . .' She had a sweet voice, soft and low.

'Did you mean to kiss me, the night after your dinner?' she asked, almost whispering.

'I didn't mean to,' he answered quickly, almost despite himself. He wanted to tell the truth. 'But then I did, very much. It seemed to come from nowhere.'

'Yes, I know,' she said. 'It seemed that way to me as well. Then I felt sorry that we stopped.'

He bent his head and kissed her neck, and felt her hands tighten on his back.

'I cursed myself for a timid fool all the way back to town,' he said. 'And then Bondino took over.'

'Ah yes, Bondino and Jacqueline. And poor Max. What a mess that girl has made.' She paused and they swayed together to the music, oblivious to the other dancers. 'Do you think we get any more sensible about love as we get older?'

'Not more sensible, no. It loses none of its power,' he said. 'Perhaps it's more quiet, more subtle, but stronger. We grow more cautious, maybe. As you and I have been more cautious.'

'Is that what it is?' she whispered. He felt her lips brush his cheek and her fingers play gently

351

with the curls at the nape of his neck. 'Or do we just think about it and talk about it more?'

'I think about it far too much,' he said, and kissed her. This time neither one of them turned away as the firelight slowly died and the stars became brilliant above.

CHAPTER 40

Between his paperwork and phone calls, Bruno had spent the morning making the arrangements for Cresseil's funeral. A Resistance veteran who had then fought his way into Germany in 1945 with the French army, he deserved military honours. Now as the *Mairie* clock chimed the last quarter before three, Bruno went down to the basement and brought out the flags and the *Route Barrée* signs for the small parade from the church to the war memorial, then to the old man's final resting place beside his Annette in the town cemetery.

The church was almost full when Bruno slipped in at the side door. Raoul, who worked part-time as a pall-bearer when he wasn't selling his wines in the market, was taking a final smoke with the other men in black ties from the funeral parlour. The coffin stood on trestles before the altar, a cushion on a stool beside it that bore the campaign and Resistance medals Bruno had brought from the old man's cottage. The Mayor and Xavier with their wives were in the front row with the Baron, and behind them a group of strangers who must be the cousins. Bruno nodded at Alphonse.

The organ was playing some doleful music that Bruno learned from the programme was a Choral Prelude by Bach. He scanned the crowd for Pamela. After the previous evening's embrace, she had left him with a lingering kiss and a look of promise in her eyes as she left the wake with Fabiola and Jacqueline. He felt a surge of excitement as he spotted her, her face half-shrouded by the dark shawl that covered her head. Jacqueline sat beside her, her head uncovered. As he studied them, the distinction was sharp between the mature and lovely woman and the more conventional prettiness of the girl. As though sensing his gaze, Pamela turned and caught his eye. She smiled and raised a discreet eyebrow, as if to ask how their relationship would now unfold. As he nodded to her in return, he felt a sense of relief that she had no regrets at their growing romance. And nor, he knew, did he.

Father Sentout, resplendent in full robes, came from the vestry to shake hands with the Mayor and the cousins before standing at the head of the coffin and beginning the service. Bruno slipped out again to ensure that Jean-Pierre and Bachelot and Marie-Louise, each almost as old as the man they were burying, were all ready with their flags. The small guard of honour from the Gendarmes was lined up with the school band for the short march to the war memorial.

As he went back to the main doors of the church, they opened and J-J emerged. 'Saw you leave,' he said and handed Bruno a computer printout. 'Here's that reply you wanted from Québec.' Bruno had sent him a text message the previous evening, asking him to send a routine 'Anything Known?' query on Jacqueline to the Québec police. 'It looks like she's clean,' J-J added. 'Which means she's in better shape than I am. The Prefect is furious with me and we've got a fancy lawyer threatening to sue me personally for wrongful arrest of Bondino.'

'Still no attestation of wrongful death from the pathologist?' Bruno asked. He resisted the temptation to remind J-J that he'd warned him of this.

'No, so they can't appoint a *juge d'instruction* and I can't hold Bondino any longer. I've got his finger-prints, and I think the DNA will show his hair under the dead man's fingernails. But until the pathologist's report there's no crime as yet so he's free, and I'm in the *merde*. I'm so deep in it that I've had to come down here to apologise to your Capitaine Duroc for misusing his Gendarmerie. The Prefect insisted. But I'm still not sure I'm wrong.'

'This reply from Québec came back very fast. I wasn't expecting an answer for a couple of days.'

'I rang our friend the Brigadier, thinking he could get it faster. I got this back within a couple of hours.'

The music swelled and the doors opened. Led

by Father Sentout and a boy in a white robe bearing a tall cross, Raoul and the other pall-bearers emerged with the coffin. The flags all rose in salute and led the procession to the war memorial across the bridge. The Mayor came out with Cresseil's medals on the cushion and the Gendarmes lined up behind him. The Baron followed with Cresseil's elderly cousins from Tulle. He caught Bruno's eye, discreetly giving him a thumbs-up. He must have reached a deal to buy their claim. The school band struck up 'Le Chant des Partisans', the Resistance anthem, and led the rest of the congregation behind the bobbing flags of France, of St Denis and of the Cross of Lorraine, the wartime symbol of Free France.

Rollo the headmaster ensured that each of the walkers from the retirement home was accompanied by a youngster to help them along. The old people scanned one another's faces as they hobbled from the church. Bruno wondered if their glances indicated relief that this was not their time while weighing which of their number might be next.

Bruno had placed the town's wreath in readiness before the statue of the French soldier from the Great War with the gleaming brass eagle perched above. There was a second wreath from the *Compagnons de la Résistance* and a third from the *Anciens Combatants*. Bruno felt a sudden glow of pride that his town and his nation still took the deaths of such old patriots so seriously, still honoured the ancient virtues of patriotism and courage, and still insisted that the young remembered at what price their liberties had been bought. It was a fine community that could generate such mutual affection between young and old strangers as had grown between Max and Cresseil. Bruno felt a weight building in his throat as he thought that Cresseil's last sight on earth might have been the floating body of the young man he had come to love like a son.

The flags dipped in salute, the Mayor laid his wreath, and then Bachelot the shoemender and veteran Gaullist laid the wreath from the *Combatants*, and his lifelong enemy Jean-Pierre of the Communist *Franc-Tireurs et Partisans* laid the wreath from the *Anciens Combatants*. It was the sort of compromise that made French politics work, and that was only made possible by the forbearance of Marie-Louise. A courier for the Resistance, she had been arrested by the Gestapo at the age of fourteen and sent to Buchenwald, and in Bruno's eyes had thus suffered more for France than Jean-Pierre and Bachelot together. But Marie-Louise never made a fuss, always volunteered for everything, and considered all the young people of St Denis as the grand-children she had never had. She stood watching impassively as the two old men straightened their backs and saluted and returned to their places. As the band struck up the *Marseillaise*, tears rolled down her cheeks.

The national anthem ended and the pall-bearers loaded the coffin into the hearse for the short drive to the cemetery. Bruno gathered up the flags, and carried them all back into the basement of the *Mairie*. Then he went upstairs to his office and took out the printout that J-J had given him. That reminded him. He picked up the phone, checking the number on the card in his drawer, and called the Brigadier in Paris.

An aide answered. When Bruno gave his name he was surprised to hear: 'You're on the approved list. I'll connect you now.' And then the Brigadier was on the line.

'Our friend J-J is in trouble,' Bruno began.

'I know. The American Ambassador came in to see the Minister and lodged a complaint. I'm taking care of it. Don't worry, the Minister understands that it wouldn't be wise to dissuade our police from showing a maximum of zeal. And I gather that thanks to you, this young American didn't even spend a night in jail. There's not a lot they can complain about. Did you get my message for you from Québec?'

'Yes, Sir. I'm looking at it now.'

'*Ça va*. Glad to help. And don't forget, there's a job for you here if you want one. And there's a message from another friend of yours on the Minister's staff, Chief Inspector Perrault. I think you knew she was on assignment in Luxembourg? She says she's looking forward to seeing you for the weekend of the rugby international against

Scotland. I got four tickets, you and J-J, Perrault and me. Dinner on me afterwards at the Tour d'Argent.'

The phone went down in Paris, but if the Brigadier said J-J would be all right, Bruno was prepared to believe him. Isabelle was another matter. He still felt a frisson of excitement at the thought of seeing her again, but he feared there was little future in it. Perhaps the invitation was the Brigadier's way of tempting him to give up St Denis and move to Paris to join his team. Or perhaps Isabelle and the Brigadier had planned it together, not understanding the bonds that kept him in Périgord. He could never leave Gigi locked up in some tiny Paris apartment. Bruno sighed and then braced himself and hauled his thoughts back to the present.

But then he thought of the new bond with Pamela that was growing and might also help to keep him in Périgord. He had no idea where their – he hunted for a word that was more than flirtation and less than affair – where their liaison was heading. It was the suspense, the prospect of different possibilities and new directions, that made it so exciting. So wherever it was heading, he was looking forward to the journey. But it wouldn't be today, he caught himself. Not when he had work to do.

He looked again at the email from Québec. Nothing known against Jacqueline Duplessis, which meant no criminal record and given the Brigadier's contacts probably meant nothing suspected against her. A blameless life. Bruno read on idly through the raw facts he had already scribbled into his note-book, date of birth, address, next of kin, mother's maiden name . . . And then he stopped. Her mother's maiden name was not listed in the pass-port. He looked again at the printout from Québec: mother's maiden name Sophia Maria Bondino; nationality United States of America.

Suddenly everything that Bruno thought he knew shifted into a different shape, and he went back to his file of material on the history of the Bondino family and its feuds and began to read carefully, taking brief notes. He checked his watch. Jacqueline would be working at the *cave* for another three hours and more. He rang Nathalie at the *cave* and asked her to check the files to find when Jacqueline had first applied to work there. He called Pamela to be sure she was back from the funeral and then his phone rang. He reached for it, expecting Nathalie's call, but froze when he heard another, far more familiar voice.

'I'm calling from a phone booth at a service station on the way back from Luxembourg,' Isabelle said. 'I don't want this call showing up on my records because I shouldn't be telling you this but it might help get J-J out of trouble.'

'Go on,' he said.

'We got hold of the bank documents for Agricolae, which is what I was sent here to do. Don't even ask how. But there's a big payment from Bondino, a hundred and twenty thousand euros, a wire transfer from their American bank on July the seventh. J-J needs to know about it, and you need to find out whether Agricolae was really the target of that fire because this means it might have been aimed at Bondino.'

'But we solved the arson case,' Bruno said. One part of his brain was focused on the conversation and the case. But elsewhere emotions were churning at the sound of her voice.

'I know. And J-J thinks your arsonist was murdered by Bondino. This deal between Bondino and Agricolae could be the link J-J needs to prove it. I've sent you a copy of the bank transfer by post so there's no computer traces.'

'Thanks, I'll let him know,' Bruno said, wondering why Isabelle had called him rather than J-J. 'Why not call him directly?'

'Not wise, given the job I do and the trouble he's in,' she said.

'The Brigadier just told me J-J's in the clear.'

'I'm glad to hear it. All the same, it's safer to go through you.' She paused. 'Besides, I wanted to hear your voice.'

Bruno closed his eyes. 'I like hearing yours, too. I thought I might hear from you earlier.'

'I had a lot of work to do, and I was thinking,' she said. 'And I reached a conclusion.'

'Go on.' Bruno was concentrating intensely, trying to divine every last scrap of meaning from the tone of her voice, the pauses between her words.

'If I see you again, it will be in Paris. That's where my life is going to be.' The words came out in a rush.

'It wouldn't work in Paris,' said Bruno. 'I don't fit there.'

'Not even for a visit?'

And prolong the agony again? Bruno shook his head in silence.

'We'll see. You don't have to spend all your life down there in the country,' she said. More silence. 'I miss you.' And she rang off.

Bruno took a deep breath, knowing his pulse was racing and telling himself that he had done the right thing by not responding to Isabelle's invitation. It was the sensible reaction, the wise decision on his part, but a part of him wanted to throw wisdom to the winds and take the next train to Paris and embrace Isabelle and all her risks.

The phone interrupted his thoughts. Nathalie called to say she had checked the files; they had received Jacqueline's application on May 30. That was six weeks before the Bondino payment to Agricolae. But it was after she had met Bondino in the professor's office and realised that he was heading for this part of France. So what had triggered Jacqueline's decision to come to work in St Denis? Bruno grabbed his cap and the keys to his van and ran down the stairs of the *Mairie*, stopping only to pose a question at the Hôtel St Denis and to phone J-J and ask him to meet at Pamela's place as soon as he could.

CHAPTER 41

Pamela was doing her accounts at the kitchen table when he arrived. A stack of bills and papers sat in front of her, and her glasses perched on the end of her nose. She looked up, startled, as he knocked and opened the door and then smiled to see him, and came forward to place her hands on his cheeks and kiss him on the lips. He responded with enthusiasm, hugged her close to him, then moved his head back.

'I'd like to carry on kissing you for some time but sadly this is a business visit,' he said. 'You know those family photos and files that you saw in Jacqueline's house? I need to look at them before she gets back so I'll need your key, please. It's official – J-J's on his way.'

'What on earth . . . ?' She whipped off her glasses and patted her hair, although it looked fine to Bruno. 'Is this legal? Do you need a warrant or something?'

'I'm working and this is official. You're the property owner. Did Jacqueline sign a lease?'

'Not yet.'

'Then it's legal. Come on, we haven't much time.'

She took a key from a row of hooks on the wall and led the way. 'Can you tell me what this is about?'

'I just found out that her mother's maiden name is Bondino. I think she must be related to the American, some kind of cousin. There was a bitter family feud over the ownership of the vineyard, really bitter. So I need to see those files and photos. And since most of them will be in English I'll need your help.'

Jacqueline's closed laptop was on the table, a row of her wine books lined up behind it. In a fat briefcase below the table Bruno found the files, all unmarked, but full of material about the Bondino family and its company. In the first file were photographs of people and on the back of each one their names were pencilled. Several depicted the man he knew from magazine photos as Bondino's father, the head of the company. Some showed him as a vigorous youth. In one photo he was holding a baby girl in the crook of his arm. On the back it said simply 'FXB, Maman, 1957.' That would be Francis X. Bondino, Fernando's father. Maman would presumably be Jacqueline's mother.

'This file is all about the Bondino company, business plans, accounts, revenue projections for this year and next year,' Pamela said, suddenly a model of brisk efficiency. 'I wonder how she got hold of that? It's all marked "confidential" but it looks pretty boring.'

'Let me see,' said Bruno. It was all small print and columns and charts and it meant nothing to him. He leafed back to the first page which was headed by a short list of names. It was dated August 20 of the current year. That was last month. How had she got hold of that? 'What's that say?' he asked, pointing at a phrase at the head of the list.

'That says "Distribution Restricted" and it lists FXB and FXB Junior, and then two more sets of initials identified as the finance director and sales director. I think that means they're the only four people supposed to have this, so how did Jacqueline get it?'

'I don't know, but she was already in France by then so she must somehow have obtained it here, maybe from Bondino.' Bruno paused. 'Can you think of some reason why he might give this confidential stuff to her?'

'Maybe she just took it,' Pamela said. 'Or maybe this was what she was after, here on the next page. It's about us in St Denis.'

'What?' Bruno came to look over her shoulder. 'What's it say about St Denis?'

'It's a report from our own Research Station on drought-resistant vines, along with the photocopy of a bank transfer from Bondino to a company called Agricolae for a hundred and twenty thousand euros to finance the research here in St Denis. There's another bank transfer, two hundred thousand euros to a Paris company called Dupuy. The transfers are dated July this year.'

'No wonder Bondino was angry about the Research Station crops being burned,' said Bruno. 'The research he was funding had gone up in smoke.'

'How did Jacqueline get hold of all this? It's like espionage. Do you think she told Max about Bondino and the Research Station?'

'That's a very good question. What's in the next file?'

It contained the details of a lawsuit, Bondino versus Bondino, that started in 1957 in California. Pamela sifted through the legal papers, affidavits, statements, notices of discovery and came to a clipping from the *San Francisco Examiner*, dated March 11, 1958. The headline read 'Bondino Will Upheld' and she began giving a rough translation as she read.

'It begins: 'The elder son of deceased Napa Valley wine magnate Silvio Bondino lost his share of the multi-million dollar inheritance when the District Court ruled that a disputed will was valid.' Shall I go on?'

'No, this is familiar stuff. That battle over the will was where the feud began. It replaced an old will that divided the Bondino estate evenly between the two brothers, but then this surprise new will turned up,' said Bruno, riffling through more photographs, some so old they were in shades of brown rather than black and white. Others had crinkled edges like ancient postcards. He held up one, an aged print in sepia. 'Here's the founder of the family fortunes, Silvio himself as a young man. He arrived in California from Italy as a babe in arms back in the late nineteenth century.'

'Quite a handsome man.'

'A tough one, too. He kept the family business going all through Prohibition when alcohol was banned, and then again through the Depression. He had two sons. The younger one now runs one of the world's biggest wine firms after inheriting everything and the elder son was left nothing in the will that he claimed was a forgery.'

'Here's another clipping – "Disinherited Bondino Son Dies in Car Crash; Foul Play Not Suspected." Somebody didn't agree with that verdict,' Pamela broke in. 'The clipping is attached to a bill from a lawyer and another to a private detective for inquiries into the car crash. The lawyer's bill is for three thousand two hundred dollars, but I imagine that was worth quite a sum back in nineteen fifty-eight. And here's the detective's report. The last page says: "We regret to inform you that our inquiries have proved inconclusive."

'The dead man's widow brought a private lawsuit claiming her husband had been murdered. It got nowhere and she ran out of money,' Bruno said. 'I was reading up about this earlier. But look, this photo, it's the same baby girl, dated nineteen fifty-seven, but this time with a woman, and on the back it says *Maman et Grand-mère*. And if you look at this family photo of everybody including old Silvio, from Christmas, nineteen fifty-six, the woman listed as *Grand-mère* is being embraced by *Grand-père*. But look at *Grand-père's* face and compare it with this portrait shot. It's the same man, so Jacqueline's *grand-père* was the elder brother, the one who should have inherited but for the disputed will. You can confirm that from that photo of him in your news clipping. *Grand-mère* was his widow, the woman who brought the failed lawsuit. So Jacqueline is the grand-daughter of the disinherited elder brother who then died in a suspicious car crash. See if you can find any names for *Grandmère* and *Maman*.'

'Right here on the private detective's bill, Mrs Maria Bondino, four two four nine Sunset Drive, Sausalito. What very long roads the Americans have. She must be *Grand-mère*. Look, here's a carbon copy of a letter from Maria to Francis, dated April the fourth, nineteen fifty-eight. That's after the court verdict, asking for money "to ensure the education of your niece Sophia". So that's the baby girl in the photo, who presumably grew up to marry a French-Canadian called Duplessis and to become Jacqueline's mother.'

'That makes Jacqueline the great-niece of our own Francis X. Bondino, the great man whose wise old face beams at us from all these company brochures. And his son would be Jacqueline's cousin, as well as her lover.'

'Her lover?' said Pamela, startled. 'You didn't tell me that. Was that while she was seeing Max or before?'

'Maybe while she was seeing Max, I'm not sure. But I do think that she set out deliberately to meet the younger Bondino. She knew exactly who he was and what he was doing in St Denis. She knew that she was sleeping with her own cousin and she knew all about the family feud. But I don't think Fernando had the slightest idea who she was or that they were related. The two branches of the family seem to have been bitterly estranged.'

'That makes it sound rather sinister.'

'Indeed it does,' said Bruno. 'What's in that next file?'

'More press clippings, but new ones, all about the Bondino company, printed out from the internet. Here's one from *Business Week* in March of this year about production problems in Australia because of the drought. And here's an interview with Bondino from a wine magazine in May, with a paragraph marked in the margin. It's about "exploring new opportunities in Europe where the industry has yet to benefit from consolidation". He mentions France and Italy and Eastern Europe. And here's another bit she's marked, about "unsustainable business model in the Bordeaux region with too many small producers making too many wines of variable quality and no consistency of product". It says here that Fernando Bondino graduated from Stanford business school.'

'So she knew back in May that Bondino was coming to Europe,' mused Bruno. 'And Hubert got her letter asking to come and work for him at the end of May. She came to St Denis on purpose, knowing that Bondino would also be here. But what did she have in mind?'

'This file looks interesting. It's about the history of wine-growing in the Dordogne and Vézère valleys by some professor at a university in California. It says he has the Bondino chair of wine studies, and she underlined the concluding paragraph that says: "History therefore suggests that the Dordogne and Vézère valleys represent the last unexploited opportunities for quality wine production in Europe, with excellent climate and terrain and inexpensive land prices." So Bondino decides to come here to St Denis just after his own professor delivers this paper. It's dated in April this year.'

Bruno looked out when he heard the crunching of gravel in the courtyard as J-J braked his car. The detective opened the door but remained in the driver's seat, his phone to his ear.

CHAPTER 42

J-J burst through the door, beaming with pleasure. 'We've got him. I was right all along,' he trumpeted. 'DNA evidence. Those hairs under Max's nails. They definitely come from Bondino.'

'But those hairs could have come from the fight at the bar earlier that evening,' Bruno objected.

'Don't you remember? He said Max never laid a hand on him. It's on tape from the interrogation. He says he punched Max on the nose but Max never laid a finger on him in the fight. So how can he explain away his own hair?'

'I don't know,' said Bruno. 'But the reason I called you here is that this Canadian girl is a lot more than she seems. Look at these family photos and these files – she's Bondino's cousin, and she knew it but he didn't. And it looks like she's been stalking him. Anyway, J-J, this is Pamela – you two meet at last!'

The two exchanged hand-shakes, smiling.

'Pamela can explain it all but I'm going to look around because Jacqueline could be back within the hour.'

Bruno found the garbage bin in the kitchen. It was empty but there was a large wicker basket beside the fire that seemed full of old newspapers. He fished among the first few, using his pen to sort through them, but they just seemed to be discarded copies of *Sud-Ouest*. He stood up, but one of the papers came with him, somehow stuck to his pen. He tried to shake it off, without success. He looked, and there were two strips of adhesive tape sticking his pen to the newsprint. Trying to peel them away he found five more small strips of the tape, about eight or ten centimetres long, all stuck to the paper.

'That's odd,' he said. Pamela looked across. He pointed to the strips of tape.

'Gift-wrapping,' she said at once. 'That's how I do it. If I'm wrapping a present, I cut off several strips of tape at a time so they're ready when I fold the paper.'

'No sign of wrapping paper and no little scraps,' said Bruno. 'The only present I know she gave was when she brought me that bottle of wine, and that was wrapped at Hubert's *cave*.'

'Maybe she was practising,' said Pamela. 'If the kitchen bin is empty, she may already have dumped stuff in the main garbage can outside. I'll take a look when I've finished explaining these files to J-J.'

Bruno went upstairs to find two bedrooms and a small bathroom filled with the usual feminine toiletries, soaps and shampoos and conditioners, toothpaste, combs and hairbrush. He took a careful look at these, but saw only the girl's own long blond hairs. Nothing else of note. Jacqueline used one of the bedrooms to sleep in, the other as a dressing room with her clothes and shoes in the cupboard. One item caught Bruno's eye, an old St Denis rugby shirt hanging forlornly from a nail. It must have belonged to Max. The chest of drawers was empty. The other room had a flimsy nightgown on the bed and a dressing gown hanging on a hook on the back of the door. A small dressing table stood by the window, stacked with cosmetics. He looked in the drawers, saw underwear and stockings. But then he saw something else, tucked away at the back, and pulled out a tightly rolled plastic bag that contained a spare hairbrush.

'J-J, can you come up here a moment?' he called. When the big Commissaire came into the room, Bruno pointed silently to the plastic bag in the drawer.

'Look carefully and you'll see short dark hairs on that brush which don't belong to Jacqueline. My guess is they're Bondino's. She told me he spent one night in her old hotel room, but just before I came here I went to check with the manageress, and she said it was two or three nights. Whenever Max wasn't with her, Bondino was. He could have used her hairbrush then. Or maybe it's his. So it's possible that Bondino never laid a hand on Max, just as he said, whatever the

DNA evidence might suggest. Somebody else put those hairs under Max's nails to incriminate Bondino. I think you'd better get your forensics boys over here.'

'That's pretty far-fetched, Bruno. I suppose your motive is that family feud and those files Pamela was explaining to me,' said J-J, looking through the items on the dressing table. 'What's that? A nail file?'

A nail file might be just the thing to put Bondino's hair under Max's fingernails, thought Bruno, as J-J pointed at the thin plastic sleeve on the dressing table.

'Got any evidence gloves in your car?'

'In the glove compartment. Help yourself,' said J-J, thumbing a number into his phone to call his forensics team.

Out in the courtyard, Pamela was poking through a large yellow plastic bag that she had pulled from the dustbin. 'No wrapping paper, but more of these strips of tape,' she called. Bruno waved an acknowledgement and grabbed two sets of gloves, ran back up the stairs and handed a pair to J-J. He blew into them to loosen the latex, slipped his hands into them and then picked up what turned out not to be a nail file. He eased a long flexible plastic strip from the sleeve.

'A strip of thin plastic protected inside plastic. What on earth could that be?' he asked, holding it up to the window and turning it. Bruno switched on the desk lamp and they looked again.

'Hang on,' said Bruno and darted down the

stairs again and returned with some of the strips of sticky tape that Pamela had rescued, holding them against the light.

'You always get fingerprints on sticky tape,' said J-J.

'Yes, but whose?' said Bruno. He went into the bathroom and came out with some talcum powder, and delicately tapped the bottom of the can, dusting a small amount onto one of the bottles of toilet water on the dressing table. 'Let's assume those are Jacqueline's prints on her scent bottle,' he said, and gently blew away the talc. The ridges of a thumbprint emerged on the glass. He placed one of the adhesive strips alongside it. 'That's the same print, right?'

'Yes, it looks like it,' said J-J dubiously. 'So what's your point?'

'Watch.' Bruno carefully unwrapped a little of the plastic bag and dusted some talcum power onto the handle of the hair-brush and then blew it away. 'That print there will belong to Bondino, and I know why she wanted his prints. His laptop computer has a security device, some kind of sensor that required his fingerprint to unlock it. That's why she needed him in her bed and asleep in her room. She wanted to get into his computer. Some of those files of hers downstairs are confidential business plans and company accounts. Maybe that's what she was after. But if she could fake his prints to get into his computer, what else could she do with them?'

'You think she could have transferred them on to that glass we found at Cresseil's place?' asked J-J.

'That's what the adhesive tape strips were for. I think she lifted the fingerprints from her hairbrush and then put them on the glass. That's one for your forensics team to check when they get here. If that's what she did, there'll be traces of the adhesive on the glass.'

'Hello,' called Pamela from downstairs, above the sound of another car arriving. 'Fabiola's here. There's nothing more in the dustbin, no wrapping paper. Are you two both upstairs?' Bruno called back and heard her footsteps coming up the stairs.

'Those bits of sticky tape,' he said when she came into the bedroom. 'I think they were used to lift fingerprints from one thing and transfer them to something else.'

'Oh yes?' she said, not in the least surprised. 'I think I remember something like that from one of the IRA bomb trials back in Britain, you remember, the Northern Ireland troubles. So whose fingerprints do you have?'

'We aren't sure yet,' said Bruno as J-J began working his phone again. 'Let's go down and say hello to Fabiola. I need to find out what's happened with the pathologist's report.'

Fabiola squeezed herself out of the loaded car. There was a suitcase on the floor of the passenger's side, a cardboard box on the seat with a large stuffed plastic bag atop it that tumbled into the driver's seat as soon as Fabiola emerged. The rear seats were down and the cargo space stuffed to the brim with suitcases, shopping bags and cardboard boxes.

'That's my life,' she grinned. 'Everything I own is in that car.'

'I'll help you unload,' said Bruno, hearing the sound of J-J's heavy tread coming down the wooden stairs. 'But first we need to know about the pathologist's report. J-J, you should listen to this.'

'The *attestation* has been filed,' Fabiola said as J-J joined them. 'Accidental death by asphyxiation, but with a cautious appendix saying the blow to the head was inflicted after death. So you have no murder.'

J-J let out a vast explosion of breath and his shoulders sagged. '*Putain, putain, putain . . .*'

'It looks like we may have another crime, though, planting false evidence,' said Bruno.

'Not to mention wasting police time and dropping me in the *merde*,' added J-J. 'But how did she come to be at the death scene to plant those fake hairs?'

'You mean the ones I found under Max's nails? I don't think there was anything fake about them,' said Fabiola. 'They were real hairs, with follicles on the end. It's not like someone got them from a barber's clippings. Remember, Bruno? I looked at them with a magnifying glass.'

'Like these?' asked J-J, holding up a plastic evidence bag that contained the hair brush.

Fabiola looked carefully, and then asked for a magnifying glass. J-J got one from the car, and she looked again, and then pulled out her phone. 'I'm calling my colleague in Bergerac. There's something we can check.'

'Jean-Claude? Listen, it's me. That autopsy we did with the asphyxiation, the one with the long delay over the head wound, can you check something for me? Yes? It's the fingernails. You remember we found hairs in them and follicles. Was there any other alien flesh under the nails, or just the hairs? There seems to be a possibility that the hairs were planted on the corpse. OK, I'll wait for your call. Thanks.'

Fabiola turned back to them. 'He'll let me know. But I can't say I remember anything except the hairs, none of those traces of flesh you usually find if the hairs have been snatched in a struggle.' She looked forlorn. 'I'm sorry, it's my fault,' she went on. 'I wasn't thinking about planted evidence so I didn't look for anything else. I won't make that mistake again.'

'Would that be definitive proof of the hair being planted, if there's no flesh in the nails?' Bruno asked her.

'No, but it's very suggestive,' she replied.

'I think we need a drink,' said Pamela. 'You help Fabiola unload the car and I'll bring the glasses. Ricard for everybody?' They nodded. 'The door to Fabiola's *gîte* is open. I put a new gas canister in the kitchen and some milk and eggs in the refrigerator. The eggs are from Bruno's hens, by the way. Just go straight in and put your stuff wherever you want.'

Two journeys were all it took between them. Fabiola's suitcases were parked upstairs, the boxes of books placed beside the shelves in the sitting room, the plastic bags put on the kitchen counter and the medical bag by the door.

'Look,' said Fabiola when they were done, pointing at a vase filled with flowers on the table. 'Pamela is so kind, welcoming me with flowers. I must go and thank her.' She went across to the refrigerator and opened the door. 'And look at this, orange juice and butter, and coffee and fruit here on the counter. She's too good.'

'She's certainly good,' said Bruno, smiling. 'But remember she's also *Périgordine*. Before you know it you'll have jars of pâté and *rillettes* and preserves and *vin de noix* presented to you by your new neighbours. Don't buy any eggs. I'll bring you some more from my hens. It's the way of things round here.'

Bruno and J-J strolled back to the courtyard as Fabiola went to thank her new landlady. The four of them gathered around Pamela's table where she had been waiting with a tray of drinks. They clinked their glasses in formal welcome to Fabiola, and J-J stole a glance at his watch.

'She'll be here any moment,' said Bruno.

'So will my lads,' J-J said. 'You realise I'm probably going to have to go back to your Capitaine Duroc and ask to use his cells again.'

'You're not taking her direct to Périgueux for questioning?' Bruno asked.

'No murder, so no *juge d'instruction*, and we'll need the forensic report on the hair and fingerprints before we can file any charge. So no, I'm not taking her to Périgueux until I have all my little soldiers lined up on parade. I've already got the American Ambassador filing complaints in Paris. I don't want the Canadian one joining in.'

Fabiola's phone trilled. 'Yes? Jean-Claude? Nothing but the hair and some splinters of wood. No flesh. OK, thanks. Can you make sure the report gets amended to say that? Right. See you, and thanks again.' She looked up at them. 'You heard that.'

'I heard,' said J-J, looking at Bruno. 'Cunning little minx, this Canadian. But why would she want Bondino charged with murder? Is there money in it for her?'

'It's the old family feud. But I don't think there's money involved, not unless she tried to marry Bondino, and then how could she stop the truth coming out that they're cousins? She'd have to present herself as an orphan and persuade her own parents to go along with it. No, greed's not the motive. It's the feud.'

'So she slept with Bondino anyway,' said Pamela. 'Just to find a way to destroy him.'

'Let's ask her,' said Bruno, looking out through the courtyard.

At the end of the lane, a figure appeared on a

bicycle, pedalling briskly, her blond hair streaming out behind her. Pamela rose, put all the glasses on to a tray and took them into the kitchen. 'Come along, Fabiola. I don't think we ought to be here for this, so I'll help you unpack.'

When they had gone, J-J went across to his car, opened the passenger door and took a pair of handcuffs from the glove compartment, and then came to join Bruno. The two men stood and waited until Jacqueline drew up before them. She stepped off her bike and lifted her cheek to Bruno as if to be kissed. Bruno ignored this and took the handlebars in one hand.

'*Bonsoir*, Jacqueline. Commissaire Jalipeau here has some questions for you and I need to see your passport again please.'

Suddenly wary, her eyes darting from Bruno's to J-J's grim face, Jacqueline lifted her shoulder bag from the wicker pannier above the bicycle's rear wheel and fished inside, pulling out her navy blue passport and handing it over. Bruno quickly checked the photo and then with his eyes fixed on hers, put it into the chest pocket of his shirt and fastened the button.

'We now know exactly what happened,' J-J said. 'We know how you put Bondino's fingerprints on to the glass you left at the cottage. We know where you got those bits of his hair that you put under Max's fingernails. We know how you broke into Bondino's computer and downloaded his files. We know how you tried to plant the evidence so that

381

Bondino would be convicted of murder. We know all this and can prove it. My top forensic team will be here shortly and will go over every inch of your house, every item of your clothing, and when you are arrested and in the cells a policewoman will be searching you very thoroughly indeed.'

J-J advanced upon her, taking one arm firmly and opening the handcuffs. 'Do you have anything to say?'

She looked helplessly at Bruno. 'Answer the question,' he told her. 'Do you have anything to say?'

'I don't know,' she said hesitantly, her eyes fixed on J-J's hand-cuffs.

'Well, let's start where you began to lie the last time I asked you about this,' Bruno began. 'You told me you spent one drunken night with Bondino in your hotel room. That wasn't true. You entertained him in your hotel room at least three nights, the hotel tells me. And yet this was your cousin, from the other side of a bitter family feud. You seduced him and got him so drunk that you could get into his computer as he slept it off.'

Jacqueline closed her eyes and shook her head but kept silent.

'We can prove that, from your own computer files,' Bruno said. 'But let's go on to your next lie. You said you left the bar with Max after the fight with Bondino and went to make love in the park by the river and then he left you to go and tread the grapes by himself. That wasn't true, was it?'

'No,' she shook her head. 'I went with him and we trod the grapes together.'

'Was that where you made love, at Cresseil's place?'

She nodded, biting her lip.

'Did you go into the house, to the bedroom upstairs?'

'No,' she said quietly. 'The old man was a light sleeper. And the dog . . .'

'In the open air, then? Were you telling the truth about that?'

'Yes I mean No,' she said urgently, her eyes very wide, a trace of panic as her voice rose. 'We were in the vat, while we were treading the grapes. We made love in the vat.'

'So what happened?' Bruno asked quietly. 'Why did Max suffocate but not you?'

'We were kissing . . .' she began. She stopped and closed her eyes. Bruno and J-J just looked at her and waited till her voice started again. Her eyes opened but seemed to focus on nothing.

'My head was over the side of the vat and I was holding the rim with both hands. Max was behind me, he was . . . he was very passionate. Then he was slumped on me, a deadweight. I was trapped, I couldn't move.'

She burst into tears, but let them fall down her cheeks. 'I couldn't move and he didn't respond. I thought he was asleep or that he'd passed out. I didn't know what was happening and even though my head was over the side of the vat I was

383

dizzy, like I was fainting. I managed to thrust him away and his head hit the side with a great thudding sound and I panicked. I climbed out and I think I was screaming because the old man came out of his house and saw me at the door of the barn and pushed me aside and went in. I saw him climb the steps and then he crumpled and fell, right from the top of the steps. He just fell and lay there.'

'So why did you not call the emergency services, the *pompiers*, the ambulance?' asked Bruno.

She shook her head. 'I don't know. It was that damned dog, yapping. It was hardly able to move, its back legs crippled, but it kept creeping across to the old man and yapping and howling and turning to snarl at me. I couldn't think. I couldn't shut it up. I didn't know what to do.'

'So you killed the dog.'

'I hit it on the head with a big stone to knock it out but the stone was so big . . .'

'Your lover was dead. The old man was dead. The dog was dead,' Bruno said flatly. 'You came here to St Denis determined to ruin Bondino's project. Max's death gave you the perfect opportunity. You began to work out in a very cold-blooded way how this could be made to damage your cousin, to have him blamed for murder and take your revenge on the family.'

'You don't know what they did to us,' she snapped back, her eyes suddenly ablaze. 'They arranged the killing of my grandfather, they cheated my mother out of what was hers. They built their fortune on fraud. They're the killers, not me. I didn't kill anybody.'

She stared defiantly into Bruno's face.

'And you know something else,' she went on. 'They're going to destroy this precious town of yours. They're going to take your land and take your water and make their usual mass-produced crap. They're going to swallow you all up, just like they devour everything else.'

Bruno just smiled and slowly shook his head. Into the silence came the sound of a distant car, drawing closer. J-J let out a deep breath and looked up the lane and said: 'My boys.' Then he looked down at Jacqueline and snapped his handcuffs on to her wrists.

CHAPTER 43

The leaves were thick on the ground at the edge of the wood, a fringe of browns and yellows and the occasional splash of red, starting to cover the charred expanse of the field. Further across the barren soil, the ruins of the large hut were slowly crumbling under the rains and wind. Bruno felt himself shiver slightly as he remembered the crumping sound of the petrol can exploding and watching Albert slump to his knees in the flames. He still feared fire. Beneath him, the grey mare twitched, perhaps feeling his brief shiver, perhaps sensing the change in his mood. Pamela had said horses could do that. He leaned forward to pat its neck.

'It's all right, Victoria. Just a memory,' he said. The horse stood calmly, patiently allowing Gigi to sniff around its feet. The horses had grown accustomed to Bruno's dog, but Bruno had yet to get comfortable with being astride an animal that seemed so much larger and more powerful beneath him than it did in the stables, that kept him so high off the ground as he looked across the field.

'This is where it started,' said Pamela, bringing Bess to a halt alongside him. 'There's an old English saying, red sky at morning, shepherd's warning. You remember the huge glow?'

'I remember. And I remember the hat you wore at the adoption ceremony. Cresseil told me you reminded him of his lovely Annette. He was right. You do look a bit like her. I saw some of Cresseil's old photos.' He looked at her. 'You're more beautiful.'

She smiled at him. 'Don't try to kiss me. Remember what happened last time you tried to lean like that?'

Bess had waited for the perfect moment, then edged a pace away so Bruno had slid slowly but inevitably down from Victoria's back. Pamela had tried to grab his arm but only managed to twist him so that at least he had landed on his rump.

'I think Bess is jealous of me,' he said, grinning.

Pamela shook her head. 'You have to realise that horses have a sense of humour. Do you feel ready to try a short canter?'

'In a moment, perhaps,' he said. 'The insides of my thighs are sore and I feel that I've scoured all the hairs off my legs.'

'Your legs are still gripping too tight. As you get more confident, you'll relax and it'll be fine.' Pamela paused, and in a different tone of voice said: 'I suppose you know what was in the paper, about Jacqueline?'

He nodded. She had been returned to Québec

under a treaty that allowed French and Canadian nationals to serve prison terms in their home country.

'Nine months wasn't much of a sentence,' Pamela went on.

'The court thought it wasn't much of a crime. Obstruction of justice, false evidence, false statement, failure to report a death. They could have given her more, but she was very good at the trial. She made the scene in the vat sound romantic and erotic and a nightmare all at once. A beautiful young woman, driven out of her wits in a tragic ordeal. She probably didn't even need the good lawyer her parents got her.'

'So next summer, she'll be out and free again,' said Pamela. 'It doesn't feel right.'

'Her real punishment will start then,' said Bruno. 'She'll never work in the wine trade again, except perhaps on her parents' place. There'll be no great career, no grand tastings, no Château Jacqueline. She'll be notorious, after all the publicity. And she'll live with the knowledge that she was defeated, that Bondino escaped her plot. The feud's over. He won.'

'You have a very idiosyncratic sense of justice, Bruno,' she said. 'Come on, let's canter . . .'

'Wait,' he whispered, pointing. 'See over there, at the edge of the field.' At the horse's feet, Gigi was pointing, one paw half raised and his head up to catch the faintest scent, his tail out horizontally behind him. Pamela peered across the field but saw nothing, and then suddenly there was a fluttering in the far hedge and a small black shape darted across the grey November sky, jinking up and down as it flew.

'*Bécasse*,' said Bruno. 'Soon be hunting season.'

'I'm looking forward to your dinner. I hope you get enough of the birds.'

'With wine like that, it probably doesn't matter much what we eat,' he said. 'It would be fitting to have *bécasses* again, and maybe venison after it. Also right that we have the same people, except for Jacqueline.'

'Fabiola will be better company,' Pamela said. 'So which wine for the venison?'

'It's an embarrassment of choice,' Bruno laughed. He still could barely believe that he was the owner of this extraordinary case of wine, even though he had been to Hubert's cellar to see the twelve bottles of Château Pétrus. There were three each from 1982, 1985 and 1990, and a single bottle from each of the great years, 1947, 1961 and 1975. It was Bondino's gift, and it had taken Hubert a month to assemble it from various cellars. It had come with a simple card saying 'Thank you, Bruno – Fernando.'

'The eighty-two with the *bécasse*, because that was how I met Dupuy, and the sixty-one with the venison because Hubert says it's the best of all. And then I don't know.'

'It's a lot of money,' said Pamela.

Bruno nodded. He had realised it was a ridiculous

amount of money when Hubert told him the case was worth more than Bruno's investment in the new company Vignerons de St Denis-sur-Vézère. 'Maybe I'll sell the rest and buy more shares in the company,' he said, knowing he wouldn't. There were some things more valuable than money. And besides, he had to save one of the great bottles to open for Bondino's promised return next year. Another dinner, another wine, and perhaps another love. He looked across gratefully at Pamela, a woman who seemed content to give him all the time in the world.

'Let's try a canter,' he said, pressing his heels into Victoria's rounded sides, and rising to the trot as he passed the ruined hut and headed for the break in the woods that led down to the valley and Pamela's home.

ACKNOWLEDGMENTS

This is a work of fiction, in which all events and characters are invented. But like the first in the Bruno series, this book once again owes everything to the kindness and generosity of the people of Périgord and the splendid way of life they and their ancestors have devised over thousands of years. Many of them have become dear friends and some deserve a special mention. The Baron and Raymond, Pierrot and René, and the staff of the inestimable cave of Julien de Savignac, have between them done wonders for my knowledge of wines and the wine trade. They also taught me a lot about the challenge of finding jobs and investment in the small towns of rural France and the hard choices involved. Michael and Gabrielle Merchez, each of whom served as a local councillor for the Green Party, taught me a great deal about the local politics of the environment and about the remaining local communes. I should stress that the many Green supporters I know are far too sensible to start fires. My wife Julia and our daughters Kate and Fanny were wonderfully helpful first readers and our basset hound keeps making us new friends. Once again, Jane and Caroline Wood with great support from Jonathan Segal whipped this book into shape and I am very grateful.